# The Pit Dragon Trilogy

# The Pit Dragon Trilogy

*Dragon's Blood*
*Heart's Blood*
*A Sending of Dragons*

## JANE YOLEN

**FANTASY**

Science Fiction Book Club edition
Published by arrangement with
Harcourt Brace & Company

First SFBC Science Fiction printing: September 1998

Illustrations by Tom McKeveny

ISBN 1-56865-900-8

Visit our website at *http://www.sfbc.com*

PRINTED IN THE UNITED STATES OF AMERICA

# Contents

AUSTAR IV IS the fourth planet of a seven-planet rim system in the Erato Galaxy. Once a penal colony, marked KK29 on the convict map system, it is a semi-arid, metal-poor world with two moons.

Austar is covered by vast deserts, some of which are cut through by small and irregularly surfacing hot springs, several small sections of fenlands, and zones of almost impenetrable mountains. There are only five major rivers: the Narrakka, the Rokk, the Brokk-bend, the Kkar, and the Left Forkk.

Few plants grow in the deserts—some fruit cacti and sparse long-trunk palm trees known as spikka. The most populous plants on Austar are two wild-flowering bushes called burnwort and blisterweed. (See color section.) The mountain vegetation is only now being cataloged but promises to be much more extensive than originally thought.

There is a variety of insect and pseudolizard life, the latter ranging from small rock-runners to elephant-size dragons. (See Holo section, Vol. 6.) Unlike Earth *reptilia*, the Austarian dragon lizards are warm-blooded, with pneumaticized bones for reduction of weight and a keeled sternum where the flight muscles are attached. They have membranous wings with jointed ribs that fold back along the animals' bodies when the dragons are earthbound. Stretched to the fullest, an adult dragon's wings are twice its body size. The "feathers" are really light scales that adjust to wind pressure. From claw to shoulder, some specimens of Austarian dragons have been measured at thirteen feet. There is increasing evidence of level 4+ intelligence and a color-coded telepathic mode of communication in the Austarian dragons. These great beasts were almost extinct when the planet was first settled by convicts (KKs being the common nickname) and guards from

Earth in 2303. But several generations later the Austarians domesticated the few remaining dragons, selectively breeding them for meat and leather and the gaming arenas—or, as they were known from earliest times, the Pits.

The dragon Pits of Austar IV were more than just the main entertainment for early KKs. Over the years the Pits became central to the Austarian economy. Betting syndicates developed and Federation starship crews on long rimworld voyages began to frequent the planet on gambling forays.

Because such gambling violated current Galaxian law, illegal offworld gamesters were expelled in 2485, from Austar IV and imprisoned on penal planet KK47, a mining colony where most of the surface is ice-covered. Under pressure from the Federation, the Austarians then drafted a Protectorate constitution spelling out the Federation's administrative role in the economy of the planet, including regulation of the gambling of offworlders and the payment of taxes (which Austarians call tithing) on gambling moneys in exchange for starship landing bases. A fluid caste system of masters and bond slaves—the remnants of the convict-guard hierarchy—was established by law, with a bond price set as an entrance fee into the master class. Established at the same time was a senate, the members of which came exclusively from the master class. The Senate performs both the executive and the legislative functions of the Austarian government and, for the most part, represents the interests of the Federation. As in all Protectorate planets, offworlders are subject to local laws and are liable to the same punishments for breaking them.

The Rokk, which was a fortress inhabited by the original ruling guards and their families when Austar IV was a penal planet, is now the capital city and the starship landfall.

The entire Erato Galaxy is still only in the first stages of Protectorate status. However, because of the fighting Pit dragons, Austar IV has become one of the better-known R & R planets in the explored universe.

Excerpt from *The Encyclopedia Galaxia,*
Thirtieth edition, vol. I: Aaabornia–BASE

# Dragon's Blood

# 1

THE TWIN MOONS cast shadows like blood scores across the sand. Jakkin hunkered down in a bowl-shaped depression and listened. Inside the wood-and-stone dragonry he could hear the mewling and scratching of hatchlings as they pipped out of their shells. One more night and the hatching would be complete. One more night and he could steal in and pick out a hatchling to raise in secret out in the sands.

As he listened, Jakkin stroked the leather bond bag that hung from his neck chain. The bag held only a few coins. But Jakkin knew that once he had trained his dragon to fight in the pits, his bag would be plump and jangling with gold. Then no one could call him bonder again, and he would answer to no master's call but his own. He would be a boy no longer, but a man.

The rustlings inside the nursery increased as more and more hatchlings caught Jakkin's scent. They began to squeak their distress, a high peeping that multiplied quickly. In the nearby stalls, the hen dragons stomped their feet. They were well used to the man-smell, but the panic of the newborn nestlings made them restless. Their huge clawed feet beat out challenges to the intruder near the clutch. Any moment now, a hen might roar, and *that* would wake any sleeping bonder within hearing.

Jakkin did not dare stay longer, but what did that matter? He had heard the sound of the hatchlings and he knew how close the pipping was to being finished. As a lower stall-boy, he was not allowed into the incubarns. His job was to clean the stud stalls and bathe the big male dragons: dust and fewmets, fewmets and dust. He was no better than a mecho garbage collector, but at least he did not clank like one, disturbing the great cock dragons in their stalls. Few of the male dragons could tolerate the sound and smell of a mechanical heapster without hackling, their collars of hardened neck flesh raising up for a fight. A hackled dragon was no good for stud. It took days to calm one down. So humans, bonders, had to serve as waste collectors even on the most modern worm farm.

Jakkin knew the stud barn well, but the incubarn he could only imagine from its sounds. Tomorrow night, when the hatching was complete, he would find his way into those half-lit, cozy compartments where the temperature was kept at a constant 34°C. He would find his way and get himself a snatchling, and begin the transformation of bond boy into master in one quick, secret, silent act.

Jakkin turned and ran, bent over, toward the northernmost corner of the building. He waded across the stone weir, knee deep in the water that was channeled through the dragonry from the Narrakka River. At the third join, he climbed out again, but kept low until he came to the dunes, another shadow in a night of shadows.

The desert air dried his legs quickly. The water had come nowhere near the bottoms of his thigh-length bonder pants. He checked the horizon for unfamiliar shapes, watchers in the night, and then he stood up, but only for a moment. He took the whisker from the sheath on his belt and began to broom his footsteps away. It made the going slow, and his back ached with the effort, but he did not dare leave prints to show that anyone had gone out across the sands. Bonders, lacking most entertainments, loved to gossip. At night in the bond-house, once the lights were out, there was little else to do until sleep claimed them.

Jakkin had a few hours before the cold of Dark-After. He planned to use them to check again on the crops of blisterweed and burnwort he was growing in his hidden oasis. Everything had to be ready for the arrival of the snatchling. He dared leave nothing to chance.

Jakkin thought, and not for the first time, how his inability to sense anything in the egg made stealing a dragon so difficult. Eggs were never counted; hatchlings were. That was because so few of the eggs actually hatched. Anyone could steal an egg unnoticed. But unless the thief could sense the living dragon within the shell, his chances of success were small.

And Jakkin did not have that sense. His talent was with the grown dragons, like his father before him. But his father had never had any time to teach Jakkin training skills. He had died out in the sands, beneath the claws of a feral dragon he had tried to train when Jakkin was very young. Jakkin's mother had buried her man and then sold

Jakkin and herself into bond for food and shelter. She had died, mourning, within the month, leaving Jakkin with scant memories, half-remembered stories his mother had told him, and a bond bag he was much too small to fill.

He thought back on his past as he whisked away his footprints, but without bitterness. What was, was. Bonders said, "You can fill no bag with regrets." What mattered now was stealing an egg, an egg containing a live dragon, without being caught. Then he had to watch over it until it hatched, and train it in secret to be a proper fighter. A champion in the pits—a big, bright, responding red with a terrible roar and flames six or seven meters long—could buy Jakkin out of bond. Such a dragon had not been seen on Austar IV for as many years as Jakkin could recall. But he was determined to find one, raise it up, train a champion, fill his bag, and become a master. And becoming a master, he would become a man.

~

JAKKIN WAS SO lost in his dreaming, he came to the oasis sooner than he expected. It was only wide enough for a wellspring and a crude reed shelter. He had found the stream by chance when wandering alone in the sands several years earlier on the anniversary of his father's death. Then he had not known enough to broom away his steps. Anyone could have followed him—and shared his find. He had been lucky that time, for his tracks had drifted back into the dunes, covered by the pervasive wind-dervishes that deviled this part of the planet.

The warm spring rose out of nowhere and disappeared as quickly, a bright ribbon of blue-white water running east to west a scant ten meters. It had no rocks or faults in the bed to make it bubble, and so it moved quietly the length of its run. Yet it shimmered against the sand unexpectedly, like dragon scales in the sun. The western end was rimmed with sand-colored kkhan reeds.

When Jakkin had first found the spring, he had begun his digging with his hands. On subsequent trips he had brought a small shovel, borrowed from the nursery supply room and long since returned there. Slowly, and with much perseverance, he had widened the western edge to make a pool. The pool was large enough for a boy to swim in, though too shallow for deep dives. And for four years the oasis had been his secret place. He came when work was finished or on his Bond-Off, the semimonthly holiday each bonder had from the dragonry. Jakkin had told no one about it, not even Slakk or Errikkin, his two closest bondmates. They chose to spend their Bond-Offs with the others, stuffing themselves at the Krakkow Stews or gaming at its minor pit. As young bonders, they mostly watched at the pit, having little in the way of coins with which to bet. Some of the older bond boys spent their time and gold at the baggeries as well, where girls waited to be filled like empty bags. But Jakkin preferred the silent, simple pleasures of his oasis and the knowledge that the few coins in his bag were in no danger of being lessened by trips into town.

It was the wellspring that had helped him decide to steal an egg. It could provide shelter and the promise of provisions. And so Jakkin had spent every free moonrise and Bond-Off at the oasis, planting a small patch of blisterweed and burnwort along the side of the spring, milking plants near Sukker's Marsh for the seeds. It had taken him the better part of the year to sow enough to provide an adequate crop for his worm.

Jakkin walked along the weed and wort patch. In the moonlight the plants sent up smoke ghosts, a healthy sign. He knew better than to touch the growing red stalks, for they could leave painful burns. Only when the plants stopped smoldering and leafed out could they be touched safely: milked for seeds, picked and crushed for dragon food, or rolled for smokers like old Likkarn, who could not do without the weed.

Jakkin looked at the weed patch critically. He was pleased. There should be more than enough for his snatchling, especially since a dragon did not start eating until it had shed its eggskin, after three or four days. By then the plants would be ready, their pale red jagged-toothed leaves veined with the protein-rich sap that showed up a deep maroon in maturity.

Glancing quickly at the sky, Jakkin saw that the second moon, Akka, had already chased its older brother, Akkhan, across to the horizon. There they sat like giant eggs on the rim of the world. Soon they would seem to break apart, spilling a pale glow across the line where land and sky met, a cold false dawn. Once that happened, there would be four hours of Dark-After, those wretched hours when it was too cold for a human to stay out unsheltered in the sand.

In the daylight the reeds could house a hatchling, keeping its sun-sensitive eggskin shadowed as easily as a hen dragon could. And once the dragon was fully scaled out, the sun could not harm it.

But the reeds were useless as protection at night. For dragons it did not matter. They did not mind the cold. But Jakkin knew he would have to hurry back, whisking away his returning tracks, before Dark-After settled its icy hold on the world.

# 2

JAKKIN WAS INTO the deepest part of his sleep, dreaming of great eggs from which red curls of silent smoke rose, when the clanging of the breakfast bell woke him. Automatically he reached under his bed and with one arm dragged out his tunic and pants. Still lying down, eyes closed, he maneuvered into his clothes. Then he sat up on the side of his bed and thrust his feet into his sandals, oblivious of Slakk's legs hanging down from the upper bunk.

"Look out, worm waste," Slakk called, and jumped, just missing Jakkin. "I almost landed on your head this time." He turned and punched Jakkin's bag companionably. "I swear, you're less awake than any bonder I know. What's the matter? Empty bag?" As if punctuating the question, he took another poke at Jakkin's bag, which clinked a quick answer. Dark, ferret-eyed Slakk bent down to tie his sandals, still talking in his insistent, whiny voice. "Less awake each day. Wonder what he's doing out half the night. Is it the pits, I ask? He doesn't answer. The stews? Will he respond? How about . . ." He stood, facing Jakkin again.

Jakkin grunted. Let Slakk think what he will. The image of the spirals of smoke signaling from the weed and wort patch filled his mind. Jakkin gave a second meaningless grunt and stood. He always found it hard to speak before he had gulped down his first cup of takk.

"Leave him alone, Slakk," called out the boy in the next bunk. "You known how he is in the morning." The boy leapt down from the bunk with an easy grace and put his hand out to Jakkin. "Never mind this talking lizard, silent one. I'll lead you straight to the takk pot. Then, perhaps, you will honor us with your words."

Jakkin refused Errikkin's hand but Errikkin was not insulted. He was never insulted. It was impossible to make him be anything but pleasant, a trait that annoyed Jakkin. He tied his sandals and then the three of them went toward the common room, with Slakk in the middle holding a nonstop monologue about pit fighting. The monologue ended only when they were seated at their table.

There were twelve tables in all, and almost all were filled. Jakkin, Slakk, and Errikkin sat with six other young bonders.

There were three girls' tables. The rest of the tables were for the older bonders, most of whom, for one reason or another, had never been able to fill their bags with enough gold to buy their way out of bond. Only one table held both free men and women: those who were walking out together or pair-bonded, and Akkhina—little, lithe, black-haired Akki, who should have been at the baggeries, Slakk said, but who preferred working around dragons and choosing her own men. Slakk always said that with a sly smile, as if there were more he could tell if he wanted, as if he had spent time with her. But Jakkin was sure it was all posture and bluff. Though Slakk was sixteen, Jakkin doubted he had ever been near a girl, any girl, not even a girl from the local baggery.

The table was set with bowls, cups, and cutlery. Unlike some breeders, Master Sarkkhan had always supplied knives as well as forks and spoons to his bonders. They were well fed and well kept, and there was rarely a fight. In the center of each table stood the takk pot, full of the rich, hot, wine-colored drink. The cook, old Kkarina, made it as thick as the mud of the stud baths; she claimed that if it were any thinner it lost much of its protein and all of its taste. Platters of lizard eggs, boiled in the shell, and heavy slabs of lizard meat sat next to the takk pot. The boys wasted little time heaping their bowls.

Jakkin was suddenly starving. He wondered if it was because of his late nights or his fears.

"I bet it's Bloody Flag and Blood Brother today," said Slakk, his mouth full of the juicy meat. "It's that time again. *Fewmets*, I hate that Brother. His is always the messiest stall, and besides, he loves to nip."

"I'll take him for you," said Jakkin. The first cup of takk had restored his tongue and burned courage through his body. "He never nips me."

"None of them ever nip *you*," said Errikkin pleasantly. "You've got something. Trainer blood. Like your dad. I bet even old Sarkkhan himself doesn't have your touch."

Jakkin looked down into his second cup of takk and stirred it

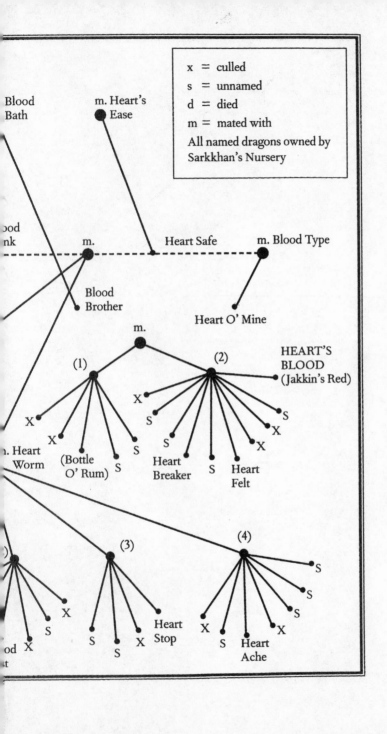

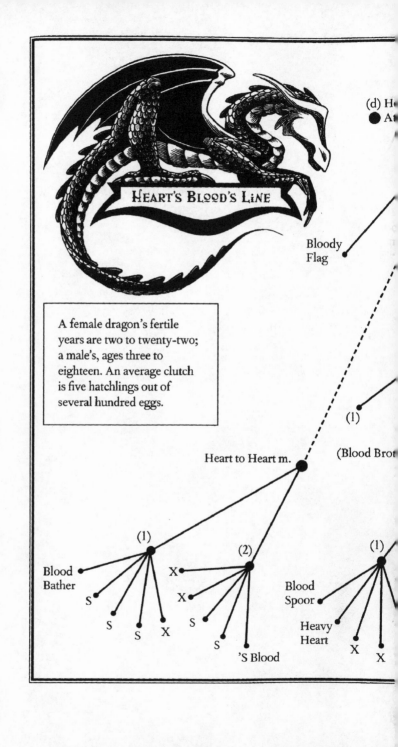

HEART'S BLOOD'S LINE

A female dragon's fertile years are two to twenty-two; a male's, ages three to eighteen. An average clutch is five hatchlings out of several hundred eggs.

(d) H
● A

Bloody
Flag

(1)

Heart to Heart m.

(Blood Brot

(1)

(2)

(1)

Blood
Bather

X

X

Blood
Spoor

S

Heavy
Heart

S

S

X

S

S

X

X

'S Blood

*For Jeff, Joan, Jim, and Scott,*
*my first SF friends*

# *The Hatchling*

slowly with a spoon. The deep red drink moved sluggishly. He knew that Errikkin was just being agreeable again, saying something to please, but it was something that Jakkin felt, too. Still he didn't dare voice it aloud. Bragging, like regrets, filled no bag.

"Will you take Brother to the bath, too?" Slakk never strayed far from his own concerns in any conversation. "His skin is getting flaky—the scales don't shine. We noticed it last time, Errikkin and me. And old Likkarn says . . ." Slakk spit expertly between his out-spread second and third fingers, the sign of dragon horns. None of the boys liked Likkarn, who was in charge of the bonders. He was too fussy and unforgiving, and quite brutal in his punishments. "Old Likkarn says, 'Scales like mud, little stud; scales like the sun, fine work done.' Old Likk-and-Spittle's full of such stuff."

Jakkin smiled into his cup.

"*Hush,*" Errikkin hissed. "He might hear you. Then where would we be?"

"Nowhere that's any worse than where we are now," replied Slakk.

Errikkin's concern was a formality. Likkarn was too many tables away to hear Slakk's complaints and Jakkin's replies, or to register Errikkin's desperate hissing. He sat with the older bonders and the free men, the ones who really ran the dragonry for the often absent Sarkkhan. They spent each morning meal working out the day's schedule, which Likkarn then scripted. Every bonder knew his or her own mark, and the marks of individual dragons, but beyond that few of them knew how to read. Or write. Likkarn, so the gossip ran, knew how to write because he had been born free. And he scripted each day's schedule with an elegant hand, though given the bonders' illiteracy, that was more ritual than anything else. Likkarn would read the day's work sheet out loud as the others filed out the door, and then hang the assignments on the wall. Even though he was a weeder, he was tolerated by Sarkkhan because he could read and script. Few bonders could read and fewer still could script. It was something taught only to free men and women.

The boys got up together. Errikkin was in the lead, Jakkin next. Several of the smaller boys slipped in between him and Slakk.

Slakk whispered at Jakkin's back, "Was I right? The schedule. Was I right?"

Jakkin checked the marks next to his name and Slakk's, reading them upside down on the chart in front of Likkarn. Jakkin's mother had taught him to read early, before they had been in bond. He could still remember the chanting tone she adopted for drilling his letters.

Jakkin had practiced faithfully, to honor her memory. The few coins he ever spent went for books, which he kept hidden with his clothes under his bed. His ability to read, which he did not trouble to hide, was one of the things that Likkarn hated. The old weeder jealously guarded his right to script the schedule. He needn't have bothered. Jakkin could read—but he could not write.

Turning, Jakkin called lightly over the heads of the younger boys, "You were right, Slakk."

Likkarn scowled and read off Jakkin's duties anyway, his voice edged with anger. " 'Jakkin: Bloody Flag and Blood Brother. Stalls and baths.' And be sure they're quieted down. If any of them hackle, you're in for it."

"Don't forget"—Slakk's whine began before they were out of the door—"you promised. You promised you'd take . . ."

Jakkin nodded and walked quickly to get away from Slakk's voice. He willed himself to remember the oasis and the sounds in the incubarns. He was halfway to the stud barn when Slakk caught up with him.

"You did promise, you know."

"Oh, lizard lumps, shut up already. I know I promised." Jakkin rarely got angry with anyone except Slakk. Then, at his friend's crestfallen look, Jakkin was immediately contrite. "I'm sorry, Slakk. I didn't mean to yell. I'm just . . ." He stopped, horrified with himself. He had been about to confess to Slakk how tired he was and why.

Errikkin turned back and interrupted them. "It's just been too many days since your last Bond-Off," he supplied. He put his arm over Jakkin's shoulder. "That's all."

Jakkin nodded. They all accepted that explanation and went on to the barn.

The stud barn was twice as high as the bondhouse, to accommodate the size of the big male dragons. Inside on the south wall were individual stalls that simulated the pumice caves where mature males lived in the wild. Since the males paired off when it was not rutting season, leaving the hen dragons to raise the hatchlings, the studs had linked stalls throughout the barn. An unpaired stud often went into a decline and was not good for mating. The north wall stalls were used for the male pit fighters.

In the center of the barn was the great hall, where hen dragons in heat were brought to the studs. The hall was an arena-sized courtyard, without a roof, to accommodate the frantic, spiraling courting flights. It had a soft, mossy floor for the act itself.

Throughout the barn was a system of stone dikes that carried water in from, and out again to, the Narrakka River. It was triple forked inside the building. One fork funneled drinking water into the individual stalls and a clear, flowing drinking stream into the mating hall. The second funneled out wastewater that had been used for cleaning the barn. The third fork ran directly into the baths, those tremendous pools of mud in which the dragons rolled and sank up to their eyes, to be cooled after mating or fights or twice a month in off-rut. The third fork also filled the cisterns in the shower room, with runoff back into the out-lying swamps.

The boys went into the barn, and the deep, cool, musky air assaulted them. Jakkin breathed deeply and smiled. Dragon smells and dragons. They were really what he loved most in the world.

"Phew," said Slakk. "The first thing I am going to do when I buy out of bond is to celebrate the end of this smell. I'm never going to work with dragons again."

"What will you do, then?" asked Errikkin. "What else do you know?"

"I know food," Slakk answered. "I might apprentice to a cook. Or run a baggery. *That* might be a job for a man. Anything but being a slave to a worm."

Jakkin shook his head and was just going to reply when an incredible roar filled the hallway. It began on a deep bass note and wound its way up and up, without hesitation, until it screamed out its defiance beyond human hearing.

"That's Blood Brother," Jakkin remarked. "He knows it's his turn."

"Just as long as he doesn't hackle," said Errikkin.

"All roar and no fight," sneered Slakk. "That's why he's here. After his first two wins, he refused to go into the pit again."

It was a cynical assessment of the great dragon's skill, but even Errikkin had to agree. Blood Brother's history was known even to the stallboys. Two tremendous fights with older, cunning dragons, and the next time the trainers had tried to lead Brother into the nursery truck to drive to a pit, he had simply collapsed at the barn door. A ton of fighting dragon lying on the ground was not something that could be moved easily. Likkarn had tried the prod-sticks and even a shot with the stinger, set below Stun. But Brother would not move until the truck had driven off without him. Only then had he stood and moved placidly back inside the barn on his own.

"But he's a fantastic stud," Jakkin reminded them. "His hatchlings have won in pits all over the world."

Slakk shrugged and Errikkin smiled. Then the three of them padded down the hall to the dragon stalls.

# 3

BLOOD BROTHER TURNED his great black shrouds of eyes toward the boys, but in the neighboring stall Bloody Flag continued to munch mindlessly on blisterwort. Brother showed his annoyance by shifting his weight back and forth and houghing.

Jakkin ran his fingers through his hair, then touched the dimple on his cheek that was as deep as a blood score. He always did that when he was nervous, and though he never would have let Slakk and Errikkin know it, Blood Brother was the one dragon he did not wholly trust. Brother was so unpredictable—one minute almost thrumming, that deep-throated purr that a contented dragon used; the next sending warning straggles of smoke through his slits. Still, it did not do to let a dragon know how nervous you were. Some bonders claimed dragons could smell fear on you. Jakkin supposed that was how his father had been killed by the feral in the sands. Besides, all dragons, he reminded himself with the conventional trainer's wisdom, all dragons are feral, even though they have been domesticated for over two centuries. And especially dragons like Blood Brother.

As if hearing his name, Brother jerked his head up. Deep inside the black eyes there was an iridescent flicker, the sign of a fighter. Involuntarily Slakk stepped back. Errikkin stood his ground. Only Jakkin went forward, holding out a hand.

"Hush, hush, beauty," he crooned, letting Brother sniff his hand. "It's the baths for you."

Jakkin kept up the soothing babble until the head of the beast started to weave back and forth and the boys could feel the thrumm of content humming along the floor. Errikkin unlatched the stall gate and Jakkin reached up, hooked his finger around the dragon's ear, and backed him out of the stall.

As Jakkin led the dragon down the hall, Slakk ran ahead to the bellpull that signaled throughout the other halls that a dragon was unstalled. No one wanted to be in the way of those great back feet or foreshortened front feet with claws as hard and yellow as old bone. On hearing the bell, anyone in the barn would press into the evenly spaced hallway niches until the dragon had gone by. Only the trainer, leading the dragon by ear or halter and pacing by its side, could be reasonably assured of safety, but even a good trainer could be accidentally clawed. Old Likkarn had a dozen scars punctuating the long, stringy sentences of veins that ran down his legs. And the rumor was that Sarkkhan himself looked like the map of Austar, pocked and pitted from his years with dragons. But that Jakkin knew only from gossip. He had never been up close to Master Sarkkhan. For all Jakkin knew, the man's body might be as smooth as a baggery girl's, though that was highly unlikely. Anyone who worked around dragons for long wore blood wounds.

Jakkin clucked with his tongue to let the dragon know he was still there. "Just be a good fellow," Jakkin sang to Brother as they went along the hall. It was early, and no one was in the niches; there was nothing to distract them as they went down to the baths. Jakkin knew that Slakk and Errikkin would use this time to clean the stall, raking out the old fewmets, patting down the dust, settling new straw for bedding. They would crush fresh wort and weed in the feed box and maybe, with extra time, polish Brother's nameplate. Sarkkhan was rich enough to afford metal ones.

Each dragon had a bath once every other week, but the stalls had to be cleaned every other day. Dust and fewmets, fewmets and dust. That was usually a stallboy's life. So Jakkin welcomed the chance to be more than a human pit cleaner, and he loved to take the dragons to their baths.

Blood Brother, smelling the mud, threw his head up; Jakkin lost his hold on the dragon's ear.

"Worm bag," Jakkin muttered under his breath as the dragon reared up slightly, fanning the close air with his front feet. There was not enough room for Brother to complete a hindleg stand, but Jakkin could feel the air currents change as the dragon lashed his tail from side to side. The thump-thumping as the tail hit the solid wooden walls was echoed in Jakkin's chest. He would have to get Brother quickly into the baths and quieted down before the dragon did damage to the building or to himself. Either way and old Likkarn would have

Jakkin back spreading fewmets on the weed and wort patches for a month. It wasn't bad work, but he preferred dragons.

Jakkin plunged between Brother's front feet and lunged for the bath door. It was a dangerous move, but unpredictable enough to shock the dragon into backing up a pace. Jakkin lifted the latch and rode the doorstep platform in and over the sunken bath room.

Blood Brother crowded in behind and plunged into the deep mud-hole. It cooled his temper at once and he began to splash and snuffle in the bath like a hatchling.

From his perch on the swinging platform Jakkin smiled. All of the dragon's ferocity seemed to slip away, and what was left was a rather silly, oversized lizard, burbling and rolling about in a pool of muck.

"And what was I scared of?" Jakkin said to Brother, but the dragon ignored him completely.

Jakkin took a large wire brush from its hook on the door and sat down on the step, his legs hanging over the side. His perch swayed back and forth. He knew that in a little while the dragon would have had enough of plunging around in the mud and would want his scales scrubbed. Dragons in the wild groomed one another with teeth and claws and tongues as rough as bristles. But domesticated dragons, though paired in stalls, were not let loose in the baths together. Their play was too rough for even the strongest wood-and-stone building. Besides, most dragons got so they preferred the wire brush, which could reach the most incredibly delightful places when wielded by a sensitive human groom.

Blood Brother sank down to the bottom of the mud bath. Only his eyes, now shuttered with their membranous second lid, showed above the brown sludge. His ears twitched constantly. After a minute, even the ears stopped moving, and Blood Brother slept.

"Pleasant dreams," mumbled Jakkin. He knew that the dragon—and not the human—would choose the time of grooming. Then, though he tried not to, he dozed off as well.

Jakkin had no idea how long they slept. One moment he was dreaming of the oasis, clean and bright and shimmering in the desert sun, and the next he was awakened by a playful, muddy nudge from Blood Brother's nose. It was forceful enough to have knocked him from his perch if the platform hadn't swung toward the far wall.

Jakkin grabbed the metal chain attached to the wall and leapt onto the catwalk. He pushed the door back with one foot and watched it lock shut with a satisfying click. His heart was racing. Falling asleep on the door was a stupid thing to have done, especially with Blood

Brother in the bath. If he had fallen into that deep mud with the dragon, there would have been little chance of his escaping. Recently, one bonder in a nursery on the far side of Krakkow had died that way. It could not have been a pleasant death.

"Come on, worm," he said aloud, amazed that his voice was not shaking. He held the brush behind him as he walked along the catwalk toward the shower room. The dragon followed, heaving himself out of the mud and onto the ramp with a loud sucking sound.

In the shower room, Jakkin stripped off his tunic and sandals but left his shorts on. And his bag. No bonder was allowed to remove the bag until it was full. Jakkin reached up and pulled the cord that started the shower. Brother was so becalmed from the mud bath, Jakkin no longer feared him.

The water began raining down on them and Jakkin moved around the great beast, heedless now of its claws. He scratched and polished the muddy scales. First the mud came off, then the patina of stall dust. Beneath were orange-red scales that shimmered in the flickering light of the shower room.

"Pretty, pretty," Jakkin crooned.

Blood Brother was not a deep wine red, which was the best color for a fighting dragon (for somehow color and ferocity were gene linked). But his color was strong, and his scales, when clean, had the sheen and polish of hundreds of small rainbow mirrors. They were not spotty or off-color as some dragon scales were.

As he worked, Jakkin smiled and even whistled through his teeth. He was enjoying the cleaning as much as the dragon.

Blood Brother languorously stretched out his wings. Unfurled, they nearly touched the opposite walls. His wingspread was the widest in the nursery, and it seemed to Jakkin that Brother enjoyed showing it off. When not confined in his stall, the dragon took every opportunity to stretch his magnificent wings.

Jakkin took a soft cloth from a hook and rubbed the silky-tough membranes that stretched between the rock-hard wing ribs. He was especially careful of the skin next to the right secondary, where a series of four puckered scars bore witness to Brother's time in the pits.

Brother began to flinch as the cloth came close to the scars, and Jakkin held on firmly to the wing. "I'll be careful, fellow. You can't tell me that still hurts after all this time. But I'll be careful." He thought to himself that he'd have to be a fool *not* to be careful. Brother had knocked one of the older bonders senseless a year ago, smashing him up against the shower wall, just for bearing down too hard on that wing.

Hanging the cloth back on the hook, Jakkin took up the brush again. He stood on tiptoe and leaned against the dragon, clicking to it with his tongue. Jakkin tried, as always, to reach Brother's mind with his. Trainers were often able to have a tenuous kind of mental bond with their worms. All Jakkin could ever sense with Brother was a dark, sluggish brooding, the color of bloody mud.

Jakkin clicked again and pushed Brother with his shoulder. Slowly the dragon turned its head to look at him and Jakkin tapped as far up Brother's back as he could reach with the brush. With a sigh, the worm lay down, first folding his short, powerful forelegs, then squatting down on the hind. Jakkin scratched the upper scales with a gentle persistence. He worked his way down the slope of the neck, leaving the head for last.

Jakkin sat down in front of Brother and cradled the dragon's head in his lap. He began to croon a silly little song that had been sung in the bondhouse that month, a kind of dragon lullaby:

> *Little flame mouths,*
> *Cool your tongues.*
> *Dreaming starts soon,*
> *Furnace lungs.*
>
> *Rest your wings now,*
> *Little flappers.*
> *Cave mouth calls*
> *To dragon nappers.*
>
> *Night is coming;*
> *Bank your fire.*
> *Time for dragons*
> *To retire.*
>
> *Hiss. Hush. Sleep.*

As he sang, Jakkin brushed Brother's ears and around his horns, over the nose and under the chin. The beast began thrumming again in the same rhythm as the song. Then, as if to thank Jakkin for the grooming, Brother tried to groom in return, holding the boy down with one foreclaw and giving him long tongue swipes along the leg. The treatment was so rough and painful, Jakkin stopped singing and began to shout.

"Cut it out, you worm pile!" He banged Brother on the nose several times with the wire brush.

With a loud, rumbled hough, the dragon let him up.

Jakkin turned off the shower, grabbed up his clothes, and put them on hastily. Then he took Brother's ear and jerked him up. Forgetting the warning bellpull because of the pain in his leg, and limping, Jakkin led Blood Brother back around to his newly cleaned stall. Luckily no one was in the hall.

Slakk and Errikkin were sitting by the stallside. Slakk was fingering his bag and talking. Errikkin was smiling and nodding his head. They jumped up when they saw the dragon coming.

"Fewmets!" Slakk yelled. "Why didn't you warn us? That big lump could have stepped on us, and then where would we have been?"

Jakkin didn't reply but shoved the dragon into the stall. Smelling the fresh food, Brother went in willingly. Jakkin latched the door and turned back to his friends.

It was Errikkin who noticed his leg. "That's awful red. You look like you've lost some skin. Does it hurt?" he asked, pointing, his bland handsome face creased with worry.

Before Jakkin could answer, Slakk said, "I *told* you he was dangerous. They ought to send him to the stews before he kills someone."

Jakkin answered angrily. "He was just being playful. And grateful. And—worm waste!"

"What is it?" asked Errikkin, parading his concern.

"I left the bagged brush in the shower."

"I'll get it!" cried Slakk, jumping up. Before Jakkin could stop him, Slakk was running down the hall, his bag bouncing crazily against his tunic. But once around the turning, he slowed down. He would walk from here. If he took enough time, the others would start on the next stall and bath without him.

# 4

AT THE SHOWER-ROOM door, Slakk hesitated, bent down, and removed his sandals. Wet feet would dry faster than wet shoes. He heard a noise and looked up. Likkarn was standing over him, glowering, the bath brush in his hand.

"I—it—wasn't me—" Slakk began under the man's hooded gaze.

"It *will* be when I get through with you, you empty-bagged piece of waste. Tossing Master Sarkkhan's property around and dodging work. I know you—bonder." Likkarn spoke it all with a quiet that exaggerated his fury, and his weed-reddened eyes seemed to grow bloodier with each word. He grabbed up Slakk's tunic and slowly raised the boy off the floor so that only his toes touched it. Then he gave Slakk three hard shakes and dropped him. Slakk fell heavily, twisting his leg and giving a sharp cry of pain.

"Now, if it isn't you, who is it?" Likkarn asked. He knew that fear and pain could control the bond boys and he used his knowledge with precision. In his blister fury, Likkarn was—like all weeders—practically unrestrainable. But during the day he did not allow himself to smoke. "Who—is—it?" he asked again, coldly, spacing the words without obvious passion—that he saved for the dragons he helped train and for his nights of blisterweed.

Again Slakk sobbed out, "It wasn't me." And then, under his breath, as if whispering might excuse his betrayal, he added, "It was Jakkin. Not me. Jakkin."

Likkarn stepped over him and went down the hallway, heedless of Slakk's sobbing. He strode eagerly, not bothering to mask his elation. Jakkin was the one boy who irritated him beyond measure: Jakkin, with his sure touch with dragons, his aloofness, his ability to read. Jakkin had already caught Sarkkhan's eye. The nursery owner had asked about Jakkin once or twice already. Such a boy, a hard worker who kept himself apart from the other bonders in their games, could not be easily manipulated. "It will be a pleasure breaking Jakkin over *this*," Likkarn told himself, knowing it would keep the other bonders in line, knowing that to empty the boy's bag over such a slight infraction would be personally sweeter than waiting for an important mistake. He allowed himself a small smile.

Errikkin was already in Bloody Flag's stall, calming the dragon in preparation for the bath. Flag was a phlegmatic beast, hard to rouse even for mating. That calmness was what Sarkkhan hoped to breed into future dragons, without Flag's habitual torpor. Breeding was an inexact science, but Sarkkhan's work had always had a high percentage of correct guesses.

Jakkin was still with Blood Brother, finishing the grooming by trimming the dragon's nails with a large hasp. It was a job that had to be done within the confines of the stall so that the dragon could not strike out if a sensitive claw was cut carelessly. Many breeders had their stud dragons declawed, since the beasts were no longer used in the pits. But according to Sarkkhan, a declawed dragon could not catch its mate easily in flight and the extra energy the stud had to expand chasing down the elusive female reduced its potency.

Jakkin did not know if such a thing were true; but still, he thought, *If Flag were declawed he'd never breed. Not if it meant an extra-long chase*. He must have said it out loud, because there was an answering chuckle from Errikkin in Flag's stall.

Neither boy heard Likkarn coming down the hall. The old trainer moved silently over to Blood Brother's stall, his fury and eagerness tight behind his smile. The dragons sensed Likkharn's heightened emotions. Flag merely houghed once and stopped. But Brother began to sway back and forth.

Jakkin stood, not knowing what was wrong. He tried to calm the worm, stroking its nose and crooning to it. But the dragon would not be soothed. Trails of smoke began to leak through his slits. Jakkin closed his eyes and again tried to reach the dragon's mind, but the dark red mud it projected was now shot through with flashes of bright yellow lightning. Brother was really disturbed. Jakkin knew that the only thing to do now was to get out of the stall as quickly as possible and bar the door. Then he would have to get one of the extinguishers—the stun guns—that hung by the main door. If necessary, he'd have to use the stinger to knock Brother out for a while. Once a dragon began thrashing, no one was safe.

Jakkin ducked under Brother's neck and slid along his side, timing his run to coincide with the sway. Just as Jakkin reached the door, Brother grunted and threw his head up, giving a soft whine. It was like the early screams of pit dragons warming to a fight. Jakkin knew that in minutes the dragon would hackle if he couldn't be put to sleep.

Jakkin clawed at the inside latch and pushed the door open. He started out and ran straight into Likkarn, who waited there.

"Messy," sneered the old bonder. "Careless and messy." He held up the bath brush like a weapon and was so intent on beating the boy, he did not notice the dragon's whine.

"Blood Brother—" began Jakkin, trying to warn the trainer out of the stall doorway.

But Likkarn lifted the brush high up over his head and brought it down with contained fury on Jakkin's shoulder. The bristles made a bloody pattern where they slipped off Jakkin's tunic and onto skin. Jakkin cried out.

The dragon answered him, scream for scream, rearing up in a hindfoot stand that pulled its leather halter out of the ring. As Brother's head touched the wooden ceiling beams, he dropped again, angered and confused, an orange light pinpointed in his black eyes. He kicked out with his rear legs, sending Jakkin tumbling into Likkarn. They fell together, the boy on top.

Blood Brother backed out of the stall screaming, and stepped slantwise on part of Jakkin's back, pressing the boy down heavily on the trainer. The dragon never noticed, but moved on, unfurling his wings until the tips touched the walls. The scarred wing scraped past a pair of hooks, and one hook caught the tender membrane, ripping it open. Frantically the dragon tried to shake his wing loose, screaming his fury over and over into the cavernous barn. Other dragons in their stalls up and down the hallway screamed back, terrifying the bonders working there. Errikkin cowered in Flag's stall, his back against the bin.

Blood Brother gave one last mighty pull and his wing tore free, the hot blood dripping down onto the dust, burning the floorboards where it fell. Three drops spattered onto Jakkin's back, leaving deep pits. But he had been unconscious since the first blow and did not feel the burns.

The dragon roared once, then stopped at the smell of his own blood and stood trembling.

Likkarn crawled out from under the boy's body and put his back against the wall. He edged toward the barn door where the extinguishers hung, three on a side. He moved slowly because he could feel that some of his ribs were broken and because he knew that any other sudden movement could send the dragon into new furies. Likkarn was breathing in great gasps by the time he reached the door. His fingers found the gun but his eyes never left the dragon. Trembling, he brought the stinger up and sighted between Brother's eyes, sliding the force regulator to Stun.

At the gun's movement, Brother moved his head up and whined once. Then he lowered it again and stared at Likkarn with shrouded eyes. He sensed, in a muddled way, the man's purpose. He whined again.

Likkarn's hand on the regulator hesitated, then rammed it right on to Kill. He fired once into the dragon's head, shattering the black eyes, and once more into the front of the neck, severing the sternum muscles and making a crimson flower burst and trickle down onto the dragon's breast. First the mighty wings collapsed, helpless, at the dragon's sides. Then slowly the great beast fell, shaking the floor of the barn. At his collapse, all the dragons in the stud barn set up a howling.

Tears, nowhere near as red as dragon's blood but colored from blisterweed, ran slowly down Likkarn's cheeks in familiar grooves.

"You gutless lizard," he hissed. "You piece of waste. Whine at me, will you? I bet everything I had on your third fight. You were going to be a champion. I was going to be a man once more. You ruined me."

Likkarn dropped the gun and walked over and began kicking the dying beast in the side. The rhythm of the blows seemed to echo in the hall. Kick after kick he delivered until the kicking tired him out. He began to shake violently, the first sign of weed hunger or shock. He turned abruptly and went out of the barn, dropping the extinguisher in the doorway. He spoke to the first bonder he saw.

"Send Brother's carcass to the stews. And get a good price for it. It's prime. Then take care of that other piece of waste, that boy Jakkin. *If* he's still alive."

Shrugging off any help and holding his sides, Likkarn went toward the bondhouse without looking back.

# 5

JAKKIN WADED THROUGH muddy nightmares and woke a dozen times. Each time, pain and drugs sent him spiraling back to blood-colored swamps, where he slogged toward the light yet one more time.

At last he came to and discovered he was staring into a starched white pillowcase and breathing through it with difficulty. Since his bunk in the bondhouse did not include such niceties, he realized groggily that he must be in the hospice. He tried to turn over, and the pain in his shoulders and down his back was so intense, he screamed weakly and buried his face in the pillow again.

"I think you'll live," came an amused voice, cool and gentle.

Jakkin lifted his head and turned slowly till he reached the outer edge of the pain. He could see the speaker now. It was Akki, the girl that Slakk said should be in the baggeries. Even in his state, Jakkin could see why. Her black hair hung straight down her back; her skin was the pale cream of a hatchling. She had a generous, mobile mouth that right now was laughing at him. Jakkin winced again and Akki moved to the head of the bed, where he could see her more easily. She held out a glass filled with iced takk.

"Here. Drink this. And now that we both know you'll make it, I have to get back to work. There are a couple of really sick people in here, you know. Not just ones with dragon footprints up and down their spines."

Jakkin groaned and managed to gasp out, "So that's what hurts." He had only a vague memory of what had happened, ending with Brother's kick.

"That and three nice deep blood scores," said Akki cheerfully. Her smile was slightly crooked. Jakkin liked that, except it made her seem to be enjoying his discomfort. "Too bad. They were the only pits on an otherwise scoreless body."

He could feel himself blushing and pushed the takk glass back into her hand. Then he buried his face in the pillow. When he raised his head again, Akki was gone. He couldn't decide if he was happy about her disappearance.

Jakkin glanced out of the window. It was shut and the blackness outside made him gasp. It was almost Dark-After. Hurt or not, he would have to get out of the bed, out of the hospice, and back to the incubarn. The hatching must be nearly complete by now. If he didn't get himself an egg or a newborn hatchling before the morning count, it might be another year before he could try again.

He eased himself into a sitting position, keeping his mouth open. He breathed deeply, willing himself to forget the pulsing ache in his back, the three hot points of searing agony that were the blood scores. He put his feet over the side of the bed and waited out the next pulse of pain. Except for some bandages on his back, and his bond bag, he was naked. His pants and tunic were folded neatly on a chair by the bed. He managed to move to them, hunching like an old man, shuffling carefully so as not to jar his wounds.

"Fewmets," he cursed. "At this rate I'll be lucky to get out of *here* by dawn."

Somehow he managed to get into his pants. He had to carry his sandals and tunic. Inching toward the door, he listened for footsteps in the hallway. He heard none, opened the door, and sighed with relief to see that his room was only about ten meters from the front door. To call it walking, he thought, was an overstatement. He moved like an injured fifty-foot, the awkward insect that went in circles if it lost even a single leg. Only, his back was not going to regenerate as quickly as a fifty-foot's foot. He was going to have this pain for a long time—and the blood scores forever.

By the glass door he hesitated once again. Pushing it open was going to require some extra effort. He saw that it was not quite Dark-After, but the two moons were squatting on the horizon and Akkhan was already leaking its color along the line. All the pain, his awkward, hurting shuffle, had been for nothing. He pounded his fist impotently on the door, almost hoping the glass would break. As he did so, he thought he felt something break open on his back. The new pain made him whimper and he slowly slid down the glass door and collapsed onto the floor.

~

JAKKIN WOKE WITH his face in the pillow again and wondered if he had dreamed his walk down the hall.

"And what were you trying to do, hero?" Akki's amused voice told him it had not been a dream after all. "You managed to rip off a bandage and start some bleeding again. And I'm the only one on night duty. Do you know how heavy you are?"

Jakkin lifted his head high enough to see Akki scripting something on a chart at the foot of his bed. He noticed that his pants and tunic were once again on the chair and his embarrassment was so great he did not even blush this time, just put his head back on the pillow and was silent.

As if she had not noticed any movement, Akki continued her monologue. "Were you planning to run around in Dark-After? Hobble-hop here and there? Why, boy, enjoy your rest. You'll be back with the dragons soon enough. You remind me of . . . Why, even old Likk-and-Spittle let his broken ribs get him off for three days. He just lay here and loved every minute of our coddling. Loved it, that is, until Sarkkhan came here with blood on his mind and broke that bagged weeder back down to stallboy again. Imagine, extinguishing a stud like Blood Brother when all he had to do was stun the worm. All he had to do was—"

Jakkin pushed himself over on his side, ignoring the dancing knives in his back. "Three days? Likkarn was here three days? I don't understand. It's Dark-After. How could it be three days? *How long have I been here?*"

Akki came around with another glass of takk, this one steaming hot. She held it out to him. Her mouth was serious. "You've been in and out of consciousness almost a week," she said. "There was even a time when we thought we might lose you. But Sarkkhan said you have too much fight in you to die young, and that your head is harder than dragon bone. He should know. He has a head like that himself."

"A week. Dark-After—a week!" Jakkin's face lost what color it had and he pushed Akki's hand away. The glass fell and splintered on the floor. The takk splattered. Jakkin threw himself down on the pillow and began to weep, heedless of Akki's hands on his hair or her soothing voice. He was fifteen and could not remember ever crying before—not as a child when his father had died so brutally; not in bond when his mother slipped away so quietly in her sleep; not when Likkarn had tormented him with the memory of his father's death under the feral's claws. He sobbed—for this lost chance, for the death of Blood Brother, for the aching scores on his back, and even with the remembered pain of his parents' loss.

Akki's voice came to him as if from far away. "It's the medicine, Jakkin. The medicine makes you weak, makes you cry."

He ignored her and let the waves of uncontrollable sorrow wash over him until he fell into a deep, troubled sleep. When he woke again, it was afternoon and Akki was gone.

~

GETTING OUT OF bed and dressing was nowhere near as hard as it had been the day before. Jakkin's back was stiff and he had a continuing headache, but the dizziness, the depression, the pinpoints of pain were gone. He decided not to wait for a visit from the doctor. He had to find out what had happened in the week missing from his life. He had to know if all the hatchlings had already been counted and settled in with their hens.

The sun was bright and hot overhead, and there was no breeze as Jakkin walked the short distance between the hospice and the barns. He met no one on the path. In the intense heat of the day, everyone either worked inside the cool barns or napped. Bonders worked.

Jakkin tried to remember back before he had been a bonder. He picked through his meager store of memories: the sight of his father bleeding on the sands while the feral dragon, a black blot in the sky, winged toward the farthest mountains; his mother threading her thin, fragile fingers through his as they walked toward Sarkkhan's Nursery, a pack filled with their few possessions on her back. Her voice came suddenly to him out of the past. "We may be bonders, but we will fill our bags ourselves." The memory of her voice was more vivid to him than the picture of his father's body. But whether that walk had occurred before they had become bonders or after, he did not know.

"I will fill my bag myself," he murmured, stroking the leather bag with two fingers.

When he entered the barn, the rush of cool air revived him. He wandered around the stalls, pausing for a minute at the empty one that had housed Blood Brother. He wondered whom they would pair with Flag now and if the dragon suffered from the loss of his companion. From the sounds of dedicated chewing coming from Flag's stall, it was hard to believe he had even noticed Brother was gone.

*I should have checked the work list*, Jakkin thought, seeing neither Slakk nor Errikkin. Then, hearing a complaining voice from farther down the hall, he followed it to the stalls where Blood Spoor and Blood Bather, a pair of red-gold four-year-olds, were housed.

Slakk's voice came from Bather's stall. Jakkin climbed up carefully, winced, and looked over. Both Slakk and Errikkin were on their knees, trimming the dragon's nails.

"These nails are butter soft," Slakk was saying. "Look, the hasp leaves grooves. I don't want to be blamed for ruining him."

"No one will blame you, Slakk," said Errikkin. "And I'll back you up."

"What's the use of trimming them anyway?" Slakk continued. "This one isn't going to be any good in the pit with those nails. Or for catching a female either. Why do you suppose Sarkkhan keeps him?"

Errikkin shrugged.

"I think he should go to the stews," Slakk finished.

"You think they *all* should go to the stews," Jakkin said from his perch. "Maybe it's a *re*-trait and not a *dom*-. Maybe the soft nails won't be passed on. Trust Master Sarkkhan to know."

"Jakkin!" both boys cried. Errikkin stood up immediately and smiled, but Slakk was suddenly very busy with the hasp again.

"Don't worry, Slakk," Jakkin added. "I don't blame you for anything. I can fill my bag myself."

Slakk looked up, but his small-eyed face was wiped free of expression. He put his hand over his bag, completely covering it. "What should you blame me for?" he asked.

Errikkin stepped between them, reached up, and touched Jakkin's hand. "We've missed you," he said. "Slakk especially. He's had to do twice as much work as before. Or so he says."

Gingerly Jakkin climbed down from the fence and walked to the stall door. Errikkin lifted the latch and came out, shutting the door behind him. Slakk remained inside, ostensibly trimming the rest of the dragon's nails.

"I seem to have missed a lot," Jakkin said slowly.

Errikkin, sensing an opportunity to please, filled him in. His tendency was to elaborate on the accident and the killing of Blood Brother. Not wanting to make Errikkin suspicious, Jakkin did not hurry him through the story. So he heard twice about the shots that had destroyed the beast and how Likkarn had sworn that, in his haste and fear, he had mistakenly pushed the regulator past Stun to Kill.

"Even though you have to push extra hard to change the setting," Errikkin added. Then he acted out Sarkkhan's reaction when he found the old trainer smoking blisterweed in the bondhouse.

"Sarkkhan said, 'You've always hated that dragon, Likkarn.'" Errikkin tried to lower his voice as deep as the nursery owner's. "'You bet your bag on him and lost and you hated him for it.' 'No,

Master Sarkkhan, I *loved* that worm. Raised him from a hatchling myself, I did,' Likkarn said as the smoke trickled out of his mouth.'' Errikkin put his hand over his bag in imitation.

''And what did Master Sarkkhan say to that?'' Jakkin asked.

''He said—''

Errikkin was interrupted by Slakk, who came out of the stall now that the story was past his part in it. ''He said, 'How many chances can I give you, Likkarn? We've known each other a long time. We were boys together. But how long can I trust a weeder?' ''

''And then Likkarn said—'' Errikkin tried to add.

''No, then Likkarn began to go into fury and jumped off his bunk screaming, *'There's no difference between us but half a bag!'* And he ripped off his bag, which really *was* half-full, and threw it into Sarkkhans's face. And then he followed the bag and leapt at Master Sarkkhan and started hitting him.'' Slakk finished the story so quickly he was out of breath.

Jakkin shook his head. ''Crazy. Weeders are crazy. Even in blister fury Likkarn's no match for Master Sarkkhan. Sarkkhan must have killed him.''

''No, that's the funny part,'' said Errikkin. ''He only held the old man's arms until the fury wore itself out. Then he pushed Likkarn back on the bed and with tears in his eyes said, 'I'm sorry, Likkarn. Sorry for all we've meant to one another. Sorry for all the years we shared. But for the sake of the others, for the sake of Blood Brother, I'm going to have to break you. It's back to stallboy.' And he emptied Likkarn's bag into his hand, pocketed all the gold but the grave coin, and put the empty bag gently on the bed beside him.''

Slakk nodded. ''That's true. And we know because Akki was there and the doctor. And the doctor told Kkarina, and she told—''

''Akki?'' Jakkin looked puzzled. ''What was she doing in the men's quarters? In Likkarn's room?''

Slakk smiled slyly. ''She gets around. Around a lot. She was with the doctor and Sarkkhan when they went looking for Likkarn. Someone said he had been injured and they had already dealt with you.''

''And I overheard some of it when I went to visit you in the hospice,'' Errikkin said.

''I don't remember you there.''

Errikkin laughed and put his arm over Jakkin's shoulder. Jakkin winced at the weight and Errikkin pulled away. ''You were out of it. For days and days. They finally made us get back to work and leave you alone.''

"Not alone," suggested Slakk slyly. "I understand Akki stayed there all night."

"Yes, all night," Jakkin said fiercely, but he added, "I was out of it, as you said. And besides, she was just being a nurse."

The boys looked down at the ground as if a gulf had suddenly opened between them. Then Jakkin asked brightly, "Well, what else happened?"

"That's it," Slakk replied, turning and going back into the stall.

"Are you going to help us finish?"

Errikkin pushed Jakkin away. "You look too white and shaky. Go on and rest. Slakk and I will finish up without you. After all, it isn't as if we had been expecting you to work today."

Suddenly Jakkin's head began to hurt again. He moved his shoulders up and down to test them. Pain shot tendrils along his spine. "Maybe I *will* go and lie down. Just today." He turned to go. Then, with as much offhandedness as he could muster, he asked, "How did the hatching go?"

Errikkin held up his hand in the wide-fingered greeting that meant everything was fine.

Slakk's voice floated back over the fence in a whine. "Come on, lizard lump, give me a hand."

Errikkin shrugged and gave a slight smile. "It went fine. Supposed to have been the best hatching in years. See you at dinner."

Jakkin nodded and left. He didn't dare ask any more. That would seem suspicious. He would, indeed, have to fill his bag himself.

tried not to wince as she popped a spoon of pulpy mash into his mouth.

"What do you think?"

"Hot!" he managed at last. He felt the heat burning all the way down his throat and settling somewhere in his chest.

"Of course it's hot, you baghead. It's right from the pot. But is it good?" She asked the question as if she knew the answer already, as if she dared him to make any judgment other than a positive one.

"It's good," he said, pushing his bag aside and rubbing his chest. "It's very good."

"Of course it is," she nodded. "But it needs a bit more skkargon." She reached up over her head to a shelf of crocks. There were no labels on any of them, but she did not waste time sorting. She knew exactly where the spice was.

Skkargon. Jakkin shuddered. That would make the mash even hotter. Skkargon was compounded of burnwort and something else. He opened his mouth and breathed in and out deeply. The aftertaste of the mash was wonderfully full on his tongue.

"Is that dinner?" he asked, suddenly hopeful.

"This? Of course not. I'll let it cool and put it down in the cellar in a big crock. In a couple of weeks it'll set and we can spread it on hot buns or slabs of bread." She spoke even as she threw two handfuls of skkargon into the mash and stirred. Without looking up at him, she added, "But if you are recovered enough to eat something solid, you'll find extra slabs of meat in the box." Her head jerked toward a series of metal lockers standing against the wall.

As he walked over to them, Jakkin heard a soft humming. He knew that in the main city of Rokk, where the original masters had lived, there was electrical power in every building. But around the countryside there were only a few small generators. The starships still landed in Rokk and rumor was that, from time to time, they brought a few extra generators to the planet. Jakkin had never seen one. He wouldn't even know what one looked like. He put his hand onto the first lockers and could feel a buzzing under his fingers. He looked up at Kkarina, ready to ask her about it, but she was tasting the mash, her eyes closed, lips moving in and out as if answering her own questions.

He opened the first locker. It was cold inside and little puffs of mist as fine as dragon's breath formed around the door. On the shelves, jars stood in silent rows. The jars were filled with red and orange liquids of varying viscosities. The next locker was equally cold. It contained loaves of bread. Jakkin found the meat in the third

# 6

MAKING HIS WAY back to the bondhouse, Jakkin was suddenly aware
of being hungry. He certainly couldn't fall asleep with his stomach
making enough noise to wake the entire nursery. Perhaps Kkarina
would let him have something to take back to his bed. She was a
funny one, old Kkarina, sometimes easygoing and other times dangerous as a hen dragon after hatching. He would have to go about it
carefully. He stroked his bag with one finger as he thought about the
best way to approach her.

The door to the kitchen was open, sending out moist, fragrant
smells. Jakkin had never been inside. It was a place of familiar mys-
teries. He stuck his head in tentatively, then let out an involuntary
sigh.

Kkarina, standing over a great black pot, looked up. She smiled.
"Come on in, come in. I can tell a hungry boy a mile away. Sit down
and be my taster. From what I hear, that's about all the work you'll
be managing for a few days."

Jakkin grinned wryly. So much for his careful approach. He sat
down on a stool by the stove and waited.

Kkarina was a short, dark woman, with shoulders as broad as a
man's and a waist that spoke of years of tasting in the kitchen. She
wore only a thin, short-sleeved jumper under a leather apron, and there
were large gray stains under each arm. When she served the food, he
neck and arms were always covered with a shapeless jacket. Jakki
was fascinated by her bare arms. They were vast but not fleshy. Sh
radiated a kind of amused power. Jakkin wasn't actually afraid of h
but he would never want to get her angry. He opened his mouth a

cold locker. He took out a bright pink slab and carried it over to the stove.

Kkarina, her eyes open now, put the spoon back into the mash and laughed at him. As she stirred, she said, "Sit down and eat. A long hunger makes a short appetite."

Jakkin sat, wrapping his legs around the stool legs, and chewed contentedly. As he thought about the cold lockers, he was distracted by the strong juices in the meat. Soon all he concentrated on was the flow of the juice into his mouth, the passage of meat down his throat. He didn't say a word until he had finished the slab, and then all he could manage was a quiet "Thank you."

Kkarina hummed an old melody as she worked. Jakkin recognized it as the song "The Little Dragon of Akkhan." He did not know all the words. He was just wondering if he dared ask for another piece of meat when Kkarina turned to him.

"Take another slab with you, and then off to bed. You look ready to fall, boy."

Jakkin was about to thank her again when he noticed something peculiar. Without meaning to, he framed a statement that was part question. "But you wear no bag."

"So?"

"But a bonder . . ." He hesitated, and kept staring at her bagless neck. It was spattered with reddish gold freckles, like her arms.

"What makes you think I'm a bonder?" She tasted another spoonful, nodding her head.

"But staying here at the nursery. And cooking. And not living in the masters' quarters, with a single room. I just thought . . ." His voice trailed off in confusion.

"You just thought what every bond boy thinks. That a master need not work—except if he wants to play at being a nursery owner or a senator, eh? That any woman lucky enough to have gold to fill her bag would lead a useless, silly life?"

Jakkin tried to shrug, but the movement hurt his back. And he wouldn't admit to Kkarina that he had never really thought much about being a master except for filling his bag and freeing himself from bond.

"Listen, boy, I had years enough of mindlessness in the baggeries. Where boys like you tried to become men in one slippery, sweaty night. When you're pretty, no one expects much more than open legs and a closed mind."

"*You?* In the baggeries?" Jakkin tried to imagine it, that large, shapeless body decked out in the filmy fripperies of a bag girl. Still, when Kkarina spoke, her voice was low and full of music.

"I'll tell you something, boy. Feeding this big family of bonders is a tough job, and I love it. Feeding them well, feeding them with the finest meals this side of Rokk. I *love* it." She smiled again and pointed to the wall. "Look at that."

His eyes followed. Above the stove there was a framed miniature, a bit sooty around the edges, with a dark jagged stain, like lightning, jetting from the right side to the left. Jakkin stood up and walked over, leaning across the corner of the warm stove to see. There was a girl in the picture, beautiful and unsmiling, with eyebrows as graceful and arched as dragon wings. He thought that if she were only smiling, she would have broken the heart of anyone who looked at her. As it was, the picture only called forth a kind of slow compassion.

"That was done of me when I was younger," Kkarina said. "I keep it around to remind me of the bad times."

Slowly Jakkin turned and looked at Kkarina, trying to find at least a ghost of that unsmiling beauty hidden in her flesh. His imagination was not that good, he decided at last. Only the eyebrows were the same.

"She was never happy, that girl," said Kkarina. "She didn't cry—but she never smiled either. She was never happy then, but she is now. It was Sarkkhan who helped me, bless that man. He's one who has never forgotten his past. Now go on, boy, and get yourself some more food."

Jakkin went over to the locker and took another slab. The cool air from the box was like the beginning of Dark-After. He wrapped the meat in a napkin and went out, careful to nod at Kkarina as he left.

In the bondhouse, he eased himself onto his bunk and ate the meat quickly. Then he snuggled inside his downer and closed his eyes. He reminded himself that he would have to wake up in the middle of the night, but he was sure that the noise of the others coming to bed would get through to him. And wondering vaguely if he should empty his bag to buy himself a timepiece at the nursery store, he fell into a sleep that was completely without dreams.

# 7

EVEN BEFORE THE others returned to the bondhouse, Jakkin awoke. He kept his eyes closed and listened while first the men and then the boys straggled in. If they guessed he was awake, they would try to get him to talk. But he wanted to listen and pick up information, not become involved in a long story-telling session.

The first voice he could identify belonged to Balakk, the old plowman, whose main duties were to the acres of weed and wort plants and the large kitchen garden. He was complaining, as usual.

"The river's going to go dry again if we don't get some rain. I've told Master Sarkkhan we'd better drill. There's water down below. I know it."

An answering grunt did not identify Balakk's partner.

"Plenty of water below. Even the worms smell it. I tell you, I fill my bag, and I'm leaving this nursery, unless Master Sarkkhan starts drilling. Got to have more reliable water than this."

Jakkin could hear Balakk's fist striking his hand, but he also knew that Balakk would not leave. The tall gaunt plowman had been making one complaint, one threat after another, for twenty years. It was said of him that he loved complaining and farming in equal measure and that, hidden away somewhere, he had gold enough to fill his bag fifty times over.

Other voices cut across Balakk's complaint, coming closer to Jakkin's bed, finally drowning out the old man's argument. Even seeing Jakkin with his eyes closed did not stop the talkers. After all, a bonder was supposed to be able to sleep through anything.

"Shh. Maybe we should . . ." That had to be Errikkin. Only Errikkin would try to hush the bonders. Then, as if he had seen something on the faces of the others, Errikkin's voice changed. "Of course, Jakkin can sleep with dragons fighting over him."

"On him," amended Slakk with a laugh.

There was general laughter then. Jakkin allowed himself to groan and turn over. The laughter increased.

The bantering went on for several minutes more, then the lights flickered. Even through closed eyes, Jakkin could see the lights dim. In five minutes, they would go out altogether.

Jakkin waited for night to claim the room before he opened his eyes. Slowly he became accustomed to the dark, could pick out the shadows of beds, of bodies. Once or twice the door opened as a late-nighter sneaked into the room. There was surprisingly little talk, mostly about old Likkarn's being broken back to stallboy. The story of Sarkkhan and the bag was told again, and a new piece of information added.

"He didn't lose his single room. Even Master Sarkkhan would not dare put that worm waste in here with us," said Balakk. He had proudly refused a single room each year it had been offered. "*We'll* not have a weeder in here." It was the last coherent sentence Jakkin heard. A few fragments drifted around the room, and then the air pulsed with heavy breathing and the light snores of sleepers.

~

JAKKIN WAITED ANOTHER half hour before rising. In the dark, the aching in his shoulders and back seemed multiplied. He suppressed a groan and stood. Carrying his sandals, he tiptoed out the door. If anyone saw him, they would suspect he was meeting a girl. Maybe even Akki. He smiled at the thought. Of all the bond girls at the nursery, she was the best looking by far. And the only one who stayed apart. He went out of the bondhouse into the night.

At first the night seemed quiet, but then Jakkin began to distinguish sounds. The *pick-buzz* of nightwings flittering around the eaves of the barn, the occasional grunting of a stud settling in his stall. Jakkin drifted toward the incubarn.

Suddenly he sensed rather than heard the silent-winged approach of a drakk, the snake-headed, deadeyed eggsucker so despised and feared by dragon breeders. As he looked up, it flew across Akkhan, its great wingspread momentarily blotting the moon from sight. He would have to report it in the morning, even though it meant exposing his own night wandering. If there was a colony of drakk nearby, it would have to be wiped out. Hundreds of eggs from one hatching could be lost to a single drakk family. The large adult drakk preyed on hatchlings, too, tearing off wings, legs, huge hunks of flesh from the living young with their razored talons. For good reason, there was a high bounty on drakk. Jakkin waited until the monster was gone from sight. It would not be back until Dark-After was past, since it had just checked the area with its sensors.

In the nursery, a hen dragon stomped her feet at Jakkin's approach, but he did not fear her roaring out. Once the nestlings were hatched, the hens were usually quiet at night, wrapped contentedly around their squirming charges. They chewed burnwort and drizzled the juices into their hatchlings' mouths. For the first month of life, after the hatchlings grew out of their eggskins, they would exist on nothing but the juice. Their little red toothbuds would grow into sharp white points, and then the hatchlings, too, could chew the leaves of blisterweed and wort, grinding out the juices for themselves and then following the juice with the mashed leaves for bulk.

Jakkin reached the door of the barn and, standing in a shadow, looked around. There was no one in sight. He lifted the latch and went in.

In the half-light supplied by the sulfur lamp, he made his way down the narrow halls. Unlike the stud barn, where wide hallways accommodated the cock dragons, these halls were used only for the human workers. Each compartment for the female and her brood had two doors, one small door opening into the hall and one wide door to the outside. The incubarn was a low, round building built around a central mow, a single column that supported the roof. Around the column was a hollow frame of slats which served as a ventilator to discharge the steam from the packed weed and wort leaves. Jakkin had once heard someone comment that the steam rising up was sometimes so dense you could wash your hands in it. At the top of the roof, the steam was caught in a series of vents that passed back through the barn to keep the individual compartments warm, even in the cold of Dark-After. It was thought that the warmer the hatchlings were kept, the faster and bigger they grew.

The workers' walkway was in between the central mow and the hens' compartments. Sweat began to trickle under Jakkin's arms, but the heat from the mow felt good on his back. It eased the ache.

Jakkin went first to the eggroom, where all the clutches were kept together for hatching. He knew at once that the hatching was finished, because the room was completely dark, but he went back into the hall and borrowed a lamp anyway, and returned. Little round shadows pitted the walls as the lamp lit the broken shells. Jakkin kicked through the sand floor, smashing pieces of the brittle casings. Jakkin knew, as any nursery bonder knew, about shells. When they were laid, they were elastic, cascading out onto the birth sands in numbers too plentiful to count. They piled up in great slippery pyramids that stuck together with birth fluids during the ice cold of Dark-After. Only when the temperatures on the planet rose again, and the fluids melted, did the eggs drop from the pyramids into the sand. That was another reason why the barn was kept heated, to hasten the hatching process.

Jakkin knew that, touched then, the eggs would break open, revealing a viscous yellow-green slime. Yet left alone the eggs hardened in a day, sheathed in a covering that even a sharpened pick could hardly open—from the outside. The growing hatchling within could break apart the shell with a horny growth on its nose. So once the egg had hardened, it was considered fair game for any human—thief, trainer, man, or boy—who thought he could sense a living dragon in the shell.

The living dragon. That was the irony. So few of the eggs held living dragons. Most were decoys for the predatory drakk. How often a bonder had had an opportunity to steal an egg, guarding it zealously, only to discover days later that it contained a heavy liquid and nothing else.

The shells were brittle now because the hens had licked the insides clean of the remaining birth fluids. One by one, the bonders had led the hens in to choose their own hatchlings and suck some sustenance from the sticky fluids. He could see the prints of hen feet in the sand. Angrily, Jakkin kicked at the shells. Then he bent down and picked one up, crunching it in his hand, delighting in the pain as parts of one scratched his palm, drawing blood. "Fewmets," he cursed, and stood.

He knew he should go back to the bondhouse. Stealing an egg was one thing, a kind of acceptable thievery. Stealing a hatchling— that was something else. Eggs were not counted, but hatchlings were, counted and recorded and set down in Likkarn's careful script on the doorway of each hen's nestroom. He had never seen it, but he knew it was so, just as he knew about eggs. It was part of every nursery bonder's knowledge, the rules and lore with which he had grown up.

He knew what he *should* do, but something drew him toward the nestrooms, some thin thread of sound. It was the peeping of a hatchling and the snuffling answer of a hen. He closed the eggroom door and moved on down the hall.

~

AT THE FIRST hen's compartment, he read Likkarn's list out loud. "Heart Worm (4) out of Heart Safe by Blood Bank. M. Blood Brother. 7 hatchlings, 5/27/07."

He lifted the latch and, holding the lamp overhead, stared in. Heart Worm was a yellowish color, not much darker than the eggskin of a newborn. She looked back at him with shrouded eyes and houghed in warning.

Jakkin squatted back on his heels and sang in that low croon, "It's all right, mother worm. It's all right."

She put her head back down and nuzzled the seven dragonlings one by one. Jakkin counted with her, saying the numbers in the same low voice. He watched her tail. The tip twitched back and forth, but he could tell that she was made only slightly anxious by his presence. He stood up slowly and backed out of the door.

The second hen was Heart to Heart, also out of Heart Safe by Blood Bank. She was a yellow-orange with a deep streak of red from her muzzle to her hindquarters. It spread like a bloodstain over her legs, then spattered like scores (or, Jakkin thought, like Kkarina's freckles) along her tail. She curled around five hatchlings, two of them still fully covered with eggskin. That meant he had missed the last of the hatchlings by only a day. Jakkin bit his lip as disappointment welled up.

Heart to Heart was even calmer than her sister had been. She barely raised her head when he entered. Jakkin took advantage of this and moved to her side, crooning to her the whole while. He put out his hand carefully and stroked the nearest of the hatchlings, a mottled little squirmer who jumped at his touch and struck at his fingers with still-soft claws. "Thou wilt be a fighter," Jakkin whispered. The best trainers, he knew, spoke *thee* and *thou* to their dragons. It was supposed to bring them closer. He had never actually tried it with the big stud dragons. He had never thought of them as *his*. He wondered if it mattered that he did not know how to speak *thee* and *thou* correctly, having only played at it with some of the other boys. Then he laughed at himself. After all, would the dragon know if he made a mistake? Would it care?

He must have been laughing out loud, because the little dragon stared at him for a long moment. Then it turned its back on him and snuggled against its mother.

Jakkin thought about the hatchling, but he could not bring himself to take it. He got up and left the room.

The next hen was Heart O'Mine, and he could hear her tail beating on the floor, an unmistakable warning. He lifted the latch anyway and slipped in. Her card said she was a half-sister to the other two hens, out of Heart Safe by Blood Type. It must have been from Blood Type's very last mating. The old stud was past mating age now, and kept somewhere far away, the other bonders said, on another farm that Sarkkhan owned. Jakkin recalled the stories of Blood Type, the fabled fighter from Sarkkhan's Nursery, his first male dragon. Fifty fights and forty-seven wins, the last a five-hour battle with a champion from the other side of the planet. Heart O'Mine had nine hatchlings this time, her second clutch. There had been a large number 2 next to her name. Nine hatchlings were a lot, especially for a second clutch. And by the sound of her tail, she was a nervous mother.

Jakkin squatted down on his heels and began the crooning that had worked so well with the first two hens, but Heart O'Mine's tail kept up its loud, irritated thumping. It was then he thought of the silly lullaby that he had sung to Blood Brother.

"Little flame mouths," he began singing, swaying a bit as he did.

The hen's tail seemed to catch his beat.

"Cool your tongues," Jakkin continued.

The tail was definitely moving in time to the song.

"Dreaming starts soon, furnace lungs."

By the song's end, the hen was quieted and Jakkin sighed. A strange peeping from the corner answered him. He saw a small yellowish hatchling there, one of its wings dragging.

"Oh, you poor thing," he murmured. It must have been hurt in the hatching. Or perhaps the hen had rolled over on it one night. It would never make a fighter. It would probably end up in the stews. A lot of people liked the meat of hatchlings. They were said to be much tenderer than old dragons. Jakkin had never tasted one.

Counting the injured hatchling as one, he numbered the rest as they squirmed closer to Heart O'Mine. He found the other eight easily.

"Bonder's luck," he whispered to the hen. "All bad." Heart O'Mine stirred at his voice. She was a strange, dark dragon with a yellowish lump above her right ear. He was wondering why Sarkkhan would breed a dragon with a deformity, when the lump moved. It stretched its oversized wings clumsily and opened its mouth to peep. No sound came out.

Jakkin was so startled he could scarcely move. His eyes made the round again. The one injured dragon in the corner, and eight at the hen's side. That made nine, and there was still the one newborn, wrinkled and yellow as custard scum. Ten. But the card outside had said nine. He was sure of it. Could Likkarn have made a mistake? Could Master Sarkkhan? He rose slowly and backed to the door, slipped through the crack, and held the lamp up to the list. "Heart O'Mine (2) out of Heart Safe by Blood Type. M. Blood Brother. 9 hatchlings, 5/29/07."

He went back into the hen's room and counted another time to be sure. On the third count, when he had reached ten again, he sat all the way down on the floor, put the lamp by his side, and let out a sound that was somewhere between a sigh and a moan. At the sound, the hen's head came up suddenly and the little dragon slid around her ear and down her nose, tumbling end over end into the sand at Jakkin's feet. It stood up shakily, stretched its wings again, and put its head to one side as if considering him. Then it trotted awkwardly over to him. Its wings were as yet too big for its body, and the weight of them dragging in the sand was so comical, Jakkin had to put his hand up over his mouth to keep from laughing out loud.

As the hatchling moved directly into the pool of light, Jakkin could see that under its yellow eggskin was a darker shadow.

"Thou," Jakkin said quietly to the hatchling in an awed voice. "Thou wilt be a red someday."

At his voice, the little dragon looked up and tried a hindfoot rise. Its heavy wings pulled it over onto its back, where its tiny legs raked ineffectually at the air. Jakkin leaned over and without thinking picked it up in his hands. The little dragon stood unsteadily and sniffed about his fingers, totally unafraid. It found the scratch from the eggshell and licked at the blood. Then it lifted its head and stared at Jakkin.

Jakkin stared back into its shiny black eyes and thought he saw a movement there.

*"Thou,"* he said again in a hushed voice, and suddenly felt a small rainbow moving in his head. It was the dragon. He had reached its mind. Jakkin drew his hands closer, up to his face, and he and the dragon stared eye to eye. The rainbow in his head danced, shooting off pale bursts of color.

Heart O'Mine gave a short, sharp hough. Her tail began its warning dance on the floor. Tucking the dragon hatchling in the crook of his elbow and cradling it against his chest, Jakkin picked up the lamp with the other hand. "You have your nine, great mother," he said to the hen. "This *one* is mine. I shall make this one a great fighter. I swear it."

He slipped back into the hallway, hung the lamp up, and pushed the door shut with his shoulder. Then he went out into the night.

# 8

THE SHOCK OF the night air, cool in comparison with the moist heat of the barn, made Jakkin shiver. The hatchling gave an answering shiver against his chest.

"There, there, little one. There, there, beauty," he said, and slipped the trembling snatchling inside his shirt. Its soft little nails caught in his skin but tickled rather than hurt, and he could feel its heart beating rapidly. He decided to keep it wrapped up until they reached the oasis.

Crossing a stone weir, one of many catch basins for the Narrakka waters, Jakkin listened again for sounds. Then he scrambled up the embankment and headed out across the sands. He traveled partly by instinct, partly by star reckoning, and cursed the light of Akkhan, which was in its brightest phase. He had to get away from the nursery's line of sight before Akka, the second moon, filled the sky as well, for then it would be as light as day, at least for a little while.

There was another way to get to the oasis. It meant going down the road almost a kilometer and then striking out across the sand. But it took longer. He did not have the time.

The dragon was quiet—sleeping, he would guess—and he stroked it lightly with one finger as he kept it cradled against his chest. Then suddenly he stopped. This was not the end—but the beginning. He had the dragon that he had prayed for, longed for, worked for, but now the hard part began.

He wondered briefly how there could have been such a mistake in the count, ten hatchlings instead of the nine listed. Perhaps they hadn't added in the one with the broken wing. If so, they would know at once that one was gone. Or perhaps this one, so obviously a newborn, with its eggskin still a bright creamy color and wrinkles even on its wrinkles, perhaps this had been a last-minute egg laid by Heart O'Mine in her own compartment instead of in the eggroom. A single. He had never heard of any such thing happening before. But then, he did not know *everything* about dragons. He laughed at himself softly. Everything? Why, he realized, he scarcely knew *anything*. Except fewmets. And did he know fewmets! He laughed again. The dragon stirred under his fingers.

*Thou*, he thought fondly, and was rewarded with a faint rainbow. *Thou art a beauty.* He began to walk again.

He approached the oasis from the southwest, and under the white eye of Akkhan it suddenly looked very large. He sat down inside the reed shelter and reached into his shirt. He had to detach the little dragon's claws from his bond bag. "There, there, let it be. I fill my bag myself," he said. Then smiling, he added, "Actually, if thou art a mighty fighter, thou wilt fill it for me. But not yet. Not quite yet."

He set the hatchling on the sand and watched it stretch. It began to stumble about, investigating its new surroundings. Enticed by the moonlight, it stuck its nose out of the shelter and seemed to sniff the air. Then it stalked over to the shelter wall and made a pounce on a shadow reed that moved across the sand. Finding nothing beneath its claws, it walked to Jakkin, wings dragging slightly. Jakkin flopped over on his stomach, his head close to the dragonling. With a tentative front foot it batted at his nose. When he did not move, it struck out again, with a greater swing, and this time connected.

"Worm waste," Jakkin cried, "that stings."

His loud voice startled the hatchling and it leapt back, moving its wings furiously and rising half an inch from the ground.

"Thou canst *fly!*" Jakkin said in a softer voice, filled with awe. But the little dragon settled down at once and did not try that particular maneuver again.

"Well, come here, then," Jakkin said at last and picked up the hatchling in his hands. He was surprised anew at how soft its skin was. It looked as if it should be slippery. It was certainly not the hard brilliance of a fully scaled-out worm. Rather, it was as soft as bag leather. Jakkin suddenly wondered what his own bag was made of. As suddenly, he decided he did not want to know.

He lay on his back, heedless of the little rivers of pain in his shoulders, and let the dragon walk about on his chest. Even with its soft claws, it managed to make some scratches through his shirt, but Jakkin did not mind. He thought of himself as being blooded by the dragon, just as one day the dragon itself would be blooded in the pit.

"Then thou shalt roar, little beauty," he said to the snatchling. "When thy life's blood first spills on the sand, then thou shalt roar for the first time, full and fierce. And the bettors will know thee for a mighty fighter. Then gold will fill our bag. And I will be a man. A man, my snatchling. And I will roar with thee, my flyer, my wonder worm, my beauty lizard."

The dragon slipped down his chest, gouging a small runnel into his armpit, and landed with all four feet firmly planted in the sand. There it promptly lost interest in Jakkin, went back into the shelter, curled up, and went to sleep.

Jakkin edged closer to it and curled around it, lending it the warmth of his own body for a while. Soon he, too, slept.

~

THE COLD WOKE him, the beginning of the bone-numbing cold of Dark-After. Jakkin crawled out of the hut on his hands and knees and stared at the sky. He could see neither moon, only the wash of white-gold that signified the start of the false dawn.

Bonders said, "Dark-After, nothing after." Very few had ever managed to remain outdoors then, even with strong constitutions and a lot more clothes on than Jakkin was wearing. The early settlers, masters and bonders alike, had stayed in their starships until housing had been built: strong stone buildings in the 150 acres that was Rokk, for the wardens and guards, cruder shelters outside Rokk's walls for the convicts. Though Jakkin had never been to the city, it was said those buildings still stood, two hundred years later, a testimony to the first Austarians. The worst punishment of the masters in the old days, before the shelters, had been to lock out a bonder all night. That was why Master Sarkkhan's nursery doors were never locked—just in case. And why the roads to the baggeries, the stews, and the pits were spotted with shelters, for late-nighters caught away from home.

Jakkin scrambled to his feet. He gazed once at the little dragon curled asleep in the sand. The cold would not bother it, not even as a newborn. He knew that. But just to be sure, he took off his shirt and wrapped it around the sleeping mite, placing the dragonling far back against the rear wall of reeds. Then, hugging his leather jerkin to him, he ran as fast as he could across the sand toward the nursery. If he kept moving, he thought, he could keep warm. If he ran fast enough, he could make it back before the worst of the cold struck. He would not bother about brooming his footsteps, but trust to the wind and pray to whatever god still watched over bond boys. Certainly the masters' god would not recognize him yet.

The sand seemed to slip away from his feet, making running even more difficult. Several times he stumbled and one time went crashing to his knees. It was hard to keep moving in the cold. The metal bond chain around his neck felt as if it were on fire, it was so cold, and the metal eyelets on his jerkin felt as though they were burning small holes wherever they touched his skin.

The cold made him want to stop and snuggle down in the sand, to build himself an earth mound and sleep. Yet he knew such a sleep would be the sleep of death. *Dark-After, nothing after*, he reminded himself, his feet moving even when his mind willed them to stop.

And then his feet were running on packed earth, and he realized he was on nursery property. But the cold befuddled him, and he was not sure where he was. His breath plumed out before him. He felt he could almost break it off and use it as a pick. Stick it on his forehead and break his way out of the egg of cold that surrounded him. He was sure his skin was becoming as hard and scaled as any lizard's. If blooded, he would roar. He found himself roaring, roaring, roaring, and he fell hard against a stone wall.

A gloved hand pulled at him, and he was suddenly wrapped in someone's downer.

"Hush. You're found. But the cold has snapped you. Just come along."

He thought he knew that voice. It came from another dream he had had.

A door opened and shut and the warmth made him hurt all over.

"Akki, what are you doing in here?" A sleepy voice.

"Bringing home a body."

"Why, it's Jakkin. Hey, Errikkin, look. It's Jakkin."

"Wonder where he's been all night."

"Look at his chest. Wonder what her name was?"

"Does he look different?"

"Like a man, you mean?" someone snickered.

"Was he coming from town?" A laugh. "You know."

A woman's laugh. "Yes, from the baggeries. Can't you see? His bag is only half-full."

"Or half-empty." More laughs.

"I heard him roaring outside the hospice. I grabbed a blanket, threw on my own thermals, and ran."

"Lucky for him."

"He's all luck. It's a wonder he's a bonder."

Jakkin opened his eyes. His body was too hot now. He threw the blanket off. He stared at Akki, who gave him a wry smile.

"Yes," she said, staring at him. "He's had himself quite a night." She winked.

They led him to his bed and he fell asleep, murmuring, "Beauty. You beauty." He heard them laugh once again before he was totally out.

# 9

MORNING SEEMED TO come too swiftly. Summoned by the clanging breakfast bell, Jakkin could scarcely rise and had to be dressed by Slakk and Errikkin. They did it good-naturedly and even tried to joke with him. Then they force-marched him down the hall to the common room.

It was the cup of takk flooding through him that gave Jakkin the strength to talk. "Did I . . . say anything in my sleep?" he asked, deciding that caution was less important than knowledge.

"Not her name," said Slakk, taking his face out of his bowl for the moment. "Nor the sign of her baggery."

"Baggery?" Jakkin was confused.

"Oh, leave him," Errikkin said. "Maybe he doesn't know her name. Maybe it wasn't so important."

"Any time you stay out so late the cold snaps you, and you leave your shirt behind, *it's important!*" said Slakk. The boys at the table laughed with him. Jakkin blushed, which made them laugh even more.

"I wasn't . . ." he began, and stopped. Better they guessed wrong than guessed where he *really* was.

Slakk heard his hesitation and stared at him slyly. "Unless, of course," he said, a grin starting across his face, "unless it was . . . Akki." As Jakkin made a stuttering protest, Slakk pounced. "It was Akki." He beat his spoon on the table and began chanting "Akki, Akki, Akki."

The rest of the boys at the table joined in, even Errikkin. "Akki. Akki. Akki."

"Stop it!" Jakkin shouted angrily. "It's not Akki. Stop it." But there was no breaking through their noise. He glanced quickly over at the pair-bonders' table, but Akki was not there. Had she heard and left? Or was she not yet at breakfast?

"Akki. Akki. Akki." The boys' chant continued unabated. Now they were all beating their spoons on the table.

Jakkin jumped up and stormed from the room, slamming the door behind him. He knew his dramatic exit would make them surer, but he didn't know what else to do. He needed time to think, time to calm down.

As he pushed through the outer door and into the yard, the bright sun made him squint. The barns seemed to shimmer and glow, heat streams rising from them. The one spikka tree in the courtyard center cast a shadow but no shade. He thought of the shadows of the night before, when he had gone, bent over, toward the incubarn.

And then, suddenly, he remembered the silent-winged eggsucker that had skimmed across the face of the moon. The drakk. He had not yet reported it. It and its family, maybe even a colony, would be somewhere close by. The dragon eggs were hatched, no longer in any danger, but there were still the hatchlings to consider. Soon the hens and hatchlings would be let out into the henyard. A drakk with its sharp, curved talons could maim or kill an unprotected hatchling before the hen was even aware of the drakk's presence. Drakk were silent, and—alive—they had no smell. Dead, they covered anyone close by with a heavy, nauseating odor of decay. Jakkin had heard that a drakk family on the hunt would circle endlessly, taunting a hen until she was drawn away from her helpless brood into a fruitless chase. He thought of his own dragon, his little beauty, out alone in the reeds.

"Stay in the shelter till I come for thee," he murmured, knowing that his thoughts could not reach so far but hoping that the young snatchling's instincts would keep it in the shelter for a while.

He turned and went back toward the bondhouse. As he went in the door, he was relieved to find that the chanting was over.

One of the younger boys, red-haired Trikko, started to call out when he saw Jakkin: "Akk—" He was stopped with an elbow in the stomach by Errikkin, who then turned and, immediately contrite, asked if Trikko had been hurt.

Jakkin nodded at his friends and walked over to the table where the older men sat: Balakk and his two helpers were there, as well as Jo-Janekk, who ran the nursery store, and Frankkalin, who was the main toolsmith and mason. At one corner of the table, surrounded by a self-imposed silence, sat Likkarn. The others ignored him and he glowered into his food bowl. Likkarn looked up only once and stared at Jakkin with such a look of distaste that Jakkin could feel a cold band of sweat start on his neck. He put his hand up to wipe it off and at the same time greeted the other men. He dried his hand on the side of his pants.

"Well, boy?" It was Balakk.

"Last night—" Jakkin began.

"Oh, we heard about your late night," chuckled Jo-Janekk, smoothing his mustache with one hand. "Woke the whole bondhouse, you did."

Jakkin's hand went up to his bag and he squeezed it, letting the tension flow out of his fingers onto the familiar soft bag surface. "Last night," he continued, "a drakk flew overhead. Near the henyard."

Likkarn looked up again. The distaste still showed in his eyes. "A drakk? Are you sure?" he asked quickly.

"Do you know what you're saying? What a drakk hunt will mean to the schedule here on the farm?" added Balakk.

"It was a drakk," Jakkin said, hoping they would not question him more.

"Describe it," said Likkarn, standing up and coming over to him. His red-rimmed eyes glistened. He was close enough so that Jakkin could see the gray-and-black beard stubble breaking through the scarred surface of his face.

Jakkin took a breath.

"What you *saw*, bonder," Likkarn added. "Not what you expected to see."

"It was a shadow. A black, silent shadow overhead. Wings stretched so." He spread his arms. "And a long snaky shadow of a head."

"A drakk," Balakk complained.

"Flying which way?" Likkarn asked, as if he did not believe a word.

Jakkin closed his eyes and saw again the great wings of the drakk. "Flying east to west, from beyond the bondhouse toward the incubarn."

"Fewmets!" Balakk's fist slammed against the table. "Those pieces of lizard waste seem to grow out of nothing. Nothing! I've a mind to quit farming and take a job in Rokk. I thought we had wiped them out seven years ago."

Likkarn's lips moved in and out purposefully. "Sometimes a new colony starts when the young are forced out by their elders," he said. "Out to find new territory . . . and new food. Across the desert sands, closer to civilization." He glared at Jakkin.

"And we were going to take the hatchlings out this very evening for their first airing," said Crikk, Balakk's right hand and his closest friend. He was a young man, just out of childhood, his arms pitted with blood scores. He had helped Sarkkhan several times in the minor pits before asking to be transferred back to the farm. "We don't dare take them out now. They'd just be meat for those monsters."

"So it's a hunt, then," said Balakk wearily. "A regular de-bagged roundup."

"Well, I've got plenty of knives, but they'll need honing," Frankkalin said as he rose. "I'll take some of the boys and get started." He went over to the table and fingered Errikkin, his special favorite, and two of the younger boys. They followed him silently; his one-word explanation was enough.

"I'll start Slakk and the other boys on the dragon food. The baths will have to wait until this is over," Likkarn said. Any sign of weed in his eyes was now gone. "I'll meet you back here in an hour. You take the boy"—he signaled with his chin at Jakkin—"and chart that flight."

Likkarn left, dragging Slakk and the others behind him.

"He acts as if he's still head here," complained Kkittakk, Balakk's second helper, a bonder new to the nursery. "And he's only a lower stallboy now."

"You've not been here long enough to know," Balakk said. "When it comes to fighting drakk, I'll stand behind Likkarn any day. He's got a nose for them, he has. He's as bloody-minded as they are. I remember once he fought a drakk bare handed . . . but there's time to tell that later." Balakk stood up. "Come, boy, show me where you saw that piece of worm waste. We'll have to take soundings." He sighed loudly and unfolded his long body from the bench.

They followed Balakk into the hall, where he unlocked a free-standing cupboard full of instruments. He took out a metal and glass object and polished the base of it with his sleeve. Then, finding a package of soft material in the cupboard, he polished the glass lens as well.

"There, that'll do for a first sounding. Now show me exactly where you were when that piece of filth passed over."

In the courtyard, Jakkin stood still for a moment, remembering. "It was night," he said softly.

"We *know* that," Kkittakk complained.

"Hush, you bonder, or I'll de-bag what little you've got," Balakk said in a fierce whisper. "He means it was dark out and he has to refeel where he stood. Fewmets, man, this thing is going to be hard enough without your interruptions.''

Grateful for Balakk's support, Jakkin closed his eyes. He was worried. If he told them exactly where he had been, he might give away the stealing of the dragon, for he had been on the path to the incubarns. But if he lied, the charting of the flight would be off by a kilometer or more, and the drakk might never be found. He thought what that could mean, picturing a hatchling squirming and peeping its fear, hot dragon blood dripping down where the talons gripped, scoring the sand below. He suddenly saw his own dragon with its life spilling out on the sands. He knew then there was no choice.

"Here," he said. "I was walking here. And the drakk flew this way." His hand cut through the air in a steady trajectory. It dipped once, just as the drakk's wings had dipped going by his head, and pointed to a spot well beyond the nursery, out in the sands.

Balakk grunted and turned the wheels of the instrument in his hand. He shouldered Jakkin aside and stood where Jakkin had stood, sighting through the eyepiece.

"There's a copse of spikka trees directly in line. And four or five kilometers farther is the edge of Sukker's Marsh. If we have to go in there to find them, it might take days.''

"And back, where it flew from?" Jakkin asked dismally, for that way lay the sands in which his own dragon was hidden.

"I'll get to that. I will." Balakk turned and sighted along the flight line. "No trees on the flight line. It's far and away across the sands before you come to anything in which a family of those baggy horrors could roost. Lucky for us they fly in such straight trajectories. Except when they're on the hunt. But with the dragons all inside right now, they'd just be making their regular straight passes. When they're hunting they can scent a dragon up to five kilometers on either side of their path and straight down as well. They have scent sensors along their bodies, covered by the wings.''

Jakkin nodded, the tightness in his chest relaxing only slightly.

"How big were its wings?" Balakk asked again.

Jakkin spread his arms apart a little, then farther.

"A small one. Pray to the gods they're all that size. I heard of a man who tackled a really big drakk, one with a wingspread longer than I'm high. Near dragon size, it was. Ripped him open as easily as a nestling pecks out of its egg." Balakk shuddered. "Let's hope they're all small ones. And that Frankkalin can get his knives honed sharp. We'll take the extinguishers, too. Sarkkhan needs to be told.

Jo, you do that. And we'll all have to get into leathers. It's some protection, at least.''

"In this heat—" Kkittakk began.

"Ripped him from here," Balakk said easily, pointing to just under his throat, "to here." He finished drawing a line down to his groin.

Kkittakk nodded. "Leathers it is," he said.

They walked back to the bondhouse in silence while Jo-Janekk disappeared toward Sarkkhan's sandbrick house. It was on a small rise overlooking the entire nursery and was surrounded by twenty-year trees. Jakkin had never been inside. Few of the bonders had. Master Sarkkhan was a solitary man who spent time training the pit fighters and running them in the major pits or off on his other farm with the retired studs. He was rarely at the nursery—and never entertained there. He gave orders—and the orders were passed along. Jakkin knew him by sight and by the sound of his voice, a big, booming gong of a voice. He doubted if Sarkkhan knew much about him.

~

THE DRAKK FIGHTERS met outside in less than an hour, dressed in leathers. Jakkin, being the youngest and unfamiliar with the pits, had never owned his own coveralls. He wore a pair of fawn-colored ones that Jo-Janekk had found for him. They were too long and had to be rolled up. There were several strange scarrings on the legs. Jakkin did not ask where the deep scratches came from. He was afraid he knew. He was grateful, though, that they let him be part of the roundup. Some bonders felt that a successful roundup changed a boy into a man. Jakkin was grateful and, though he wouldn't admit it out loud, very frightened. He had heard a lot about drakk, none of it good.

"Master Sarkkhan was not in his house. He's away at the pits—" Jo-Janekk began.

"Fewmets, that's right," Balakk cursed. "I forgot. He's got two fighters. Hoping to have a winner at the minor pits with them. He's hungry, is Master Sarkkhan. Hasn't had a winner in months. Not even at a minor. Well, I hope he has them today, or that we find those pieces of waste. Otherwise, I'd not bet a coin to fill a dead man's bag against a sack of gold but that he'll have us on half rations before nightfall.''

"Now, Bal," Jo-Janekk began, "you know he's not that kind of master. He came up from bond himself.''

"The worst kind are gold masters, they say," Kkittakk put in. "Worse than born masters.''

"You haven't been here long enough to know," said Frankkalin. "Save your fire for the drakk," Likkarn warned them. "We can't wait till Sarkkhan comes back, win or no win." He rubbed his hand over the bib of his coverall, touching the place where his bag lumped. "You can't wait with drakk flying out there." He looked at Jakkin. "Do we have to take this bag of waste?"

"Yes." Balakk gave the answer without hesitation, and as he was now senior, Likkarn could not quarrel with him.

Jakkin could feel the cold sweat begin again, beading his neck and running down the crease of his back. He wondered that he could feel so cold when he should be hot in the confining leathers.

Wordlessly, Frankkalin gave out the knives. Long, straight bladed, they resembled machetes with bone handles. Each man got one. Likkarn, Balakk, and Frankkalin carried extinguishers as well, the three that could be spared from the hallways.

"Stingers for stunning, but finish them with knives," Balakk cautioned. "We can't waste power. There's not another shipment of power packs due into Rokk till next year, and we're already low." He did not have to mention Likkarn's killing of Blood Brother. It was on everyone's mind.

Likkarn grunted and looked away.

Balakk continued as if there had been no interruption. "And once the drakk are down, they can be cut easily enough. Just be sure they *are* down, though, and always come at them from behind. Even a downed drakk can sometimes make a pass at you with his claws, a reflex like. Knew a man once, had his leg near took off by a drakk he thought was dead." He shivered. "Those . . . those . . ." Even his curse words seemed inadequate. He spit to one side. "I hate them."

Though they all knew the basics of hunting drakk, no one minded the extra warning. Then Jo-Janekk handed out the masks. "Clip them to your shoulder straps and snap them on at the last," he explained. "There's no smell like a dead drakk. It'll fair incapacitate you. Let's hope we get lots of them today."

"*Drakk!*" they shouted together, lifting their knives and stingers overhead. As if the shouted word guaranteed success, they shouted it again, Jakkin louder than the rest. He put his fear into the word and hurled it from him, then pumped his arm high, catching the sunlight with the blade. "*Drakk! Drakk! Drakk!*"

The ululation continued to echo as they marched out of the yard, a band of seven in gray-and-tan leathers. The other bonders stood by the barn doors to watch them pass.

Jakkin wondered suddenly if Akki, too, watched from the hospice or if she were away on some errand of her own. He threw his chest out and strutted down the road like the rest.

# *10*

THE GRIM PARADE, sweating freely under the eye of Austar's red sun, marched out the two kilometers to the copse of spikka trees. Jakkin had minded well what Jo-Janekk had said to him in the bondhouse, before he had dressed in his leathers: "It is no shame to be afraid, but it is foolish to go out with a full bladder." He only wished they could stop now, but he did not dare break the silence to ask.

Likkarn gestured as they came close to the trees. He chose three hunters—Balakk, Frankkalin, and Jakkin—to circle to the right, and three—Jo-Janekk, Crikk, and Kkittakk—to the left. Likkarn's fingers signaled that he would remain at the point.

They obeyed him at once, moving on silent feet into the circle. If the drakk were flying, the men would be scented. But drakk had notoriously bad ears and eyes. If the marchers were careful, they could catch the colony by surprise just as it rose from the nests.

There were not more than forty trees in the copse, though it was a large stand by Austar standards. Being so near Sukker's Marsh meant that there was water feeding into an underground stream. Each tree would have to be approached, shaken, searched. Drakk adult males were fairly easy to spot. They always sat hunched over like dark fruit high up on the top side of the broad, spiky leaves. The females, however, squatted in the nests and had to be shaken out. And the young drakk within the nests were the most difficult to find. The tallest trees had to be climbed; and Jakkin, being the youngest and lightest of the hunters, was to be the climber.

The ground directly under the trees was spongy. The men's steps down were silent, cushioned by the wet, sandy soil. But each time they pulled their feet up again, the sucking noise seemed as loud as a dragon's roar.

At Likkarn's signal, they stopped and listened. Then Likkarn put his fingers to his mouth, wiggled his fingers, and made a peculiar peeping sound. Jakkin was startled. He had never heard anyone call in that way. It sounded just like a dragon hatchling in trouble. The mewling cry of a nestling just out of the shell echoed around the oasis, but there was no answering hiss from a drakk on the hunt.

Jakkin looked over at Frankkalin, who mouthed back: "Daylight." Drakk did not ordinarily hunt by day. Only a rare drakk could be goaded or fooled into a day flight. But if these were young drakk, and they were in the copse and they were hungry, perhaps . . . It was a chance they had to take. Likkarn gave the cry again. It was greeted with more silence.

He gestured them forward, each to the foot of a small tree. Jakkin watched the others before tackling his own tree. First the top was scanned carefully, then the trunk was shaken. If there was no hiss from the treetop, no drakk shaken into a diving flight from the tree, a slashing X with the knife on the trunk marked it as having been searched.

They scanned and shook some twenty-seven small trees, the last two large enough to need two men for the shaking. It was all done silently.

Thirteen trees in the copse remained. They were too large and thick for shaking. They would have to be climbed.

Jo-Janekk reached into his pack and drew out two sets of pitons—knifelike clamps. One set was to be tied onto sandals and the other was already sewn into leather gloves. Jakkin had heard of them but he had never used them before. Jo-Janekk showed him the best way to secure the pitons to his shoes and mimed the climbing, whispering in his ear, "Just find them. Don't be a hero. Leave the rest to us. When you find them, drop straight down and show by fingers how many." Then he gave Jakkin a boost up the tree.

Jakkin clamped first his hand pitons, then the feet, into the slippery-smooth gray bark of the tree. The knives dug easily into the trunk, their thudding impact the only sound in the oasis. He began a slow ascent, moving one arm, then one leg at a time, rocking the knife a bit to free it from the trunk, drawing it out, clamping it in again. He was halfway up the tree when the first real wave of fear hit him. If there were drakk in the toothed leaves above him, they could rake him with their razored claws before he could remove his knife from his coverall belt. Rip him, he remembered Balakk's saying, "from here''—and drawing his hand down to below his stomach—''to here.'' Jakkin gripped the tree with his arms as well as the knives, closed his eyes, and could not move.

A sharp hiss from below made him open his eyes again. It was not a drakk but Likkarn, pointing the extinguisher directly at him. Jakkin shook his head, and Likkarn answered with a shake of the stinger. Next to Likkarn stood Balakk, his knife drawn, his mouth forming the words ''Move, boy.''

Jakkin moved. He was less afraid of the drakk than of the stinger in Likkarn's hands. The drakk were only a possibility, but the narrowing of the old weeder's eyes was a certainty. Jakkin climbed.

The trunk of the spikka tree was long and crisscrossed with old knife cuts, though whether from other drakk hunts or from climbing games or from the lopping of limbs of wood, Jakkin could not be sure. The scars had healed black against the gray trunk, and already the oozing cuts his pitons inflicted upon the wood were closing behind him, a dark trail of scars. The spikka allowed little moisture to escape.

Jakkin climbed until the men below were the size of small boys. He could see that Balakk had a bald spot the size of a gold coin and that Likkarn had an egg-shaped one. His own head touched the first leaves. He stopped and scanned, peering through the ragged edges of the leaves that fanned around the treetop like a crown. His eyes saw nothing, though his heart continued to thump loudly at every shadow.

He pulled one hand loose and, balancing carefully, took the glove off his hand with his teeth. He let it drop to his chest. Then he detached the knife from the belt slipknot with an easy motion. Silently he pushed the knife up through two leaves, bending one back slowly. Now he could see the rest of the leaves clearly. There were no drakk. He put the knife between his teeth, managed to get the glove back on his hand, and went down much faster than he had gone up.

The ground felt solid and welcoming. He turned to the others and made a zero between his thumb and forefinger, saying the word silently to them, and tied his knife back on his belt. They nodded, and Balakk added a fresh slash of an X to the tree, chest high.

The climb up the second tree was easier, both on his muscles and his mind. He went up without stopping, scanned the leaves, and descended. The third tree was the same.

The fourth tree was longer and more fully leafed out. One leaf was blackened as if it had caught on fire. Occasionally, when the droughts were at their worst, a spikka tree had been known to burst into flame spontaneously. At first Jakkin had thought the black leaf was a drakk. He had been ready to drop from the tree like a stone.

But squinting his eyes, he could make out the jagged edges, and when it did not fly off, even under prodding from his knife, he knew it was just a leaf. He climbed down slowly, his heart beating strangely in his chest.

He took some deep draughts from the water bottle Balakk proffered and squatted back on his heels as the men whispered above him. They were trying to decide which trees seemed the most promising or the least difficult to climb.

"Are you all right, boy?" Jo-Janekk mouthed at him, ruffling his sweaty hair.

Jakkin nodded. Even with the water, his mouth was dry.

Up the fifth tree, he could feel the water sloshing in his tightened stomach, remembering too late Jo-Janekk's message about his bladder. He should have gone without the drink. He was thinking about that, and not about the climb, when his head touched the leaves and a sharp hiss caught him by surprise. He dropped by reflex, his arms up, the pitons flashing above his head. He heard the shouting of the men and the sharp retort of the stinger.

It was the awful smell, dark, penetrating, searing his nose, fighting its way down his throat, that woke him to action. He reached up to his shoulder, found the mask dangling there, and jammed it on. Several quick breaths revived him. He stripped off the gloves, grabbed up his knife, and looked around.

On the ground near him was a drakk. Its oily green snakehead was severed from its body, but the body still flapped its enormous wings, uncovering the scabrous, pulsing sensor organs. The near-blind snake eyes glowed with a dark malevolence that went out slowly, like the embers of a dying fire. The talons of the body gripped and ungripped on an invisible prey.

Jakkin walked around the back of the drakk and suddenly stabbed at it with his knife. He cut into the drakk body again and again, as if he could, by his actions, cut away his own fears. A viscous blood pulsed out at each cut. He jabbed at the drakk until his arm was tired. Then, finally exhausted, he stopped and looked around for the others.

The six bonders stood in a circle under the tree, knives drawn, waiting. When no other drakk flew down, Likkarn gestured them away. He walked around the tree, girdling it quickly with the stinger. The tree fell, heavily, its descent slowed by its close neighbors. At last its leafy crown was caught securely between two other trees. It hung there low enough for their knives.

The bonders moved toward the tree, circling it. Jakkin stood behind them, peering over Jo-Janekk's shoulder. Likkarn pointed with his stinger and grunted.

In the topmost leaves was a nest of kkhan reeds plastered together with dragon fewmets. The reed tops were arranged in such a way that the nest looked exactly like a spikka leaf. Even close up, it was difficult to distinguish it. Suddenly a small snakehead peered over the side of the nest. Then another. Jakkin counted quickly. There were seven young drakk hissing furiously up at them. They could not fly yet and tried to hide under one another.

"Seven," called out Likkarn in a doomsday voice slightly obscured by his mask. "Be sure. Seven."

The men marched into the leaves and stabbed the squirming little horrors with their knives, severing the heads from the bodies. The drakklings died quickly, leaving the dreadful stench behind. Their thick, dark blood coated the knives and had to be washed off immediately in the sand. Even then, the blood left pits and ruts in the shine.

They buried the remains of the drakk and their nest in a great hole they dug out beneath the fallen tree. Reluctantly Jakkin climbed the rest of the trees, his knife always at the ready in his clenched teeth, but he found nothing else.

On their march back to the bondhouse for hour-long showers in hot water with strong yellow soap, Likkarn spoke only once.

"I don't like it," he said. "The female and the young. Where was the male? I don't like it."

"Perhaps she had mated before she came here," offered Crikk.

"Yes, that's it," said Kkittakk.

"Perhaps," said Balakk. But like Likkarn he was not happy.

Likkarn took out some weed and, with one hand, rolled it mechanically into a thin red cylinder. He had already started smoking it by the time they entered the courtyard. They left him alone and hurried into their showers.

Old Likk-and-Spittle may have been worried, Jakkin thought, but not enough to lay off the weed. So Jakkin wasn't worried either. He had dipped his knife into a drakk's blood and come out a man. Surely he was ready to tackle anything now. He thought of his dragon waiting out in the sand.

*See, thou mighty fighter*, he called to it in his mind. *I am a mighty fighter, too.*

~

AT THE DINNER table, the talk was all about the fight with the drakk. The boys had the story from Jakkin at least three times, in three different versions. Each time the tale ended with his killing the drakk and then the hour-long attempt at scrubbing the smell from his hide.

"It lingers," said Jakkin. "Gods, how it lingers."

"You're telling me," Slakk put in, holding his nose.

Errikkin jabbed Slakk in the ribs, and they all laughed.

"And my jaw still aches from holding the knife in my teeth." Jakkin waggled his jaw at them and they nodded admiringly.

"I wish *I* had been there," Errikkin said wistfully.

Jakkin did not tell them how he had bloodied his knife in the back of a *dead* drakk, and how wet the inside of his coveralls had been, and how next time, if there were a next time, he would never take a drink in the middle of a roundup. But he did add, "Each of the men on the march is going to get part of the bounty. Eight drakks. I'm to have a full seventh share." He did not have to say a *man*'s share. That was understood.

Errikkin interrupted. "You *should* get it. After all, you were in the most danger, climbing up the tree."

"Not really," Slakk said. "Remember, he was dropping fast, while the others were standing still below."

"But he was closest," said Errikkin.

The boys began to take sides, some supporting Errikkin with great vehemence, and one or two restating Slakk's argument. Jakkin stopped them by banging his spoon on the table.

"Enough," he said. "What matters is that I have filled my bag with this fight. Or at least," he added truthfully, "a bit more gold will clink in it. And . . ." He paused for effect.

They listened.

"And?" asked Errikkin, right on cue.

"And I have been given tomorrow as an additional Bond-Off day. I don't have to work. I can go where I want." Jakkin spoke the words with a kind of sly joy.

"And where will you go?" The questioner was one of the youngest boys, little L'erikk, Frankkalin's son.

"Do you need to ask?" said Slakk. He began pounding his fist on the table. "Akki, Akki, Akki."

The others laughingly joined in.

Jakkin looked quickly over at the pair-bonders' table. Since Akki was not there, he smiled and let them go on. What did it matter how wrong they were? *He* knew he would be spending first his night and then his Bond-Off day out on the sands with his dragon.

# The Snatchling

# *11*

JAKKIN LEFT DIRECTLY after dinner, strolling off down the road as if going toward the town for an evening at the local stews. It was a long walk, nearly fifteen kilometers, but he shrugged off a ride with some of the others. Let them think what they liked; he had jangled his bag at them, clanking with the bounty coins. Let them make false guesses.

When he was passed by no more nursery trucks (bought dearly, he knew, from the star traders at Rokk) and he could see no road dust deviling up from tires or feet either ahead of him or behind, Jakkin doubled back halfway, crossed the weir, and headed out over the sand.

Once, hearing the noise of a vehicle far off down the road, and seeing the telltale dust spiraling up, he had dug a quick depression in the sand and snuggled into it. But the truck roared by without stopping, and he realized that he had not really needed to hide. He was already far enough away from the road. Still, he knew that care was more important now than ever. Bending over and brooming his footsteps, he scuttled like a lizard over the ocean of sand. He noticed that his prints from the night before were gone, and he thanked the intermittent south wind for helping him keep his secret.

He reached the oasis before the first moon had lipped the horizon. That gave him four hours at the very least. Nothing stirred. The air was incredibly still. The weed and wort patch had stopped smoldering except for one lone stalk that sent a gentle puff of smoke into the air. Without wind to move it off, the smoke cloud hung around the tip of the plant. From where he stood, Jakkin could see the toothed leaves of the plant partially unrolled, maroon sap veins like road maps running through them. Tomorrow he would start crushing the most mature leaves.

A sudden little wind squalled through the patch, coming from nowhere. The leaves trembled, dipped. As quickly as it had come, the wind puffed itself out in the patch.

Jakkin smiled and went over to the reed shelter. Before he got there, a cascade of muted colors burst into his head. "Thou mighty snatchling!" he cried. "Thou hast sensed my coming." He bent over and started in and was tripped by the dragonling.

Its size startled him. It was fully a body size larger than the night before, coming almost to his knees. Its eggskin was still the dirty yellow color, but now it was stretched taut over the dragon's growing muscle and bone. Underneath, the dark patches that he had only sensed were beginning to show through. And there were tears in the custard-scum-colored skin where the dragon had begun to molt. Inside the shelter, Jakkin found swatches of the eggskin hanging from snags on the wall. The snatchling had apparently rubbed against the reeds to ease the itching of its shedding skin.

Jakkin picked up one of the swatches of skin and pulled it between his hands. It stretched easily and had a soft, almost furry feel. When he let it go, it snapped back to its original shape.

Jakkin walked out of the shelter to the spring and took off his sandals. He put his feet into the warm water. The dragon held back, as if waiting for a signal.

"Come on, then," he called to it softly, making enticing little trails in the sand with his hand.

The dragon watched his fingers for a moment, then trotted out of the shelter and pounced. It caught his hand in its mouth, and the red ridge of tooth bumps clamped down. One tooth must have already broken through, for there was a sharp piercing pain in Jakkin's palm, but he did not take his hand away. "Fight, thou wonder," he said, and was rewarded with another burst of color in his head. The dragon opened its mouth and backed off for a moment. Then, raising its trailing wings, it launched itself with a leap into the stream.

Jakkin was up in an instant, ready to follow the snatchling and rescue it, when he realized that it was paddling down the ribbon of water as easily as if it were a fish. He sat down again and watched it. Obviously it had tried this maneuver before. There was nothing casual or tentative in its swimming. When the dragon came to the stream's end, it climbed up through the kkhan reeds and trotted back to Jakkin's side, where it shook itself thoroughly, wetting Jakkin in the process.

"Thou didst that on purpose!" shouted Jakkin, cuffing the little dragon lightly, a love tap. The dragon, in the same spirit, tapped

Jakkin back with its still-soft claws. It followed this attack by leaping onto Jakkin's chest. Jakkin tumbled back, and they rolled over and over, and down into the stream.

Jakkin paddled after the dragonling with more splashing and less grace. When they climbed out through the reeds, Jakkin took off his shirt and shorts and spread them out to dry on the sand.

"Listen," he said, "if thou art going to be such a rowdy, thou must eat to gather strength." He walked over to the weed and wort patch with the dragon at his heels. Carefully choosing a fully leafed-out stalk, he plucked three leaves. They were warm to the touch.

Back at the spring, he squeezed a leaf between his fingers. Only a little juice ran out of the veins. The dragon snuggled in his lap. Jakkin tickled it under the chin. The dragon opened its mouth and Jakkin drizzled what juice he could into its mouth and on its nose.

At first the hatchling looked surprised. Then it sent a long, red-ribbed tongue out to explore its muzzle for whatever juice remained.

Jakkin crushed the second leaf, puncturing the vein at several places with his fingernail. This time he was able to extract more juice from the plant.

The snatchling slurped it eagerly, licking Jakkin's fingers for whatever was left.

The third round of juice seemed to satisfy the dragon's hunger completely, and it fell asleep as soon as it had finished giving Jakkin's red-stained fingers a perfunctory lick.

Jakkin sat for almost an hour with the little dragon on his legs, stroking its head and working carefully at a tear in the eggskin over its left ear. He crooned old songs and hummed new melodies he made up himself. He murmured names to it. But when Akka and Akkhan sat high in the sky, making double shadows in the sand, Jakkin lifted the little dragon in his arms and carried it back into the hut. He covered it again with his old shirt.

"Sleep well, thou mighty snatchling," he whispered to it. "For I shall come to thee in the morning. And bring a bowl and a bone knife to make thee a proper meal. I promise."

The dragon answered him only with slight, hissing snores.

Jakkin put on his clothes, now dried in the heat, and left the oasis, brooming away his trail. A slight wind, rising in the east, finished the job for him. He was back in the bondhouse and asleep long before the rest had returned from the town.

# 12

BOWL AND BONE knife. Those were Jakkin's very first thoughts when the morning sun streamed across his face. He was lying half in and half out of his bunk, well awake before the bell. Bowl and bone knife. How would he ever find them? What excuse would he use to get them?

In the end, he simply got dressed early and found his way into the kitchen before the other bonders had risen. Kkarina was stirring the takk in a gigantic pot, tasting it every three or four stirs.

"Good morning," Jakkin said brightly.

She turned and looked at him, raising her eyebrows but keeping her mouth on the spoon. Kkarina would never hurry her tasting. At last she finished and put the spoon back in to stir some more. "Another few minutes," she said, meaning the takk.

Jakkin nodded.

"Get a bowl and have a taste," she said, pointing at a small room off the kitchen.

Jakkin walked where directed and found a room of shelves with all the bowls and spoons and cutlery he could want. He slipped a bone-handled knife inside his shirt, then took a bowl and spoon and went out. It had been easy.

"Come here," Kkarina said. "You need some meat on you."

She jabbed at him with the spoon. He jumped back, and the knife inside his shirt slapped his ribs. He had a sudden fear that it would fall out. Hugging the bowl against his shirt, imprisoning the knife between it and his ribs, he went over to Kkarina.

"Drakk killer," she said affectionately, and smiled. "Hero." She touched his bag, making it jangle.

Jakkin smiled back. He knew it was a false smile and hated himself for it.

"Want to tell me the story of the hunt?"

Jakkin began the story as Kkarina filled his bowl. But when he got to the part where the mother drakk had been killed, he quickly glossed over the stabbing, not really wanting to tell Kkarina that all he had done was dip his knife into the dead drakk. But he did not want to lie to her, either. That other knife, the one under his shirt, seemed to burn a brand across his front.

"I didn't do that much," he ended lamely, remembering with shame the wet coveralls that he had stuffed into the laundry. The more he remembered, the less he wanted to remember. Some hero.

"You must have done something to have filled your bag, to have been given an extra Bond-Off."

Jakkin looked down at the full bowl. The takk was hot enough to send up bubbles that burst into a deep pink froth. He shrugged.

"Go on and eat. I'll pack you a lunch. Most men, after their first roundup, want to get as far away from work as possible. Must be something, that hunt." She turned her back on him and went to the cold lockers, coming back with a basket of paper-wrapped food packages. "Here. Go. This won't be the only one of these I'll be fixing today."

Jakkin took the bowl in one hand, the basket in the other, and went out into the common room. He drank the takk as quickly as he could, letting the hot, thick liquid sear a trail down his throat. Then, rinsing out the bowl and spoon, he thrust them into the basket, covering them with one of the food bundles. If anyone asked, he would say . . . He could not think of what he would say.

The alarm bell rang loudly and Jakkin jumped. He could hear the sounds of bonders waking on both sides of the house.

Hoisting the basket onto his back and adjusting the leather straps to fit his shoulders, he pushed open the heavy door and went out into the daylight.

As he left, Kkarina's voice echoed again in his thoughts: "Most men, after their first roundup . . ." *Most men.* Was the passage from boy to man really that easy? And was it always built upon lies?

Then, pushing the thought away, he bent his head and trudged off down the road as if he were going into town.

~

THE DRAGON MUST have sensed his coming, for it was out of the shelter and waiting for him. It had only shreds of eggskin still clinging to its body, a strange patchwork of dull brown and yellow. Jakkin had a moment of disappointment. Dull brown. He had thought it was going to be a red. Browns were usually solid fighters, aggressive but without much imagination. Reds, on the other hand . . . He beat down the thought. Perhaps, it might still change color. Hadn't he heard that "color fast does not last," meaning a dragon's true color often did not show early? He could still hope.

He shifted his pack on his back and the coins in his bag clinked together.

At the sound, the dragon lifted its oversized wings. They still had a crumpled appearance and the effort of moving them seemed to tire the little lizard. It settled down again on its stomach and waited, head on front claws, for Jakkin to come nearer.

Jakkin smiled at the dragon and thought at it, *The morning becomes thee, my wonder worm.*

The dragon's muted rainbow signature ran through Jakkin's head once more, as clear and identifying as if it were a mark on paper.

Jakkin knelt for a moment by the dragon's side and scratched it behind the ears and then down its long neck. The hatchling raised its back up, arching under his hand.

"Not yet, thou beauty," he said. He stood and walked into the shelter, where he shrugged out of the basket, unpacking the bowl and bone-handled knife. "First we must feed thee. Come on."

The dragon followed confidently at his heels as he walked to the weed and wort patch. In the direct sun, the leaves were all open, as if turning every vein to catch the light. At the head of the patch, the dragon halted, digging its claws into the sand. It stood still, watching the movement of the wind through the stalks.

Jakkin was about to enter the patch but stopped himself. This was the time, he thought suddenly, for the dragon's first lesson. He turned and faced it and held his hands toward it, palms up. "Good *stand*," he said, and then thought at it as well. STAND *still, thou mighty fighter.* STAND. He repeated the hand signals again and the spoken words, all the while thinking the sentence.

The dragon cocked its head to one side as if considering, but remained in the clawed-in stance.

Jakkin watched it carefully. After a minute, he could see it tiring, one leg beginning to waver. *Good* STAND, he thought at it one more time and went over and hugged it to him, rubbing it under the chin. "Thou mighty young snatchling. Thou great worm."

The dragon's tongue wrapped around his little finger and licked.

"Now for some food," Jakkin said. He walked back into the

patch, careful not to touch the red stalks, which were still hotter than was comfortable; nor to brush against the seed pods, which until they were covered with a gray film could give a bad burn. He plucked a handful of leaves and went back to the shelter, where he got out the bowl and knife.

Sitting down, feet in the stream, Jakkin cut the leaves, piercing the veins with the knife. Then he crushed the leaves with the bone handle. Before long, he had a half a bowl of juice.

"Here, eat this," he called to the snatchling, who was pouncing on shadows thrown by the kkhan reeds at the end of the pool.

The dragon looked over at his voice, but did not move.

"Come," said Jakkin, again, holding the bowl down so the dragon could see it.

The snatchling put its head to one side and lashed its ridged tail.

Jakkin thought at the dragon, *Come, thou hungry worm. Come.* The dragon trotted over to him.

"So, thou needest an official invitation," said Jakkin, laughing as the dragon settled on its haunches and opened its mouth. He spooned the juice onto its tongue, missing whenever the dragon moved its head. Soon the two of them were covered with the dark maroon juice.

"Aw, fewmets," Jakkin said when the bowl was finished. "Look at this mess." Quickly he stripped off his clothes and washed the shirt and pants in the warm stream. His bag, too, was spattered with spots as dark as blood. He tried to rinse it as best he could, bending over the stream. As he was bent over, unbalanced, he felt a sharp nudge from behind, strong enough to thrust him forward. He tumbled head first into the water, went under, and came up spluttering to find the dragon in a hindfoot rise, its wings braced on the ground behind. It raked at the air with its soft claws. Jakkin could feel a rainbow laugh forming in his mind.

His moment of anger dissolved. The dragonling was so comical and fierce at once, he started to laugh instead. Then he realized what it was doing, and thought at it, *Steady. Steady.* Then, when he saw the dragon begin to falter, he cried out, "Good. Now."

The dragon lifted its overlarge wings and leaped into the river, landing next to him with a tremendous splash.

Jakkin laughed and splashed back.

At last they climbed out of the river together and flopped onto the sand. The sun on his back and shoulders and legs felt good. Jakkin lay on his stomach and thought about the dragon and about the possible fights ahead. "It will not be easy, little one," he said. "There is much I do not know. I was too young to learn much from my father. I am not old enough yet to be apprenticed to a trainer. And watching badly trained dragons in the pits only teaches bad habits— I heard Master Sarkkhan say that once. He was talking to Likkarn, but I overheard him. Master Sarkkhan said there were only two ways to learn about dragons—from a good trainer or from a good dragon. Likkarn *is* a good trainer, even if he is an awful weeder. But he hates me, I know. He would never take me on, even though he knows I am the best of the bonders with dragons. Maybe I should try to smile and be nice to him, like Errikkin. Only, that's Errikkin's way, not mine. Or I could run away from dragons entirely, like Slakk. Only, how can I? Dragons are my life. If Likkarn will not teach me, *I will fill my bag myself.*"

Jakkin sat up and stared at the hatchling. "If I cannot learn from a good trainer, then I will learn it all from thee, who comes from a line of fighters, great fighters, from Heart O'Mine out of Heart Safe by Blood Type. Blood Brother was thy father and he was my special charge. And what I learn from thee, I will teach thee back. Together, heart of my heart, blood of my blood, we will be unbeatable. In time. In time." He lay back down and crooned the last words over and over and soon put the both of them to sleep.

~

JAKKIN WOKE WHEN the sun was high overhead. The dragon was standing guard beside him. He plucked some more leaves from the stalk and crushed out the juices, and only then took out his own lunch. It consisted of great hunks of brown bread spread liberally with the jellied protein that Kkarina made and a bottle of cold juice. There was cake for dessert.

Jakkin lay on his side eating and watched as the dragon ripped off the last shreds of its eggskin with its claws.

The claws were not as soft as they had been the day before, but were halfway between brittle and hard, and a strange yellow. They looked like the jingle shells found in Sukker's Marsh.

Jakkin loosened one particularly difficult piece of skin up behind the snatchling's hackle, and the dragon rewarded him by licking his hand with its tongue.

"Thy tongue is getting rougher each day," Jakkin commented. "Soon I will not find thy thanks such a pleasure." He remembered, suddenly, how Blood Brother had tried to groom him in the baths, lifting off skin with his rough tongue. And he remembered what had happened to Blood Brother after. He shuddered.

"No one shall do such a thing to thee, little wormling," Jakkin promised. "I will not allow it. Not ever."

The dragon turned its black eyes toward him and Jakkin felt as if he could see strange constellations being born in the endless night of its eyes. "Be thou ever my friend," he whispered.

The dragon answered him with a weak trickle of smoke through its nose slits. It was no more than a patch of light fog that for a moment obscured the dragon's mouth, then was gone. But that it *was* smoke, the first conjurings of the fire of a fighting dragon, Jakkin was sure.

He laughed, a loud eruption that startled the snatchling into backing up.

"No, no, thou fire breather, do it once again," said Jakkin, his voice alive with laughter. "A great pit dragon must breathe fire and smoke. I will give thee *more* juice to stoke thy furnace, for blisterweed and burnwort are the fuel for thy flames." He stood up and started for the weed patch, chattering at the dragon as he went. He continued his monologue down one row, looking for the healthiest, most mature plants, and up the next until he found the plant he wanted at the row's end.

He stopped abruptly. In the sand by the stalk, almost hidden by a leaf, was a single shoeprint. For a moment, Jakkin was ready to dismiss it. He himself had walked around the weed and wort patch in sandals. But the fact that there was only the tip of the print showing, as if the rest had been broomed away, puzzled him. He turned and ran back to the shelter and picked up his own sandals. Then, reluctantly, he walked back to the patch.

Kneeling down, he matched up the toe of his sandal with the print. The print was slightly smaller than his own.

Jakkin sat down in the sand to consider. Bigfoot was a name that the boys had often called him, for he had had enormous feet since he was very young. His mother, he remembered, used to say that someday he would grow into his feet, and he was growing still. But if his own sandal had not made that print, then someone else's had.

He tried to think who it might be. Had any of the boys said anything to make him think they knew of the oasis and the snatchling? He recalled them teasing him about Akki. Had Slakk been a little less sarcastic than usual? Or Errikkin a little more willing to please? Or any of the younger boys too familiar? Perhaps . . . yet he couldn't imagine them spying on him. He thought about the men, listing them in his mind. Balakk and his two were busy in the fields today. And Jo-Janekk was inventorying the store—or so he said. Frankkalin had been given the day as Bond-Off. Perhaps it had been Frankkalin. Or old Likkarn. What had he said before their march back? He had turned to Jakkin and spit out: "You'll have tomorrow as Bond-Off. I'm sure you'll *need* it, boy." At the time, Jakkin had thought old Likk-and-Spittle had meant he would need the time to recover from the bloody roundup. "But perhaps," Jakkin said aloud, "perhaps what Likkarn meant was that I would need the time for my dragon."

And Likkarn was a small man, small and wiry. He would have a smallish foot. Jakkin thought about it, and the more he thought, the more it all fit. Likkarn must have followed him out and watched as he and the dragon slept. It all fit except for one piece. Why, if Likkarn knew about the dragon, had he not reported it? What subtle motives did the old man have in keeping such a thing secret?

Jakkin got back on his knees and held his sandal over the print again. There was no mistake. His sandal *was* bigger, though not by much. Likkarn must have been there at some point, all right, watching. Watching and waiting. Jakkin looked around the oasis. It was no longer as bright, as clean, as beautiful. Likkarn's presence there cast a long shadow.

Reluctantly, Jakkin stood up and went to the shelter. He dressed slowly, trying to think out his next steps. He would have to return to the nursery and see if he could find out what Likkarn was up to. He was not afraid for himself. After all, what could Likkarn do to him? He was already a bond boy. Though his bag might be emptied, he could not be broken further. But Jakkin worried what the old weeder might do to the hatchling. If he could kill a great stud like Brother, how easy it would be for him to slaughter the defenseless dragonling. Kill it—or have it killed in the stews.

Jakkin walked to the top of a dune, escorted by the dragon. It ran around him, its legs having to work twice as fast to pull the weight of its wings.

"Stay," Jakkin told it sharply. Then he knelt down by its side. "Stay, my beauty, till I come to thee again." He touched its nose.

The dragon seemed to understand. It crouched down, head on its front legs, wings folded back along its sides.

Jakkin turned back only once to look at it, and by then it was fast asleep in the sand.

# 13

JAKKIN SCRAMBLED ONTO the road once he was sure it was free of dust clouds, and turned to broom away his final steps. As he walked briskly toward the nursery turnoff, the basket banging against his back, he tried again to sort out the possible meaning of the toeprint he had found. He was convinced it belonged to Likkarn. But what if it did not?

If it belonged to one of the young boys—Errikkin or Slakk or Trikko, for example—he could probably buy the boy off with the coins from his bag. He jangled the bag, listening to the clank and nodding his head at how full it seemed.

If the footprint belonged to an older bonder, things would be more difficult. Perhaps he would have to offer a half share in the dragon, besides the gold. But he would make it clear that he, Jakkin, was to be the trainer. After all, the dragon already responded to him, already knew *his* mind.

But if it was Likkarn spying on him, then that would be the worst of all. The old man already blamed Jakkin for his latest de-bagging. He had made that quite clear.

Shifting the basket on his back, Jakkin turned onto the road lined with spikka trees that led to the nursery. It was said that there were more spikka trees planted at Sarkkhan's Nursery than anywhere else on Austar. They were expensive, Jakkin knew, but they also helped make the ground fertile by drawing and holding water with their roots.

As Jakkin rounded the last turning, he saw the nursery buildings spread out before him and, to the right, the red haze of the wort and weed patches. He let out an involuntary sigh and stopped. Except for a few snatches of memory, Sarkkhan's Nursery was all he knew. It was his home. And yet *not* his home, for when he had filled his bag, when he had trained his dragon and won his fights, he would leave and start the life of a master. On his own. Instinctively, his hand went first through his hair, then touched the dimple on his cheek, and at last rested on his bond bag, a habitual round he was not aware of.

He laughed out loud. "You can face drakk and dragons, but not your own waking dreams."

He had started up again, determined not to fall prey to such fears, when a strange cackling sounded from behind the incubarn to his right. For a moment Jakkin did not recognize the noise. It was a combination of a hen chuckle and the frantic peep-peeping of hatchlings. Then he remembered. Today was the day of the first airing, when the hens and their broods were let out of the barn into the corral.

Jakkin took off the basket and set it by the side of the barn, where he would pick it up later. He loved to watch the first airing. There was nothing funnier than the rush of hatchlings as they ran about, watched over by the mother dragons and the bond boys.

The henyard was an open corral surrounded by a fence of planed spikka wood. A full-grown hen could easily step over or fly across the man-made border. But the mother dragons would not leave their broods, and the hatchlings would not be able to make more than a few wing-hops for several months yet. So they all stayed inside the enclosing arms of the fence. The hens crouched down like great stone statues, keeping their fathomless black eyes on the antics of the young. And bond boys scattered at intervals on the fence top made sure no injuries occurred, using long prod-sticks to separate overeager hatchlings, who were already establishing a pecking order that would last the rest of their brood lives.

Jakkin climbed up the fence and, holding on, peered over the top. He scanned the broods quickly. They were all out of their eggskins, the hens having helped remove the last patches. Jakkin knew that the bond girls had already collected the pieces of eggskin and begun the long task of sewing them together for clothes and coverlets and the hundred other items the soft, stretchable fragments could be used for. Jakkin looked in particular for the crippled hatchling in Heart O'Mine's brood, but he could not find it. It had probably already been culled. There were one or two runts that would be culled soon as well: a nearly white one cowered by the barn gate, smaller than the rest by half; and a finely spotted yellow weakling lay covered with dust by the foot of its mother, Heart to Heart. There was little doubt those two hatchlings would be early culls.

Jakkin sighed. He hated the thought of the culling, when the weakest dragon hatchlings were taken from their hens, squealing and peeping, and thrown into the truck bound for the stews. He knew it had to be done, that such dragons would die before year's end anyway, stepped on or pecked into a stupor by their broodmates. If they were allowed to live long enough to stud or bear young, the resulting hatchlings would be even weaker than their parents. Jakkin knew all this, but it didn't make the terrible cries in the culling trucks any easier to bear.

He compared the hatchlings in the yard to his own dragon, and they all suffered by the comparison. These young dragons were spotted and marked with splotches of color. Not a dark red in the lot. One hatchling was all orange, one deep mustard-colored, and two gray-browns with yellow paws. His dragon, with its dull brown skin, had the best markings of them all. Of course, he reminded himself, color was not the only clue to a dragon's worth. And first color was not last. But he could not stop himself from smiling when he thought of his own, as he had last seen it, a brown mound asleep on the sand.

Some of the hatchlings began to give mock battle, prancing around their hens and stepping on one another's dragging wings. The all-orange dragonling seemed the most ferocious, and it already could trickle straggles of fog from its nose slits when approaching an enemy. But it was the deep mustard dragon that had the best control of its wings. It could hover for several heartbeats above the ground, confounding its broodmates.

The lethargic hens occasionally stuck out their massive paws to separate two fighters when the going got too rough and the agonized peeping of a loser become too harsh on the ear. More often it was the bond boys who did the separating, with the prod-sticks. In the end, only the orange, the yellow, and one of the gray-brown hatchlings were awake, pawing at the hens' tails while their brothers and sisters curled up under the hens' outspread wings to sleep.

Jakkin felt an elbow in his side and, turning his head, came face-to-face with Errikkin. "Back so soon?"

Jakkin nodded.

"I thought you might want the whole day off. Considering . . ."

"Considering?" Involuntarily, Jakkin looked down to check Errikkin's shoes. He was barefoot, one leg stuck through the gap in the fence.

"Considering . . . you know." Errikkin grinned and punched Jakkin's bag.

"Hey," called Slakk across the yard, his voice disturbing several of the sleeping hatchlings who stirred next to their hens. "Empty your bag again?"

"Oh, considering," mumbled Jakkin. They were talking about Akki. They thought he had spent the day with her. He was suddenly sure that neither of the two of them had been spying on him. Flushing with guilt, he climbed down from the fence and started to walk back to the bondhouse to get his basket.

"Wait," said Errikkin, "don't go yet. I have something to ask you. I know you'll probably be the first of us to fill your bag . . ." Errikkin stumbled over his words.

Jakkin was cold; his words came out in icy formality. "What makes you say that?"

Errikkin did not seem to notice his coolness. "You got extra gold for the roundup and now that everyone knows you're almost a man, you'll probably have other extras as well. It's only natural."

"Oh." Jakkin felt ashamed. He had thought again, for a moment, that Errikkin had been the spy. In a rush of companionship compounded in equal parts of relief and chagrin, he put his arm over Errikkin's shoulder. "Ask away, you baggy bonder. Ask—and it shall be given unto you."

Errikkin flushed. "Well, I was wondering. When you become a master, I'll still be in bond. I can't seem to save anything. I mean, I love the stews. And the pits." Errikkin's hands went up in mock dismay. "And if you have extra gold and all. Well, I mean, would you consider buying *my* bag? I'd rather work for you than old Sark-khan. I mean, not that he's a bad master. It's just that I don't really *know* him. He's never here. And I do know you. And . . ." Errikkin smiled and shrugged.

Jakkin was stunned. Slowly he pulled his arm away from Errikkin and looked at the ground.

"Fewmets," said Errikkin. "I hope I didn't say anything to make you mad."

Jakkin looked up again and said, as much to Errikkin as himself, "I never considered. I never considered—" he began. "I mean, I never thought that once I was a master, it meant I could own bonders. I don't think I want that. I don't think I want that at all."

"Well, what did you think being a master meant?" asked Errik-kin, incredulously.

"I thought it meant, well, being free. And doing *what* you wanted *when* you wanted. Like sleeping late. Or like training your own dragon. Or . . ."

Slakk, coming up behind them, overheard only part of the conversation and interrupted. "And how could any of us train a dragon on our own, unless it's a feral? And *you* should know the results of that piece of folly better than any of us. Didn't your father get gaffed by a feral yellow in the sands? I'd rather be a live bonder than a dead master, any day."

"You're going to be a dead bonder if you don't get back up on that fence," came a voice behind them. It was Likkarn, his eyes red with weed tears. "You, too, Jakk-boy. If you're here, your Bond-Off is over. Keep an eye on those hatchlings, or by the time I'm through with you, you'll stink as bad as a drakk." He jabbed a prod-stick at them.

The boys went back to the fence, but Jakkin couldn't stop thinking about all that had been said. It was only at dinner, after the broods had been herded back into the barn, that he realized he hadn't tried to match up the shoeprints with any of the bonders' feet. In fact, except for one quick peek at Errikkin's bare feet, he hadn't even looked. He would have to find out who had been spying—and quickly.

# *14*

ALL THE WAY back to the oasis that evening, Jakkin tried to sort things out. Then it occurred to him that returning to the bondhouse late at night afforded him the greatest of opportunities. He would simply take off his sandals before entering the sleep room and quietly match up his shoes against the others. The sleeping bonders would have their sandals neatly lined up by their beds. If he was quick enough, and silent, he could know in minutes who the possible suspects were. Except for Likkarn and Jo-Janekk, who had single rooms. He would have to think of another method for them.

Jakkin was so deep in thought, he almost tripped over the brown mound of dragon waiting for him.

"Fewmets, you nearly killed me," he complained. But the use of the word "you" confused the little dragon, and it sent tendrils of color questing into his mind.

Immediately contrite, Jakkin knelt down by the dragon and cradled it to him. "I'm sorry, thou mighty one." The snatchling nuzzled his bond bag and licked him under the chin. Then it butted him in the chest, and the force of its blow knocked him over.

"Is that how thou treats a friend?" Jakkin asked, pretending anger. But the dragon could hear the laugh in his mind over the false anger of his words, and it blew several small strands of smoke at him. Then it turned and trotted across the dune toward the weed and wort patch.

Jakkin followed. "Art hungry again, thou bag of lard? I shall go through this patch of weed too quickly if thou canst not control thyself." He laughed out loud, both at his own awkward use of *thou* and at the dragonling who waited, jaws wide, by the patch.

Quickly Jakkin stripped the largest leaves from two stalks, pleased to see new buds growing from the stalks he had plucked earlier. Bonders said, "Springtime is sprout time," meaning dragons and weeds both grew incredibly fast in the spring. And watching his own snatchling, now as high as his thigh, Jakkin could believe it. The little dragon followed him closely back to the shelter, where Jakkin got out the bowl and the bone knife.

Sitting in the sand, Jakkin began the work of crushing the leaf veins, with the dragon snuggled, mouth open, by his elbow. Jakkin had to push the hatchling away. "Move, thou wonder worm, otherwise I cannot get thy dinner ready." The dragon moved inches away, then settled down again, nose in the sand. Stretched out, the dragon was as long from tip to tail as Jakkin was high. Its wings, which that afternoon had still looked crumpled and weak, were already beginning to take on the rubbery sheen of maturity. In the fading sunlight, the dragon's skin was a mud brown color, but when Jakkin squinted his eyes and took a closer look, he could detect a reddish glow beneath. Jakkin thought: *Another boy seeing that ugly brown skin might have taken the snatchling to the stews right away. It would mean a few coins. Maybe even more than a few. The younger the dragon, the more coins. "The meat is sweeter nearer the eggs,"* as the stewards like to say. And besides, training a fighter was sure to be a long, uncertain process, a year at least till a dragon's first fight.

Suddenly the enormity of what he had done by snatching the dragon was borne down on him. A year. A year of sneaking out by himself and hiding the dragon in the sands. A year of training it in secret. A year . . . But what was a year to a bonder? Just never ending days of work. In the nursery the seasons were struck off in threes: the season of stud, the season of eggs and hatchlings, the season of training the new fighters and selling the rest. And Jakkin's part of the year was only dust and fewmets, fewmets and dust. But this year, the year of Jakkin's dragon, things would be different. He finished crushing the juice out of the leaves and poured some of it into the dragon's mouth. The snatchling lapped it eagerly and waited for the rest. Around its muzzle, drops of the red liquid still glistened.

"See that thou turneth that color all over," said Jakkin sternly, drizzling the rest into the dragon's open maw.

The hatchling's tongue licked away the last of the juice, and its tail twitched in reply.

~

LATER THEY PADDLED together in the warm spring, watching the sun go below the horizon. The sky seemed stained with blood. As he floated on his back in the spring, the bond bag heavy on his chest, Jakkin felt surprisingly at peace. He closed his eyes and let the light rainbows of the dragon's mind float by his closed lids. Mauve and pink and a color slightly paler than eggskin arced across the dreamscape. It was an unruffled reflection of the little dragon's world.

Suddenly the rainbows broke apart in a fever of tiny slashing red streaks and Jakkin heard a screaming hiss. He opened his eyes and automatically clutched the bond bag with his right hand. A dark shadow was crossing the red-drenched sky, and Jakkin saw eight feet of outstretched wings and talons fixed for battle. It was a male drakk. The water of the spring mirrored the blood color of the sky. The dragon was nowhere to be seen.

Above the spring the drakk began circling, catching the currents of air and dipping first one wing and then the other. Its body sensors picked up the scent of dragon. But it could not trace the dragon smell on water; what it caught was the odor of the hatchling that still clung to the sand and the reeds.

"Where art thou, beauty?" Jakkin called to the dragon, desperately afraid.

In answer, down by the kkhan reeds, from under the water, an earth-colored mound rose up, shaking itself furiously. The hatchling had sensed the attack and had escaped underwater, where the drakk could not find it.

*Stay in the water*, Jakkin thought at the hatchling, wondering if, in its fear, the young dragon would even hear him. *Stay* under *the water, my wonder worm*. Then he scrabbled onto the bank and ran, crouching over, to the shelter. He knew that any minute the drakk might make a slashing run at him. Without his clothes he had no defense at all. But the drakk, intent on the dragonling below, paid him no mind.

Frantically he dressed in his shirt and short bonder's pants, which would afford him only slight protection. On the floor of the shelter lay his old shirt, the one he had left for his snatchling. It smelled strongly of dragon. He put it on. Two layers were surely better than one. He picked up the bowl and the bone-handled knife. Then, taking a deep breath, he plunged back outside.

The circling drakk cast continually for the scent of its prey. Suddenly the dragon smell was strong again, emerging from the shelter. The drakk took aim at the smell, trying to distinguish the unfamiliar outline with its nearsighted eyes. It swept its wings back along its sides, cutting off the sensors, and dove.

Jakkin heard the cleaving of air above him and looked up just in time. He raised the wooden bowl as a shield. The rush of the drakk's attack knocked him down and its wings scraped across his face, but the thick bowl blunted the drakk's first charge, breaking off one of its talons.

Hissing furiously, the drakk winged away, banked sharply, and turned back for a second run.

Jakkin planted himself firmly in the sand, knife raised, and waited.

The drakk dove again but pulled up short. Standing up straight, Jakkin's outline was nothing like a dragon's. The confused drakk veered away at the last moment, but not before Jakkin's knife had sliced into its wingtip. Hissing in pain, the drakk charged again, heedless of the lies its eyes told. It raked the air above Jakkin's head with its razor talons.

Jakkin lifted his arm and plunged the knife upward. The blade slid through drakk feathers and cut into the air. The drakk's talon found his wrist and left a cruel gash in it along the inner arm, nearly to the elbow crease. If the one talon had not just been broken, it would have taken his hand off at the wrist.

Jakkin screamed in pain and fell to the ground as the drakk wheeled back above the treeline. His involuntary cry called the dragon out of the water, and it ran to him, its tail lashing in dismay.

"Go back!" Jakkin shouted. "To the water. Go back." But the little dragon stood by his side and urged him up with its nose.

Jakkin stood unsteadily, dizzy with pain, just as the drakk started down again. He leaned against the dragon, trying at once to shield it and to use it as a support. He held the knife in his other hand and waited. He knew that he would have only one more chance at the horror, and he knew he dared not fail.

The drakk dove. Its hissing preceded it and its snaky head was as straight as a spear. It counted on the hypnotic effect of its milky eyes to keep its prey still.

Jakkin thought at his dragon, *Do not look straight on it. Look to one side. And when I move, move away from me. But not till I cry it.* Only the faintest wisp of color came back in reply, and Jakkin prayed that the hatchling understood.

He could feel his jaw tighten and a sickness compounded of pain and fear growing in his belly. What he had felt on the roundup was nothing compared to this. And he knew that if he and the dragon died out in the sands, they might never be found. He remembered his mother crying over his father's bloody corpse. No one would cry over his.

The diving drakk seemed to hang in the air, unmoving, yet careening toward him at a speed too fast for reckoning. Jakkin stood still for moments, for hours, for eternities. Then at the last minute, he shoved the dragon one way, threw himself the other, screaming, "Move. Move, thou beauty!"

The dragon shot away from him, and Jakkin planted both feet wide to steady himself. He held the knife overhead.

The drakk, torn between the dragon smells and the true and false dragon forms, broke its dive for an instant, as if to veer off. In that instant, Jakkin thrust the blade under and into the drakk's neck where it joined the body.

Hot, foul-smelling drakk blood poured out over Jakkin's sleeve, coating it with a greasy, purplish color. The odor made Jakkin gag, then gasp, then collapse. He never saw the drakk fall, but it landed heavily next to him, its talons opening and closing in its death throes. One talon caught on Jakkin's outer shirt and ripped it open from neck to hem.

Cautiously, the dragon trotted over to the drakk. It shook its head as if to rid its nose slits of the terrible smell, then, carefully, from behind, it shoved the drakk body with one foot as far from the shelter as it could. Then it went back to Jakkin and nudged him with its nose. When there was no response, the dragon lay down next to Jakkin and began, purposefully, to lick his bloody wrist and arm with its rough tongue. One swipe, two, three, and the wound was clean, though blood continued to seep. The dragon curled its body around the boy, but it did not sleep. Every now and then its tongue touched the edges of the wound as if, by licking, it could close them.

Jakkin came to, once, to a great sunburst of color in his head, then passed out again, his face half-buried in the sand.

~

JAKKIN WOKE IN pain. There was a vise on one wrist and a burning ache along his other arm. And there was a horrible smell all around him that, combined with the constant pain, made him want to throw up. With an effort, he controlled his stomach. He moaned, almost experimentally, and there was a sudden cool hand on his forehead.

"Shhh. Hush. It's all right," a voice whispered in his ear. Recognizing the voice, he opened his eyes, expecting to see the white walls of the hospice and to find that he had been dreaming. He saw instead the dark, shadowy outline of the shelter nearby. He turned his head toward the voice and stared.

"You." He couldn't think for a moment. The awful smell confused him. "You . . ."

Akki smiled down at him, her dark hair falling over one eye. She brushed it back with her hand. "This is getting to be a habit," she said.

Suddenly it all fit together. The one person he had not suspected of spying on him.

"You have awfully large feet for a girl," he said, and pushed himself up to a sitting position, despite the pain. "Almost as big as mine."

She laughed. "That's funny, I think. What does it mean?"

"It means I found one of your footprints by the weed patch. One you neglected to broom away. Only I thought it was Likkarn's," Jakkin said, still surprised.

"I didn't think I missed any," she answered.

"Sloppy," he said, and laughed.

"I learned my bad habits from you," Akki said. "How do you think I found you in the first place?"

"That night you pulled me in out of the cold?"

"Yes. I got up extra early and broomed away your steps."

"And tracked them back at the same time," he said. There was admiration in his voice.

"Yes." She smiled again, acknowledging his admiration.

"I guess I have a lot to be grateful to you for," he said slowly, looking around casually. He hoped that in all her snooping she had never actually *seen* the dragon. Maybe she just thought he had built himself a retreat here, an oasis for his days of Bond-Off.

"It's outside," she said.

He shifted the weight off his aching arm and looked at his wrist, which was expertly bandaged. "The drakk?"

"What's left of the drakk. You nearly took the neck off its body," she said. "And with a blunt kitchen knife that's impressive."

This time Jakkin smiled. "Left-handed, too," he said, glad to be able to boast about something to her.

"And your dragon is still standing guard over the drakk's body. Kicking sand in its face every now and then. The sand seems to help keep the smell down." She wrinkled her nose. "It's still pretty awful, but the dragon keeps kicking. What a wonder worm."

"Oh." All his fears were contained in the one word. Akki heard it and looked at him slowly.

"I won't tell," she said. "I'll *never* tell."

Jakkin kept staring at the bandage on his wrist rather than looking again at Akki. The bandage material was unusual. He looked up and for the first time realized that Akki was wearing his old shirt, the one he had given the dragon. It had no buttons left and was tied up in front in a big knot. Her bond bag showed. And a lot of her skin. He looked away. Then he looked back shyly.

She seemed to guess his thoughts and gestured toward herself. "This shirt was too dirty to put around your wrist, so I tore my own up. Then I used this. It was split up the front, from the hem to the neck. The drakk got it, I guess. So I had to tie it like this. It smells, though. And so do you." She hesitated a moment and added, "And so do I." She actually blushed under his stare.

His wrist suddenly throbbed, and he winced.

"The wound was clean," Akki went on, speaking in the same amused voice she had used in the hospice. "The dragon was licking it and it had already started to heal over. There are lots of old stories about that, though I had never seen it in real life. That dragon tongues can heal, I mean. Your other arm was burned a bit from the drakk's blood, but the shirt helped. And the dragon had kicked sand on it, too. That seemed to help as well."

Jakkin grunted and got to his knees. He was dizzy and started to tumble back. Akki was at his side and helped him up. He wasn't sure he wanted to have to lean on her, but he had no choice: It was either lean or fall. He would rather have died than fall in front of her, so he leaned. She was both soft and hard and they both blushed. This time she looked away first.

"I fed your dragon," she said.

"What?"

"Juice from the wort patch. Wouldn't you know, I burned myself on one of the stalks." She held up her hand but it was already too dark to see the burn clearly.

"We'd better get back to the bondhouse. The moons have both risen." She helped him stand and put her arm around his waist and under his arm. She came no higher than his shoulder.

"You must have *very* big feet for such a small girl," he said.

She laughed again. "I do."

They stopped a moment, and he called out loud to the dragon, "Take care, my mighty healer." He was unprepared for the great rising bursts of color that came into his head, reds and oranges and shining golds. He stumbled and put his hand to his temples.

"What's wrong?"

"The dragon . . . my head . . ." He was confused for a moment. Then he realized that the colors filled him up—made him stronger— but did not threaten to overflow his mind. *Bank thy fires a bit*, he thought at the dragon. The colors ebbed slightly. "That's better," he said out loud.

"You must be weak from blood loss," Akki said.

The dragon came over and nuzzled against his thigh, turning its black eyes on Akki for a moment. Then it walked over to her and licked her free hand.

"It likes you," said Jakkin, surprised at how jealous that made him feel.

"Only because I have been helping you," she said. But she tickled the dragon behind its ears, and the dragon began a gentle thrumming under her hands.

*Thou fickle worm*, Jakkin thought at the dragon, but aloud he said, "Look, Akkhan has started down. We had better get back."

"Not without the drakk," Akki said.

"The drakk!"

"Listen: You stink, I stink. And it's not a smell that usually accompanies a boy and girl out at night together. If we bring the drakk back, they'll just think we were out pair-bonding and got set upon by that . . . that horror. Oh, I'll tell them quite a tale about how you saved me and . . ."

Jakkin interrupted. "But they'll know. Drakks don't attack humans."

Akki thought a minute, running her free hand through her hair. "But hadn't you been out with the hatchlings this afternoon?"

"Well, yes, but how did you know?"

"I know . . . a lot," she said. "We'll tell them we think the drakk smelled the hatchlings on you."

"And knew that I had had a hand in killing his mate and chicks," Jakkin finished.

"I don't know if drakk think that way," said Akki.

"Or think at all," added Jakkin. "But who can say? That baggy piece of waste attacked us and I fought it off. And you, being a nurse, nursed me." He was really enjoying the story.

"And we'll bring the stinking carcass home and be heroes." She smiled.

"Until someone asks where I got the knife."

Akki frowned. "Oh, that."

Jakkin nodded his head. "That."

"This will take a bit more thinking," said Akki.

Jakkin stood apart from her, feeling stronger. "We'd better think as we go."

"You take the drakk. If you can. I don't want to touch it. And the knife. I'll do the brooming," Akki said.

He went over to the sand-covered drakk, circling from the back and kicking it several times to be sure it was really dead. He looked at Akki in case she was laughing, but drakk were no laughing matter. The drakk did not move. He picked it up by its talons with his left hand and slung it over his shoulder. It must have weighed over five kilos and it still smelled. He hated the feel of it against his back. He wondered if he would ever get the stench out of his skin.

Akki followed behind, brooming their path. She used a long broomer with a collapsible handle. "See," she said brightly, "no bending."

"I never thought of that," Jakkin said ruefully. She seemed to think of a lot of things he had never considered. He wondered how many other things she knew about: brooms and hospices, dragons— and men. There had been talk about her at the nursery, about her and Sarkkhan. Guesses, really. Nursery gossip. No one knew much about her for sure, though Slakk often supplied tidbits he swore were true. She had arrived at the nursery about three years earlier, Jakkin seemed to remember. Someone said Sarkkhan had found her at a baggery. Someone else had once suggested she was the doctor's girl. She seemed to go where she wanted and when she wanted, almost as if she were free. But she was a bonder; her bag said as much. Jakkin suddenly remembered her standing by his bed at the hospice and scripting something. If she could script, she could read. And if she could read, she was either free, or very close to someone free. The doctor. Or Master Sarkkhan. Yet the way she had been acting this evening didn't sound as if she were Sarkkhan's girl. She talked about a boy and girl out together. She had followed Jakkin's tracks. She had rescued *him*. She had promised not to tell. If she were a free man's mate, pair-bonding with someone, surely she wouldn't act that way. Or would she? It was a riddle, a puzzle that Jakkin could not answer.

They walked most of the way in silence. Jakkin even stopped thinking after a while, because walking and carrying the heavy drakk took most of his remaining strength.

Near the nursery road, Akki spoke at last. "I still haven't thought of any way to explain the knife," she said.

"Nor have I."

But in the end, no one asked. There was a great fuss when they set the dead drakk on the bondhouse steps and the smell woke the other bonders and set the hen dragons roaring. Jakkin and Errikkin, accompanied by a complaining Slakk and a sleepy Trikko, were sent to bury the drakk beyond the compound. They finished just before Dark-After and hurried back for showers.

Jakkin was allowed to sleep the morning away. He did not see Akki again until that night.

# 15

DINNER WAS A special occasion, the first party since the twenty-fifth anniversary of the nursery's founding. In honor of the drakk killers, Kkarina had made an elaborate cake covered with a deep red frosting and a candied figure of a dead eggsucker, complete with caramelized eyes and a bone-handled kitchen knife rising out of its stomach.

Even Master Sarkkhan ate with the bonders. Just back from a successful trip to a minor pit, the nursery owner sat with the older bonders and regaled them with stories of his early fights. Only Likkarn was absent. Rumor had it that he had cursed Sarkkhan to his face, calling him "gold master" and "drakk dodger." Jakkin wondered if the old man had been smoking weed again or if he were really jealous of Jakkin's success.

*Let him sulk in his room*, Jakkin thought to himself. But he suddenly felt sorry for the old man who had led them all so fearlessly against the drakk colony. Now that he no longer thought that Likkarn was spying on him, threatening his hatchling, Jakkin could afford to feel sympathy.

At the dinner's end, Jakkin was summoned to Sarkkhan's table, where the master, still in the red-and-gold suit he had worn to the pit, presented him with a handful of gold. Jakkin had never been face-to-face with the nursery owner before. The man was big, massive, with broad shoulders and large hands that were covered with red-gold hair. He had an expansive smile.

"Here," Sarkkhan said, his bushy red beard waggling as he spoke. "Your bag is not yet full. Fill it with the thanks of the nursery. One dead drakk means many live dragons."

Jakkin took the gold and opened his bag with two fingers, never taking his eyes off Sarkkhan. He slid the coins into the pouch and heard them clink, one after another: one, two, three, four, five. Then he murmured his embarrassed thanks.

"The thanks are entirely on our side, young Jakkin," said Sarkkhan. "I've had my eye on you for some time."

Jakkin wondered briefly what Sarkkhan meant by that. Then he managed to smile back and add, boldly, "Some thanks and coin belong to Akki as well," he said, appending the ritual words: "Her bag is not yet full."

Sarkkhan houghed through his nose like a disgruntled stud dragon. From the boys' table there came a giggle. Jakkin recognized Slakk's laugh.

Sarkkhan's eyes narrowed and his mouth grew thin, though it still smiled.

"She *was* there with me. She helped," Jakkin said.

"So I've heard," Sarkkhan replied. "We appreciate your fairness. As to paying her gold . . ."

Akki stood at the pair-bonders' table and called out loudly, "I do not fill my bag with Sarkkhan gold." Then she walked out of the room.

Jakkin watched her leave. He started to go after her, but Sarkkhan's hand on his arm stopped him.

"Let her go," the nursery owner said. "She has a head harder than dragon bone, and Fool's Pride to match. Like her mother. Go back to your seat." It was not a suggestion but a command.

Jakkin sat down again between Errikkin and Slakk and replayed the scene in his mind. It was all suggestion; it could be read many ways. Was Sarkkhan jealous? Was he angry? Or was he merely amused? The other boys chattered around him as they finished off extra helpings of the cake. Jakkin seemed to be in two places at once: running through the conversation with Sarkkhan once again and sitting next to the boys. As he heard Sarkkhan's voice saying "Fool's Pride," Trikko was eating a second slice of cake—Trikko, who usually seemed to exist on takk and water.

"Couldn't you have left me some scrapings of icing?" asked Slakk.

"Have a heart," Errikkin said. "You've had three helpings already. Jakkin . . ."

Jakkin turned slowly and focused on Errikkin. "Yes?"

"Tell us again. How did you manage to kill it?"

Jakkin repeated the tale once again, but his mind was really wandering outside with Akki. He could hardly wait for dinner to be over to find her.

~

AKKI WAS NOT in the bondhouse at all. Jakkin finally came upon her by the southwest corner of the building. She was sitting in the sand, her back against the wall. She was fiddling with her bond bag and looking out into the distance, beyond the copse of spikka trees where the first drakk had been killed.

"Akki," he said quietly, and slid down the wall to sit next to her.

She didn't bother looking at him, but let the bag fall against her chest. It didn't make a sound. "Leave me alone."

"But you didn't leave me alone when I needed it."

"He knows I won't take his gold. I've told him so before. There is always a hidden price to pay. No man's gold will go into *my* bag." She placed her hand protectively over the leather pouch and spoke in a fierce undertone.

"Sarkkhan?" He found himself whispering back.

"That bullheaded, stone-prided . . . I hate him." Her voice was loud again, and hard.

Jakkin sat up on his knees and turned to face her. "Now, wait a minute," he said, putting his hands on her face and forcing her to look right at him. "The gold in your bag was my idea, not Master Sarkkhan's."

*"Master!"* she spit the word out.

"Yes, *Master* Sarkkhan. Until I am a master, he is mine. And yours."

"No man is my master," she said.

He was shocked into silence.

"No man's gold will fill my bag," she said, and jangled her bag at him. It was totally empty. He reached over and crumpled it in his hand. Not even a grave coin. He had never known any bonder without that single coin.

"My mother was a baggery girl," she said. "She died at my birth. The other bag girls raised me. But when I was twelve and knew that I wanted to doctor—people and dragons—and not live a bag girl's life, I left. So here I work. And learn. I am only fifteen. I have years of learning ahead. But no man's gold will fill *my* bag."

"I see," Jakkin said, though he didn't really.

"Come on. Never mind me. Let's go see your little beauty," Akki said, brushing her hair from her face and giving a swipe at her eyes as well.

Jakkin pretended not to notice. He had a feeling she wouldn't want him to see that she had been crying.

"All right," he said at last, standing up. He was about to reach down and give her a hand when she stood up without his help. "Do you have the broom?"

"Don't I always?" she asked.

He nodded, and they walked down the road, slightly apart, but not so far that Jakkin could not feel the warmth of her by his side.

~

THE DRAGON WAS asleep in the shelter. It did not even wake when they entered. They sat down next to it, listening to its hissing snore and watching the rise and fall, rise and fall, of its mud brown sides. Its wings twitched slightly, as if it dreamed of flying.

"Look," Akki said, pointing to the tail, "there's red coming through. A berry red, I think."

Jakkin looked. There was a patch of red showing, like a halo around the tail's tip. "Red. But deeper than berry."

Akki moved closer and stared.

"You're right," she said. "It *is* deeper. It's the same color as your blood was on the sand."

"Are you sure?"

"Didn't I see enough of it yesterday?" she asked.

Jakkin nodded and held up his wrist. It was only lightly bandaged and no longer hurt. "Dragon's tongue and heart's blood," he said.

The dragon gave a long, slow yawn and woke, stretching its wings and scrabbling with its claws on the sand.

"Up, thou lazy worm," Jakkin said aloud.

"Do you always speak *thou* to your dragon?"

Jakkin nodded. "At least I try, though I get my *thees* and *thous* mixed up a lot. My father knew dragons and he said the best trainers always use *thou*. It's supposed to bring me closer to the dragon. It seems to work."

She thought about that a moment. "I expect that's true with people, too," she said.

"Should I call you *thee?*" he asked impulsively.

"I'm not sure either of us wants to be *that* close," she said, laughing. "Yet."

For some reason, her laughter hurt. He answered quickly, "Besides, which of us would be the dragon, and which the trainer?"

"Well, I have the claws for it," she said, holding up her hands. They were large, sturdy hands. "But you have the bonehead."

"Funny, that's what Master Sarkkhan said about you," Jakkin retorted.

"He should know."

Jakkin wondered what she meant.

"Come on, show me what this worm can do. Besides eat, sleep, and cover drakks with sand." She got up and ran out of the shelter, and the dragon followed her, nipping playfully at her heels.

Jakkin stood and went outside. For a minute he watched the two of them playing. As Akki moved, her long, dark, hip-length hair swung around her body. The dragon caught a hank of the hair and pulled. She fell to the ground and the dragon jumped on her, and they rolled over and over to the edge of the spring.

"Look out!" Jakkin warned. But he was too late.

They fell in together and swam apart.

Jakkin kicked off his sandals and took off his shirt and leapt in after them, dousing them both with more water. Akki splashed back with her hands, and the dragon fanned the water with its wings.

"Enough," Akki called at last and climbed up the bank on her hands and knees.

Jakkin reached out, caught her ankle, and dragged her down again. When she resurfaced he said, "I was only able to do that because your feet are so big."

The last part of the sentence was lost in coughing, as he swallowed a wave she pushed toward him. When the coughing fit was over, he saw Akki and the dragon stretched out on the sand, drying in the warmth of the desert breeze. He climbed up after them and lay down a little ways apart.

Akki turned on her side and leaned on one elbow, facing him. The sand clung to her clothes and bond bag. "Now show me what this dragon can do. After all, you *are* trying to train a fighter, aren't you?"

Jakkin called the dragon to him and showed her its stance. He had to hold the young dragon in place, but once the snatchling got the idea, it stood waiting for his nod of release. Then came the hind-foot. And finally, on command, it blew a few weak, damp straggles of smoke.

"Not much yet," said Jakkin. "But we've got a year. And this mighty worm is already way ahead of its clutchmates. They've just had their first airing. It's already bonded with me, fought a drakk, hovered, and blown smoke. Quite a dragon, don't you think?"

"But you've never trained a dragon before . . . ," she began.

"Of course not."

"Or seen one trained?"

"My father worked with ferals in the sands," Jakkin said. "I think I remember something of that. And I've sneaked about some in the nursery. Last year I watched Likkarn in a session. And I'll try this year as well."

"What about going to a fight?"

"Well, I heard Sarkkhan say once that the dragon itself is the best teacher. And I'll need my gold for food and stuff."

Akki nodded. "I'll get you a book. Can you read? You were born free."

He nodded. "Some."

"Good," she said. "Or else I would have taught you."

"You *can* read," he said, more a statement than a question.

She ignored it. "I've seen several books on training at the hospice and some in Sarkkhan's cottage. I think I can get them for you without anyone suspecting."

Jakkin did not ask her why she had been in Sarkkhan's house. Perhaps she had helped treat him for an illness. She seemed to know him well—and hate him, too. Maybe the nursery rumors were true. After all, she had been brought up in a baggery. And though she had left at twelve . . . well, some girls started early. Sarkkhan had no wife, and Akki was beautiful. Maybe not as beautiful as the girl in Kkarina's portrait, but . . .

"Let's feed this beastie and go back home," said Akki. "I'm tired. And wet."

"We'll dry," said Jakkin, happy that she had changed the subject. "Long before we reach the nursery and our beds, we'll be dry."

They stripped the leaves from three stalks and pressed out the juices with their nails, for they no longer had the kitchen knife. Then they washed their hands in the warm spring and went back.

# 16

AKKI WAS AS good as her word, bringing him three books on training over the next few weeks and white trainer suits for them both. Jakkin did not ask her where she got everything, or what she had to do to get it all. He did not want to know—and she did not volunteer the information.

He read the books with painstaking slowness, sounding out some of the harder technical words. And Akki, the few times she came out to the oasis with him, gave him lessons in dragon anatomy.

"Here, in the haunch," she said, pointing to the dragon's upper leg, "the big bone inside is called humerus. And the bending bone is the carpus, like our wrist bone."

He recited all the bones after her; humerus, ulna, radius, carpus, pointing to his own body and then the dragon's body, marveling at all the similarities. He wanted to know everything about dragons, inside and out. He learned the scientific names of the dragon's five claws from one of the books: the large double claws were the lanceae, the back three were called unum, secundum, and tricept, strange otherworldly words that he had to chant in order to remember. Akki tested him on the scientific names, and then he demonstrated the week's lesson with the dragon to her in return.

But Akki was not there as often as Jakkin would have liked. Most evenings she would start off with him, sometimes even holding his hand as they left the bondhouse. Then, at the main road, she would suddenly shake her head and pull her hand away, as if the hand holding had only been a show for the others. She would leave him to go east toward the oasis while she took off on a more northerly path toward the Narrakka River. She warned him not to follow her. He never did.

He never did, because the dragon needed him. Even when it had outgrown the drizzled juice and could graze on the leaves and stalks of the blisterweed and burnwort that he picked for it—even when it was chest high and then past his shoulder—he could feel it calling to him in his head. It was a siren call he could not resist.

And so the season of the eggs passed.

During the day Jakkin joined Slakk and Errikkin, Trikko and the rest in cleaning the stud barns and mud-bathing the cock dragons. Likkarn was absent more and more from the barns, off to the pits, it was said, his differences with Sarkkhan patched up once again. Jakkin did not miss him.

A new song was going the rounds of the nursery now, called "The Minor Minor Pits" about a dragon who lost all his fights but one, and that one with the greatest champion of the world. Jakkin adopted the song for the mud baths and found its haunting tune with the slow rises and falls of the melody line wonderfully soothing to the excitable males. Even Bloody Flag, who had been unmanageable quite often since his stallmate's death, seemed to calm down and thrumm when the song floated by him.

Dust and fewmets and mud baths filled Jakkin's days, but at night he worked with his own dragon, teaching it the rudiments of fighting in the pits. All those feints and passes and stands that a dragon does naturally Jakkin gave names to, and he taught the names to his worm. By the end of the egg season, when the days grew shorter and the nights became a pavane of moons across the sky, Jakkin's dragon could respond to his every thought. He put it through its paces two or three times a week: left-claw pass, right, hindfoot rise, stand. And the little dragon obeyed and improved at every lesson.

By the season of training and selling, Jakkin's dragon was far ahead of the dragonlings at the nursery. They were just being separated into fighters and culls. The topmost hatchlings in the pecking order, those who had shown an instinct for blood, were automatically chosen for training. The quieter, frightened dragons were chosen for the stews, though an occasional beauty, one marked with attractive spots or streakings, was set aside. Often baggery girls or the masters' wives enjoyed such as pets. Gelded or spayed, the beauty-dragons never grew more than shoulder high and were gentle creatures of tidy habits.

Culling Day was always a horror. Great trucks drove onto the nursery grounds, painted with the blood-red logo of the Rokk Stews:

a dragon silhouette with crossed knives beneath, and the single word *Quality* outlined in gold paint like an aura above the dragon head. The bonders' foul mood communicated itself to the dragons. The hens stomped back and forth on their great feet, heaving and rocking their weight from side to side. They houghed and groaned. The hatchlings were silent beneath their feet; even the top of the order shivered, cowering next to their mothers' tree-trunk legs. In the stud barn came the bellowing of the males as if some memory of their own hatchling days were triggered there.

The food then was predictably bad, for Kkarina always absented herself on Culling Day, leaving the bonders to sort out her verbal instructions on their own. Something always went terribly wrong in the kitchen without her: the meat would be spoiled or the takk would not boil or the stoves would not function properly.

Only old Likkarn seemed to enjoy the culling. He preceded it every year with a night of blister fury. Jo-Janekk's swollen left eye and a bruise on Balakk's cheek testified to Likkarn's blisterweed strength. It had taken four of them to put him to bed. In the morning they all followed his orders sullenly. He was a weeder—but he knew dragons. His fingers pointed to one hatchling after another, sorting, hesitating only once at a well-spotted orange that was assigned, at last, to the beauty group. Jakkin was secretly pleased that he had guessed all but that last correctly. His eye was as good as Likkarn's.

He also knew that all over Austar IV similar Culling Days were held. It was reasonable to select the best dragons for breeding. Once, so the books told him, the great Austar dragons had been on the edge of extinction and the first settlers had slowly brought them back. The encyclopedia had a whole article on the dragons. They used to fight one another to the death, and it had taken men to train them—retrain them, really—to their old instincts of fighting only until dominance was assured. But that didn't make Culling Day any easier to bear.

Jakkin wondered briefly why the culling had to be so violent, why the hens and hatchlings had to be subjected to such a hard separation. But he knew that the only way to choose the hatchlings properly was to see them all together. And there was no practical way to quiet the culls' terror. Stunning the hatchlings would ruin the tender young meat for the stews and could disorder the beauty-dragons completely. Besides, as Jakkin knew full well, there were very few power cells for the extinguishers to be had. They were used sparingly, and only in life-and-death situations.

That night, out on the oasis, Jakkin sat with his dragon's head in his lap. He sang it all the old songs he knew and tried to think pleasure at it while he scratched behind its ears. But the darker side of Culling Day must have nuzzled through his thoughts, for the dragon pushed his hand aside, stood up, and trotted beyond the weed patch. He heard it snuffling as it went. Leaving it to its own thoughts, he returned to the nursery early.

Two days later, the nursery had settled down again, the hens starting the long process of weaning their remaining hatchlings. In the oasis, Jakkin had to do the same. He made himself stay away, going back every third or fourth night with dread, fearing to find that the dragon had died of starvation without him. Each time he returned, the dragon greeted him joyfully, larger by another handbreadth than the last visit, and the weed and wort patch full of signs of its browsing. Jakkin was torn between pleasure at his dragon's growth—it was now as tall as he was—and a lingering disappointment that the snatchling did not seem to have needed him during his absence. But his pride in the growing strength and ability of his dragon soon overshadowed everything.

It was on the last day of the training season that he taught it a move that was in none of the books. It was an accident, really. They had been playing, though Jakkin now had to play with the dragon much more carefully. It was a little higher than his head, and its legs were the width of half-grown spikka trees. The scales of its back and neck and tail were as hard and shiny as new-minted coins. Only along the belly and where its legs met the firm trunk were the scales still butter soft.

Jakkin had rolled on the ground, propelled by a light tap from the dragon's tail, and had ended up on its left wing. The wing's ribs were encased in the hard grayish skin that contrasted sharply with the dragon's dark red body. Only at the knobby part of the wings, where the rubbery skin stretched taut, was there a hint of red in the gray. Shakily Jakkin stood up on the dragon's wing, careful not to scrape or tear it.

The dragon turned its head slowly to look at him, its eyes black shrouds.

"See, mighty worm, if thou canst free thyself of this encumbrance," said Jakkin, standing very still.

The dragon opened its mouth and yawned, then fluttered its free wing slowly.

Jakkin began to relax. "Nothing? Canst do nothing?" he taunted gently. He watched the fluttering free wing.

Suddenly the tail came around and swept him off the pinioned wing in a single fluid motion. Caught unaware, Jakkin tumbled backward and rolled into the embrace of the dragon's left leg. For a full minute it would not let him go. He could feel its laughter in his head, great churning waves of blue and green.

"And that," said Jakkin when the dragon let him up at last, "*that* we will call the Great Upset." He dusted his clothes off with his hands. "I *let* you knock me down. A dragon in the pits will not be so easily fooled." He had started to walk away when the dragon's tail came up behind him and pushed him into the sand once again.

Jakkin laughed and turned over on his back. "You win. You win," he said as the tail came down and nudged under his arm, where the dragon knew he was especially ticklish.

~

AND THEN IT was the season of stud.

The bonders were kept busy day and night, helping the studs to preen, leading them one at a time into the arena-sized courtyards where the chosen hen waited. As the humans watched, the dragon courtship began.

The female stood, seemingly uninterested, while the male paced around the yard, measuring it with his eye. Every once in a while, he stopped and sprayed the floor with the extended scent glands on the underside of his tail or breathed smoky gusts onto the sand. His hackles rose. The circling continued until the hen either curled into a ball, pretending to sleep—which indicated that she was uninterested in the male—or until she leapt several feet in the air, pumping her great wings and lifting her tail.

If she turned down the courting male's offers, the bonders would jump into the ring and take the deflated dragon away. Deflated was the word, Slakk commented once, as he led Bloody Flag out of the ring. The male dragon's scent gland hung as loose as a coinless bag and his hackles had returned to normal size.

But once a hen accepted the male, showing her preference by her leap above the ring, the male winged into the air after her. Then they both shot into the sky, above the roofless courtyard, the female screaming her challenge to the male, who followed always slightly behind. They rose screaming and spiraling above the nursery, higher and higher, until they were merely black, swirling specks in the sky.

An hour later, the frantic courting flight over, the two returned together, wingtip to wingtip, to the courtyard, where a moss-covered floor pad had been rolled out by the bonders. There, in full view of the watchers, the cock dragon mounted and mated with the hen. Then they lay side by side for the rest of the night. The following morning, separated by mutual consent and the prod-sticks of the bonders, the stud went back to his own stall, the female to the incubarn.

Jakkin only managed to get to the oasis one evening a week during the season of stud, for he was suddenly promoted to helping with the matings, under Likkarn's direct supervision. It was not an easy job. It also meant that he shared Bond-Off with Likkarn. Jakkin's one worry was that the old man would track him over the sands just for spite, to get even with him for every mistake—real and imagined—that Jakkin made in the mating courtyards. But each Bond-Off Likkarn disappeared first. After the third Bond-Off, Jakkin relaxed his guard. He guessed that Likkarn had found someplace away from the nursery to spend the day smoking blisterweed, since each morning after Bond-Off Likkarn's eyes were a furious red.

It was on that third Bond-Off, as Jakkin and his dragon were lazing in the sand after a hard session of training, that Jakkin thought about the latest mating flight he had seen.

"Canst use thy wings yet?" he asked, picturing the wild mating spiral in his mind. "Canst thou do more than a hover?"

The dragon responded by pumping its wings strongly, stirring the sand and making little frothy eddies in the stream. Then, as Jakkin watched, the dragon began to rise. Its great wings pumped mightily and Jakkin could see the powerful breast muscles moving under the shield of skin. The dragon rose as high as the shelter roof; then two more pumps brought it above the treeline, where it hovered a minute. Suddenly it caught a current of air and rode off into the sea of sky.

Jakkin stood, one hand over his eyes, straining to follow the disappearing dragon. He bit his lip and touched his bag. Now that it knew what its wings were for, the dragon might never return. It might go feral, finding a colony of wild dragons out beyond the mountains. Loosing a feral—that had always been a possibility. And yet he hadn't believed it. Not with his dragon, not really.

In the nursery only the mating dragons were ever allowed to fly. And since they were not ready for mating until the females were two years old, the males three and quite settled into nursery routines, there was rarely a nursery dragon that went feral. Only one that Jakkin could remember had ever gone from Sarkkhan's nursery—a red-gold stud on its first mating flight, a stud named, appropriately, Blood's A Rover. It had happened when Jakkin had first helped in the barns. Likkarn had raged for days, and everyone had felt the back of his hand or the lash of his tongue.

For over an hour the sky was empty and Jakkin was near despair. And then the dragon was back, wheeling and diving and cresting the waves of air with the same buoyant grace with which it had ridden the stream. Finally it settled down, landing on the ground with an earth-shaking thump right next to Jakkin.

He looked at it with a great smile on his face. "There is none like thee," he said, moving to it and circling its neck with his arms. He put his cheek on its scaly jaw. "None."

He was rewarded with a cascade, a waterfall, a sunburst of color, and this time he did not ask it to mute its fiery show.

# *The Fighter*

# 17

THE YEAR TRAVELED straight across the season, but Jakkin saw only the wavy lines of progress that his dragon made. By year's end, the dragon towered above him, and it was hard to recall the little hatchling in its yellowish eggskin that had staggered around the oasis under the weight of its oversized wings. This yearling dragon was a beautiful dull red. Not the red of holly berry or the red of the wild flowering trillium that grew at the edge of Sukker's Marsh, but the deep red of life's blood spilled upon the sand. The nails on its forepaws, which had been as brittle as jingle shells, were now hard—the lanceae were almost indestructible. Its eyes were two black shrouds. It had not roared yet. But Jakkin knew the roar would come, loud and full and fierce, when it was first blooded in the ring. The quality of that roar would start the betting rippling again through the crowd at the pits, for they judged a fighter partly by the timbre of its voice.

Jakkin dreamed of the pits at night, fretted about them by day. The closest minor pit—for a First Fighter could never start in a major pit; that was only for champions—was past Krakkow, the town that was fifteen kilometers from the nursery. Jakkin had tried to ask seemingly innocent questions of the other bonders about the route to Krakkow and beyond, because Akki had never been to the minor pit there. But Likkarn had overheard one such conversation and had interrupted it as he passed by, asking, "Checking out the fighting dragons for some purpose, boy?" as if he knew something. So Jakkin had stopped asking anything. He had debated going one Bond-Off to the minor pit to check them out himself. But the trip by truck cost a coin, as did the entrance fee to the pit, though Slakk said there were ways to sneak in. And he might have walked there and back in a long day, but he needed the Bond-Off to train and he had little enough gold left in his bag. Most had gone with Akki to buy more burnwort and blisterweed seeds. He never asked her how she got them, only thanked her when she handed him the precious paper packets of seeds.

He could have stolen what he needed from the nursery stores. Just a handful of seeds seemed an insignificant thing. But he never even considered it, just as he never considered sneaking into the pits. Taking an egg was acceptable thievery, the mark of a possible master. But taking supplies from a nursery might condemn an older dragon to short rations in a bad year. It could even mean death to the nursery worms. And sneaking into the pits meant cutting into the most basic part of Austarian economy. Besides, if he was caught it was punishable by a prison term on another planet. Jakkin simply would not do such a thing.

One evening, while Jakkin was putting the red through its paces, Akki came slipping quietly through the weed and wort patch. The old shoots were mostly all grazed down, but the new crop, planted with the purchased seed, was sending smoky signals into the still air. Akki's passage moved the gray smoke away from the stalks, and some of the clouds clung to her dark hair, crowning it with fuzzy gray jewels. She tried to brush the stuff off her hair and bond bag with impatient hands.

"Akki," Jakkin cried out when he saw her, unable to disguise the pleasure in his voice. It had been many days since she had visited the oasis.

She grinned lopsidedly. "I've brought you a present."

"A present? For me? What?" He sounded like a child, and willed himself to stop chattering.

She opened her bond bag and reached into it, withdrawing some crumpled pieces of paper.

"Registration papers. For the Krakkow Minor," she said, holding them out to him.

"I don't understand," Jakkin began.

"I didn't think you would. You have to sign these papers in order to fight your dragon at the pit. They don't just let *anyone* in, you know." She shook her head at him.

"But my father never . . ."

"Your father was training a feral," she reminded him. "And he never got far enough along with it to register it. Ever since—well, the Constitution at least—there have been rules about this sort of thing."

Jakkin suddenly felt as crumpled as the paper. "I didn't realize.

What would I have done?'' He began half a dozen other sentences and finished none of them, mumbling half to himself and half to Akki.

"Never mind,'' said Akki. "I've gotten the papers all filled out. All you have to do is sign them with your mark."

"That's all?"

"That's all. I'll take the papers in and file them with the right people,'' Akki said. "And then, on the right day, you and the dragon will be there. At the pit. *If* you think your dragon is ready."

"Ready?'' Jakkin gestured at the dragon. "Just look.'' The yearling dragon was lying by the side of the stream. It stretched out parallel to the bright ribbon of water, its red contrasting with the blue-white. In the moonlight, both the water and the dragon scales shone equally. Slowly its tail rose and fell, weaving little fantasies in the air.

Akki nodded slowly. "Thou art a beauty, in truth. In truth,'' she said, her voice free of its usual mocking tone.

At her voice, the dragon stirred and looked around at them.

"So,'' said Akki, turning back quickly to Jakkin. "How do you propose to get the dragon there? Walk along the main road with that great thing galumphing at your side? Or sneak it under the cover of darkness and get frozen during Dark-After?"

Jakkin looked down at his feet. It had been a question that had troubled him frequently and he had put off thinking about it.

"Perhaps . . . I thought . . .'' he began, then finished with a rush. "That the dragon could carry me."

"Look,'' said Akki, and she pulled him along by the hand to where the dragon lay in the sand. Then, as if giving a fairly stupid child a lesson in spelling, she pointed: "The dragon's shoulders, here and here, are too thin and smooth scaled for sitting. The hackles would be damaged by pressure there. And if you tried to hold on there or there''—she touched the dragon along its long, sinuous back—"the slightest turn of its body would send those sharp-edged scales slicing into you at your most tender points."

Under the withering lecture, Jakkin held his shoulders rigid and fingered his bond bag with one hand. Akki was right. And the worst of it was, he had already figured that out for himself.

"It's been tried before, dragon riding,'' said Akki. "And the men who tried it had scars they would not even show the bag girls.'' Her voice got hard. "The ones that lived."

"I was thinking more of a harness,'' he said quietly. "With a swing of some kind."

Akki was silent for a moment. "Hmmm. You know. It might just work. If . . . if you had more training time. And a dragon whose claws you didn't mind ruining while you practiced. But this, my boy, this dragon is a *fighter*.''

"You don't need to remind me," said Jakkin, straightening up and walking away. Akki made him feel two ways. He was happy to see her but he was angry at her long lecture, at her calling him a boy. He had already proven his manhood—fighting drakks, stealing and training a dragon. What more did *she* want, anyway? His anger communicated itself to the dragon, who blew a sudden hot breath at Akki's foot.

Akki caught up to Jakkin and touched his shoulder. "Then what are you going to do?"

Jakkin flinched from her touch and sat down suddenly in the sand, his head and arms on his knees. "I . . . don't . . . know." He said it with a finality that precluded pity.

Akki sat down opposite him, her toes touching his. She pushed his head up with the palm of one hand. "I do!" she said, and waited.

He looked at her but could not speak.

"I have . . . friends with a dragon truck," she almost whispered. "A big hauler."

"You said," Jakkin began, each word an accusation, "you said you would tell no one."

"I haven't. Yet."

"Then don't. *I fill my bag myself.*"

She heard her own voice echoed in his and nodded. "But what else can you do? Your fight is scheduled in three days." She held out the papers again.

"What?" He grabbed the papers and smoothed them out. Slowly he read the print by the weak light of Akka.

*AGREEMENT made this 127th day of Stud, 2507, between the management of the Krakkow Minor Pit and Jakkin Stewart of Sarkkhan's Nursery. WITNESSETH*

   *In consideration of the mutual covenants herein contained, the parties agree as follows . . .*

"Where does it say that?" Jakkin asked, the words on the page a jumble. Some of the words he had never even *heard* before, much less spelled out.

"There," said Akki, her finger pointing halfway down the first page.

Jakkin looked. In between the words "Jakkin's Red" and "First Fight" was a date. "It *is* in three days," Jakkin said.

"It was the only opening," Akki explained. "The season is already booked up with dragons from all the major and minor nurseries. But in this one fight, a dragon dropped out, a promising Second Fighter. The dragon escaped somehow. Went feral. Its owners are wild themselves. They've even accused someone of pirating, of setting the dragon free. Anyway, I was able to get the place for you. Don't ask how. It wasn't easy. But it's your only chance at Krakkow this season."

Jakkin looked up. He was about to thank her when he stopped, remembering her words of nearly a year ago. "You once said to me that letting another person fill your bag meant that there would be a hidden price to pay."

Akki smiled crookedly at him. "What a memory you have," she said. He felt, oddly, like a small child being praised. "It all depends whether you think that what you are getting is worth the price, I guess."

Jakkin looked over at his dragon. "A First Fight. In three days," he said. "It's worth it." He hesitated. "It's worth anything."

"Are you ready?"

"The question is really whether the dragon is ready," Jakkin answered, wondering why she shook her head at his reply.

At his voice, the dragon looked up and shot a single flame at them, neatly parting the two.

"Ready," said Akki, and she began to laugh.

# *18*

AKKI'S PLANNING WAS perfect. Jakkin's Bond-Off coincided with the day of the fight. He was dressed and off to the oasis as the cold of Dark-After was still receding, a paper sack containing a slab of meat between two slices of bread inside his shirt. It was left over from the evening's meal. He had been too excited to eat it, almost too excited to sleep.

At the oasis he polished the red's scales from tip of tail to nostril slits. The first polishing was in the stream, where he made a mud bath of the sand, stirring up the stream-bed until the water ran brown. The second was on shore, where he dried the dragon with an extra shirt Akki had provided.

Well before the full sunrise, Jakkin was walking out across the desert, the dragon trotting docilely at his heels, heading first north and then west, well away from the nursery, to a ford in the Narrakka River. He had promised to meet Akki and her friend there.

The truck was waiting. He recognized it from Akki's description, but caution, an old habit, claimed him. He warned the dragon, "Drop. Stay." The dragon squatted down on its haunches, waiting.

Jakkin went ahead on his own, conscious of the great silent mound of dragon behind him. He was ready, at an instant's notice, to send the dragon a silent command that would have it winging into the air, past the oasis, to the far mountains, where it could live free. He walked up to the truck and knocked tentatively on the door.

A man looked out of the cab. His eyes were a calculating blue, his mustache full, and his skin neatly tailored over his bones. "Jakkin, is it?" he asked.

Jakkin nodded and, hearing steps behind him, turned quickly.

"Hello," Akki said. "This is Ardru." She pointed to the man in the truck, who opened the cab door and stepped down.

He was a bit taller than Jakkin, with an old scar that ran from the corner of his right eye to his sideburns. It gave him a piratical look. Ardru put out his hand. "I'm always happy to help Akki's friends," he said. His voice was low and he spoke the language so precisely that Jakkin could hear each syllable. Ardru smiled. "She appears to have a lot of friends."

Jakkin hesitated a moment. Ardru's name—if it was his whole name—lacked the double *k* that would identify him as a bonder, a son of bonders, a grandson of bonders. Only those whose ancestors had been the original masters—and there were very few left—had names free of the jailer's brand, *kk*. Jakkin had never met one before. He touched his bond bag with two fingers while he decided, then suddenly he put out his hand. Ardru's grasp was cool and firm. Jakkin thought at his dragon, *Fly to me, now, thou First Fighter.*

The air hummed with the sound of dragon wings and the sand stirred around the wheels of the truck as the red flew in and hovered. Then it turned tail down and, using the tail as a rudder, settled slowly to earth, backwinging carefully.

"Thou art an impressive worm," said Ardru aloud, fearlessly walking up to the dragon. He held out his hand for the dragon to sniff. Satisfied, the dragon houghed once and sat down.

Jakkin, too, was satisfied. The dragon filled his head with cool green-and-beige landscapes.

Ardru unzipped the back doors of the truck and gestured to Jakkin. Jakkin climbed into the cavernous canvas-and-frame body of the truck, checking the insides for anything sharp that might injure the dragon. When he found nothing, he coaxed the red in after him. The red responded at once, climbing into the truck with an eagerness that matched Jakkin's own. The whole truck shook as the dragon settled down with its tail tucked around its feet and its nose on Jakkin's sandaled feet.

"Come ride up front with us," said Akki, peering into the darkness.

"No," Jakkin replied. "The worm needs me here."

"It will do just fine without you," said Akki.

"The boy knows best, Akki," said Ardru, putting his hand on her arm.

The easy familiarity with Akki and the smooth way Ardru called him a boy angered Jakkin. He started forward, but the doors were zipped shut on his movement. And then everything was black. He could see nothing through the heavy dark canvas, but he could hear the dragon's tail pound a sudden warning tattoo as it read the anger in his mind.

The ride to the pit was a series of thudding bumps and shimmies. Jakkin leaned against the dragon's side and tried not to absorb the shocks through his bottom, but by the trip's end he ached in every bone.

The sudden shuddering stop of the truck and the zigzag of light through the opening door seemed to happen simultaneously.

"Come on out. Hurry." It was Akki.

He got shakily to his feet and went to the door, his eyes drawn into thin slits to keep out the sun. Together Akki and Jakkin backed the dragon out of the truck.

"Where's your friend?" he asked as the red lumbered out and stretched.

"Standing watch," she answered.

Jakkin looked around. They were still in the desert, the tan truck disguised by the dunes. But ahead, about a kilometer away, he could see a large building squatting like a monstrous round beast on the sand.

"That's the pit," said Akki, nodding at the horizon with her head. "We didn't want to dump you out there. We can't have anyone know we helped you. I'd get into trouble—real trouble—at the nursery. And Ardru—well, he has to remain anonymous in all this. Do you understand?"

"Then that's not his real name?" asked Jakkin.

"Real enough," Akki answered. "And *that's* all you need to know. In fact, you should probably forget all about him. If I had been able to drive, I never would have asked him to help."

"I'll never tell," Jakkin said, looking at her. "That was a promise you gave me once. Remember? Only, I keep my promises."

"And if I had kept it completely, would you be here now?" she asked. "Or if I had not been the watcher, but Likkarn? Or Slakk? Or even Errikkin?"

Jakkin said nothing.

"Oh, go on, Jakkin. I *have* kept my promise to you—in substance, if not in words. Go on. Besides, both of you could probably use the walk."

Feeling the tightness in his muscles echoing the tightness in his throat, Jakkin nodded. He did not trust himself to speak.

A piercing whistle recalled Akki to the truck's cab. Ardru came around from the other side.

"All is clear," he said to Jakkin as he climbed into the cab. "And, boy . . ."

Jakkin looked up into the man's coolly assessing eyes. "Yes," he said, his voice hesitating between resentment and thanks.

"That is a mighty fighting dragon you have there. You must treat your dragon as you would a woman—with respect as well as love."

Before Jakkin could think of an answer, the truck had started with a muffled roar and pulled away, leaving great ruts in the sand.

Jakkin put his feet in the ruts and walked slowly along. When he looked behind, the dragon was following him docilely.

~

THE KRAKKOW MINOR PIT was a huge, round two-story building constructed between two small cities but within the jurisdiction of only one—Krakkow. Jakkin could see a great center bubble illuminated from within, probably containing the pit itself. He had been told that there were tiers of stands where bettors sat, and a series of stalls on the lower floors.

He checked the contract once again, and the letter that Akki had given him. It told him nothing beyond the number of his fight—tenth draw—and the number of the stall to which "Jakkin's Red" was assigned. First Fighters usually had the master's name and color description as identification. Naming would be done later.

"Stall twenty-four," he whispered over his shoulder to the dragon. In the early-morning light, the dragon's red scales were lustrous, even with their patina of road dust.

As they came nearer the pit, there was an explosion of sounds and smells and a flash of colors as dragons were unloaded from trucks, pushed and chivvied through two wooden gates. Jakkin heard the high-pitched scream of an angry dragon and watched as a gigantic brown with a splash of yellow across its muzzle went into a hindfoot rise. It towered over the truck it had come in. A scattering of men with smaller dragons warned Jakkin to hold his red close.

*Steady, steady*, he thought at it, but his own tenseness communicated itself to the dragon. It sent a series of lightning strokes jetting through his head.

The great brown was calmed at last by a man who struck it on the sensitive end of the nose with a prod-stick. The dragon slinked through the gate with several well-dressed men after it. Nearby an orange dragon shifted its weight back and forth and houghed its distress. The sound was picked up by others.

Jakkin's dragon sat for a moment and looked around. Jakkin went back to it and stroked its muzzle, then scratched behind its ears. "There's weed and wort for you inside, my beauty," he said. "And then you can show them all what you can do. But come. Come. Calmly."

The dragon turned its black eyes on Jakkin and they stared at one another for a long time. Something very like a bridge formed in Jakkin's mind and he fancied that two colors, a primary red and a primary blue, met in the middle of it. Then the dragon stood and followed Jakkin across the hard-packed earth and through the gates, where a bored guard stamped the papers that Jakkin carried in his bag. The guard took a quick picture of the dragon, affixing it to a badge that he pinned onto Jakkin's shirt so carelessly that it fell off before Jakkin had taken two steps. Jakkin picked up the facs badge and pinned it back on himself.

~

THE UNDERPIT STALL number twenty-four was a solid wooden affair, and the food bin was piled high with fresh stalks and leaves. The dragon munched happily on them while Jakkin took the meat and bread from inside his shirt. Even wrapped in brown paper, the meat drippings had spotted his clean shirtfront. Jakkin tried unsuccessfully to rub the spots out.

"Maybe," he mumbled to himself, "maybe they look like dragon blood." But what they smelled like, he knew, was sandwich. He had dressed carefully that morning, but now he looked like a poor bonder. Shrugging the annoyance away, he settled down to grooming the red with a cloth he found on a hook in the stall.

Noises came through the wooden ceiling. Jakkin could hear the groans of the floor joists as bettors and onlookers crowded into their seats. A disembodied voice called the names of the dragons for the opening fight: "Sarkkhan's Heavy Heart and Nokkar's Gold Digger."

Sarkkhan, here at the pit! And with a named dragon! Jakkin found himself suddenly aware of the loud drumroll of his own heartbeats. Why hadn't Akki warned him? She must have known. Why hadn't he found it out himself? Surely he could have asked Balakk or Jo-Janekk or any of the other older bonders. It was information that was easy to discover. But he had been so afraid of being discovered that he himself had discovered nothing. He cursed his own incompetence, his own inadequacies. He was a *boy*, indeed. And now he could only hope—hope that Sarkkhan would win and leave, or lose and leave. He did not know what he would do if the Master recognized the red.

Suddenly he laughed out loud. How *could* Master Sarkkhan recognize the red? He had never seen it. "Thou art mine," he whispered fiercely at the dragon. "*I* took thee and *I* raised thee and *I* trained thee." He attacked the dragon's scales with the cloth as if they were an enemy to be rubbed out. "And thy name is *Jakkin's* Red."

The dragon was too busy munching on the wort to reply.

Then the noises overhead changed. Jakkin could hear cheers and an occasional raucous call. He could not distinguish the words, but the intentions were clear. And above it all were the loud thumps and screeches and roars of the dragons as they battled for supremacy in the pit.

A pattern developed, and Jakkin, still cleaning his own dragon, heard it and made it a part of his own respiration. In the reactions of the crowd he could hear attack and counterattack, feint and thrust. He could translate the dragon screams into passes and charges, the thuds into wing-leaps and an occasional hindfoot rise. But he was unprepared for the sudden stillness at the fight's end, and when it came, he held his breath.

Then, floating into the silence, violating the peace, the mechanical voice called out: "Game to Heavy Heart."

Sarkkhan's worm had won the first draw. Jakkin did not know whether that was good or bad. He bent down over the red's claws and polished the lanceae of the right front foot with special care. He did not even notice when Sarkkhan's winner flowed through the dragonlock and went back into its stall.

# 19

JAKKIN LOST COUNT after the sixth fight, but he could hear, overhead, the pit cleaners circling noisily, gobbling up old fewmets with their iron mouths. They spit out fresh sawdust and moved on. It generally took several minutes between fights, and the mechanical clanking of the cleaners was matched by the roars of the pit-wise dragons and the last-minute betting calls of their masters.

Jakkin's fingers betrayed his nervousness. He simply could not keep them still. They picked off bits of dust and flicked at specks on the dragon's already gleaming scales. They polished and smoothed and polished again.

For the moment the red dragon seemed impervious to first-fight jitters and arched up under Jakkin's hands.

The cleaners clanked out of the ring through the mecho holes and Jakkin looked up. He ran his fingers through his hair and tried to swallow; then he touched the dimple on his cheek. Finally his hand found the bond bag and kneaded it several times for luck.

"Soon now," he promised the dragon in a hoarse whisper, his hand still on the bag. "Soon. We will show them a first fight they will remember."

The only sounds came from the dragon's jaws as it munched on the remaining stalks in its bin.

The disembodied voice announced the next fight. "Jakkin's Red, Mekkle's Bottle O'Rum."

Jakkin winced. He had overheard a little about Bottle O'Rum that morning when he had gone out once to find more wort leaves. (Burnwort stoked a dragon's internal fires and made its flame hotter in a fight.) The dragon masters and trainers did not chatter while they groomed their fighters, but the bettors did, and Jakkin had chanced upon a knot of them by a stall. There were three in the fancy coveralls that the Austarian free men at the pits affected, and one offworlder, the first Jakkin had ever seen. He was wearing a sky blue suit covered with gold braid. Jakkin had known him for a rocket jockey at once because of the planet name and number emblazoned on his pocket.

The bettors had said, among other things, that Mekkle's Bottle O'Rum was a light-colored orange male that favored its left side and had won three of its seven fights—the last three. It would never be great, the whispers had run, but it was good enough in the minor pits. Jakkin had stored that bit of information away in his head, along with a lot else.

And now, Jakkin thought miserably, he could use what he knew. Bottle O'Rum was a hard draw for a new dragon, and possibly disastrous for a would-be dragon master. If Mekkle could afford to run his dragon for four losing fights, until it was pit-wise and old enough and strong enough to win, then he must own a nursery. Jakkin, with a bag now almost empty of even its grave coin, had no such option.

Jakkin knew his red would be good in time, even great, given the luck of the draw. It had all the things a fighter was supposed to have: It listened well, it had heart, it did all that was asked of it. "And more," he whispered. "And more."

But the red was not a particularly large dragon and this was its first fight. Not only that, but it was unused to the company of other dragons. It was starting to get really nervous, rolling its eyes, houghing at loud noises. It had even begun to hackle when he had first brought it into the stall, though he had been able to calm it quickly. It had never been in a ring, not even in a corral or training ring behind a barn. What chance would it have fighting a pit-wise three-time winner? The red had never been blooded or given roar. He had been crazy to think they had a chance.

Already, Jakkin supposed, the betting would be running way against the young red. He thought he could hear the murmur of new bets following the announcement of the fight. The odds would be so awful, he might never get a sponsor for a second match, even if the red showed well in the pit. First fights were free, Akki had told him. But seconds cost gold. And if he had no sponsor and no gold, that would leave only the stews for the dragon—and a return to bond for himself.

Jakkin stroked the bond bag once more, then buttoned his shirt over it to conceal it. He did not know yet what it felt like to be free. He had had a year of pretending in the oasis, a year of short nights and an occasional Bond-Off away from bonders' gossip and Likkarn's hard hand. But he could still endure years more as a bond boy if he had to. Balakk and Jo-Janekk had stood it well. And there would be other chances for him to steal an egg, other years. Or he could apprentice under Likkarn as a trainer, swallowing his pride and bowing and smiling like Errikkin to buy favors from the old man.

He could stand it—if he had to. But how could he give up the red to the stews? It was not any old dragon—an enraged stud like Brother or a young cull. It was his beauty, his red. They had already shared a year together, nights and a few precious days out in the sands. He knew its mind better than his own: a deep, glowing cavern of colors and sights and sounds.

He remembered the first time he had really felt his way into it, not just been assaulted by the jets and passionate lightnings it chose to send him.

He had been lying on his side, slightly winded from running. The red lay down beside him, a small mountain in the sand. Closing his eyes, Jakkin had tried to reach out for the red, and suddenly he felt it open to him and it was as if he were walking down a glowing path into a cavern where colors dripped like large hanging crystals from a roof of the deepest purple. Rainbow puddles were on the cavern floor and multicolored fish leapt up from the water, singing. There had been a resonant thrumming, a humming that filled the air and then filled him.

The red calmed him when he was not calm, cheered him when he thought he could not be cheered. Linked as he was with it now, how could he ever bear to hear its last screams in the stews as the sharp-bladed knack-knife cut across its tender throat links and the hot blood dripped away into the cauldrons? How could he hear that and stay sane?

Perhaps, he thought suddenly, perhaps that was why Likkarn was always yelling at the younger bonders, why he smoked blisterweed that turned his mind foggy and made him cry red tears. And perhaps that was why most dragons in the stews were early culls or untrained yearlings. Not because they were softer, more succulent, but because no one would be linked with them to hear them when they screamed.

Jakkin's skin felt slimed with perspiration and the dragon turned and sniffed it on him. It gave out a few straggles of smoke from its slits. Jakkin fought down his own fear. If he could not control it, his red would have no chance at all. "A dragon is only as good as its master," bonders liked to say. He took several deep breaths and then moved over to the red's head, staring into its unblinking eyes.

"Thou art a fine one, my Red," he whispered. "First fight for us both, but I trust thee." He hesitated a moment. "Trust me?"

The dragon responded with slightly rounded smokes. Deep within its eyes Jakkin thought he detected small lights.

"Dragon's fire!" he breathed. "The nearness of the other dragons must have brought it out. Thou art a fighter. I knew it!"

Jakkin slipped the stall ring from the red's neck and rubbed its scales underneath. They were not yet as hard as a mature fighter's—still tender enough for the knack-knife. For a moment Jakkin worried that the older Bottle O'Rum might tear the red beyond repair. He pulled the dragon's head down and whispered into its ear. "Guard thyself here," he said, rubbing with his fingers under the throat links, thinking *Danger* at it.

The dragon shook its head playfully and Jakkin slapped it lightly on the neck, pushing it backward and out of the stall.

The dragonlock on the wall irised open, and with a surge the red flowed through it and up into the empty pit.

# 20

"IT'S EAGER." THE whisper ran around the crowd. They always liked that in young dragons. Time enough to grow cautious in the pit. Older dragons often were reluctant and had to be prodded with sticks, behind the wings or in the tender underparts of the tail. The bettors considered it a great fault. Jakkin heard the crowd's appreciation of the red as he came up into the stands.

It would have been safer for Jakkin to remain below, guiding his dragon by mind. That way there would be no chance for Master Sarkkhan to find him.

Many trainers, Mekkle being one of them, stayed down below in the stalls drinking and eating and guiding their dragons where the sounds and looks of the crowd could not influence them. But Jakkin needed to see the red as well as feel it, to watch the fight through his own eyes as well as the red's. They had practiced too long, just the two of them, in the sands. Neither Jakkin nor his red knew how another dragon in a real fight would respond. Jakkin had to be up in the stands to understand it all. And the red was used to seeing him close by. He did not want to change that now. Not now. Besides, unlike many of the other bonders, Jakkin had never been to a fight, only read about them in the books and heard about them from Akki and his bondmates. This, he thought bitterly, might be his only chance to watch. He further rationalized that up in the stands he might find out more about Mekkle's orange, and what he learned could help him help the red.

Jakkin looked around the stands cautiously from the stairwell. He saw no one he knew, neither fellow bonders in the upper tiers nor masters who traded with Sarkkhan in the pitside seats. He edged quietly into the lower stands, just one more free boy at the fights. Nothing could call attention to him in the masters' boxes but the near-empty bond bag beneath his shirt. He checked his buttons carefully to make sure they were closed. Then he leaned forward, hands on the seat back in front of him, and watched as his red circled the ring.

It held its head high and measured the size of the pit, the height of the walls. It looked over the bettors as if to count them, and an appreciative chuckle ran through the crowd. The red scratched in the sawdust several times, testing its depth. And still Bottle O'Rum had not appeared.

Then with an explosion Bottle O'Rum came through the dragon-lock and landed with all four feet planted well beneath the level of the sawdust, his claws fastened immovably to the boards.

"Good stance," shouted someone in the crowd, and the betting began anew.

The red gave a little flutter with its wings, a flapping that might indicate nervousness, and Jakkin thought at it, *He is a naught. A stander. But thy nails and wings are fresh. Do not be afraid. Remember thy training.* At that the little red's head went high and its neck scales glittered in the artificial sun of the pit.

"Watch that neck," shouted a heckler. "There's one that'll be blooded soon."

"Too soon," shouted another from across the stands at him.

Bottle O'Rum charged the inviting neck.

It was just as Jakkin hoped, for charging from the fighting stance is a clumsy maneuver at best. The claws must all be retracted simultaneously, or one will catch in the boards. And the younger the dragon, the more brittle its claws. The orange might have been seven fights older than the red, but it was not yet fully mature. As Rum charged, one of the nails on his front right foot, probably the unum, Jakkin thought, did catch in the floorboards, and it splintered, causing him to falter for a second. The red shifted its position slightly. Instead of blooding the red on the vulnerable neck, Rum's charge brought him headlong onto the younger dragon's chest plates, the hardest and slipperiest part of a fighting dragon's armor. The screech of tooth on scale sent winces through the crowd. Only Jakkin was ready, for it was a maneuver he had taught his dragon out in the sands.

"*Now!*" he cried out and thought at once.

The young red needed no urging. It bent its neck around in a fast, vicious slash, and blood spurted from behind the ears of Mekkle's Rum.

"First blood!" cried the crowd.

*Now the betting will change*, Jakkin thought with a certain plea-sure, and he touched the bond bag through the thin cloth of his shirt. Ear bites bled profusely but were not important. It would hurt the orange dragon a little, like a pinprick or a splinter does a man. It would make the dragon mad and—more important—a bit more cau-tious. But first blood! It looked good to the bettors.

Bottle O'Rum roared with the bite, loud and piercing. It was too high up in the throat yet, but surprisingly strong. Jakkin listened care-fully, trying to judge. He had heard dragons roar at the nursery in anger or fear or when Likkarn had blooded one of them for a customer intent on hearing the timbre before buying. To him the roar sounded as if it had all its power in the top tones and none that resonated. Perhaps he was wrong, but if his red could make this a long fight with the orange, it might impress this crowd.

In his eagerness to help his dragon, Jakkin moved to the pit rail, elbowing his way through some older men.

"Here, boy, what do you think you're doing?" A man in a gray leather coverall spoke. He was obviously familiar with the pits. Any-one in all leather knew his way around. And his face, what could be seen behind the gray beard, was scored with dragon-blood scars.

"Get back up in the stands. Leave ringside to the masters and money men," said his companion, taking in Jakkin's patched, food-spotted shirt and short bonder's pants with a dismissing look. He ostentatiously jounced a full bag that hung from his wrist on a leather thong; an ex-bonder often wore his old bag on his wrist.

Jakkin ignored them, fingering his badge with the facs picture of the red on it. He leaned over the rail. *Away, away, good Red*, he thought at his dragon, and smiled when the red immediately wheeled and winged up from its blooded foe. Only then did he turn and address the two scowling bettors. "Pit right, good sirs," he said with defer-ence, pointing at the same time to his badge.

They mumbled, but moved aside for him. A trainer, even though he had no money, had precedence at the pit.

The orange dragon in the pit shook its head and the blood beaded its ears like a crown. A few drops spattered over the walls and into the stands. Each place a drop touched burned with that glow peculiar to the acidic dragon's blood. The onlookers ducked. One watcher in the third row of the stands was not quick enough and was seared on the cheek. He reached up a hand to the wound but did not move from his place.

The orange Rum stood up tall again and dug back into the dust.

"Another stand," said the gray-leather man to Jakkin's right.

"Pah, that's all it knows," said a dark-skinned offworlder beside him. "That's how it won its three fights. Good stance, but that's it. I wonder why I bet it at all. Let's go and get something to drink. This fight's a bore."

Jakkin watched them leave from the corner of his eye, but he absorbed their information. If the orange were a stander, if the information were true, it would help him with the fight.

The red dragon's leap back had taken it to the north side of the pit. When it saw that Bottle O'Rum had chosen to stand, it circled closer warily.

Jakkin thought at it, *He's good in the stance. Do not force him there. Make him come to thee.*

The dragon's thoughts, as always, came back clearly to Jakkin, wordless but full of color and emotion. The red wanted to charge; the dragon it had blooded was waiting. The overwhelming urge was to carry the fight to the foe.

*No, my Red. Trust me. Be eager, but not foolish*, cautioned Jakkin, looking for an opening.

But the crowd, as eager as the young dragon, was communicating with it, too. The yells of the men, their thoughts of charging, overpowered Jakkin's single line of calm. The red started to move.

When he saw the red bunching for a charge, Rum solidified his stance. His shoulders went rigid with the strain.

Jakkin knew that if his red dived at that standing rock, it could quite easily break a small bone in its neck. And he knew from Akki's lessons in anatomy that a dragon rarely came back to the pit once its neck bones had been reset. Then it was good only for the breeding nurseries—if it had a fine pit record—or the stews.

"Steady, steady," Jakkin said aloud. Then he shouted and waved a hand. *"No!"*

The red had already started its dive, but the movement of Jakkin's hand and his shout were signals too powerful for it to ignore, and at the last possible minute it pulled to one side. As it passed, Rum slashed at it with a gaping mouth and shredded its wing tip.

"Blood," the crowd roared, and waited for the red dragon to roar back.

Jakkin felt its confusion, and his head swam with the red of dragon's blood as his dragon's thoughts came to him. He watched as it soared to the top of the building and scorched its wing tip on the artificial sun, cauterizing the wound. Then, still hovering, it opened its mouth for its first blooded roar.

There was no sound.

"A mute!" called a man from the stands. He spit angrily to one side. "Never saw one before."

A wit near him shouted back, "Never heard one, either."

The crowd laughed at this and passed the quip around the stands. But Jakkin only stared up at his red. *A mute*, he thought at it. *Oh, my poor Red. You are as powerless as I.*

His use of the distancing pronoun *you* further confused the young dragon, and it began to circle downward in a disconsolate spiral, closer and closer to the waiting Rum, its mind a maelstrom of blacks and grays.

Jakkin realized his mistake in time. *It does not matter*, he cried out in his mind. *Even with no roar, even voiceless, thou wilt be great.* He thought it with more conviction than he really felt. But it was enough for the red. It broke out of its spiral and hovered, wings working evenly.

The maneuver, however, was so unexpected that the pit-wise Bottle O'Rum was bewildered. He came out of his stance with a splattering of dust and fewmets, stopped, then charged again. The red avoided him easily, landing on his back and raking the orange scales with its claws. That drew no blood, but it frightened the older dragon into a hindfoot rise. Balancing on his tail, Rum towered nearly three meters high, his front claws scoring the air, a single shot of fire streaking from his slits.

The red backwinged away from the flames and waited.

*Steady, steady*, thought Jakkin, in control again. He let his mind recall for them both the quiet sands and the cool nights when they had practiced against the reed shelter a game of charges and clawing. Then he repeated out loud, "Steady, steady."

A hard hand on his shoulder broke through his thoughts and the sweet-strong smell of blisterweed assailed him. Jakkin turned.

"Not so steady yourself," came a familiar voice.

Jakkin stared up at the ravaged face, pocked with blood scores and stained with tear lines.

"Likkarn," breathed Jakkin, suddenly panic-stricken. He tried to turn back to the pit, where his red waited. The hand on his shoulder was too firm, the fingers like claws through his shirt.

"And when did *you* become a dragon trainer?" the man asked.

At first Jakkin thought to bluff. The old stallboy was too sunk in his smoke dreams to really listen. Bluff and run, for the wild anger that came after blister dreams never gave a smoker time to reason. "I found . . . found an egg, Likkarn," he said. And it could be true. There were a few wild dragons, bred from escapees that had gone feral.

Sometimes a lucky bonder came upon a dragon-egg cache out in the sand.

The man said nothing but shook his head.

Jakkin stared at him. This was a new Likkarn—harder, full of purpose. Then Jakkin noticed. Likkarn's eyes were clearer than he had ever seen them, no longer the furious pink of the weeder's, but a softer rose. Obviously he had not smoked for several days. This end of the season, Jakkin had been so intent on his own dragon that the workdays at the nursery, monitoring the mating flights, had slipped by. But Likkarn was too alert. It was useless to bluff—or to run. "I took it from the nursery, Likkarn. I raised it in the sands. I trained it at night, by the moons."

"That's better, boy. Much better. Liars are an abomination," the man said with a bitter laugh. "And you fed it what? Goods stolen from the master, I wager. You born-bonders know nothing. Nothing."

Jakkin's cheeks were burning now. "I am no born-bonder. My father and his father were born free. That's two times." He did not mention the great-grandfather after whom he was named, the reason for the double *k*. "And I would never steal from the master's stores. I planted swamp seeds in the sands last year and grew blisterweed and burnwort. And bought new seeds with my drakk bounty. *On my own time.*" He added that fiercely.

"Bonders have no time of their own," Likkarn muttered savagely. "Or supplements."

"The master says adding supplements to the food is bad for a fighter. They make a fighter fast in the beginning, but they dilute the blood." Jakkin looked into Likkarn's eyes more boldly now. "The master said that. To a buyer." He did not add that it was Akki who had told him.

Likkarn's smile was wry and twisted. "And you eavesdrop as well." He gave Jakkin's shoulder a particularly vicious wrench.

Jakkin gasped and closed his eyes with the pain. He wanted to cry out, and he thought he had, when he realized it was not his own voice he heard but a scream from the pit. He pulled away from Likkarn and stared. The scream was Bottle O'Rum's, a triumphant roar as he stood over the red, whose injured wing was pinioned beneath Rum's right front claw.

"*Jakkin . . .*" came Likkarn's voice behind him, full of warning. How often Jakkin had heard that tone right before Likkarn had roused from a weed dream to the fury that always followed. Likkarn was old, but his fist was still solid.

Jakkin trembled, but he willed his focus onto the red, whose thoughts came tumbling back into his head now in a tangle of muted colors and whines. He touched his hand to the small lump under his shirt where the limp bond bag hung. He could feel his own heart beating through the leather shield. *Never mind, my Red,* soothed Jakkin. *Never mind the pain. Recall the time I stood upon thy wing and we played at the Great Upset. Recall it well, thou mighty fighter. Remember. Remember.*

The red stirred only slightly and made a flutter with its free wing. The crowd saw this as a gesture of submission. So did Rum, and through him, his master, Mekkle. But Jakkin did not. He knew the red had listened well and understood. The game was not over yet. Pit fighting was not all brawn; how often the books had said that. The best fighters, the ones who lasted for years, did not have to be big. They did not have to be overly strong. But they did have to be cunning gamesters, and it was this he had known about his red from the first— its love of play.

The fluttering of the unpinioned wing caught Bottle O'Rum's eye and the orange dragon turned toward it, relaxing his hold by a single nail.

The red fluttered its free wing again. Flutter and feint. Flutter and feint. It needed the orange's attention totally on that wing. Then its tail could do the silent stalking it had learned in the sands with Jakkin.

Bottle O'Rum followed the fluttering as though laughing for his own coming triumph. His dragon jaws opened slightly in a deadly grin. If Mekkle had been in the stands instead of below in the stalls, the trick might not have worked. But the orange dragon, intent on the fluttering wing, leaned his head way back and fully opened his jaws, readying for the winning stroke. He was unaware of what was going on behind him.

*Now!* shouted Jakkin in his mind, later realizing that the entire stands had roared the words with him. Only the crowd had been roaring for the wrong dragon.

The red's tail came around with a snap, as vicious and as accurate as a driver's whip. It caught the orange on its injured ear and across an eye.

Rum screamed instead of roaring and let go of the red's wing. The red was up in an instant and leapt for Bottle O'Rum's throat.

One, two, and the ritual slashes were made. The orange throat coruscated with blood, and instantly Rum dropped to the ground.

Jakkin's dragon backed at once, slightly akilter because of the wound in its wing.

"Game to Jakkin's Red," said the disembodied voice over the speaker.

# 21

THE CROWD WAS strangely silent. Then a loud whoop sounded from one voice buried in the stands, a bettor who had taken a chance on the First Fighter.

That single voice seemed to rouse Bottle O'Rum. He raised his head from the ground groggily. Only his head and half his neck cleared the dust. He strained to arch his neck over, exposing the underside to the light. The two red slashes glistened like thin, hungry mouths. Then Rum began a strange, horrible humming that changed to a high-pitched whine. His body began to shake, and the shaking became part of the sound as the dust eddied around him.

The red dragon swooped down and stood before the fallen Rum, as still as stone. Then it, too, began to shake.

The sound of the orange's keening changed from a whine to a high roar. Jakkin had never heard anything like it before. He put his hands to the bond bag, then to his ears.

"What is it? What is happening?" he cried out, but the men on either side of him had moved away. Palms to ears, they backed toward the exits. Many in the crowd had already gone down the stairs, setting the thick wood walls between themselves and the noise.

Jakkin tried to reach the red dragon's mind, but all he felt were storms of orange winds, hot and blinding, and a shaft of burning white light. As he watched, the red rose up on its hind legs and raked the air frantically with its claws, as if getting ready for some last deadly blow.

"Fool's Pride," came Likkarn's defeated voice behind him, close enough to his ear to hear. "That damnable orange dragon wants death. He has been shamed, and he'll scream your red into it. Then you'll know. All you'll have left is a killer on your hands. I lost three that way. *Three.* Three dragons and three fortunes. Fool's Pride.'' He shouted the last at Jakkin's back, for at his first words, Jakkin had thrown himself over the railing into the pit. He landed on all fours, but was up and running at once.

He had heard of Fool's Pride, that part of the fighting dragon's bloody past that was not always bred out. Fool's Pride that led some defeated dragons to demand death. It had nearly caused the dragons to become extinct. If men had not carefully watched the lines, trained the fighters to lose with grace, there would have been no dragons left on Austar IV.

He could not let his red kill. A good fighter should have a love of blooding, yes. But killing made dragons unmanageable, made them feral, made them wild. In his mind suddenly was the image of his father dying under the slashing claws of a wild orange worm. Jakkin heard a scream, thought it was an echo of his mother's voice, and realized at last it was his own.

He crashed into the red's side. ''No, no,'' he called up at it, beating on its body with his fists. ''Do not wet thy jaws in his death.'' He reached as high as he could and held on to the red's neck. The scales slashed his left palm cruelly, but he did not let go.

It was his touch more than his voice or his thoughts that stopped the young red. It turned slowly, sluggishly, as if rousing from a dream. Jakkin fell from its neck to the ground.

The movement shattered Bottle O'Rum's concentration. He slipped from screaming to unconsciousness in an instant.

The red nuzzled Jakkin, its eyes unfathomable, its mind still clouded. The boy stood up. Without bothering to brush the pit dust from his clothes, he thought at it, *Thou mighty First.*

The red suddenly crowded his mind with victorious sunbursts, turned, then streaked back through the open hole to its stall and the waiting burnwort supplied by the masters of the pit.

As Jakkin stood there, too weary to move, Mekkle and two friends came through the stands, glowering, and leapt into the pit. They wrestled the fainting orange onto a low-wheeled cart and dragged him over to the open mecho hole by his tail. Then they shoved the beast through the hole.

Only then did Jakkin walk back to ringside, holding his cut hand palm up. It had just begun to sting.

Likkarn, still standing by the railing, was already smoking a short strand of blisterweed. He stared blankly as the red smoke circled his head.

"I owe you," Jakkin said slowly up to him, hating to admit it. "I did not know Fool's Pride when I saw it. Another minute and the red would have been good for nothing but the stews. If I ever get a Second Fight, I will give you some of the gold. Your bag is not yet full."

Jakkin meant the last phrase simply as ritual, but Likkarn's eyes suddenly roused to weed fury. His hand went to his bag. "You owe me nothing," said the old man. He held his head high and the age lines on his neck crisscrossed like old fight scars. "*Nothing.* You owe the master everything. I need no reminder that I am a bonder. A boy. *I fill my bag myself.*"

Jakkin bowed his head under the old man's assault. "Let me tend the red's wounds. Then do with me as you will." He bowed and, without waiting for an answer, ducked through the mecho hole and slid down the shaft.

~

JAKKIN CAME TO the stall where the red was already at work grooming itself, polishing its scales with a combination of fire and spit. He slipped the ring around its neck and knelt down by its side. Briskly he put his hand out to touch its wounded wing, in a hurry to finish the examination before Likkarn came down. The red drew back at his touch, sending into his mind a mauve landscape dripping with gray tears.

"Hush, little flame-tongue," crooned Jakkin, using the lullaby sounds he had invented to soothe the hatchling of the sands. "I won't hurt thee. I want to help."

But the red continued to retreat from him, crouching against the wall.

Puzzled, Jakkin pulled his hand back. Yet still the red huddled away, and a spurt of yellow-red fire flamed from its slits. "Not here, furnace lung," said Jakkin, annoyed. "That will set the stall on fire."

A rough hand pushed him aside. It was Likkarn, no longer in the weed dream but starting into the uncontrollable fury that capped a weed sequence. The dragon, its mind wide open with the pain of its wound and the finish of the fight, had picked up Likkarn's growing anger and reacted to it.

"You don't know wounds, boy," growled Likkarn. "How could you? I'll show you what a *real* trainer knows." He grabbed the dragon's torn wing and held it firmly, then with a quick motion, and before Jakkin could stop him, he set his mouth on the jagged tear.

The dragon reared back in alarm and pain and tried to whip its tail around, but the stalls were purposely built small to curb such motion. Its tail scraped along the wall and barely tapped the man. Jakkin grabbed at Likkarn's arm with both hands and furiously tore him from the red's wing. "I'll kill you, you weeder," he screamed. "Can't you wait till a dragon is in the stews before you try to eat it? I'll kill you." He slammed at Likkarn with his fists and feet, knowing as he did it that the man's weed anger would be turned on him and he might be killed by it, and not caring.

Suddenly Jakkin felt himself being lifted up from behind, his legs dangling, kicking uselessly at the air. A man's strong arm around his waist held him fast. At the same time, the man pushed Likkarn back against the wall.

"Hold off, boy. Hold off. He was a good trainer—once."

# 22

JAKKIN TWISTED AROUND as best he could and saw the man he had most feared seeing. It was Master Sarkkhan himself, dressed in a leather suit of the red and gold nursery colors. His red beard was brushed out, making it twice as bushy as normal. He looked grim.

"Hold off," Sarkkhan said again. "And hear me. Likkarn is right about the best way to deal with a wing wound. An open tear, filled with dragon's blood, will burn the tongue surely. But a man's tongue heals quickly, and there is something in human saliva that closes these small rips."

Sarkkhan put Jakkin down but held on to his shoulder with one large hand.

"It's the other way around, too," Jakkin heard his voice saying in a rush. "The dragon licked my wound and it healed clean."

"Well, now, that I never saw myself, though it's been folk wisdom around here for a while." Sarkkhan brushed his hair back from a forehead that was pitted with blood scores as evenly spaced as a bonder's chain. "Now, promise me you will let this old man look to the red's wing."

"I will not," Jakkin said hotly. "He's a weeder and he's as likely to rip the wing as heal it. And the red hates him—just as I do." Suddenly realizing who he was talking to, Jakkin put his hand up before his mouth.

Likkarn turned toward him and raised a fist, aiming it at Jakkin's head. Before it could land, the dragon had pulled the ring chain free of the stall and nosed the trainer to the ground, putting a front foot on him to hold him still.

Master Sarkkhan let go of Jakkin's shoulder and considered the red for a moment. "Likkarn," he said at last, nodding his head at the old man, "I think the boy is right. The dragon won't have you. It's too closely linked. I had wondered at that, by its actions in the pit. This confirms it. Wish I knew how Jakkin did it. That close a linkage is rare. I can control my dragons somewhat. But a fresh dragon and a trainer are never that close. It takes years to establish such a bond. Never mind now. Best leave this to the boy and me."

Jakkin nodded, saying, "Let him go, my worm."

At his words, the dragon lifted its foot slowly.

Likkarn got up clumsily and brushed off his clothes. One button of his shirt had been ripped off and the bond bag had slipped out in the scuffle. Jakkin was surprised to see that it was more than halfway plump, jangling with coins. How could he have filled his bag that way in less than a year? Betting? Perhaps he had spent his Bond-Offs not weeding but playing the dragons at Krakkow Pit.

Likkarn caught Jakkin's look and angrily stuffed that bag back inside his shirt, then jabbed at the outline of Jakkin's thin bag with a weed-reddened finger. "And how much have *you* got there? Not even a baby's portion, I warrant." He walked off with as much dignity as he could muster, then slumped by the stairwell to watch.

Sarkkhan, ignoring them both, was crouching down by the dragon, letting it get the smell of him. He caressed its jaws and under its neck with his large, scarred hands. Slowly the big man worked his way back toward the wings, crooning at the dragon in low tones, smoothing its scales, all the while staring into its eyes. Slowly the membranes, top and bottom, shuttered the red's eyes, and it relaxed. Only then did Sarkkhan let his hand close over the wounded wing. The dragon gave a small shudder but was otherwise quite still.

"Your Red did a good job searing its wound on the light. Did you teach it that?"

"No," the boy admitted.

"Of course not. Foolish of me. How could you? No lamps in the sands. Good breeding, then," said Sarkkhan with a small chuckle of appreciation. "And I should know. After all, your dragon's mother is my best—Heart O'Mine."

"You . . . you knew all along, then." Jakkin suddenly felt as confused as a blooded First.

Sarkkhan stood up and stretched. In the confines of the stall he seemed enormous, a red-gold giant. Jakkin suddenly felt smaller than his fifteen years.

"*Fewmets*, boy, of course I knew," Sarkkhan answered. "Even when I'm not around, I know *everything* that happens at my nursery. Everything. Make it my business to know.''

Jakkin collapsed down next to his dragon and put his arm over its neck. Akki. It had to have been Akki, because who but Akki had known everything about him? She had sold him to Sarkkhan and this was the price he had to pay: the knowledge that all of his manhood was the gift of the girl with the mocking mouth and her red-bearded lover. What had she said? "I have kept my promise in substance—if not in words." And she lied then, too. He had believed each one of her lies, believed them because he wanted to, because it was dark-haired Akki who told them. Well, he would not think about it any longer. It was too shameful, too painful.

When Jakkin finally spoke again, it was in a very small voice. "Then why did you let me do it? Were you trying to get me in trouble? Do you want me in jail? Or did you just find it all terribly funny, your own private entertainment?"

The man threw back his head and roared, and the dragons in neighboring stalls stirred uneasily at the sound. Even Likkarn started at the laugh, and a trainer six stalls down growled in disapproval. Sarkkhan looked down at the boy. "I'm sorry, boy, I keep forgetting how young you are. Never known anyone quite that young to train a hatchling successfully. But everyone gets a chance to steal an egg. It's a kind of test, you might say. The only way to break out of bond. Some are meant to be bonders, some masters. How else can you tell which is which? Likkarn's tried it—endless times—but he just can't make it, eh, old boy?" The master glanced over at Likkarn with a look akin to affection, but Likkarn only glared back. "Steal an egg and try. The only things wrong to steal are a bad egg or your master's provisions." Sarkkhan stopped talking for a minute and mused. Idly he ran a hand over the red dragon's back as it chewed contentedly on its burnwort, little gray straggles of smoke easing from its slits. "Of course most *do* steal bad eggs or are too impatient to train what comes out, and instead they make a quick sale to the stews just for a few coins to jangle in their bags. Then it's back to bond again before a month is out.''

Jakkin interrupted. "I didn't steal an egg, sir."

"I know, boy. I always had high hopes for you. You kept yourself apart from the others. Had a kind of *dedication* about you. A dream you wouldn't dilute with cheap, boyish pleasures. Your coins went into your own bag, not into someone else's. You filled your bag your-self. I like that. I admire that. So I left one late hatcher uncounted, just in case. I knew you could read—and count. I had high hopes and you didn't let me down, even though you lay a week in the hospice. And didn't I give Likkarn a de-bagging for that, for killing Brother and nearly killing you. And you bounced back. Stole a hatchling from my best hen. Probably the best hatchling in the bunch. None of that false compassion—picking a runt or one with an injured wing. You went right to the best. I like that. I'd do it myself."

Jakkin started to say something, but Sarkkhan went on.

"That's all you stole, I hope. The ones who steal provisions land in jail. And the next time, it's off planet for good."

"You wouldn't put me in jail, then? Or the red in the stews? I couldn't let you do that, Master Sarkkhan. Not even you," Jakkin said.

"Send a First Fighter, a *winner*, to the stews? *Fewmets*, boy. Where's your brain? Been smoking blisterweed?" Sarkkhan hunkered down next to him.

Jakkin looked down at his sandals; his feet were soiled from the dust of the pit. He ordered his stomach to calm down and felt an answering muted rainbow of calm from the dragon. Then a sudden, peculiar thought came to him.

"Did you have to steal an egg, Master Sarkkhan?"

The big redheaded man laughed again and thrust his right hand into Jakkin's face. Jakkin drew back, but Sarkkhan was holding up two fingers and waggling them before his eyes.

"Two! I stole two. A male and a female. Blood Type and Heart's Ease. And it was not mere chance. Even then I knew the difference. *In the egg.* I knew. I can tell in the egg, and by a hatchling. Even before the first mating season exposes the difference. And *that's* why I'm the best breeder on Austar IV." He stood up abruptly and held out his hand to the boy. "But enough. The red is fine and you are due upstairs." He yanked Jakkin to his feet and seemed at once to lose his friendliness.

"Upstairs?" Jakkin could not think what that meant. "You said I was not to go to jail. I want to stay with the red. I want—"

"*Wormwort*, boy, have you been listening or not? You have to register that dragon. Give her a name. Record her as a First Fighter, a winner."

"Her?" Jakkin heard only the one word.

"Yes, a her. Do you challenge *me* on that? Me? And I want to come with you and collect my gold. I bet a bagful on that red of yours—on Likkarn's advice. He's been watching you train, my orders. He said she was looking good, and *sometimes* I believe him."

Jakkin pulled his hand back. "Likkarn? Likkarn watched? But it was Akki. It had to be. Her footprints. Akki who told . . ." He trailed off into a confused silence.

Sarkkhan shook his head. "That little piece of baggage. Just like her mother, boy. But when she's a woman, she'll be something, I'll tell you. Oh, I knew she'd been sneaking out there to be with you. As I said, there's not much I don't know about my nursery. And when I first heard about it from Likkarn, about you staying out half the night making love to my girl . . ."

Jakkin started to protest, but Master Sarkkhan's voice overrode his. "Well, you can bet I was ready to kick your tail up between your shoulder blades till your bond shirt rattled up your backbone like a window shade. I'm not an easy father, I'm not."

"Father!"

"And her refusing to let me claim her officially, to write it into the books. Akkhina out of Rakki by Sarkkhan James. I'm not supposed to let anyone know. She's got a temper, that one. Just like her father." He laughed. "Won't have anything to do with me. Me! The best breeder on the planet. Pretending to be a bonder and wearing that damned foolish empty bag after I bought off her bond. Fool's Pride, I shouldn't wonder. Damnably silly. There are masters and there are bonders in this world and no one *wants* to be a bonder. 'Let her try to fill her bag alone,' Likkarn said. 'Then she'll come crawling back,' he said. And *sometimes* I listen to him. Sometimes. I owe him still. He took me in, taught me everything."

The day seemed made up of never-ending surprises. Jakkin kept hearing himself repeat Sarkkhan's last words like a common-mocker, the little lizard that mimicked the tail-end of its enemy's challenges and, in the ensuing confusion, often got away. Only Jakkin could not tear himself away from Sarkkhan's endless stream of revelations. "You owe him? Likkarn? *He* taught *you*?"

"*Fewmets*, boy, you sound like a mocker. Yes, I owe him. He found me, a runaway bond boy, out in the sand near Rokk with two eggs. Trying to hatch them with my own body warmth. Damn near froze to death in Dark-After. He found me and dragged me to a shelter and warmed me with his own clothes. Didn't turn me in either, though it could have bought him out of bond. Took three of my hatchlings in exchange when the two mated, and that's the first time he was a master. I owe him." Sarkkhan walked toward the stairwell where the old trainer still waited.

They stopped by Likkarn, who was slumped again in another blisterweed dream. Sarkkhan reached out and took the stringy red weed ash from the old man's hand. He threw it on the floor and ground it savagely into the dust. "He wasn't born a weeder, boy. And he hasn't forgotten all he once knew. But he'll never be a *real* man. Hasn't got the guts to stay out of bond. I hope you do." Then, shaking his head, Master Sarkkhan moved up the stairs, impatiently waving a hand at the boy to follow.

A stray strand of color pearls passed through Jakkin's mind and he turned around to look at the dragon's stall. Then he gulped and said in a rush at Sarkkhan's back, "But she's a mute, Master Sarkkhan. She may have won this fight by wiles, but she's a mute. No one will bet on a dragon that cannot roar."

The man reached down and grabbed Jakkin's hand, yanking him through the doorway and up the stairs. They mounted two at a time. "You really are lizard waste," said Sarkkhan, punctuating his sentences with another step. "Why do you think I sent a half-blind weeder skulking around the sands at night watching you train a snatchling and make love to my girl? Because I'd lost my mind? *Fewmets*, boy. Likkarn was the only bonder I could trust to keep his mouth shut. And I need to know what is happening to every damned dragon I have bred. I have had a hunch and a hope these past twenty-five years, breeding small-voiced dragons together. I've been *trying* to breed a mute. Think of it, a mute fighter—why, it would give nothing away, not to pit foes or to bettors. A mute fighter and its trainer . . ." And Sarkkhan stopped on the stairs, looking down at the boy. "Why, they'd rule the pits, boy."

They finished the stairs and turned down the hallway. Sarkkhan strode ahead and Jakkin had to double-time in order to keep up with the big man's strides.

"Master Sarkkhan—" he began at the man's back.

Sarkkhan did not break stride but growled, "I'm no longer your master, Jakkin. *You* are a master now. A master trainer. That dragon will speak only to you, go only on your command. Remember that and act accordingly. Never have seen such a linkage as you have with that worm. It's a wonder, it is. If I were a jealous man . . . but I'm not."

Jakkin blinked twice and touched his chest. "But . . . but my bag is empty. I have no gold to fill it. I have no sponsor for my next fight. I . . ."

Sarkkhan whirled, and his eyes were fierce. "*I* am sponsor for your next fight. I thought that much, at least, was clear. And when your bag is full, you will pay me no gold for your bond. Instead I want pick of the first hatching when the red is bred—to a mate of my choosing. If she is a complete mute, she may breed true, and *I* mean to have a hatchling.''

"Oh, Master Sarkkhan," Jakkin cried, suddenly realizing that all his dreams were realities, that there was no price to pay at all, "you may have the pick of the first *three* hatchings." He grabbed the man's hand and tried to shake his thanks into it.

"*Fewmets!*" the man yelled, startling some of the passersby. He shook the boy's hand loose. "How can you ever become a bettor if you offer it all up front. You have to disguise your feelings better than that. Offer me the pick of the *third* hatching. Counter me. Make me work for whatever I get."

Jakkin said softly, testing, "The pick of the third."

"First two," said Sarkkhan, softly back, and his smile came slowly. Then he roared, "Or I'll have you in jail and the red in the stews."

A crowd began to gather around them, betting on the outcome of the uneven match. Sarkkhan was a popular figure at pit fights and the boy was leather patched, obviously a bonder, an unknown, worm waste.

All at once Jakkin felt as if he were pitside. He felt the red's mind flooding into his, a rainbow effect that gave him a rush of courage. It was a game, then, all a game. Being a master, being a man, just meant learning the rules and how far to go. And he knew how to play. "The second," said Jakkin, smiling back. "After all, Heart's Blood is a First Fighter, and a winner. And," he hissed at Sarkkhan so that only the two of them could hear, "she's a mute." Then he stood straight and said loudly so that it carried to the crowd. "You'll be lucky to have pick of the second."

Sarkkhan stood silently, as if considering both the boy and the crowd. He brushed his hair back from his forehead, exposing the blood scores; nodded. "Done," he said. "A hard bargain." Then he reached over and ruffled Jakkin's hair, saying back, "And I'll be glad to give my girl Akki to you. She needs a strong master." They walked off together.

The crowd, settling their bets, let them through.

"I *thought* you were a good learner," Sarkkhan said to the boy. "Second it is. Though," and he chuckled quietly, "you should remember this. There is rarely anything very good in a first hatching. That is something Likkarn has never learned. Second is the best by far."

"I didn't know that," said Jakkin.

"Why should you?" countered Sarkkhan. "*You* are not the best breeder on Austar IV. I am. But I like the name you picked. Heart's Blood out of Heart O'Mine. It suits.''

They went through the doorway together to register the red and to stuff Jakkin's bag with his hard-earned dragon's gold.

# 23

THE TWIN MOONS cast shadows like blood scores across the sand. Jakkin hunkered down in the bowl-shaped depression and listened. Inside the wood-and-stone dragonry he could hear the mewling and scratching of hatchlings as they pipped out of their shells. One more night, maybe two, and the hatching would be complete.

Near the stud barn was a newer, smaller barn. In that building Heart's Blood stayed apart from the other hens. She was still too young to breed, though under Sarkkhan's tutelage she and Jakkin had won two more fights. Sarkkhan said that Heart's Blood would command the best mating prices if she fought at least ten times in a variety of minor pits. After that, if she could win a championship in a major pit, she would be known all over the world.

*Sleep, my worm*, Jakkin thought as he stood and walked past the barn. A cool river of greens meandered slowly through his mind in response. He knew that Likkarn was asleep in the bondhouse and no other watchers had been set on his track. Sarkkhan trusted him. Jakkin would not betray that trust. Brooming his footsteps away for the first kilometer would not keep Likkarn or Sarkkhan from his private spot, but it would keep the other bonders from finding it. He still needed a place he could go. And he hoped that Akki might be waiting for him there.

He remembered the first time he had gone back, several weeks after the fight with Rum. Wanting to claim the remaining rows of weed and wort plants in order to keep his debt to Sarkkhan down, he stripped the stalks with care. He had been at work for only a few minutes when he heard a familiar mocking laugh. He turned and had seen Akki standing near the shelter, her hands on her hips.

"I hear you won," she said. "Ardru was there. In the Master Box. Did you see him? Was it exciting? Was it worth the risk?"

He had walked over to her slowly. "Why haven't you returned to the nursery?" he asked.

"Do you always answer questions with a question?" she countered. They had both laughed.

Later she told him she would never come back. "I only stayed as long as I did to help you. Because you had a dream, just like me. If dreamers don't help one another . . . But once *your* dream came true, it was time for me to go. I don't really belong in a nursery. Not anymore. I am both master and bonder," she said. "And I will let no man fill my bag."

Then she added, almost under her breath, "I left the gold Sarkkhan paid for my bond on his pillow."

Jakkin did not ask her how she got the gold.

"I know Sarkkhan is your father," he said quietly.

"I am not responsible for that."

"Then why must you go away?" he asked.

"I just told you," she said. "Weren't you listening?"

"You answered my question with a question," Jakkin whispered. "I don't want you to go."

She said nothing, just looked at him strangely and left.

~

THE SECOND TIME she had come during the day when Jakkin had taken Heart's Blood for a run and a day of training. The dragon was often restless if he left her confined too long in the barn. She needed to fly in great wheeling arcs over the oasis. And Jakkin always felt he had passed some kind of important test each time the dragon returned to his side.

It was Heart's Blood who had first sensed Akki's approach, casting a gold silhouette in Jakkin's mind. He recognized it immediately as Akki, though it was many minutes more before she actually came into view.

"How do you know when I am going to be here?" he asked.

"I don't. Sometimes I come when you aren't here," she said. "And I lie down by the pool and remember. Or forget."

He wanted to ask, "Remember what? Forget what?" But he didn't. Instead, he lay down in the sand with his head resting on the dragon's flank. Akki sat beside him. They held hands. That was the day they hardly spoke at all.

~

THE LAST TIME he had seen Akki was a night when he had come out
to the oasis to sit and think and be by himself. He had been worrying
about an approaching fight and his nervousness had communicated
itself to Heart's Blood. So he had come alone, expecting no one.

It had been a night of many breezes, and the swirling patterns of
sand had changed over and over, a kaleidoscope whose pieces were
shaken by the winds.

Jakkin had been sitting by the shelter with his eyes closed when
suddenly he felt Akki by his side. She had moved up close to him
without warning, putting her hands on either side of his face. Her
palms felt as hot as dragon's blood on his cheeks.

She pulled him toward her and kissed him slowly, gently. She
seemed to know what she was doing and he let himself almost drown
in the sweetness of her kiss. Then she pulled away suddenly and said,
"I have to go away. *Really* go away this time."

He had laughed nervously, saying, "You can't, you know. You
belong here. With me. Your father gave you to me. He said you
needed a master."

She stood up. "You're such a boy, sometimes, Jakkin Stewart.
Such a child. And so is he." She turned and walked away.

Jakkin had scrambled up after her, but she had run from him
across the sand. He tried to follow her and suddenly heard the roar
of a truck engine ahead of him. All he found were deep tire ruts in
the sand.

~

JAKKIN CAME UPON the oasis and listened, stroking the bond bag he
still wore around his neck. It was plump and jangling with coins. He
had earned enough from the three fights to pay Sarkkhan his bond
and to buy Errikkin's bond paper as well. He still owed Sarkkhan:
gold for the barn and for feed, and the choice of the second hatching.
But he owed it freely, master to master. He was his own master now.
He need not wear his bag.

But Jakkin had sworn to himself that he would wear it until he
could pour out the gold from the bag into Akki's hands and she accepted him as a master and a man. It was a promise he made to
himself, and he was a man who kept his promises. He hoped he would
not have to wait too long.

# Heart's
# Blood

*For Adam Stemple,*
*dragon master*

THE THREE CAVES

NARRAKKA CHASM

SUKKER'S
MARSH

SPIKKA
COPSE

SARKKHAN
HOUSE

JOURNEY INTO
THE MOUNTAINS

TOM McKEVENY

O ROKK 320 KM.

INCUBARN

JAKKIN'S BARN

STUD BARN

BONDHOUSE

# *The Hatchlings*

# 1

THE SECOND MOON had just lipped the horizon when Jakkin checked the barn again. His great red dragon, Heart's Blood, was near her birthing time, and he was more nervous than she. All day he had wandered uneasily, walking from bondhouse to the fields, then back to the barn, looking in on the dragon frequently as she lay in her birth stall, grooming herself. He had rubbed her nose, patted her head between the vestigial earflaps, crooned old nursery lullabies. Then, tight with inexpressible feelings, he would leap up and run out of the barn, threading his way across the fields of shoulder-high burnwort or bursting into the bondhouse to watch fat Kkarina cook.

"Get out," Kkarina had shouted at him the last time he had invaded her kitchen. She waved a large wooden spoon at him. "You're making me nervous with your pacing. Don't worry so. The dragon will know what to do when the eggs come. Believe me."

Jakkin believed her all right. But He doubted *he* would know what to do. Should he crowd into the room with Heart's Blood? Or should he observe the egg laying from the peephole in the door, as Master Sarkkhan advised? Or should he stay away from the barn altogether, as old Likkarn had pointedly told him to do?

"You'll only send her your own fears," Likkarn said. "You transmit well with that worm. She'll add your worries to her own. Don't be more of an idiot, boy, than you already are."

But Jakkin couldn't stay away from the barn and his red. They had been together almost two years, but in those two years they had grown up together, their thoughts linked in great colored patterns. He wouldn't desert her now.

As he opened the barn door, he was hit with the blood-red tide of her sending and knew it was time. Running down the corridor, he called, "Easy, easy, my beauty." But there was no recognition in her churning reply.

He threw open the door of the birthing room and was almost overwhelmed by the power of her thoughts. Suddenly he felt as she felt; for the first time there seemed no separation between them. He was engulfed in the colors as if he himself were a great dragon hen.

The pressure in her birth canal sent waves rolling under the sternum and along her heavy stomach muscles. She fluttered her wings, then pressed them against her sides, letting the edges touch her belly. Stretching her neck to its fullest, she looked around, scouting the area for danger, an unconscious gesture left over from the eons when dragons had given birth in mountain caves. The skin protrusions over her ear holes fluttered.

Jakkin spoke again, making the sounds into a soothing chant. "Easy, easy, my beauty, easy, easy, my red."

Heart's Blood opened her mouth as if to scream an answer into the dry air, but because she was a mute, the only sounds that came out were a hungry panting: in and out, in and out.

As Jakkin watched, she circled the cavernous room three times in a halting rhythm, squatting at last over a shallow hole she had dug in the sandy floor only that day. Then, with one final push, she began to lay.

The eggs popped out between her hind legs, a continuous production, cascading down into the sandy nest, piling on top of one another, and quickly building up into a shaky cream-colored pyramid.

Jakkin could scarcely breathe as he watched. He leaned back against the wooden wall, waiting, running his fingers through his hair, and stroking the leather bondbag at his neck. He longed to stroke the dragon's neck as well but feared to distract her, though he guessed she wouldn't have even noticed his touch. She was too far caught up in the birthing rhythms.

"Easy, easy," he crooned again.

The dragon shook her head, and Jakkin felt a spillage of her usual rainbow sending patterns shoot through his mind in colors that were a riot of reds: scarlet, carnation, crimson, and rose; fiery gems strung on a strand of thought. For each egg, another ruby-colored jewel, and he knew there would be upward of a hundred eggs.

Perhaps Likkarn was right, and he shouldn't be here in the room with her. Jakkin's instant of uneasiness made the dragon look up for a moment, causing a halt in the laying.

Jakkin smiled at her and let his thoughts gentle. She looked away, and the eggs started out again. Sliding down to the ground, Jakkin wondered, *Maybe old Likkarn was right for ordinary dragons, but Heart's Blood is not ordinary.*

"Thou art a rare beast indeed," he whispered, comforting both himself and the red with the archaic language trainers used with the big beasts. He stroked the bondbag again and, feeling a large measure of calm now within himself, concentrated on sending Heart's Blood a single image to help ease the passage of the eggs. He thought of a ribbon of clear blue water lying across a sun-flecked base of sand. One edge of the ribbon was lined with sand-colored kkhan reeds. The image was cool, quiet, familiar. It was a picture of the oasis where, for a year, Jakkin had raised the dragon, watching her change from a scum-colored, wrinkled-skin hatchling into a great responding red.

The dragon's muscles never ceased their straining, but her massive head turned once again toward the boy. The black shrouds of her eyes lit for a moment with the crackle of red light known as dragon's fire. Then the eyes went dark again as she turned her thoughts inward and attended to the laying of her eggs.

Jakkin knew it would take her the better part of the night. The barn was heated for the egg laying and warmed as well by the dragon's body. It would be hot enough, even in the fiercest cold of Dark After, for him to stay. But first he wanted to tell his friends, the bonders in the nursery, that she had started to lay.

~

"Early laid, early paid." Slakk greeted the news with the old saying. "What luck you have, Jakkin." He was sitting in the dining room, playing a hand of Four-man Flikk with the other boys.

Jakkin stumbled against the table.

"Lucky, you mean, that he's not the one with the eggs," shouted red-haired Trikko. "They'd all be splattered by now."

"How many so far?" asked Slakk.

"Worm waste, they're just now laid, not hatched," growled Balakk from the table where the older man sat talking. "You've lived all your life in a nursery, boy, and still you know nothing."

Slakk ignored him. "How many do you think will hatch? There's good coins there."

Jakkin rubbed his arm thoughtfully, tracing the thin bracelet of scar tissue that ran around his wrist. "I don't know, Slakk."

"Guess."

"I hope for five or six live, of course. But I'll be thankful for any."

"I bet nine," said Slakk. "A gold says nine." He dug into his bondbag and pulled out a coin, letting it drop onto the table.

"It's a first birth," Jo-Janekk called from the other table. Next to him Balakk nodded. "And that means fewer live. My gold to yours that he gets only three worth selling and one to keep." He opened his bag, drew out a coin, and slammed it down on the table in front of him.

"*My* master," said Errikkin, standing up and putting his hand on Jakkin's shoulder, "*my* master's beast will outbreed any on the farm. Just as she can outfight them. I'll go one higher than Slakk. One higher than any of you. A gold for ten."

"Oh for God's sake," muttered Jakkin to Errikkin, "save your coins. Don't waste them on such foolishness. Of course, she's not going to have ten live. They never do."

But Errikkin shook his head and smiled brightly. "Ten, I say."

Slakk laughed. "You should have had Jakkin buy your brains when he bought your bond, Errikkin. I'll take your gold—as always."

"Lend me a gold, Slakk. I'm flat," Trikko begged. "I want to bet, too."

"No."

Balakk called out, "Three. Put me down for three."

Quickly the others placed bets.

From the corner where he was sitting alone, Likkarn rose. His weed-reddened eyes were rheumy, hazed over as if with a smoky film, but his voice was steady and low. "My guess is she'll have five. And one born crooked. It's all in the way you read the breed lines, boys. I'll take your one gold and add another for you to match. And I'll spend your money in Krakkow next Bond-Off, laughing at you all." He slammed the two coins on the table in front of Slakk, then went out the door.

"Old Likk-and-Spittle," said Slakk as the door shut, but he was careful to say nothing until Likkarn was out of hearing. "What does he know?"

"More than you ever will, bonder," Balakk said. "Put your money down."

Jakkin left, too, the sound of coins on the table accompanying him. The bickering was getting on his nerves, but what bothered him the most was the callous betting on Heart's Blood's eggs. All that dragons meant to the bondboys was money. "First laid, first paid," indeed. Heart's Blood was more than just a brood hen, more than just a mighty Pit fighter. She was—his other self, he supposed.

He went into his room, grabbed the blanket from the bed, and went back to the barn.

# 2

THE EGG LAYING and the night were done. Jakkin had hardly slept, dozing fitfully in the overwarm barn. Still groggy, he watched as a sticky, yellow-white liquid afterbirth trickled out of the dragon's birth canal, coating the pyramid of eggs and holding them together. He knew that after this, she would leave the clutch of eggs and retreat to the farthest corner of the room to clean herself thoroughly with her long, rough-ribbed tongue. Then she would fall asleep for a full day and night.

Jakkin had been a bonder in a dragon nursery most of his life. He knew what to expect. In the wild the birthing would have been done on the sandy floor of a pumice cave, and the hen would have slept in the cave mouth, her warm bulk raising the temperature in the cave during the cold of Dark After. Nothing would wake her in that comalike sleep as she recovered from the hard work of egg laying. Some of the first wild dragons captured by the early KKs had been taken while they slept such birth-sleeps.

Jakkin had a sudden illuminating thought. It must have been because of that sleep that so many eggs had to be dropped. There was always danger while the dragon slept that one of the many egg-eaters would find the clutch. Perhaps the fierce flying drakk would sniff out the dragon's cave. Or the tiny cave-dwelling flikka, all teeth and tail, which could pierce even the hard shell of a dragon's egg, might already be living there. That *had* to be why most of the eggs were empty. They were decoys for the suckers. Of the hundreds dropped, no more than eight or nine ever actually contained live hatchlings. And no wild dragons had ever been seen with more than one or two young.

Most of Jakkin's information had been gathered from bonder gossip, or from the few books he had read, or from talking with Master Sarkkhan. Bonders were always open and giving with their information. Some of it Jakkin had found correct, and some of it, he had discovered this past year, was spectacularly wrong. The books all were scientifically accurate but much too dry and technical for easy reading. And they were surprisingly cautious about some things that any trainer knew. For example, one book had said, "Trainers often claim to understand dragon thought."

"*Claim!*" Jakkin smiled as Heart's Blood reacted to his mood with a slight shiver and a sending that showed a solitary dark, jagged blob racing across an otherwise bland sand-colored landscape.

Master Sarkkhan, who owned the nursery and knew so much after a lifetime with dragons, was stingy with his facts because he believed any good breeder or trainer should find his own way in the world. "Grow up with your worm" was the way he put it.

Jakkin had been slowly piecing it all together—with the help of Heart's Blood. The dragon *was* teaching him, teaching him more than had the rest. *And that is how it* should *be*, he reminded himself, unconsciously echoing Sarkkhan. "A man should learn from his dragon just as the dragon should learn from the man."

He ran his hand through his hair once again, wondering if Heart's Blood was learning anything from him at all. Although he was seventeen and no longer a bonder, he did not feel much like a man. The other bonders called him a man, but then they called anyone who could buy himself out of bond that. And he had fought a drakk by himself, which Kkarina said was confirmation of manhood. But he was still waiting for a shift in feelings, some sure recognition that boyhood had ended and manhood begun, as sure a demarcation as the lines on a map.

He touched the leather at his neck. The very fact that he still wore a bondbag when he was a master was his own sign to himself that he didn't feel like a man. Not yet.

His hand stayed on the bag while he watched the hen dragon heave herself to her feet and shuffle off to the darkest corner of the room. She houghed once and lay down. As the dragon settled into the rhythm of cleaning herself, Jakkin slipped out through the door. There was nothing more for him to watch. In the superheated room the eggs would start to hatch in a day or two. Until that time he would have to find other things to do.

His stomach suddenly reminded him that it was breakfast time.

The dark passageway in the barn made one small turning. It was only a few more steps to the outside door.

Jakkin could see the rim of light under the door frame. He stopped for a moment, closed his eyes to make everything darker still, and concentrated on a final sending. Before he could push a gentle memory of their oasis days toward Heart's Blood, he felt her mind reach out first. As always, it was a wordless color display that was easy enough for him to translate. He could touch the minds of the other dragons in the nursery, but none was so clear to him.

What Heart's Blood was saying was that she was . . . *satisfied*. "Happy" was too strong a word, too human a word to describe what she felt. Her thinking, her emotions were very different from his. She was, simply, alien. However, Jakkin could always make a quick, rough translation, and he knew what she meant. The egg laying was completed. She would finish cleaning herself, then lie down for the long sleep. Everything was as it should be, and she was . . . *satisfied*.

The colors of her sending faded off into a peaceful rose landscape, a replica of the farm as it was seen from above.

Jakkin, satisfied as well, pushed through the door and out into the assaulting, harsher colors of the day.

# 3

"MASTER SARKKHAN WANTS you to eat with him tonight," Errikkin said as Jakkin came into the bondhouse. His smile turned what must have been a command into an invitation, but he delivered it with the half bow, half bob he had affected ever since Jakkin had bought his bond. "Dinner at his house."

"Fewmets!" muttered Jakkin. "I wish you'd stop that bowing. It embarrasses me."

Errikkin shrugged and bobbed again, almost imperceptible this time. "But I *like* doing it," he said, still smiling. "I like showing you how I feel. After all, you promised to buy my bond from Master Sarkkhan when you had enough gold, and you did. I bow because I'm grateful. They say a good master makes a grateful servant, so you must be a good master." He paused, then added, "And you pay me more for less work."

"Because I *want* you to pay off your bond and be free. But you just spend it every chance you get," Jakkin said, his voice lowering to a near growl. "Or bet it stupidly." He stopped himself from mentioning that he actually had very little money to spare, what with feed costs and Pit fees. Errikkin would consider such talk unmasterly. If he could only get Errikkin to buy off his bond or let Jakkin simply manumit him—set him free. But Errikkin sidestepped the issue with a smile whenever he brought it up. That smile—and that constant good humor—annoyed Jakkin. He snapped, "I keep telling you— don't spend your gold. Save it for freedom."

"Why? I don't want to be free." Errikkin smiled more broadly. "I'm perfectly happy with you as my master. I know you'll never let me starve. I get room and food and gold in my bag. What more do I need?''

Jakkin was silent. What more? When he was a bonder, all he had ever wanted was to own a dragon and be free. Errikkin somehow wanted neither of those things. All these years they had worked together, side by side, as bonders in the nursery, eaten together in the dining room, slept in the same bunk bed. It seemed incredible to Jakkin that they could be so different, want such different things. His hand went to the bag under his shirt, and he made a face.

For the whole of the past year Errikkin had argued against Jakkin's wearing a bag. ''It isn't masterly,'' he complained. But this time he ignored Jakkin's gesture. ''You've been with that dragon all night. Let's get you cleaned up.'' He gestured with his hands in a shooing movement toward the corridor.

Jakkin nodded distractedly and marched down the hall. Only as he turned into his single room did it occur to him that sometimes he seemed the bonder and Errikkin the master, so quickly did he jump to Errikkin's tune.

As a freeman Jakkin no longer had to share quarters with the others. Although he knew it was a privilege, he often missed his friends, missed having someone to talk with just before falling asleep. But when he saw Errikkin coming toward him with a washcloth, he remembered the one advantage to having his own room. He could throw someone out of it. He held up his hand.

''No!'' he said. ''I'm perfectly able to clean myself. I'm not a child, you know.'' His voice was sharp. All the contentment he had felt with the dragon had been leached away by Errikkin's smiling attentions.

''But I like helping you,'' Errikkin said, his bland handsome face set in its smile.

''Out!'' said Jakkin.

''Now, Master Jakkin . . .'' Errikkin said.

''Out!''

''As you wish.'' Errikkin left, bowing, his face triumphant.

By the time the door shut, Jakkin was as angry with himself for the outburst as he was with Errikkin. He hated losing his temper and sounding like an outraged old master. He had certainly seen enough of *them* at the Pits. They screamed and hit their bonders at any provocation. Jakkin had a sneaking suspicion that Errikkin wouldn't mind a smack now and then. But if he had to become *that* kind of master, he wanted nothing to do with the bond system at all.

Jakkin bit his lip and calmed down by forcing himself to take stock of his room, an old trick that usually worked. This time, though, the neatness of the place—all Errikkin's doing—annoyed him anew. He ticked off the bonder's additions to his Spartan surroundings: a bone pitcher filled with kkhan reeds; the facs badges and tickets from three Minor fights arranged on a board by the door; a bowl of jingle shells from Sukker's Marsh. There was nothing wrong with any of them. In fact, they were quite handsomely displayed. But he preferred doing such things on his own.

"I fill my bag myself," he murmured. That was something his mother had taught him before she died, and it was something he believed in. Having Errikkin—or anyone else—tidying up after him, toadying up to him, annoyed Jakkin almost beyond the telling of it.

He set to scrubbing off the accumulated barn dirt with a ferocity that left him no energy to think about Errikkin or any other petty annoyances.

~

THE DINING ROOM was full and noisy. Jakkin made his way to the table where the younger boys—Slakk, Errikkin, Trikko, and L'Erikk— sat eating. At his arrival Errikkin jumped up subserviently, and Jakkin rolled his eyes toward the ceiling.

*"Sit down!"*

"Yes, Master," Errikkin said.

"Yes, Master," the boys all mimicked, further embarrassing Jakkin but not seeming to bother Errikkin at all.

A girl laughed at another table.

Jakkin did not look to see who it was.

"Done?" Slakk asked.

"All done," Jakkin said. He grimaced as Errikkin slid a glass of hot, thick takk in front of him but drank it nonetheless, hunger getting the better of indignation. But he reached quickly for a pair of boiled lizard eggs before Errikkin could serve him. Trikko slid the basket of bread down the table toward him, and he nodded his thanks. "Now we wait for the hatchlings to come out."

"How long?" Slakk began.

Jakkin shrugged. "When they come."

Slakk smiled and pushed away from the table, rocking back on the hind legs of his chair. "When they come. I know, I know. Don't lecture me. 'The dragon chooses the time.' Haven't I heard that before! I just don't have the patience for worm farming. When I can buy out of bond, I'm moving to the city. I'll own a stewbar. Or a baggery."

The boys laughed.

"You'll die broke, sampling your own wares," warned L'Erikk.

"But what a way to go," Slakk answered quickly, his dark, fer-rety eyes lighting up.

"I want to be a senator," Trikko said. "And live in a big house in The Rokk. And have people wait on me and wash my clothes and have more to eat than lizard meat and takk and eggs and bread. And—"

"Pah, boy," said Crikk, one of the farmhands, as he passed by the table, two platters of lizard meat carefully balanced. "Whoever heard of a senator who smelled of the farm? Even Master Sarkkhan knows better than to make a run for it. They'd sniff you out."

"Why would you want to be a senator anyway? Overbred, un-derprincipled, soft-handed wardenbrats." It was Balakk. Overhearing the boys, he had come to their table to continue the old argument. He folded his arms over his chest, and the muscles on his forearms bulged. "To be a senator means being for the Federation. A pawn of the Galaxian Empire. And I say *that*"—he spat on the floor—"for the beslimed Feders."

L'Erikk and Trikko slammed their mugs on the tables. "Feder, no! Feder, no!" they chanted loud enough to be heard throughout the room.

Pots and pans clattered suddenly in the kitchen. Kkarina, the only one at the farm who openly supported the Federation, was angry. No one, not even Sarkkhan, whom she worshiped, could change her mind. She was convinced that if Austar joined the Federation, she would be able to purchase all the materials she needed to modernize her kitchen and generate reliable electric power.

The boys chanted louder, Slakk and Errikkin joining in, hoping to make Kkarina storm out of the kitchen and shake a spoon at them. The older bonders watched the kitchen door in silent amusement. They liked Kkarina, but they loved her wild displays as well. This time the only indication of her political displeasure was the rattling of pans. The ineffective chanting slowly died. Slakk's was the last voice to be heard.

Only Jakkin, of the boys, had been silent, methodically chewing the tough eggs and sipping the spicy takk. He hated dinner-table pol-itics. It was all slogans and no sense. He knew that membership in the Federation would mean Austarians would have to conform to Gal-axian rules and Galaxian laws instead of their own. They would be ruled by a Federation-selected governor instead of the loose system of country senators. The Federation definitely outlawed a master class, and Jakkin secretly thought that would be just fine. But it didn't prohibit a class of rich hereditary overlords, which meant, he thought, that you had to be born into it. Like most Austarians, Jakkin was fiercely independent, a legacy of his convict ancestors. If there was bond—well, a boy could always buy his way out. But you couldn't change your birth.

"Maybe Kkarina's a secret rebel," whispered L'Erikk. "Maybe she's plotting to put something in our stew."

Slakk guffawed, slapping L'Erikk on the back.

Balakk's face turned purple. "You piece of worm dottle," he called. "Watch what you say. Kkarina—a rebel? That gal couldn't sneak about if she wanted to." He had meant it as a compliment to Kkarina's honesty, but they all took it as a measure of her vast girth and laughed.

L'Erikk laughed the loudest, his boy's voice cracking on the highest note. And Balakk, realizing he was being teased, shut up.

Jakkin thought about the rebels. What few of them there were wanted neither system—no masters but no Federation either. But they offered nothing to put in its place. Every week the rebels littered the Pit fights with pamphlets, badly written stuff full of slogans, all of which Jakkin found stupid, especially since most bonders—at whom the pamphlets were aimed—couldn't read.

He stood up, taking the takk cup with him. Once these political games started at the table, they went on until chore time, and were boring and predictable. Federation, rebels, senators—the whole lot could rot in fewmets as far as he was concerned. He was a dragon master and would rather talk about the changing of the seasons and the raising of dragons, the price of wort seed and the bloodlines of worms.

He left the room.

# 4

THE DAY WENT slowly, and though Jakkin helped in the barns bathing the stud dragons, his thoughts were constantly with Heart's Blood. She, however, was in such a deep sleep that the only sendings he got from her were a low, constant hum of rose with thin lines of quiet blue marching across the unchanging landscape.

His inattention to his work caused him to be nipped once, quite painfully, by the usually phlegmatic Bloody Flag. And he received a rope burn from mishandling a bale of wort. Then he forgot to eat lunch. And turning too quickly in the tool room, he bumped his head hard enough on a low beam to raise a small lump.

"Worm spit," he called himself when the pain on the top of his head subsided. It was the last of a long line of curses he had aimed at himself all day.

He found himself looking forward to dressing for dinner with Sarkkhan, not only because it was something different but also because it was the least dangerous thing that he could do in a day that had been filled with small hazards. And it would certainly keep his mind off the moment that Heart's Blood would wake and pick over the hatching eggs.

He found that Errikkin had laid out his Pit suit, with the red and gold trimmings, Sarkkhan's colors. Although he tried not to let it bother him, Errikkin's attentions were yet another annoyance in a day of petty and painful annoyances. He jerked off his shirt and dropped it onto the floor, shoving it under the bed with his foot.

*There*, he thought wryly, conjuring up Errikkin's smiling face. *Work for your gold, bonder!*

Then, immediately contrite, he knelt and retrieved the shirt. It had bits of dust sticking to it. That commentary on Errikkin's housekeeping skills made Jakkin smile for the first time that day.

*A not-so-perfect bondservant*, he thought. *For a not-so-perfect master.*

He scrubbed his skin with a wet cloth until all traces of barn dirt were gone, though the dragon smell still lingered. Crikk was right about that. The tart musk of dragons got into human pores and stayed. Even city folk, who lived on slabs of lizard and dragon meat from the Stews, seemed coated with the smell. Offworlders sometimes found the odor offensive, or so they said. At one Pit fight Jakkin had heard a starship trooper call a trainer "worm breath," and the fight that had followed had engulfed the betting crowd, ending in thirteen arrests and six men—including the trooper—being hospitalized.

Putting on the heavy red-and-gold suit, Jakkin grimaced. He much preferred his trainer whites or the leather bonder pants he was no longer allowed to wear. Only masters could afford the more uncomfortable dress. He bent down to tie his sandals with the ornate master knot, then checked his longish, unruly hair in the mirror. Patting it in place, he thought that he must have left his comb in the barn. Or maybe it was under the bed, covered with dust.

Out loud he mused, "And what would Errikkin do if I just simply *gave* him his freedom without asking? Would he sell himself back into bond immediately to the highest bidder?"

Shrugging slightly at his image in the glass, Jakkin turned and walked out of the room. He had no sooner reached the end of the corridor when he heard, rather than saw, Errikkin slip into the room to straighten it up. Briefly he wondered if this time Errikkin would notice the dust under the bed.

"Wait," he muttered. "As soon as I know how many eggs are hatched, I'm going to see if I can sell a hatchling and set you free."

~

THE WALK UP to Sarkkhan's stone and sandbrick house had a calming effect on him. The twenty-year-old spikka trees lining the walkway threw sharp-edged shadows onto the road.

For the first time Jakkin wondered why he had been summoned to Sarkkhan's to eat. Could the nursery owner want to discuss Heart's Blood's next fight? A week after hatching, she could go. But they might have discussed that anywhere—in the bondhouse, in the barn, in the fields. Perhaps Sarkkhan had a guest. That would be unusual, but it had been known to happen. Usually, though, he transacted his business in the cities, on his trips to the Pit. When he was home, he was in the barns or at the training yards. For all his bulk, Sarkkhan was not a big eater; rather, he grabbed his meals on the run. He often said that eating while you worked was a necessity, and Jakkin had learned, in the past year, how true that was. If you were grooming a dragon for a fight or keeping watch at egg laying or calculating the readiness of the mating studs, it was hard to find time for regular meals. "The dragon chooses the time." Slakk might hate to hear it, but it was true. And trainers, linked with their dragons, often chose to eat crouched amid the fewmets and dust.

Fewmets and dust! That was a dragon master's life. A few moments of glory in the Pit, then back to the dust and fewmets again.

Jakkin knocked on the carved front door of Sarkkhan's house, delighting as always in the panels of dragons expertly etched in the wood.

The door was flung open.

"Well, at last, young Jakkin," said Sarkkhan, walking toward him. Sarkkhan was a red-gold figure, his beard almost orange in the flickering candlelight and the backs of his hands covered with a matting of red-gold hair. He was so massive across the chest and shoulders that most men looked puny beside him. The man sitting in the window seat with a glass in his hand was no exception.

"Golden and I have gone on to our third drinks waiting for you." He gestured toward the slim, beardless figure by the window. "Were you with your worm? Has she finished laying?"

"Laying, yes. Hatching, no."

"You were *with* her? Your hen dragon? I thought all that was natural. That you did not have to *do* anything to help them." The man near the window spoke with a high, unnatural fluting to his voice. Each word was so precise Jakkin could distinguish every syllable.

"It *is*. It is natural." Sarkkhan spoke quickly. His hearty booming suddenly seemed too loud for the small room. "But we breeders, we like to be there, though we watch through a peephole. Just in case. And this is Jakkin's first dragon and her first laying. Under the circumstances, I'd do the same."

Jakkin was surprised at Sarkkhan's apologies. "You do the same with all your worms, not just on their first layings."

"Yes, yes," Sarkkhan said. "Of course. But Golden doesn't know that. He's not a dragon master, though I'm sure he's been to an occasional Pit."

The man rose as if careful of his bones. "Yes, yes," he said, almost parodying Sarkkhan but smiling to show he meant no offense. "I do like watching those great brutes in the Pit. But it's the people

I really go to see. I fancy myself a people master actually. Not a dragon master." He laughed. "They quite terrify me. Dragons."

Jakkin watched the man as if he were watching a performance. Something did not seem quite right about this Golden, this man who had no double *k* to his name. A wardenbrat? He was too careful with his words, dealing them out for their effect. And *too* careful with his movements. Yet his blue eyes were infinitely calculating.

"But my manners are showing," Sarkkhan boomed again. "Jakkin Stewart, this is Durrah Golden, first senator from The Rokk."

A senator. He *was* a wardenbrat. His ancestors had never been convicts. It also explained Sarkkhan's strange behavior. He was uncomfortable in his own house because it had been invaded by a senator and Sarkkhan had often—and publicly—railed against the Senate and its laws. "Too many laws already" was a favorite line of his.

Golden held out his hand, and Jakkin was forced to take it. The senator had lizards' hands, a handshake that seemed to slip away as soon as you touched it, like a marsh streaker. Yet, in that brief touch, Jakkin thought the hand was not as soft as its owner would have him believe. There was also a strange, subtle scent to the man, not a dragon smell but a lack of any natural odor at all.

"Golden was born offplanet and educated on shipboard," Sarkkhan concluded. "But he's one of us."

"I am an Austarian by choice," Golden added quickly.

*So that is why he has no smell*, Jakkin thought.

"And being from an original master family," Sarkkhan continued, avoiding the use of the slang *wardenbrat*, "he was appointed a senator in place of Master Crompton, who died suddenly last year."

Jakkin wrinkled his nose involuntarily. Politics again. It seemed he couldn't get away from it. But he couldn't very well walk out of Sarkkhan's house the way he had left the bondhouse dining room. Some politeness was expected of him. He murmured congratulations to Golden on his appointment.

His distance must have been reflected in his voice, for Golden smiled lazily and said, "I see Master Jakkin is less than interested in politics. So let us not bore him with unnecessary talk of it." He sipped the takk.

Jakkin looked at him gratefully.

"But he should be interested!" roared Sarkkhan. "What affects Austar affects dragons. As a Protectorate we make our own laws but can still be visited by Federation ships. We'll lose that autonomy if we become a state, the way you senators would have it. We'd have to bow to Galaxian rules. How can a Galaxian Senate, hundreds of light-years away from here, know what is best for Austar?''

Jakkin looked down at the floor. He had heard it all before. Including the suggestion that the senators were being well paid for their support of the Federation.

"Ah, my friend Sarkkhan,'' Golden drawled, "the Federation is set up precisely to rule places hundreds of light-years away. And for the most part it has done its job well,'' Golden said quietly.

"What about the coup on Io? What about the seven suns that blew up, destroying Caliban? How quickly did the Federation move then?'' Sarkkhan's face was red with anger.

Jakkin thought: *Next he'll mention the freighter that incinerated half of Isis's moon and the race against time that was lost when the mining colony on Rattigan VI died from a mutated plague. It's all so predictable.*

"Now, Master Sarkkhan, you know I have not taken a stand on the question of the Federation yet,'' Golden answered companionably. "I am trying to sound out *all* my constituents. And you, Master Sarkkhan—as well as you, Master Jakkin—are part of them.'' He put his hand on the nursery owner's shoulder, but Sarkkhan shrugged it off. "Come now, wouldn't the Federation be of some help here? We could use the trade, especially metals and power cells. And those Austarians who wanted to leave could get travel permits. Think of those things.''

"That kind of help has an awesome price tag,'' Sarkkhan said. "And while you senators sit around The Rokk, arguing whether to sell us into bond to a bunch of offworlders, the rebel numbers are growing. If we don't deal swiftly with them, the Federation will step in whether we like it or not. Its way of dealing with a planet at war with itself is to turn a united Federated shoulder against it. Slap on an embargo. No starships for up to fifty years. What will that do to the dragon business, I ask you? No starships, no Pit fights. No Pit fights, and the dragons will be good only for meat. It's quite simple.''

Sarkkhan turned and looked directly at Jakkin. "And that's why, like it or not, Jakkin Stewart, politics affects you.''

The senator waved his glass in a lazy movement toward Sarkkhan. "My dear man, I hardly think it will come to that. The great Federation—though I can hardly speak for it—is not likely to worry itself about a small, minor, so far bloodless rebellion of a disgruntled few.'' He paused. "Unless you know something more than I know. Is it, do you think, neither minor nor bloodless?''

Sarkkhan looked down into his glass. "I know only what I hear. I've never actually met anyone who professed to be a rebel.''

Jakkin had to laugh. "Do you think anyone would walk up to the greatest dragon breeder on the planet and say, 'Hello, there, I'm a rebel'?"

"There, you see," Golden said. "You *do* know something about politics."

Sarkkhan houghed through his nose like a disgruntled dragon. "Don't be naive. You're *already* affected. If the rebels had their way, they'd make every man a master and set every bonder free."

Thinking of Errikkin, Jakkin replied, "I don't think that would be so awful."

"And then who'd deal with the fewmets, I ask you?" Sarkkhan's voice rose to a shout again. "The world is filled with dirty jobs that no one really wants to do. Still, the jobs have got to be done. So start at the bottom and work your way to the top. How else can you test a man?"

It was exactly the kind of argument Jakkin always tried to avoid, complete with shouting and arm waving and no one really listening to anyone else.

"And what would *you* have us do, Master Sarkkhan?" Golden asked smoothly. Jakkin could see that he had done this sort of thing many times before.

Sarkkhan looked away from them and suddenly threw his glass into the fireplace. He laughed when it shattered against the stones.

"Break them. As easily as that glass. Break the leaders of the rebels, and throw them offworld. They're used to this dry heat, so send them to KK Forty-seven. That ice world should cool them off soon enough."

Golden laughed flutily. "You know better than that. The Federation can condemn a man only on a Federation planet. Criminals can be transported offplanet only if the planet is a Galaxian world. Protectorates are off limits to Federation transporters."

"You brought us here originally," said Jakkin.

"This is no longer a penal colony, and you are not a convict," Golden reminded him.

"Nor you a warden," Jakkin countered.

Golden smiled.

Sarkkhan continued to stare at the glass. "Break them anyway. We'll throw them off ourselves. We need no such trash here."

Golden crossed his arms and leaned against the table. "You cannot break a movement by breaking a few heads."

"Don't dignify them by calling a few men and their pamphlets a movement."

Golden laughed again. "Young Jakkin here has just said that doing away with the bond system might not be so awful," Golden said smoothly. "Yet he writes no pamphlets and he is no rebel."

"What does he know about such things?" Sarkkhan asked. "He's still young. All he knows is dragons."

"Now wait a minute," Jakkin interrupted. "How do you know what I am and am not interested in?"

"I know *you* because I was just like you when I was young," Sarkkhan said. "Dragons, dragons, dragons. They were my whole world. Nothing you do, Jakkin, surprises me because you *are* me. That's how I was able to help you steal your Heart's Blood." Sarkkhan deliberately turned his back on Jakkin.

"I fill my bag myself," Jakkin said angrily.

Golden chuckled, and both Sarkkhan and Jakkin turned toward him. "Perfect," he said. "It is precisely because he is so obviously uninterested in anything but dragons that he is perfect."

"Perfect for what?" the other two asked together.

"Perfect to infiltrate the rebels, of course. To join one of their cells."

"Don't be absurd," said Sarkkhan.

"I'm not being absurd. Not in the slightest," replied Golden. "Why did you think I came here, contrived to get your invitation? I was hoping that Jakkin would be as perfect as I had been told. And he is."

Jakkin sputtered. "Why should I join the rebels for you? I have no interest in them and no interest in you. I have a dragon fight coming and soon new hatchlings to raise. I owe money to Master Sarkkhan, and I have a duty to my bonder. And . . ." His voice trailed off as his anger turned to bewilderment. "If the rebels are so unimportant, why do you need to infiltrate them? And if they *are* important, why do you need me? Who told you I was perfect for anything? Why me? I don't know any rebels. I don't know where they are or why they are, and I really don't care. Politics is just slogans and talk. So give me one good reason, Senator Golden, one good reason why I should be your spy."

Golden looked into Jakkin's eyes for a long moment. Then he spoke, choosing his words with great care.

"As for the rebels," he said slowly, his high voice softened by the intensity with which he spoke, "they are indeed a small number. But they are growing fast. They are certainly not large enough really to worry the Federation, but they can trouble Austar. So far they have worked within the present system with a minimum of violence. Loud arguments and messy pamphlets are an annoyance, nothing more. But we have reason to believe that things are starting to change. The few informants we have in place—"

"You mean spies," said Jakkin, "so say spies."

"Very well, the few spies we have in place have already been compromised. We need some new, seemingly innocents there to watch what the rebels are doing. If we know ahead of time, we can stop them from hurting Austar and use their love of country in a positive way."

"Love of country!" Sarkkhan's sarcasm was unmistakable.

"Masters have no monopoly on love of country," Golden said gently. "Nor do senators or bonders."

Jakkin listened intently.

"Don't confuse method and message, my friend," Golden said. "They *mean* well, though they may very well end up doing ill. Violence breeds only violence, and this planet, like any expenal colony, has a legacy of blood. It is in the chromosomes, even hundreds of years later. We do not want the Federation to be forced to act. It would be best, I agree, if Austar could solve Austar's problems. So our game must be to watch, to contain, to stop. When change comes, it must come peacefully."

"Or not come at all," Sarkkhan said, his voice gravelly.

"An old Earth philosopher once said that there is nothing permanent except change." Golden's tone was suddenly mild. "Believe me, Master Sarkkhan, change *is* inevitable." He turned back to Jakkin and took his shoulder in a firm grip. There was to be no more play-acting. The man beneath the casual, foppish manners was really as hard as dragon bone. His blue eyes, coolly assessing, stared into Jakkin's. He seemed to read Jakkin as easily as a map. Then he gave a short, sharp, low laugh without a trace of humor in it. "So much for the rebels, Jakkin. As for the reason why *you* should be my inform—excuse me, my spy—I will give you just one reason. Her name is Akki."

# 5

AKKI. BACK IN the barn with his dragon, Jakkin repeated the name out loud and was rewarded by a faint fluttering golden image. Heart's Blood was still fast asleep, but Jakkin's reaction to Akki's name had got through to her.

*Akki.* Jakkin sat close to the dragon and put his hand on her flank. Her scales were cool to the touch. He ran his hand carefully down her leg, feeling the jagged edge of a long, zigzagging scar, one of the legacies of her Pit fights. For a full year he'd schooled himself not to think of Akki, Sarkkhan's dark-haired daughter. He'd thrown himself into his work at the farm, training Heart's Blood with a dedication the others had marveled at. And for most of the time he'd forgotten Akki—or at least not remembered her. But now the memories came flooding back.

*Akki.* The last time he'd seen her they had kissed—and they had quarreled. The kiss had been her doing. He'd been too much in awe of her to try. She'd knelt beside him and taken his head in her hands, her palms as hot as dragon's blood burning his cheeks. She'd leaned over and touched her lips to his. And then, before he could tell her how he really felt, she'd gone away, spurred on by some unnamed mission of her own and by his own clumsiness. He hadn't followed her because he hadn't known where she was going or if she wanted him to come, and besides, he'd had a dragon to train and a life to build.

And now more than a year later this stranger, this unnatural, scent-less, ship-born senator, came with Akki's name in his mouth and a strange story of what she'd been doing in the intervening seasons.

Akki, Golden claimed, had been living and working in The Rokk in a baggery.

"Not a baggery!" Sarkkhan had boomed out. Jakkin's denial had been just a moment behind. They both knew it was the easiest and best-paying job for a young, good-looking girl, and there was no shame attached to it. But Sarkkhan's daughter hadn't needed to earn money. She was no bonder. Sarkkhan would have given her anything she wanted, he said.

At that Jakkin had laughed, remembering how emphatically Akki had wanted to do things on her own.

"I fill my bag with no man's gold," she'd said last year, refusing payment from Sarkkhan for her role in helping Jakkin kill a drakk.

But baggery girls took money from men, all kinds of men. It was that darker image that horrified Jakkin. What if some other man, some bonder as blood-scored and smelling of blisterweed as old Likkarn, or some starship trooper, scentless and bloodless, had been buying her kisses at the baggery?

"Not a baggery," he had said aloud again.

"As a doctor's assistant," Golden answered, a strange smile playing around his mouth. "She's quite a midwife by now."

Jakkin couldn't fully explain the relief and embarrassment he'd felt then. How could he have misjudged Akki when he knew she'd always wanted to be a doctor? And was it his business, anyway, if she wanted to sell or give her kisses away? He had started to say something else when Golden spoke again.

"But she's disappeared."

"Disappeared?" Sarkkhan interrupted. "What do you mean?"

"She has often gone off by herself. No one keeps an eye on her. When she was needed, she was always there, but essentially she had always been a loner."

Sarkkhan smiled heavily. "She's my daughter, all right."

"The fact is, no one knew she *was* your daughter. She wore a bag, so it was assumed that she was a bonder. A runaway from a nursery, perhaps, or an escapee from a baggery in one of the smaller cities."

Sarkkhan looked at him. "And you didn't turn her in? You, the lawmaker?"

Golden pulled the slow smile across his face again, a now familiar gesture. "There are laws . . . and laws. She was a fine doctor's assistant, even if she was a bonder, was what we all thought. And she was useful."

"An empty bag," Jakkin said suddenly. "She wore an empty bag. She said it helped remind her."

"Just so," Golden said smoothly. "That is what we finally figured out *after* she had disappeared. But still, we thought we were dealing with an independent-minded bonder, a hardworking loner. It was quite a while before we discovered she was gone. Most of the bag-girls had shrugged it off. No one had mentioned that she hadn't been around for days. So what if another young bondgirl disappears? It happens all the time. There are underground baggeries that serve the rebels, staffed with young runaways. Everyone knows about that. And some of the girls, it is rumored, are shipped offworld, though we have no evidence of that. The Federation would have to be called in if such a thing were true. But the doctor Akki worked for noticed her absence and mentioned it to me because she knew I had taken a liking to the girl. And then a note came, a note that said, 'Ask Jakkin Stewart at my father's nursery—are you a man yet? If so, I need you.' The bond records showed Jakkin was here. So I am here to ask him that very question."

Sarkkhan blustered, "A man? Of course, he's a man. A fine trainer. A young master. Just look at him. What kind of question is that?"

Jakkin felt his face flush, and he turned away to stare out the window. The first of the twin moons had risen. Sand-colored, slightly egg-shaped, it was beginning its passage across the sky.

"I—I need to think about what she means," Jakkin stuttered, though his heart was thundering madly and he had a sweet-sour taste in his mouth. "I need to think what all this means."

Then he had walked out of Sarkkhan's house with the nursery owner calling after him, "What do you mean—think about it? Fewmets, boy, of course, you're going. And I'm going with you."

The heavy door had swung shut on the rest of Sarkkhan's tirade as Jakkin had walked purposefully into the night. Sarkkhan was right about one thing. Of course, he was going. But everything else was a blur. His mind kept repeating Akki's name over and over, almost like a chant. Before he realized it, he found himself sitting by the sleeping dragon in the heat of the incubarn, not even aware that he had missed his dinner.

*Akki.* It had been well over a year since he'd had any word of her, and now she needed him. Her face, once reduced to a blurred outline in his mind, sprang sharply into focus: the straight black hair; the cream-colored skin; the generous, mobile, mocking mouth.

*Akki.* He would have to puzzle out her cryptic message, then arrange things here at the nursery. Whether he was by his dragon's side or not, her eggs would be hatching in a day or two. If they hatched without him, his chance to imprint the new worms would be gone. Oh, he would still be able to reach their minds, but not with the unique closeness he'd developed with Heart's Blood. And did he dare trust them to Errikkin's care? Still, Akki's safety was the most important thing.

The dragon stirred uneasily at his thought, and a soft grey sending laced with black came into his mind.

"I'm sorry, beauty. Thou art first. And thy hatchlings." But he knew he lied, and the dragon knew, too, for the grey landscape broke into pieces, like storm clouds, and drifted away.

Jakkin stood and stretched, patting Heart's Blood on the flank. The message. He had to think about it. What had she meant when she asked if he was a man?

Her final words to him after their quarrel had been about that. For a year he had pushed the scene from his mind, banished it. But now it returned to embarrass him.

It had begun as teasing. He had said, "You can't leave the nursery. You belong here with me. Your father gave you to me. He said you were too strong-willed for a woman, that you needed a master." But he had said it laughingly because one of the things he liked about her was her forwardness, her ability to speak her mind. And after all, it was she who had kissed him.

But somehow what he said had angered her beyond believing. She'd stood up and, nearly shaking, said, "You are such a boy, such a child, Jakkin Stewart. And so is my father. Talk to me when you are a man."

Then she had run off across the sand and disappeared, apparently into The Rokk and a baggery, if Senator Golden was to be believed.

And now Golden had come bearing a message from her, a message that no one but Jakkin and Akki could have deciphered. But where was she? Why did she need him? Why had she sent the message through Golden? How well did she know him? And what did the message really mean?

Jakkin knew he was as strong as any man on the farm, strong from carting dust and fewmets, from handling the stud dragons, from working out with the fighters in their training sessions by holding the heavy steel-tipped wands. He'd fought a drakk; trained and run a dexad, a ten-time winner in the Pits. But none of those answers would have satisfied Akki last year, and he guessed none would satisfy her now.

"Are you a man yet?" The only honest answer he could give was that he really didn't know. But the end of the message had been "I need you." So he'd go. And the rest would happen as it must. He believed that, believed in the inevitability of consequence. Just as the fertile eggs in a pyramid would hatch if you didn't disturb them . . .

Jakkin walked over to the pile of eggs. He touched the top one with his finger hard enough to punch a hole in its shell. The egg slid down the pyramid, leaking a viscous liquid. When it reached the floor, it broke open. Inside was a yellow slime with no hint of a growing dragon inside.

If left alone, the fertile eggs in the pyramid would hatch. First they would harden, their elastic shells becoming so strong almost nothing could break them open from the outside. Only the hatchling within could break the shell when it was time, using a horny growth on its nose.

Jakkin looked again at the sleeping dragon and at the clutch of eggs. He touched the broken egg on the floor with his foot. No one would do that to him. He'd let no one break his life open. He'd do what had to be done and emerge from this thing intact.

*Akki.* He promised himself he'd find her, and he prided himself on keeping his promises.

# 6

JAKKIN NEVER KNEW a day could go so slowly. He had his answer
ready for Golden, and he ached to give it. The skin above his eyes
seemed tight, and there had been a throbbing in his head from the
moment he'd got up. But Golden didn't appear, and Jakkin was forced
to go through the rounds at the nursery while Heart's Blood slept.

He helped L'Erikk trim the nails of three of the older studs, en-
during the string of endless jokes the young bondboy used for conversation. He tried to laugh. He was really fond of L'Erikk, but
somehow every single joke fell flat.

Then he took his turn in the dining room, setting up the racks of
silverware and swabbing down the floor. It was part of his bargain
with Sarkkhan, partial payment for his continuing board at the farm.
He was so silent, not even teasing with Terakkina, the blond bondgirl
who was the current pet of the nursery, that Kkarina came out of the
kitchen and remarked on it.

"Oh, don't mind him," Terakkina said. "He's clutched." She
held her stomach and made a face, and the two women laughed at
the double meaning.

Jakkin just pushed the mop over the floor and ignored them.

"Worse than a brooding hen," said Kkarina.

"Much worse," Terakkina agreed, and went into the kitchen to
help her.

By afternoon Jakkin's temper was as foul as the taste in his
mouth, but still, the work continued. He even took Slakk's turn with
the roughest dragons in the mud bath, winning a measure of sarcastic
thanks from Slakk plus a promise of a coin. Jakkin could have used
the coin, but he knew better than to expect it. Slakk's promises, like

his gold, had a habit of disappearing. But Jakkin did the extra work because to sit with nothing to do but worry on this particular day would have been worse.

When he went to check on Heart's Blood, expecting her to be sleeping, he was surprised to find her stomping around the room. She houghed continuously and shook her head. He had been so immersed in his own worries he had not been open to her sendings.

Suddenly he was afraid she would step on the eggs.

"Quiet, my worm," he said in his most soothing voice, but the dragon had picked up so much of his agitation she couldn't be stilled. Her tail drummed on the floor; her tree-trunk legs pounded into the sand, raising puffs as heavy as smoke signals. And all the while she sent angry bleeding rainbows through his head, arcs of red across a maroon-and-black landscape.

Jakkin had never seen her like this, and he knew he couldn't handle her in such close quarters, not without endangering the entire pyramid of eggs. He opened the big wooden door and herded her through it into the hen yard. Reluctantly she moved outside.

Once in the hen yard she turned to Jakkin and nuzzled him, bringing her great scaled head across his chest and licking his arm with her sandpaper tongue. He was wearing short sleeves and—though he was not supposed to—short leather bonder pants as well. She gave his left calf a swipe, leaving a red spot raw enough to ache. Then she curled her tail around his feet and lay down. All the while she sent soft, wavery grey clouds into his head, clouds that seemed to weep pink-grey tears.

"I know, I know thee cares," Jakkin said to her. "And I'm sorry to have given thee such a day of sendings. But fewmets! Where is that man?"

He worried a bit of caked dirt from the inside of the dragon's left hind leg and hummed a snatch of tune, one of the oldest Austarian love songs:

> *The dragon arcs across the sky.*
> *It sits on Akkhan.*
> *It breaks, the moon; my heart breaks, too.*
> *What do we need of the moon,*
> *We who once shimmered*
> *In one another's arms?*

The dragon shifted, and Jakkin looked up. Errikkin was standing at Heart's Blood's head.

"This came for you," he said, bobbing his head quickly and holding out a folded piece of paper. He could scarcely disguise his interest. Standing first on one foot and then on the other, he smiled his brightest, toothiest smile and waited to be told the contents of the note, for he could read little beyond his own name and a few of the names of the nursery dragons.

Jakkin scanned the message quickly, reading the signature first. It was from Golden.

*There has been a delay. You are not to worry. She has been located, is still in The Rokk. Arrange to go to next week's fight at Rokk Major. I will see you there.*

*D. Golden, Master*

A week! He could never wait a week. And how could he not worry? Golden wrote: "She has been located." Well, it wasn't good enough. Did she still need him? Golden hadn't mentioned that, the most important part.

Yet, he thought guiltily, he felt relieved at the note because a week would give him a chance to imprint the hatchlings, let them know him as their master. It would also give him time to be sure that Heart's Blood had fully recovered from the laying.

Suddenly he laughed out loud, a sharp, staccato bark that had little humor in it. A week would also give him time to get ready to face Akki.

"Is it funny then?" asked Errikkin, smiling, ready to be let in on the joke.

"Funny?" Jakkin stared at him. He had been laughing at his own guilt and his own innocence, for it was suddenly clear to him that Golden had known all along what Jakkin's decision would be.

"Just a private joke," Jakkin murmured. Then he added in a firmer tone, "I'll be going to Rokk Major next week. Who's up for that?"

Errikkin stuck his tongue between his teeth, a sure sign that he was thinking. Because he couldn't read, he memorized schedules and had become very good at it.

"S'Blood," he said. "He's up for Rokk Major, and Heart Stop will be at one of the Minor Pits. Maybe Krakkow. She didn't mate this year, rejected all the studs. Rejected S'Blood twice, come to think of it." He chuckled, as much at the memory as to show he knew a private joke, too. "The boys think she's got a good chance at a string of wins, maybe even make dexad this year." He bobbed his head again, not enough of a bow for Jakkin to fuss at, just enough to be annoying. "She's not really Heart's Blood's class, of course, but then—what dragon is?"

At the sound of her name the great red hen uncurled her tail from around Jakkin's feet and stretched. She pushed her wings out to their fullest. The ribs pulled the membranes taut, and the crisscross of scars showed plainly. Jakkin could read the history of her fights in those scars, and he loved and hated every lesion.

"I'll take her in now," Jakkin said. "She—she needed some air." He wondered why he bothered to lie.

"Likkarn says you're spoiling her. He says a dragon spoiled won't fight."

"A lot old Likk-and-Spittle knows," growled Jakkin, guiding the dragon by holding on to her ear.

"Well, *you* said he was a fine trainer," Errikkin began. "Even though—"

"Even though he's a weeder. Yes, I did say that. Sure he *knows* dragons. But he's lizard drool, and even though he *knows* dragons, he doesn't *like* them."

"Oh, Jakkin," Errikkin said disgustedly, dropping the humble servant pose for a moment, "of course he likes dragons. We all do. They're great animals, except—" He stopped purposefully.

"Except for the fewmets," Jakkin finished for him. It was the oldest nursery joke around. There had always been jokes and songs and riddles and stories about the way to plug up a dragon properly. To get a nursery bonder's attention, all a storyteller had to do was invent a novel way of getting rid of worm waste. The best-beloved tall tales swapped at night in the nursery revolved around the legendary Fewmets Ferkkin, who had tried to breed a totally clean dragon, a dragon that took in at one end but never gave out at the other. But— so the story continued—when he ran it in its first fight, one swipe from the opposing dragon's claw, and Ferkkin's dragon exploded in the Pit. The punch line, "It rained fewmets for three days and three nights," was a favorite catchphrase among bonders.

Jakkin shook his head. "You don't understand either. No one does. Not even Sarkkhan. We all call dragons animals and beasts and worms. I do, too. But sometimes I think—" And he remembered suddenly how he had felt when Heart's Blood had begun to lay: that there was no separation between them; that for a wonderful moment he himself had been a dragon hen. "Well, I'm not quite sure what I think except that they're more than just overgrown lizards. Heart's

Blood can talk to me; she really can. Oh, not with words, of course. But I can understand everything she says. And she understands me."

Errikkin smiled again, agreeing.

"Oh, worm dottle," Jakkin swore. "She understands me a good deal better than *you* do. She doesn't try to humor me either." He made a wry face and watched the dragon move away to stand patiently, her nose pressed against the door.

Jakkin went over to her and unlatched the door, and she lumbered inside. Jakkin turned back to his bonder. "And speaking of fewmets . . ."

Without another word, they walked toward the stud barn, where they both knew work waited. Jakkin went eagerly, but Errikkin hung back, dogging his heels, to reemphasize the gap between master and bonder.

Slakk and L'Erikk greeted them without interest, merely nodding because their hands were busy with the big waste buckets. It took two boys to unload each bucket into the wheeled handcarts; four boys were needed to push and pull the carts. Each day the carts were emptied into the wort patches, the combination of fewmets and straw being the finest fertilizer available on the planet. It was not pleasant work. Fewmets stank. But it was important. "Waste not—grow not" was a nursery axiom. Jakkin grabbed on to a bucket and quickly got into a familiar rhythm of filling and emptying.

As he worked, he felt the tentative minds of the nursery dragons reach out to him. L'Erikk was in the middle of a new Fewmets Ferkkin joke, but Jakkin never heard the punch line. He was more intent on the individual patterns the dragons threw.

Heart Breaker, one of Heart's Blood's clutchmates, had a similar rainbow signal, but with the colors faded, drifting off around the edges. As he passed S'Blood's stall, the big brown fighter gave off sharp, jagged images. His body worked in the Pit in that same jagged way, with little fluidity in his motions. He fought with a series of strikes of such slashing intensity that he had won twenty-two of twenty-six fights—a wonderful Pit record—losing three early fights because of immaturity and one recent one when he was exhausted from having fought two days in a row. Heart Worm, the best brood hen in the nursery, had a signal that was a series of yellow globes. Every sending from her contained these golden auras somewhere: sometimes as free-floating bubbles; sometimes stacked like a clutch of golden eggs; sometimes as balls bounding in intricate rhythms. She had that same sunny personality.

"... which is why"—L'Erikk was finishing yet another joke—"Ferkkin had no nose."

Slakk and Errikkin howled.

"That's new," Slakk said.

"Brand-new," L'Erikk admitted.

"Where do you *get* them?" asked Errikkin.

"Straight from the Fewmets factory," answered L'Erikk. "Signed, sealed, and delivered."

"Delivered is right," Slakk said. "You have the best delivery in the nursery. I've got a *great* idea. Let's switch and get Bond-Off together. I'd like to take you into Krakkow to this terrific stewbar I know. It's called The Pits! And I'll lay a bet that you can tell jokes without stopping for, say, three hours."

"Four," said L'Erikk.

"Four then. And we'll get some gold to back us from the boys here. And—"

"I've got a better idea," interrupted Jakkin. "Why don't you *save* your money and buy yourselves out of bond? Four hours is a long time for jokes. And you'll probably lose. L'Erikk needs only one or two drinks and he forgets his name, much less his jokes, and you know it."

"Where's your sense of adventure, Jakkin?" said Slakk.

"In my nose," Jakkin answered. "And it tells me these fewmets are growing riper by the hour. As are L'Erikk's jokes. So let's get to it."

"Yes, *Master*," the three said in unison, bobbing their heads together.

Jakkin gritted his teeth but didn't answer back. Anything he said now would make things worse. Ever since he had become a master, a distance had opened up between him and his old friends. He hated that.

The boys worked in silence, and even the dragons refused to send.

*It is a conspiracy*, Jakkin thought. He was being forced to think about the one thing he didn't want to think about. He remembered Akki's hovering over him at the hospice when she had tended his wounds, the black wings of her hair, her crooked smile. He shook his head. Despite what Golden had written, Jakkin *was* worried. A week was an awfully long time.

Then he pushed the thoughts of Akki out of his mind. The dragons needed every bit of his attention. *Dragon time is now*.

As he let his mind fill up with dragons, he came to S'Blood's stall. This time the big brown responded. A jagged stroke of yellow lightning flashed through his head, and Jakkin smiled at last.

"I've got a week with you coming," he whispered to S'Blood. "A week of training and waiting for the eggs to hatch."

The same flash of lightning jagged through his head, less an answer to what he had said than an emotional response to his presence.

"A week," he said again, the smile suddenly gone.

# 7

S'BLOOD WAS SLUGGISH at first. The morning mud baths had cooled his temper and dulled the sharper movements of his body. But as Jakkin put the great brown through his paces, he knew the dragon would soon be back to normal. Normal for S'Blood meant slashing at the dummies with the erratic, jagged movement that was his hallmark, dodging and feinting abruptly when Jakkin made passes at him with the metal-tipped reed wands.

Jakkin tried to reach way into S'Blood's mind the way he did with his own red, but he was always stopped at what he called the landscape level. He could see a general signature of the particular dragon drawn in his head, as if it were a picture of a foreign country. But the many mood changes and colorations, the actual pictures that he could receive from Heart's Blood, were missing. He wondered if it was because he had imprinted Heart's Blood so early and had come to the big brown fighter only when they both were adults. Or, he thought, it might have had something to do with his having shared blood with his hen. She had licked his wounds, first when she was a day-old hatchling and he had cut himself on an eggshell and then again when he had been gashed badly by a drakk, and ever after her mind had been as open to him as his own.

S'Blood gathered himself into a hind-foot rise and slashed quickly at the dragon-form. He roared his defiance, a sound as sharp as his movements. It was a good roar, and Jakkin praised him. S'Blood was never as reluctant as some to sound. Many dragons needed to be blooded before giving roar.

"Sing out, thou mighty worm," Jakkin called, encouraging the big lizard, for punters in the Pits judged a fighter in part by the timbre of its voice.

S'Blood roared again in response. Then he dropped suddenly and whipped his tail around with a loud, wind-whistling sound. The tail snapped against the heavy yellow-hide dummy, which toppled over, part of its reed skeleton crushed. Quickly S'Blood straddled it and made the ritual slashes on its neck, adding to the many other scars there. One slash was so deep it tore open the skin, allowing several small stone weights to spill out. There would have to be a lot of work done on that dummy to salvage it for another practice.

Immediately S'Blood backed away and stood trembling near the fallen form. His shaking was a reminder of the days when dragons had fought to the death. Careful breeding and training kept them from dealing deathblows now. A fight ended with only ritual shallow slashes to the neck, but it was an effort, even for a well-trained dragon, to resist moving in for the kill.

A noise behind Jakkin startled him. He turned. Standing by the door was Likkarn. His face was in shadows, so Jakkin could read neither its expression nor the map of Likkarn's weed addiction.

Likkarn's voice, haggard from years of weed smoke, came to him. "Look at him, boy. Watch him shake. Just remember, all dragons are feral." The old trainer limped back into the barn.

Jakkin felt a pulse of red anger surge through him. A whine from the dragon reminded him that they were still linked. He turned to look at S'Blood. The dragon was trembling harder than before, fed by Jakkin's emotions as well as his own.

"Quiet, boy, quiet," Jakkin said, knowing his mind and voice would help ease the brown into the next period, that of overwhelming hunger. After fights—even after hard training sessions—a dragon always gorged, feeding a different sort of appetite. He led S'Blood back to his stall and left him there to munch on extra portions of burnweed and wort. The red-veined plants fueled dragon's fire, and S'Blood needed help, for his flames were generally not very bright or very long.

Besides, it was time to check up on Heart's Blood. Eagerly Jakkin left the brown fighter. It had been three days since the laying. The warmth of the incubarn encouraged early hatchings, and he'd already checked the heaters twice that morning. Perhaps the first of the eggs would be ready to hatch.

~

IT WAS MYSTERIOUSLY quiet in Heart's Blood's barn. Jakkin hurried into the egg room.

The red dragon was standing over the pyramid, touching each egg with her nose. The shells were hard now, and she rolled the eggs off the pyramid and onto the floor without breaking any of them. The floor was already covered with cream-colored shapes.

Heart's Blood looked up at Jakkin for a moment, flooding him with a rosy glow. Then she returned to sorting through the eggs as if counting them. Jakkin wondered if she could tell which held dragons and which were the dead, slime-filled decoys.

At last she stopped at one and tapped it lightly with her lanceae, the twin front nails on her foot.

It seemed to Jakkin that there was an answering tap from within. She tapped again.

Again there was a tiny echo.

Then, as Jakkin watched, a slight crack appeared in the egg. It jetted across the rounded side, leaving a scarlike trail that looked like an old river and its tributaries.

Heart's Blood tapped the egg once more. This time there was an unmistakable tap in return, and the egg split open into uneven halves. In the larger half lay a curled form: tiny, wrinkled, the color of custard scum and covered with the remains of green-yellow birth fluids. Slowly it lifted its heavy head, and Jakkin saw a horny bump on its nose.

The dragonling stretched one front foot and then the other, then heaved itself to its feet. The eggshell rocked, and the little dragon tumbled out, landing on its nose. Its eyes were still sealed shut by the fluids.

Heart's Blood licked the little dragon clean. Each swipe with her tongue knocked the hatchling over, and it gamely struggled up again after each tumble. One tongue polishing even removed the bump on its nose. The little dragon hiccuped and opened its eyes.

For a moment Jakkin hesitated, almost trembling with awe. Then he reached out a hand and touched the pea-size bit of horn. It crumbled into a fine dust.

He breathed a sigh and looked up at Heart's Blood. "Oh thou amazing creature," he whispered. "To have done such a marvelous thing."

Heart's Blood greeted his praise with a cascade of rainbows. Then she turned back to her work. It took more than a dozen licks before the red hen was satisfied with the hatchling. When it seemed ready to her, she turned to the pieces of shell and licked the insides clean.

After she had finished with the shells, she went back to the scattered eggs on the floor and began picking through them again.

Jakkin gathered the hatchling to him with exquisite care. He examined it closely. Its wings were twice as long as its body, and its skin hung loosely in wrinkles and folds. He smiled, remembering that once Heart's Blood had looked as ugly and as ungainly. He tried to reach into the little dragon's mind but could sense only a bright blankness.

Then, on impulse, he picked up a bit of eggshell and dug it into the tip of his left forefinger, drawing blood. He put the bloody finger up to the little dragon's nose. Tentatively it stuck out its tongue and tasted. Once, twice it licked at the bead of blood, and suddenly Jakkin was rewarded with a tiny, cool rainbow of light blues and greys across the blank landscape. It was a sending like—yet not like—Heart's Blood's.

"I am thy brother," he whispered.

He heard a tapping and looked over his shoulder. The red hen had started on another egg. Cradling the little dragon in his palm, Jakkin sat down on the floor to watch.

~

BY THE END of the day there were five live hatchlings and one that had emerged deformed, with an open spine and only one wing. It had died quickly, and Heart's Blood had moved it to the side of the room with her great claw.

*Five and one*, Jakkin thought, suddenly remembering the bet. *How could Likkarn have guessed?*

Heart's Blood cracked open the remaining eggs and cleaned out each one with her tongue. Afterward she lay on her side, exhausted, while the five hatchlings snuggled next to her. They were alike on the outside, each with yellowish, wrinkled skin, oversize wings, and butter-soft claws. But Jakkin could already tell them apart because their minds were startlingly different.

Blood called to blood, he was sure of that now. He shook his left hand. The fingers ached from the five separate bloodlettings. His back ached, too, with the tension of the day. His legs hurt from squatting so long near Heart's Blood as she went through all the parts of the hatchling. But the rest of him felt wonderful.

He stood and stretched, and the red dragon watched him with an interested but slightly wary eye.

As he stood, Jakkin suddenly remembered. "Akki!" he said aloud. He hadn't thought of her all afternoon.

In answer, the dragon sent a golden rainbow silhouette that was unmistakably an image of Akki. In the dragon's sending she was enclosed and safe.

"Oh, I hope so, I hope so, my wonder worm. Because there's nothing I can do about it until it's time to go to The Rokk." He thought he'd kept the bitterness out of his words, to keep from spoiling the marvel of the day, but his fears about Akki had now surfaced clearly in his thoughts.

Heart's Blood's answering picture, rimmed with grey, told him that she understood.

"Sleep well, thou great mother," Jakkin said. "And I will try to do likewise."

He gathered up the shells and the body of the one dead hatchling and put them in the cart that stood outside the egg room door. Then he went out of the barn.

~

HE WAS SURPRISED to find it was only midday. Across the yard he saw Jo-Janekk entering the tool room. A group of bonders were trooping into the fields.

He thought about calling out to them with the news of the hatching. "Five and one," he could tell them, and watch them calculate who had won the bets.

But suddenly he only wanted to be alone with the wonder of it and with the ache of the days before he could look for Akki. He turned and set off to the east, across the stone weirs, to the oasis where he had, a long year ago, raised Heart's Blood.

# 8

THE HOT AIR dried his legs, wet from the water in the dikes, and because it was daylight and he no longer had to hide where he was going, the sand dunes posed few problems. When he'd been a bonder, he'd had to sneak away to the oasis, going at night alone, running bent over, and brooming away his footprints. But now, a master, he could go where he willed. Still, walking in the desert sands, with the slight gusts of warm wind sending puffs of dust up around him, he was reminded of those cautious days past. He was surprised to find he missed the tinge of fear, the prickle of danger.

He daydreamed all the way to the wellspring, and it came as a shock when he reached the oasis so quickly.

The bubbling blue of the spring stood out against the pale sand. At the western edge of the stream, the little pool he had so carefully dug out by hand was almost hidden by a border of shoulder-high kkhan reeds that waved in the wind. The once carefully tended wort patch was a haze of volunteer plants growing in haphazard rows. The plants themselves were healthy enough, sending up the smoke that signaled they were ripening, but without straight rows, he didn't dare walk among them for fear of getting burned.

The shelter still stood by the stream, although sand had been driven by the winds against one inside wall in such a large drift that the hut was untenantable. Jakkin considered digging it out, then shrugged. He had no need of it—why bother? But it was *his* past that was buried there in the sand, and without exactly willing it, he suddenly found himself kneeling and digging furiously, throwing the sand behind him like a gakko at its burrow.

After a few minutes of digging he was exhausted, less from the work than from the emotions of the long day. He lay down on his stomach by the side of the stream and let his hand drift in the water.

The setting yellow-green sun was bright, and a few dark dots moved slowly across the cloudless expanse as dragons or other flying lizards scripted their signatures on the blank slate of reflected sky.

As he watched, one dot grew larger than the rest. Before he could read it clearly in the water or turn over onto his back and see it face-to-face, a rainbow sending trumpeted ahead.

It was Heart's Blood! Red and glowing with the fading sun at her back, she arrived with her wings fanned out, stirring a mighty dust storm in the little oasis.

Jakkin leaped to his feet and put his arm up over his eyes because of the swirling sand.

*"Fewmets!"* he cried out. "Thee could have made a slightly quieter entrance." But he laughed as he said it, keeping his eyes shut tightly and reaching out for her. His hands encountered her head and neck, and he gave her a rough, quick hug.

She lifted her head suddenly and tumbled him backward into the stream. Then she plunged in next to him, and the displaced water splashed into the air, raining down on top of them. Something very much like a chuckle pattered through Jakkin's mind in cataracts of red and gold.

Jakkin let the water settle, and then he floated on his back. The water rocked him. He put his hand gently on the dragon's nose.

*"This,"* he said at last, "this is perfection. I could ask for nothing better than this."

Akki's golden silhouette teased into his mind.

"Thou art right. There is still one thing missing. But soon we shall have her home."

After a while he stood up and shook his head like an animal. Then, suddenly, he turned and kicked water into the dragon's face.

Heart's Blood rose over him and tried to look menacing, but all the while she sent rainbowed waterfalls into his head.

"Thou big fake," he said, pushing at her leg with his shoulder. "Thou monstrous bag of pudding. It is a wonder to me that thee can fight at all, so loving thou art."

Her tail crept around and snapped at his legs.

"Ow—that hurt! Dost think I am a child that needs spanking?" he cried. And then he stopped. "But thy own children, my red, thy hatchlings. Thee has left them. How?"

The dragon climbed out of the stream and lay down in the sand, first folding her front legs and then collapsing like a mountain avalanche. She sent a picture of five tired hatchlings fast asleep in a darkened barn, rainbow halos dancing over their heads.

"Oh, I know they're asleep. They'd have to be after hatching. Thee slept most of thy first days away here in the shelter. How I remember. Eat, sleep—and grow. My, how thee grew. But I meant, how did thee get out? I left the door to the barn closed."

There was a momentary blank in Heart's Blood's sending, a black space about a blink long. Then a picture of someone bent over at the waist, bobbing along, creeping; someone blanketed with a grey aura, opening the door. Slowly the grey bobber stood up. The bland-handsome face smiled slyly and bowed.

"Errikkin? What was he doing there at thy stall?" Jakkin asked. He climbed up the side of the stream bank and touched the dragon lovingly under the chin, her scarless chin where none of the slashes that spoke of a lost fight could be found. "Never mind. He did me a favor, whatever he planned. This time with thee, stolen from thy hatchlings, back in our oasis, has been precious to me. But now—go back to them. Go back quickly. They need thee as I do not now. Go, and I will follow."

The red dragon stood and spent a few minutes grooming the sand from her wings. Then she stretched the mighty ribs to their fullest, until the grey membranes between were iridescent and backlit by the setting sun. She pumped the wings once, then twice, pushed off with her legs, and leaped into the air.

Sand swirled around Jakkin and settled into his hair. He rubbed his eyes. When he opened them again, Heart's Blood was just a dark dot winging home.

~

THE RED DRAGON was standing impatiently at the barn door, flailing at it with her tail. If she had not been a mute, she would have been trumpeting her distress loud enough for everyone in the bondhouse to hear.

The door was shut and barred.

Jakkin, who had been clearly receiving her distressed sending for more than two kilometers, was exhausted by running. He had not known what was wrong, only that Heart's Blood was in trouble.

He flung himself at the door, pushed away the wooden bar, and swung the door open.

She plunged inside.

From the egg room came a frantic peeping, and she rushed in to comfort her hatchlings and lay down so that they could scramble up to her. Her presence calmed them almost at once, and Jakkin hauled in an extra bale of wort.

Soon Heart's Blood was chewing up the wort and drizzling the juices into the open mouths of the little dragons.

*I'll kill him for this*, Jakkin thought when he at last had a moment. *I'll show him what a master* can *do*.

Then he remembered Errikkin's shining face when Jakkin had raised his voice. *No*, he thought. *He wants me to yell at him. He wants me to beat him. That would make me his kind of master, and I won't do it.*

Jakkin closed the door quietly behind the dragon. "Sleep well, my beauty. And do not worry about this. This I will tend to."

The dragon, busy with her hatchlings, sent only the briefest of colors.

~

JAKKIN STRODE INTO the bondhouse. He could see down the long hallway that the door to his room was open. Keeping his anger in control, he went in.

Errikkin was waiting, his mouth playing with a smile. "Master Jakkin?" he said, bowing his head.

"I'll be your master for only a few more weeks," Jakkin said. "Come culling, I'll sell a hatchling—one of five, as you well know since you sneaked into the barn."

"But, Master—"

"Don't 'Master' me. I won't have you around my dragons. I'll sell a hatchling, give you the money for the bond, which you will give back to me at once. At once, do you hear? And then you will be free. I won't manumit you because that's what a friend does, and we are friends no longer. And I want you to know that you bought yourself out of bond, that you purchased your own freedom, whatever else you decide to do with it later."

Errikkin stared at him, his eyes furious.

"Now get out. Get out of my room." He hadn't meant to raise his voice. He hadn't meant to let his anger show. Letting any of it show let Errikkin win just a little.

The door closed, and Jakkin lay down on his bed. *Why this?* he wondered. *Why now?* It seemed that just as he had almost everything he wanted, things were falling apart. He closed his eyes, and a red-gold thread, like a lifeline, teased into his head. He envisioned putting his hand on the thread. It pulled tight, pulled him up.

He stood. "All right," he said aloud. There was much to do and little time to get ready. He would eat, sleep, and start the new day.

# 9

WITH SO MUCH to do to prepare the brown dragon for his fight and to keep a constant watch on Heart's Blood and her hatchlings, Jakkin was surprised how the rest of the week sped by. Only at night, as he lay alone, waiting for sleep to claim him, did time move in slow, bitter inches. When he finally slept, his dreams were filled with images that were blood-drenched and frightening, but when he awoke, shivering and wet in his bed, he could not recall them.

He was snappish all the time, treating the bonders with quick, unusual displays of temper—when he talked to them at all. Errikkin he ignored so obviously it became the talk of the nursery. And gossip being the common coin in a dragonry, there were soon enormous bets on the reasons, but neither Jakkin nor Errikkin supplied them.

Sarkkhan was equally testy, but that was usual enough before a fight to occasion no wagers. Only Likkarn, his bag flush with coins from the Heart's Blood's hatch bet, was in good humor. And *this* so disconcerted the bonders that dinnertimes became strangely silent affairs, with glances and shifting eyes becoming the mode of communication.

For Jakkin, the training sessions under Sarkkhan's testy tongue were difficult. The nursery owner criticized every step.

"More to the left, the left," Sarkkhan would roar. "He keeps his guard down. His chest is open. His neck links are exposed. Get him to protect those links."

But when Jakkin went for the tender links with the metal-tipped wands, trying to force the dragon's guard up, Sarkkhan roared again.

"Hind end. Keep the tail moving. Up and over with that tail.

Slash. Slash. Have him slash. Fewmets, boy, what kind of performance is that?"

The result was that S'Blood, confused by the contradictory signals coming to him from the two voices and minds he trusted the most, squatted and refused to move until Slakk was sent to bring a bucketful of burnwort into the ring. Slakk, who hated the big worms, refused to get into the ring with the sulking—and therefore dangerous—dragon. S'Blood, reading his fear, lashed about with his enormous ridged tail.

Jakkin had to drop the heavy wands, pull them out of their holders on the wand belt, and take the bucket from the cowering Slakk.

"You're about as useful," he hissed at his old bondmate, "as a flikka in an egg room. Even L'Erikk would be better."

Slakk started to answer back, then remembered Jakkin was a master. He made a face, left the ring, and slammed the door behind him.

As the sound of the dragon munching wort leaves filled the ring, Sarkkhan voiced his own fears to Jakkin.

"All he sent was the one note. Worm waste! One fewmety note saying she's been located and nothing more. And I should bring you to The Rokk. For that spying, I guess. But Akki's *my* daughter, and I mean to know more." He rubbed his massive hands through his red-gold hair. Jakkin was surprised to see that the hair was thinner than he had realized.

"I—I got a note, too," Jakkin said.

"That's the note I mean."

Jakkin felt his jaw drop. Sarkkhan had read a note meant for him just as if he were still a bonder. He knew he should make a protest, but nothing came out.

"I went to The Rokk, looking for him," Sarkkhan added. "But he was gone. Off again on one of those beslimed Federation rocket ships. I say, if the gods had wanted me to fly, I would have been born with dragon wings. Anyway, I went through the baggeries looking for Akki. Didn't find her, though."

Still angry about the note, Jakkin turned away. Sarkkhan, at least, had *done* something. He had gone looking for Akki, while Jakkin, like a bonder, like a *boy*, had stayed home, playing with worms and worrying over Errikkin's silly little trick. His fists clenched, and his nails made little marks in his palms. The fingers of his left hand still ached from the blooding, and that made him think of the hatchlings. As if in answer, he felt an immediate soothing colorburst followed by five miniature echoes.

He turned back. Sarkkhan was still speaking.

". . . some doctor she worked with. Even went to the old baggery where her mother had been. I hadn't visited there since she died. Since *before* she died. Her mother wouldn't see me, you know, not at the end. She didn't want me to know about the baby, thought I might not believe it was mine—or care. So none of the girls told me about Akki for years. I found out by accident. It was Kkarina let it slip. She'd been best friends with—with Akki's mother."

His voice sounded wistful, and he looked at Jakkin. Jakkin nodded.

"Her old room looked the same. Our old room. But I didn't know any of the girls anymore."

"Sarkkhan." Jakkin said his name in the same tone of voice he used to soothe a hackling dragon.

Sarkkhan shook his head. "Akki wasn't there." His eyes had a strange, moist look to them. He cleared his throat. "Looks a lot like her mother, you know. Same mouth. But she's got my temper. My stubborn nature. My eyes." His voice had suddenly gone very quiet.

"I'll find her," said Jakkin just as quietly. "I promise."

"Fewmets, boy!" The old roar was back. "*We'll* find her. I'm not worried. Seeing the old place, so familiar, yet not, just got me to remembering, that's all. Memories can make a man weak. Can't let that happen now. We've got to be strong. Got to clean out a whole nest of rebels if we have to. They're no better than drakk, whatever Golden and his laws say. Egg suckers, all of them. Treat them as such." His hands made the familiar chopping motion worm farmers used when talking about the killing of drakk.

Jakkin nodded distractedly. The dragon had finished the wort and was listening to them intently, sending little slivers of yellow light into Jakkin's mind, testing.

"Listen," Jakkin said.

"I hear him. Come on, worm waste, off your belly and back to your stall." Sarkkhan walked over to the dragon and twisted the ear-flap.

The dragon got up to his feet.

"No more practice. We don't want him overtired. Tomorrow we go to The Rokk, and we *all* need some rest. I'll get him ready; you tend to your hen." As an afterthought he added, "You've never seen The Rokk, have you?"

Jakkin shook his head.

"It'll put your eye out," Sarkkhan boomed. He wiped a hand across his eyes. "Getting hot," he said, and turned away, pulling the dragon along with him.

~

THEY STARTED EARLY enough the next morning. There was still a touch of frost in the air from Dark After. As Jakkin walked to the barn to say a farewell to his own dragons, having instructed L'Erikk in their care, he could see the smudgy haze over the weed and wort fields, where the plants smoldered in the morning cold.

Heart's Blood's good-bye was punctuated with color, and Jakkin hated to leave her. He chucked each of the hatchlings, now almost knee-high, under the chin. They were a shabby-looking lot, the egg-skin stretched over the growing muscle and bone. Two of them were already beginning to shed the skin. Patches of it littered the floor.

One hatchling swatted at Jakkin's hand over and over with its claw, the nails still butter-soft.

Jakkin smiled wryly. "Mighty fighter," he whispered, and shadowboxed for a minute with the little dragon.

Unused to such exertion, the hatchling suddenly toppled over and fell asleep, its tail tucked around its belly. The others walked over it, but it slept on.

Heart's Blood showered him with a rosy rain shot through with gold, and Jakkin smiled. "Good luck to thee, too," he said, then left the smaller barn to walk across the compound and fetch S'Blood.

The brown dragon greeted him with dark, unfathomable eyes. Jakkin backed him out of the stall and guided him along the hall, a hand on the dragon's ear.

The nursery truck was waiting at the barn door, close enough so that the dragon would have little chance to grow wary and hackle so far from the Pit. But S'Blood was a dragon who loved the Pits, and as the old memory linking the truck with the fights moved into his slow brain, reinforced by Jakkin's and Sarkkhan's thoughts, his head went up. He shook off Jakkin's hand and charged eagerly into the back of the truck, sticking his head into the baled burnwort. Then he knelt heavily, short front legs first, and began munching.

"Done," Jakkin said as he slid into the cab next to Sarkkhan. The one word did not begin to communicate the excitement flooding through him.

"I have all the papers. And the equipment bag," Sarkkhan said, patting a satchel between them. "Let's go."

After slipping the truck into gear, Sarkkhan guided the big rig along the farm driveways with an ease Jakkin envied. He'd never learned to drive.

The spikka trees lining the road seemed to bounce past them. By the time they came to the main highway, the sun had already poked its head over the rim of the mountains.

Jakkin had been on nine trips to Krakkow with Sarkkhan and with Likkarn. Each time but one he'd chosen to stay in the underpit stall with his dragon instead of visiting the city. That one time he'd been unnerved by the sour smells, the loud noises, the constant edginess of the people in the streets. But The Rokk was a masters' city, unlike Krakkow, which had been built by convicts. He was sure it would be grander and cleaner and quieter, built as it was with offworld materials rather than just the sand and stone of Austar. Despite his lingering worries about Akki, he was excited and eager to go.

The trip to Krakkow was relatively short. Jakkin knew that road intimately. The raised pavement, always in danger of being buried by the drifting rosy desert sands, was clear this time because of a strong northern wind. Along the way there was only one major stand of trees, the Krakkow Copse, though smaller forty-tree copses dotted the landscape. Occasionally the Narrakka River could be glimpsed: a dark ribbon stretched parallel to the road and contained within high, nearly vertical sand cliffs.

To the north Jakkin could see the mountains, spiky, brooding shadows that seemed to be hunched over like mammoth drakk awaiting weary travelers. The foothills, too, were forbidding and honeycombed with unexplored caves. Wild dragons nested in the mountains, and drakk often patrolled the night skies. Tame as the flatlands were after two hundred years of human habitation, the mountain strongholds were not. Jakkin's father had died at the foot of those same mountains, killed by a gigantic feral dragon, an escapee from a nursery that had lived many years in the wild. Jakkin gave an involuntary shudder as he looked at the near hills. He closed his eyes. The jagged mountains formed dark impressions on his lids.

The truck rolled on, and Jakkin fought the urge to sleep. He had wanted to see every inch of the road between Krakkow and The Rokk, but most of it was depressingly the same. By mid-morning the sameness of the landscape had lulled him into a half stupor. Evidently the road had the same effect on Sarkkhan. He pulled the truck to the side of the road, stopped, and got out.

Jakkin woke abruptly.

"Walk it off, boy," Sarkkhan called in to him.

Jakkin got out and walked over to the nursery owner. Sarkkhan opened a small covered crock, lifted it to his lips, drank. Then he passed it to Jakkin.

The crock contained takk, and it was still hot. It burned down

Jakkin's throat. He opened his mouth and roared like a blooded dragon.

"Roar again, hatchling!" Sarkkhan said with a laugh. He clapped Jakkin on the back, capped the crock, and gestured at the truck. "Ah, boy, you remind me of myself on my first trip to a Major—scared, happy, half-dreaming, half-awake. In we go."

The walk and the takk had done their work. The soporific desert lost its claim on Jakkin, and he listened contentedly the rest of the morning as Sarkkhan held forth on matters of the farm. By afternoon Jakkin had made it a conversation, speaking of the hatching and the thrill of holding the cream-colored dragons in his hand. But he kept the secret of the blood sharing to himself.

"I bet you'll have some special fighting material in those five," Sarkkhan said. "Maybe you'll get away with no culls at all. That would be rare, but it does happen. Never happened to me, though. I always had some keepers, some sales, some culls."

The culling. Jakkin had pushed that thought out of his mind. To buy off Errikkin's bond he'd have to choose one of Heart's Blood's hatchlings to sell. He wondered if he could do it: forcibly separate the hatchling from its hen and listen to it scream as it was carted off . . .

"Have you ever come across one of the dragons you sold?"

"Went up against two of them at Minors. Even lost to one once." He laughed. "You lose track after a while, though. But every now and then I wonder what's become of them. Of course, when another owner says to you that he just beat you with a worm you sold him . . . well, it makes you mad. I nearly drowned myself in drink the night that happened. Likkarn had to wring me out and drag me back. He said I'd torn up two stewbars, claiming to be Fewmets Ferkkin! I told him I could remember breaking up one." He laughed again and slapped his hand on the wheel. "I always wonder if I've lost something good in the culling. Bad days, culling. Especially when the stewmen come."

Jakkin shivered. He couldn't imagine sending any of Heart's Blood's hatchlings to the Stews. Young as they were, sweet as the meat would be, they were already individuals to him. He knew their minds. There was no way he could ship any of them to their deaths. But maybe he could manage to sell one to another owner to raise as a fighter or a stud or a hen. After all, a bonder's life was surely worth a dragon. "How—how can you stand it?" he asked at last.

For a moment Sarkkhan said nothing. Then he shrugged. "You just do it," he said. "If you didn't, the farm would be overrun with bad bloodlines and weak stock, and that wouldn't be good for business. But I'll give you a hint.''

"A hint?"

"Something Likkarn said to me when I was your age and romantically inclined: Don't listen in too much to hatchling sendings, and don't name any of them until after culling day. It helps.''

They rode a way in silence, and Jakkin thought about Sarkkhan's hint. It had come too late for him. He already knew each hatchling's mind. And even if it meant keeping Errikkin on or manumitting him instead, Jakkin realized he couldn't sell any of the hatchlings. They didn't belong to him. They were Heart's Blood's children. You didn't sell a child.

~

AS IF BY unspoken agreement, they changed the subject. They discussed the fight to come and S'Blood's chances. Then they started rating the other dragons in the nursery. Sarkkhan mentioned Heart Breaker and Blood Spoor as dragons to watch, and Jakkin agreed. They talked of the price of wort and where the best weed seeds could be bought. While Sarkkhan harangued Jakkin on the hidden costs of running a worm farm, Jakkin marveled at how many facts and figures the nursery owner could keep in his head. As they drove on, the one subject they didn't bring up was Akki, though her name seemed to hang heavily between them.

Jakkin was about to hazard that name when he looked through the windshield.

Ahead, as if waiting to swallow them up, was a great walled citadel. Towers stretched out on either side like stone wings, and a series of smaller humps along its back resembled the ridges of a hackling dragon's neck. A great egg-shaped dome was on one side, staring at Jakkin like a blind eye.

"What's that?" he asked.

"The Rokk!'' Sarkkhan said in a voice that announced both possession and pride. "It rises out of the sand suddenlike. The first time I saw it, I said the same thing. 'What's that?' I asked Likkarn, though I almost meant, 'Who's that?' Everyone I've brought here says it, too. And it's as fierce and as untamable as a wild dragon. Takes a lifetime to know it. Quite a place, The Rokk.''

As they drove closer, the walls of the city assumed the aspect of giant open jaws, for the tops of the high barricades were jagged with glass and old, rusted barbed wire. The Rokk was still a fortress, an armed camp, but whether it had been meant to keep the wardens in or the convicts out, Jakkin was unable to say.

And somewhere, he thought suddenly, not able to keep her from his mind any longer, somewhere in that fortress there was a crooked-smiled, dark-haired, familiar stranger named Akki. For the first time he was worried that when she saw him, she'd know at once that he wasn't the man she needed or wanted.

# *10*

THE STREETS IN The Rokk were mazelike: winding and crisscrossed with overhead ramps. Jakkin had trouble with his sense of direction, twice losing even the position of the sun as it reflected crazily off the many windows. But Sarkkhan drove through the streets unhesitatingly.

"Never mind. You'll get used to it. Orient yourself by that dome." He nodded his head at the egg-shaped stadium roof. "The roads turn back on themselves, and the windows were made like mirrors on purpose. They bend the light back to you and show you hundreds of suns and moons. In the old days only the wardens had the master maps of the city, and there was no single central dome. If a convict got into The Rokk, he was quickly confused and easily caught."

Jakkin nodded, staring.

The truck made a sudden right-hand turn, and there, directly before them, rising seven stories high, was the Pit. Jakkin had heard many things about it, but nothing had prepared him for his first close sight of it.

"Rokk Major," Sarkkhan said and smiled. "Some say that Brokka Major is a better Pit. Certainly it's newer. But for size and sturdiness, I'll choose this one any day."

Jakkin nodded again, trying to take in the bulk of the place.

"We'll leave S'Blood here," Sarkkhan continued. "Get him bedded down. Then you and I've got a party to go to."

"A party?"

"Golden's party. We talked of it—after you had left that night."

Jakkin suddenly wondered what else the two men had talked about after his abrupt departure. He realized only now that he should have stayed with them and made plans rather than run off to sulk like a small boy.

Sarkkhan inched the truck into a back alley, and Jakkin felt a bright slash of color zigzag across his mind. He jerked his head around to look at the back of the truck, as if he could see through the cab and into the trailer behind. Then, sheepishly, he turned to Sarkkhan, but the man was busy maneuvering the truck through a dark doorway.

Had he heard nothing? Felt nothing? Jakkin couldn't believe that. S'Blood was Sarkkhan's own dragon. Surely he had registered that joyous lightning stroke.

"Noisy thing, isn't he?" Sarkkhan commented. "A bit like static in the mind. Just ignore him." He braked the truck to a stop and handed some papers to a leather-garbed guard at the gate.

Jakkin fingered the dimple in his cheek and didn't reply.

"Here," Sarkkhan said, handing two facs badges to Jakkin. "We're in stall twenty-seven at my request. It's a quiet corner, and S'Blood needs some gentle persuasion. Seniority has some privileges here at The Rokk. We'll unload him and stall him and walk to Golden's place. It's not far."

~

THEY FOUND THE well-appointed stall and guided the brown dragon into it, but S'Blood had needed more than *some* gentle persuasion. Jakkin had spent almost an hour rubbing the dragon's scarred neck links and legs, belly and back in an effort to settle him in. The smells and sounds of the Pit had aroused him to fighting spirit, and he didn't understand waiting.

Sarkkhan had stoked the dragon with extra portions of wort and weed to fire his flames. Then he had talked nose to nose with S'Blood for another hour. Jakkin's head was full of the brown dragon's sendings, but it was not until the lightning strikes had become a brassy yellow and steady that Sarkkhan had smiled.

"Now I hear you," he had said, chucking the dragon under the chin. He stood and signaled to Jakkin. They changed clothes right there in the stall, then left for the party.

The streets to Golden's house were of hard paving separated into squares by wooden forms. Every tenth square there was a spindly spikka tree set into dirt and surrounded by a wire fence, reflected time after time in the mirror windows. The spikkas were practically leafless, with mustard-colored trunks instead of the deep green-gold of healthy trees. They made Jakkin think of the beauty dragons, culls that were gelded and sold to city folk. The beauty dragons never grew very large, and their minds were of a uniform pastel shade.

The transplanted spikkas might be dreary, but Jakkin thought the three-story houses quite fine. They sat shoulder to shoulder along the road, each with a colorful front door and small reflecting windows looking warily on to the street. The gaudily painted housefronts mirrored by the windows gave the street a crazy-quilt appearance.

They stopped in front of a house with the number 17 splashed in red paint across its door.

"Here," Sarkkhan said. His hands wrangled with one another for an instant, and Jakkin realized with a sudden shock that the nursery owner was nervous.

"Mind your manners, boy. Don't let these city folk and offworlders judge trainers badly by what they see of you. Remember, *you* are a master now."

Jakkin repressed a smile. In Sarkkhan's voice there had been a warning tone that he had never heard before. It occurred to him that this was something Sarkkhan had once had to go through himself. Jakkin thrust his chin and chest out and nodded. He'd show any offworlders what being an Austarian dragon master meant.

The door was suddenly opened, and they went in.

If the outside of the house had seemed garish, the inside was a maelstrom of color. Oranges and pinks, purples and reds fought for space on papered walls. Heavy brocaded curtains framed the windows, and an enormous tapestry depicting three dragons and a rocket ship hid one entire wall. There was a mirrored ceiling reflecting the startling color display. Colored lights pulsed off and on in time to a rhythmic pipe-and-drum song. Making slits of his eyes, Jakkin had to fight an urge to cover his ears as well.

The most astonishing thing was a fountain of red-and-yellow water that seemed to squat in the center of the room. The waters ran through a series of transparent pipes shaped like a man and woman embracing. The man was outlined in red water, the woman, in yellow. The subject matter didn't shock Jakkin, but the lavish use of water did. He had been brought up believing that on this desert planet water was too precious to be wasted on frivolities.

He turned away in disgust and bumped into one of the many serving women. To be polite, he was forced to take a couple of light green berries from a bowl she was carrying. He popped one in his mouth and bit down. The skin of the berry popped open, flooding his mouth with a cool, tart taste. He decided he liked it and ate another quickly.

The serving woman, a tiny blond with her hair braided on top of her head like a crown, smiled at him. "A grape," she said. "Do you like it?"

He started to nod, then coughed as he realized he could see right through the gown she was wearing.

"Pits," he said, pointing to his mouth. "There are little pits in this fruit."

"Welcome," came a voice behind him. A hand on his shoulder turned him around. "Welcome to grapes and to The Rokk and to my house. I see you have decided you *are* a man after all." It was Golden, his voice as forced and as unnatural as his house. "Do you like what you see?" He gestured with his arm, more a choreographed movement than a natural act. The arm took in the blond girl as well as the house, the fruit, the fountain.

"I'm not here for *this*," Jakkin replied, his voice louder than he intended.

"Of course not," Golden drawled. "You are here for the dragons and the Pit." He laughed in his fluttering way, but his meaning was clear. Akki's name was not to be mentioned.

A smallish man with strange green paint above his eyes seemed to materialize at Jakkin's elbow. "Are you a trainer then?"

"One of the best," assured Golden, "even though he is young."

"And will your great beast win?" the painted man asked.

Jakkin hesitated, not knowing what to say to such a bizarre-looking creature. He glanced around for Sarkkhan, but the nursery owner was lost in the crowded room.

"Should I bet on your beastie?" the man pressed.

"Go ahead. Answer him. Master Trikkion is one of the richest men on Austar. He owns the baggeries and The Rokk Stews. He always gets his way!" Golden smiled broadly, patting the painted man on the shoulder.

Jakkin swallowed, remembering Sarkkhan's warning before they had entered the house. Then, openly sullen, he answered, "If twenty-two wins out of twenty-six fights is any indication, S'Blood is a good bet. He has a strong, slashing attack. He's unpredictable. And he never gives up." He ended almost angrily with a strange smile that didn't reach his eyes.

"That sounds like a description of you, young man," said Master Trikkion. "I like that in humans as well as in worms." He put his hand on Jakkin's forearm.

Golden laughed loudly. "This one knows what he is talking

about, Trikk. He is the youngest dragon master on the planet. Do you recall Heart's Blood?''

"The mute?'' Another man, devoid of paint but with a face pocked with dragon scores, joined the conversation. ''I bet on her first fight. Just an instinct, but I'm often right. What a beauty she is. Is she bred?''

The question took Jakkin's anger away. He always enjoyed talking about Heart's Blood, and before he knew it, he found himself in a complex discussion of breed lines and fighting skills with the pocked man. He entered it with passion and was soon the center of a small circle of men who listened to him intently. They interrupted with knowledgeable questions, then with anecdotes of past fights they'd seen. Despite the body paint and the embroidered clothes, they were not so different from the bonders, Jakkin decided. Only they knew more about the Pits and less about the dragons. He entertained them with the story of Heart's Blood's first three fights and life on a worm farm. Then the painted man told the latest Fewmets Ferkkin story. It involved three dragons, a baggery girl, and an offworld seller of iron Pit cleaners. Though he laughed with the others, Jakkin didn't find the joke funny.

Golden had disappeared sometime before the joke, and Jakkin didn't even notice until the blond came by and took his arm. ''Senator Golden has asked for you,'' she said.

In the middle of a forced laugh, Jakkin stopped and turned his head. He felt himself blush again at the girl's dress, though she seemed unconcerned, herding him expertly from the men who'd already begun a new Ferkkin story. Jakkin followed the girl into the hallway where Golden waited.

"Come with me,'' Golden said, dismissing the girl with a nod. ''The others have got a good sense of your politics and your expertise—with dragons. And I'm sure Bekka's dress made you blush prettily. But now you and I have something more important to talk about.''

They walked down the corridor, and at each step the noise from the party receded. They turned right and went through a door into a room. Golden shut the door, and it was as if the party had ended.

Jakkin took in the room with a swift look. Spartan, it bore no resemblance to the rest of the house. Three of the four whitewashed walls were empty; the fourth was hidden behind an immense, filled bookshelf. By the hearth were a pair of comfortable chairs, and over the hearth was a wood-framed mirror. Hanging from the ceiling was a mobile of the heavens. Jakkin recognized Austar IV and its two moons, nothing else.

"This is better," Golden said. "That other house belongs to Senator Golden. But this"—he gestured at the room—"belongs to me. Sit." His voice was no longer high-pitched but low and natural. Jakkin thought he had heard it somewhere before.

"Sit, Jakkin," Golden said again.

Jakkin took the closest chair, and as he sat, something stirred at the hearthside. His mind was touched at that same instant by a soft violet glow, not a landscape but a warm pastel feeling. He looked down and saw a thigh-high yellow dragon yawning. It had a spattering of red freckles on its nose and a ring of red freckles like a jeweled collar around its neck. He realized it was a beauty dragon, though he had never seen one before.

"Her name is Libertas. That means freedom in one of the old languages of Earth," Golden said. "They used to prize freedom there so highly they set imprisonment as the final punishment—a punishment they considered far worse than death. Hence Austar Four and the other KK planets." He stopped for a minute, cleared his throat. "Akki got Libertas for me."

"Akki!" Jakkin almost stumbled over the name. "Where is she? What's happening? And who *are* you?" The last came out in a rush. "I know you from somewhere. Oh, not Senator Golden from out there." And he gestured with his hand, a deliberate parody of the man's early motion. "But whoever you are here. In this room."

Golden smiled and leaned against the fireplace. "Very good. Very observant. You might do very well indeed. I'd been worried. But you must learn not to blurt things out, Jakkin, if you're to be of any help. You must keep your own counsel. You must frame the right questions."

Jakkin leaned forward. "I *do* know you," he said again. His eyes drew down into slits as he concentrated.

"The question," Golden continued, "is not who am I now, but who have I been?" He turned and looked into the mirror over the hearth, then reached into his pocket. Having drawn out a small box, he opened it and picked out a piece of flesh-colored rubber, which he placed against his cheek. Then he began kneading it onto his face. When he finished, he plucked two small patches of hair from the box and stuck them in front of his ears.

As he began to turn, Jakkin jumped up. "Ardru. You're Akki's friend Ardru. You drove the truck to Heart's Blood's first fight. But how?"

"Again the wrong question. Don't disappoint me, Jakkin. Ask, rather, *why?* The how is simple. A bit of stagecraft learned offworld." He removed the scar and sideburns with several quick motions of his hand. "Of course, when I do it for real, I take a good deal of time because the sideburns and scar must remain in place whatever I'm doing."

Golden squeezed the scar down to a flesh-colored lump, smoothed the hairpieces together, and stored them back in the box. "Only Akki and you on this world know about my two faces. She has known for more than a year. And you—I am trusting you now because there's suddenly so little time and I need you. I need someone the rebels don't know but whom Akki will recognize at once. You're younger and more naive than I'd hoped, although your recognition of me gives me some confidence in your skills. When you ran out of Sarkkhan's house last week, I tried to rethink the whole plan. But I couldn't come up with a better person. There was simply no one else to fit the bill."

"You mean, if you'd found someone else, you'd never have sent me that note?" Jakkin could feel his face flush with anger.

Golden came over to him, bent, and put his hands on either arm of the chair, effectively pinning Jakkin. "I mean exactly that. We're not playing games here. Not running dragons in mock battles. This, Jakkin Stewart, is real."

"I'd have come anyway. Akki needs me."

"Akki needs a strong man, not a runaway boy. She needs someone who will listen and act—react quickly and decisively. I'm counting . . . I *have* to count . . . on you to be that man."

Jakkin felt his jaw tighten. "I can try."

"Good. Good." Golden straightened up and walked back to the hearth.

Jakkin wanted to stand; but he was afraid that his legs would shake, and he wouldn't give Golden the opportunity to mock him. "Where is Akki?"

"She's been located. She's part of a rebel cell, which, of course, was in the original plan. But she was supposed to keep in touch with me, and when she dropped out of sight, I was worried."

Jakkin muttered, "I bet you were."

Golden stared at him. "You *must* learn to keep your thoughts hidden."

Jakkin started to answer, caught himself, stared back.

"That's better. Listen carefully. Now that we've found where these particular rebels are keeping her, we must get her away from them without compromising her. We have to know what she's learned there. That's why I need your help. But you must trust me."

"I don't understand . . ." Jakkin began.

"I'm not asking you to understand," interrupted Golden. "I'm asking you to be strong and to help me."

Angrily Jakkin jumped up. "I'll help because of Akki—not because of you or your rebels. Just Akki."

Golden smiled again. "*My* rebels? Do you really think they're mine?"

"Well, you certainly seem to know a lot about them," Jakkin replied sullenly.

"That I do. It's my business to know about them. But I need to know more. And so I need Akki back."

"You may *need* to get her back, but I *want* to get her back," Jakkin said.

Golden turned from him and stared into the mirror. His reflected face was bleak, white, drawn. "Never mind. It's just words. I understand you, Jakkin. And I accept your terms. You'll do this not for me but for Akki."

"Yes," Jakkin answered, not trusting himself to say more.

Golden turned again and leaned against the hearth, casual, foppish. "This, then," he said, his voice a mockery of the senator's careful pitch, "is the plan."

# *11*

WHAT JAKKIN HAD to do first, it seemed, was to go on with the dragon fight. Golden had sketched out the possibilities. If S'Blood lost, Jakkin was to become so distraught that he would wander out into the streets. There he would be picked up by one of the rebels and brought into their bar hideout. That rebel, who worked for Golden, would use Golden's name somewhere in his initial greeting so Jakkin would know him. He would introduce Jakkin to the cell.

And if S'Blood won—as was more likely—then Jakkin would follow Sarkkhan to whatever celebrations were planned and pretend to get drunk, wander into the streets, and . . .

". . . get found by your rebel," Jakkin had finished.

Golden had smiled at him then like a fond teacher. "There are, after all, only those two possibilities." He held up two fingers and waggled them at Jakkin. "A fight has to end with either a win or a loss. But don't tell Sarkkhan about our little plan. His hatred of the rebels is well known. He has been so outspoken against them that if you stay with him, there will be no possibility of getting you into the rebel cell. You will have to appear to break with him since if he suspects anything, he'll try to become part of our plan, be the center of it. So he must know nothing."

Jakkin nodded. Then, with Golden's help, he found his way back to the noise and lights of the party. After the quiet of Ardru's room, the assault on his eyes and ears was unbearable. He'd just made up his mind to leave when he was grabbed from behind.

"Did you talk to him?" It was Sarkkhan. "I've been looking and can't find him anywhere. The girl says he's around. Senators, bah!"

Jakkin whispered, "I saw him briefly. In passing. He said we should go on to the fight and he would—would be in touch." The lie was as close to the truth as he dared.

"Well, that's all right then, though he *should* have talked to me. Akki is *my* daughter, after all. I believe he knows what he's doing, though I don't really trust him too far. Trust yourself, boy. Fill your own bag, I say." His hands began their silent wrangling.

They left the party, pushing through a knot of people at the door.

~

THE WALK BACK to the Pit seemed to take less time than the walk there, for they were guided by the glowing dome.

The guard demanded to see their badges, though he obviously recognized Sarkkhan. Pit security had been tight ever since the famous Kkhmer betting scandals in 2483 and the destruction of the original Brokka Major Pit. A syndicate of offworlders had managed to slip, disguised, into the stalls and drug several of the dragons, hoping to weaken them. Instead, the dragons had gone wild in the Pit. One had jumped the barrier, and before it was subdued, had killed seventeen in the crowd, including a starship commander. Three other dragons had broken the stalls apart. These days—with rebels about—no one questioned the need for guards.

Making their way down the dimly lit stairs, Jakkin and Sarkkhan were silent. They knew that dragons slept only in the half-light when it was quiet, and before a big fight the dragons needed their few hours of deep sleep.

Jakkin could hear the little hiccuping snores of trainers napping near their beasts and the occasional *pick-buzz* of nightwings beating against the stall walls. Into his mind came occasional colors from the nearby dragons, the landscape sendings evened out by sleep.

Sarkkhan, who had drunk quite a bit at the party, was asleep almost at once with a stuttering snore. Jakkin could not fall into such an easy oblivion. He kept thinking about Golden's plan. It seemed too simple, and he distrusted it. Bonders always said, "Plans fill no man's bag."

~

HALFWAY THROUGH THE morning, after four fights had rocked the boards overhead, Jakkin heard the call for S'Blood over the loud-speakers. He had watched only the very first fight, in order to get a feel for the Pit. Then he went back below to stay with S'Blood. Sarkkhan had remained in the owners' part of the stands, willing to leave S'Blood's care to Jakkin.

When the brown's name was called, it was paired with Bankkar's Mighty Mo. Jakkin knew that Mo was one of Bankkar Smith's line of sluggish stayers, huge dragons that moved slowly but often managed to outlast many of the quicker fighters like S'Blood. Jakkin's job would be to pace S'Blood, to make sure he did not tire himself out against the stone wall of Mighty Mo.

Jakkin untied S'Blood and yanked his head away from the bale of wort.

"Enough, worm," he said, reaching S'Blood with his mind as well. "Thy fires will be long enough to reach that rock. It is time thee earned thy keep."

S'Blood followed eagerly and, being an old hand at fighting, went immediately to the dragonlock without further encouragement, waiting there until Jakkin had mounted the stairs.

Jakkin fought his way through the crowd and took a stand at the railing, where he could watch every aspect of the fight.

His thoughts reached down to the lock below, where S'Blood was hackled and waiting. "Now, come up to me."

S'Blood flowed up through the dragonlock and flashed into the ring. The artificial lights reflecting on his brown scales cast a warm halo around his entire body. He lashed his tail and stretched his neck to its fullest.

It was a good entrance, and the spectators applauded. They always enjoyed a display. S'Blood, who loved to please the crowd, paced up and down at the ten-meter line near the other lock, his tail whipping back and forth furiously. By the rules of the fight he could go no closer until the opposing dragon appeared, and it took some control on Jakkin's part to hold him there. But S'Blood *could* blast the lock with his fire, heating it up and making it uncomfortable for Mo. His flames shot out, locking the edges of the opening of the lock. The flames were not long, and S'Blood probably should not have wasted his fires at the first, but Jakkin let him do as he pleased, for the color of the flame was good—orange and yellow with a bright blue heart. The bets would increase, and in any case, the hot lock might serve to slow Mo down even more.

"Now wait," Jakkin cautioned at last.

S'Blood stopped flaming, though he continued to pace. Fired up by the extra wort, he was impatient to begin. His hackles rippled, his shoulders bunched.

Bankkar, an old competitor, was obviously counting on S'Blood's eagerness to thin out his fighting edge, so he delayed Mo's entrance into the Pit until the very last moment. Just before the final bell Mo flowed up through the lock—and the crowd roared.

S'Blood was a large dragon, but Mo was enormous. Red and yellow, with a mustard-colored body and large splashes of crimson like blood clots all over, he would have been comical if he hadn't been so huge.

For a moment Jakkin blanked mentally, but S'Blood did not. He gave Mo no time to set himself out of the lock but led an immediate slashing raid on the giant's back. He winged up above Mo and feinted to the head, then dived at Mo's hind end.

Finally Mo moved, his yellow-and-red tail beginning to lash, and Jakkin saw what the Pit gossip had meant by sluggish. Mo's tail did not snap around like a whip but rather moved over his back like a heavy, unwieldy rope. S'Blood had no trouble avoiding it, but his movements were so quick he expended more energy than he needed to. Jakkin saw the trap in that.

"Slow, slow, my worm," he cautioned. "Do not skip about so. Save thy power."

This time S'Blood heard and backed away, wagging his head from side to side as if taunting Mo.

Mo lumbered forward, and S'Blood made a half turn, as if afraid.

"Go! Now!" Jakkin screamed aloud.

S'Blood turned back so suddenly the movement was a blur, and his right paw slashed out and up. The twin lanceae sliced two shallow trails through Mo's tender nose, and hot dragon's blood dripped onto the sand, sending up gouts of steam.

At the cuts, Mo roared. It was deep and full and agonizingly slow. The roar sent punters back to the touts, and a surge of excitement made a circle of the stands.

The big dragon stopped roaring, letting the sound fade away like a rocket receding into the distance. S'Blood caracoled across the Pit, his jaw hanging open, giving the impression that he was laughing. The crowd applauded.

"Once again, swift worm!" someone called out.

"That's not a worm. That's a brown lightning bolt," answered a voice.

"Brown Bolt!" a man in the upper stands shouted, standing and waving his arms.

The cry was instantly taken up. "Brown Bolt! Brown Bolt! Brown Bolt!" The name pounded against the walls, the rhythm so insistent that even Mo responded to it, lumbering into the center of the Pit in step to the crowd's chant.

"Brown Bolt! Brown Bolt! Brown Bolt!"

There was no holding S'Blood's attention now. Jakkin feared the dragon would be exhausted if he insisted on playing to the crowd, and again and again he tried to get through; but all he could feel was a hurricane of yellow-and-red flashings across an ultrabright landscape.

Both dragons flared at once, and tongues of fire lashed the sand, turning the old blood into crystals.

S'Blood spread his wings and soared to the Pit roof, where he circled, dipping his wings first to one section of the stands, then to the other, while below him Mighty Mo rested, and the small wounds on his nose crusted over and began to heal.

S'Blood started a downward spiral. Mo suddenly stood in a heavy hind-foot rise, one front claw lifted. He swatted at S'Blood, and the two front nails scraped along the full length of the brown's body, lodging for an instant in a weak tail link. It was enough to disrupt S'Blood's flight and send him crashing to the floor. If Mo had been faster, he could have finished S'Blood then; but the jarring fall was enough to waken S'Blood from his crowd-induced fever, and Jakkin's anguished calling came through.

"Up! Up quickly, my beauty!"

S'Blood pumped his wings without taking time to see where Mo was and lifted. He was slower than Jakkin had ever seen him, but still fast enough to avoid the indolent Mo. Hovering out of reach, S'Blood beat his wings in great sweeps.

Jakkin looked at Mo even more closely now. He seemed to have a film of some sort over one eye, a legacy of an earlier fight or else sand and dust from this one. He thought carefully at S'Blood: "To his left, thou fighter. To the wall. The wall." It was an unlikely move because the dangers of being cornered against the wall were great. S'Blood recognized that, shaking his head as if arguing, but Jakkin persisted.

"The wall."

S'Blood flew to the wall, then dropped swiftly, standing on his hind legs and momentarily exposing his tender neck. Mo swung his head around slowly, and at the same time S'Blood brought his claws together in a pincers movement and slashed from above and below with a lightning stroke.

Jakkin winced at the sound of nails on scales, then smiled at the next sound, a rip. One of the lanceae had caught on Mo's underchin, the most vulnerable part of a dragon.

Mo looked up, stunned, his one good eye beginning to glaze.

S'Blood delivered the ritual slashes to the neck—one, two, three, and foolishly tried to streak beneath Mo, who was collapsing. Mo's outstretched claws caught S'Blood on his back legs, causing him to stumble. He managed to crawl out from under Mo's front claws, but despite the cheers of the crowd he did not get up.

Jakkin stared at the two fallen dragons, then looked for Sarkkhan. The nursery owner was standing, shaking his head. Then he pushed through the crowd, put one hand on the railing, and leaped into the Pit.

Jakkin followed.

They walked over to S'Blood's side, and Jakkin knelt beside the dragon and touched his massive head.

Sarkkhan bent over, examining S'Blood's hind legs. "By the moons," he growled, "he's been hamstrung."

"Maybe he's just tired," Jakkin said, though he had never seen a dragon tired enough to act this way.

"Hamstrung," Sarkkhan said. "Fewmets! Fit only for the Stews."

Jakkin heard the agonizing flashes of pale yellow crying in his head. "Maybe he could be saved. He's just won you lots of money. I'll work with him. I'll—"

"Save your breath, boy," Sarkkhan said angrily. "I'm not blaming you. This piece of worm waste did himself in, all that grandstanding. I should have known when he got confused between us in training. He listens to too much—and not enough. And a hamstrung dragon is worthless. He can't stand up, and if he can't stand up, eventually he can't breathe. His body is so heavy, he simply crushes himself to death. There's *no* saving them, no matter how hard you work. You know that, boy." He turned suddenly and waved to a man in a blue-green suit who was in the stands. "Here, Sharkky."

The man vaulted the railing and came over. Jakkin saw an emblem over the man's left pocket, a dragon with a knife and fork crossed over it. He was from The Rokk Stews.

"No!" Jakkin cried, and in his head came an answering, painful stab of yellow, trembling but still bright.

Sarkkhan gave him a hard, silencing look, then walked over to the stewman. They talked briefly, and the man offered his hand, which Sarkkhan ignored. Undaunted, the stewman smiled and left.

"You come with me," said Sarkkhan, turning to Jakkin.

"Where?" It was all Jakkin could manage without his voice breaking.

"To the Stews. They'll cheat us if they can. Fighting dragon's meat is not the sweetest, but it's worth a lot to *certain* people." He drew a breath. "If you want to be a real master, a real trainer, a real owner—a man—you are going to have to know the bad of it as well as the good." He breathed out heavily. "Culling's nothing to this."

Sarkkhan turned and walked out of the Pit, his face set in a mask.

Jakkin followed and tried, without success, to blot out the pale yellow cry in his head, S'Blood's pain-filled calling, that went on and on and on.

# *12*

IT WAS A fifteen-minute walk over the ramps as well as through the streets. Jakkin smelled the Stews before he saw it. The smell, dark and fleshy, was part cooked and part rotting meat. Smoke hung over a windowless three-story building that sprawled over two streets. The blood-red knife-and-fork insignia was emblazoned on the north wall and on the doors.

Jakkin drew in a deep breath, then gagged. His head ached, remembering the last flash of pale yellow, both defiant and pained, that he had had from S'Blood. He'd tried to send a comforting thought back but had been unable to do it. The sight of the four men from the Stews, in light green suits that aped his trainer whites, shoving S'Blood's unprotesting body onto a large wheeled cart had shocked Jakkin into a mental silence. The stewmen had wheeled the cart through a pair of enormous double doors that led from the arena, working in oily synchronization. It was their obvious unconcern that so chilled him.

The crowd in the stands had been chilled, too, their silence complete. The ending had been so sudden, and until that moment S'Blood had been so flashily alive. Then he lay there, not dead, but somehow not really alive either. Dragons did sometimes die in the Pit. Occasionally a loser was too severely hurt, the ritual slashes too deep or other wounds too great. But S'Blood had been the winner—not the loser. The loser, Mo, still lay in his faint, but it hadn't been his body so hastily carted away.

Sarkkhan had also been silent, though Jakkin couldn't tell if his speechlessness came from anger or pain. Sarkkhan had merely guided

Jakkin out with a touch on the arm, out the door and along the maze of streets and ramps.

Once they reached the Stews, Sarkkhan had been rougher, propelling Jakkin through a series of doors, past a paneled outer office lined with pastel paintings of smiling, wide-eyed dragons that bore little resemblance to any worms Jakkin had ever known.

They came at last to a balcony that overlooked a room as large as a Minor Pit.

Overhead were lights as bright as a hundred suns, illuminating the slaughterhouse below. To the right there were pens for holding the dragons. In one was a knot of late culls, overgrown dragonlings whose early promise had not been fulfilled. Too ugly for beauty dragons or too low in the pecking order to be successful fighters, the culls were useless for anything but meat. They moved restlessly, occasionally challenging one another with feeble hind-foot rises.

In another pen was a single older dragon, its greying muzzle and the smooth, rounded humps on its tail indicating that it was well past mating or fighting age. Some nursery owner had decided it was not worth feeding that worm anymore.

The other pens were empty.

The young culls were herded from their pen by a green-suited man who carried a stinger in one hand, a prod stick in the other. He urged them into a passageway. One by one the culls trotted down the passageway and through a door where they were met by a hulking man, who led them over to a great white vat. With one economical movement, he shot the dragon through its ear hole with the stinger. Then he checked a watch on his wrist. After a minute he slit the cull's throat, and the blood gouted into the vat.

While the blood was flowing, the man turned his head briefly and shouted something to the other green suit by the door—some joke or instruction. Then he turned back, checked the cull's eyes, and smiled. Jakkin could see the smile as the man dipped his hand into the vat and wiped a smear of blood into his mouth.

"How—how can he do that?" Jakkin asked, remembering suddenly the steaks Kkarina served at dinner, smothered in rich red sauce.

Sarkkhan ignored the real question. "Once the dragon's been dead a minute," he said, "the blood loses its heat and no longer burns."

Jakkin could feel tears, hot as dragon's blood, starting in his eyes. He blinked them away. He had heard almost nothing from the cull when it died; just a brief spit of color, and it was gone. He recalled the nursery culling sessions and how he had helped, feeling only the smallest agony, hearing Likkarn remark matter-of-factly, "The meat is sweeter nearer the egg." It was an old farm saying. He promised himself again that he wouldn't make culls of *any* of Heart's Blood's hatchlings. He would *not* be party to their deaths.

The men were sending in the next cull, having disposed of the first body onto a cart that was pulled through a dark doorway. They joked and moved with ease. Jakkin thought they couldn't possibly have heard the dragon. No one could do this kind of work if he were linked to the cull.

He turned away. If he looked anymore, he'd be sick and disgrace himself.

Sarkkhan remained facing the slaughterhouse, legs spread apart, arms folded, jaw tight, watching.

Several more times Jakkin's mind was touched by the briefest moment of color, which he knew to be a dying cull's only protest. One was almost a rainbow, and he shuddered. What if that had been Heart's Blood's own?

Then Sarkkhan spoke. "They're bringing him in."

Jakkin knew he meant S'Blood, and one part of him wanted to run away as far and as fast as he could go. But another part issued a clear reminder: Be a man—and stay. There was one thing he could do to help S'Blood still. He could touch the brown dragon's mind and send him some measure of peace.

Jakkin shut his eyes. S'Blood's groggy protests were slow slashes of yellow against a grey, foggy backdrop.

"Good-bye, brave worm," Jakkin whispered, letting the thought fly like an arrow toward S'Blood.

He had time for only that one quick sending before there was an agonizing streak of bright yellow pain. It blotted out all other colors, all other sensations. Then the yellow began a slow leakage off to the left-hand side, draining away to a somber grey background. Only one small, bright, flickering bit of yellow remained in the center of the grey, a candle flame that suddenly guttered and went out, leaving a wisp of lighter grey in the dark, like smoke from a candle snuff.

"I'll never forgive you for this," Jakkin said quietly.

"Would you rather have watched him die slowly over the days in agony? Suffocation is not an easy death for a dragon."

"I could have explained it to him," Jakkin said.

"You mean you'd have looked for forgiveness," said Sarkkhan. "I've lost dragons before. I know."

Jakkin didn't answer, but he refused to cry. He wiped his nose once on his sleeve. Men didn't cry.

"Come on," Sarkkhan said, returning to the Stew.

Jakkin went past him and out of the building without looking back. He turned right, then left, then right and right again until he was thoroughly lost in the mirrored maze of the city, and not caring that he was lost.

"Lost!" He laughed bitterly at himself. "Just as Golden wanted it." He was standing in a small, poorly lit square, wondering what to do next when a hand on his shoulder turned him. He wasn't startled, having half expected it and expecting, too, to meet a rebel with Golden's name on his lips.

It was no hard-faced rebel but the girl from the party, the blond with the hair like a crown. This time her dress was opaque and covered further with a light cloak. She was smiling.

"I'm a friend of Akki's," she said. "Come with me. There's someone who wants to meet you. I followed you from the Pit."

"Did you?" he asked distractedly.

"It's easy to follow someone who's a stranger in The Rokk," she said. "The mirrors slow him down."

Without hesitation, he went with her. She had said Akki's name, not Golden's, but then S'Blood's death had not been in either of the senator's original plans. Obviously Golden had changed things. Bonders were right. Plans filled no bags.

# The Snatchlings

# 13

IT WAS LUCKY Jakkin had someone to follow, for it was beginning to get dark, and the maze of windowed streets was alternately shadow and light. The light, coming from the gaudy bars and steamy stewhouses, made the black alleys under the ramps blacker. The mirrors multiplied shadows until it was hard to know what was real and what was not.

Jakkin stayed as close to the girl as he dared without ever once touching her. She seemed to know every bend and turning, never once making a mistake. At last she slipped into a narrow alleyway between two indistinguishable sandbrick buildings, both painted with wild designs.

Jakkin caught his breath quickly and went after her. She opened a door that blazed with sudden light and pulled him in.

He knew at once he was in a baggery by the filtered lights, the gauzy curtains on the barred windows, the profusion of low couches and pillows on the floor, and the gentle pulsations of a hidden band. He swore at himself, calling himself all sorts of lizard scum. He guessed he'd mistaken the girl's invitation, wanting so much to hear Akki's name that he convinced himself the planned password had been changed.

"Worm waste. That's what I am. Lizard drizzle."

But at his voice the girl turned and smiled, holding out her hand. It was soft-looking, and he remembered, suddenly, Akki's calloused, capable hands. He moved back.

The girl laughed. "Oh, don't worry. I won't bite. Not you anyway. Akki would kill me. With her it's always 'Jakkin this' and 'Jakkin that.' "

Jakkin's cheeks burned suddenly.

"Come on. She's upstairs." She gestured with her head.

"Akki?"

"*Akki?*" Momentarily the girl looked puzzled. "Oh, no, it's the doctor who wants to see you."

He remembered then that Akki had worked for a doctor in a baggery, and with things starting to fall into place in his mind, he followed the girl up the stairs.

There was a long hall at the top with doors branching off. The girl walked into the last door and pointed in. Jakkin entered, and it was immediately obvious that it was a doctor's office. There was a small desk, a table spread with a roll of white paper, several hardback chairs. The doctor sat on one, perched as if ready for flight, reading a book. Under a cap of dark hair, two lively eyes looked up at him out of a face as tan as a kkhan reed.

"Dr. Henkky," the girl whispered from the door before leaving.

Jakkin inclined his head toward the doctor, who nodded back. Then she spoke without preliminaries, as though the sentences had been long rehearsed. "Don't trust Golden. Akki did, and now she's missing."

"But Golden knows where she is. He says she's all right."

"Don't trust Golden," the doctor said again. "He is an offworlder, perhaps even a Federation spy. He's . . . unreadable. Unknowable. Unnatural." The wooden quality was gone from her speech, and she spoke passionately. "He sent Akki to the rebels without adequate explanation or preparation, and now he can't get her out safely. Not without jeopardizing himself. He uses people and throws them away when he's done."

Jakkin walked into the room and closed the door. His hand found the bondbag beneath his shirt and touched it for reassurance. "I'll get her out. That's why I'm here in The Rokk."

Dr. Henkky let out a staccato laugh and rubbed her finger along her nose. "Think, boy, think logically about your chances. You don't know this city. Or the rebels. You're disposable to Golden. If you get her out, fine. If not, it doesn't matter to him."

"You're wrong."

"I'm right. He's Federation, I'm sure of it. And think of what the Federation has done to Austarians from the first. They used this planet as a dumping ground two hundred years ago, dumping human beings onto a desert. Oh, yes, those human beings were thieves and murderers and psychopaths and whores. But they were human beings nonetheless. And then the Federation set wardens in a city of stone and wire to watch the results. Well, the wardens ate stores shipped in from offworld and kept themselves warm during the cold of Dark After in heated houses while the KKs scratched out what they could from the sands. The wardens grew fat and went home on leave while the KKs died, killed by hunger and wild dragons and heat and cold—and each other.''

"You sound like a rebel," commented Jakkin.

"Then you've never heard a rebel," said Dr. Henkky. "Me, I'm an Austarian and proud to be a survivor. I'm the great-great-great-grand-daughter of a pair of thieves who had their crimes marked in colored brands on their backs. I may not like the bond system, but I've worked my own way out of it. I wouldn't level what civilization our ancestors managed to achieve despite the Federation. And I surely wouldn't kill off anyone labeled a master or that which makes most masters—the dragons.''

"The rebels want to kill the dragons?" Jakkin could hardly believe it. "I thought they wanted to do away with bond. That's not really a bad idea—no masters and no bonders. But to kill dragons . . ." His voice trailed off.

"Not to mention masters," Dr. Henkky added. "Like me. Like you. Like . . ."

"Akki is a master, though she wears a bag. An empty bag," said Jakkin.

Dr. Henkky nodded. "So."

"I *will* find her."

"Then you mustn't trust Golden. I did once—and he betrayed me.'' She didn't explain further.

Jakkin shook his head. "But Golden knows how to put me in touch with the rebels," he protested.

"At what price?" Henkky asked. "With him there is always a hidden price. Besides, you don't need Golden to find rebels. They're everywhere in The Rokk.''

"But I need to find the specific cell that's holding Akki. And as you pointed out, I don't know my way around this city, and I have so little time. I'm supposed to go back to the nursery tomorrow with Sarkkhan. It was tonight I was to meet—" He stopped suddenly. He knew Henkky no better than he knew Golden. What if he had just given away precious information?

"And so you should go home—but return soon. You have a reason—your own dragon. Akki told me about her. Heart's Brood.''

"Blood," Jakkin corrected automatically. "Heart's Blood.''

"Isn't that like a man?" The doctor chuckled. "Blood all the time.'' She stood. "Listen well, Jakkin. All you have to pretend to be is what you are—a new young master ill at ease with that role. Stick close to the truth, for that's always better than telling complicated, outrageous lies. And if you're half the man that Akki believes you to be, you'll find truth-telling the easier way. Ask questions, but keep your own counsel.''

Jakkin nodded, but her advice sounded familiar. Where had he heard it before?

"The Stews and baggeries and fighting Pits are symptoms of a sick society. That's why the Federation starships find us so fascinating. They're allowed no blood sports on their own planets anymore. War has been illegal for many centuries. Violence has been outlawed. The Federation planets do chromosome tests on all newborns, weeding out potential murderers, exiling them as babies to the Protectorate worlds, where—ironically—many of them become leaders. But there's still that ever-present human longing to see blood spilled. So they come to us, in the Protectorates, for their shot of violence. And we Austarians certainly have plenty to give them. Do you read?''

The sudden shift startled Jakkin, and he nodded warily.

Dr. Henkky held up a small volume. "It's called *Dragon, Man, and the Warrior Society* and was written by our friend Senator Durrah Golden. You should read it. It says, among other things, that Austarians are drenched in blood, that it's our legacy but that the Federation, for its own needs, encourages us in blood sports as long as it's within legal acceptable bounds. This book is not allowed on Austar. The Federation forbids it. I stole it from Golden's bookcase.''

Jakkin could remember only one bookcase in Golden's house. How well had the doctor known him?

"Drenched in blood and death,'' Dr. Henkky continued.

"I don't believe you,'' Jakkin said suddenly. "We train our dragons *not* to kill. We saved them from extinction. They were fighting to the death, and we retaught them how to fight only for domination.''

"But do we train people?'' muttered Henkky. "Every Bond-Off I patch up knife wounds and strap broken bones.''

"But—''

"And we wear our blood scores proudly.'' She reached out quickly and grabbed Jakkin's hand. Twisting it, she forced his wrist up. The bracelet of scarred flesh showed white against his tanned arm. Without letting go, she said, "Tell me about this.''

Jakkin mumbled, "A fight with a drakk.''

"So—a fight.''

"But it was necessary. It could have killed our hatchlings.''

"A necessary killing then," Dr. Henkky said. "And did you enjoy it?"

Remembering his fear, the cold sweat of panic that had bathed his limbs, Jakkin shook his head. But then, recalling the triumphal march home and the party afterward, he was no longer so sure.

"Some of us do enjoy the killing," the doctor said. "And these marks on your arms, these little pocks."

"You know they're blood scores from dragon's blood."

"Yes—dragon's blood. Did you know that the stewmen hear the dragons they kill?"

Jakkin pulled his arm away. "Hear?"

"What is it you dragoners say? They are *linked* with the beasts."

"You mean," Jakkin said, stunned, "that they get sendings from the dragons and *still* kill them?"

"Yes, that's exactly what I mean." Dr. Henkky nodded.

"But why?"

"Why? Not because it's their work but because they enjoy the cries. We're still paying a debt for the sins of our ancestors."

Jakkin spun away and stared at the wall, seeing again the stewman wiping the smear of blood across his mouth, hearing again the fading yellow landscape flickering out as S'Blood died. Something sour rose in his throat.

"You see," Dr. Henkky said, "it'll be easy for you. You will not have to do much pretending. You're sick at the thought."

"But why pretend at all? Why wait? Golden has it set up to get me directly in touch with the rebels."

Dr. Henkky put her hands up, palms together, as if in prayer. "Believe me when I tell you not to trust Golden. I know him *very* well."

Jakkin nodded.

"Ask yourself how a man who is a senator, a master, can be so well connected to the rebels."

The scarred face of Ardru came instantly to Jakkin's mind.

"Ask yourself what a man who has been offplanet and reared on a Federation ship hopes to gain. If we stay a Protectorate—even with a bond system—the Federation has a perfect planet for its crews to play at bloody-mindedness. If we become a Federation state, it will be the end of the dragon Pits as we know them. Either way the Federation gains something—a playpen or a member state paying taxes and trade. But if the rebels take over, the Federation has nothing— no more Pits, no state to tax, no land to plunder and mine."

Jakkin thought for a minute. "But then what does Golden have to do with the rebels?"

"Think, Jakkin, think. By its own laws the Federation cannot come legally, openly into our world and break up a homegrown rebellion, but it needs a stable world here. So someone like Golden must be found, an Austarian by birth but a Federation man by upbringing. He can track the rebels and push them into stupid enough acts so that we're forced to come down on them ourselves."

Jakkin suddenly shivered. "What kinds of stupid acts?"

"Murder perhaps."

"Of a master's daughter?" Jakkin whispered.

Dr. Henkky did not answer but restlessly pushed her fingers through her hair, then rubbed the back of one hand with the other.

"Do you *really* think that?" Jakkin asked.

"I don't know," Dr. Henkky said. "Golden uses everyone and doesn't even realize it. Even with me . . ." She stopped, drew in a breath. "He's not really one of us, though his ancestors may have been born here. He's an offworlder, not an Austarian."

"And you are," said Jakkin.

"I am. And you are. And Akki. We're what is best in Austar. We want to save and build, not break down things like the rebels or play with things, like the Federation and like Golden."

Jakkin's hand went again to the bondbag. "Dr. Henkky, all I've ever wanted to be is a dragon master, not a master of men. I hate politics. I don't enjoy the games that people seem to play. Give me a great worm to run in the Pit—even with cleaning the dust and the fewmets—and I'm happy." He shook his head. "But if you're right, then I guess it's politics time—not dragon time—that is now."

She laughed abruptly, and her face underwent a change of such magnitude that Jakkin realized with a shock that she was a beautiful woman. "No, Jakkin, there you're wrong. Politics is a waiting game, and you'll have to get used to that. I know how hard it is for someone your age to wait, so listen to me and do this: Go home *now*. Think about all I've said about the stewmen and the blood thirst *now*. Work with your worm *now*. The moment I have real word of Akki's whereabouts—and I think I can find it out from Golden—I'll send word through Bekka to you."

Jakkin stared at her. "But what will Golden do when I don't meet . . ." he began.

"I'll tell him that you were brought here to me with a bump on the head. Here a bandage will help our story." Her competent hands quickly affixed a large bandage on his forehead as she spoke. "You see, it wasn't your fault that you were set upon in an alley as you wandered unhappily after your trip to the Stews."

"But that's a lie," said Jakkin.

"Believe me, Golden understands lies. Don't be so naive, my young friend." She finished the bandage and patted his head.

Jakkin moved away from her and went to the door. With his hand on the latch, he turned again to look at the doctor. Her eyes were glittering like those of a trainer whose dragon was running well in the Pit. Jakkin felt uneasy.

"No," he said, "don't send Bekka to me. I won't trust Golden, but I don't trust you either. I fill my bag myself." He tore the bandage from his forehead, wincing as the tape pulled some hair. "I won't play the political waiting game."

Henkky's eyes were suddenly opaque. She shrugged. "Unfortunately politics plays people as much as people play politics," she warned. "There are times when no amount of wishing will speed things along."

Jakkin stared angrily at her. "I don't need any more advice, Doctor. After all, I'm not sick." He opened the door and found his way back down the hall and stairs. Once out on the street, he managed to get a bearing on the light-filled dome of the Pit and started to thread his way slowly, and with much backtracking, through the maze. But though it took him hours, no one with Golden's name found him, and he had to concede the period of Dark After and sleep it away in the underpit stalls.

# 14

WITHOUT THE HEAVY dragon in the back of the truck, the return trip to the nursery was swift, but the two men barely spoke to each other. What Sarkkhan was thinking Jakkin didn't know. His own thoughts, like a takk pot at full boil, bubbled furiously.

He didn't know whether to believe Dr. Henkky or Golden or neither, and he wished he understood the animosity between them. He wondered what Golden had concluded when he'd missed the meeting with the rebel. *Some spy*, he thought bitterly. Then, remembering S'Blood's guttering yellow flame, he thought: *Some trainer*. Finally, as the miles between the truck and The Rokk grew greater, he had a final anguished thought: *Some man*.

The landscape was dull, as if a grey wash had been painted over everything: grey roads, grey sand, grey trees. Only the mountains stood out, dark and brooding against the slate-colored sky.

Jakkin was sunk in self-misery and hardly noticed when they turned into the nursery drive, so he was unprepared for the sudden assault of reds and rainbows in his head.

Greeting and cheering him in the only way she could, Heart's Blood heralded his arrival. For the first time in more than a day, Jakkin found he could really smile.

"Go to your worm," Sarkkhan said abruptly. It was clear that he had felt a spillover of Heart's Blood's sending. It was also clear that he was issuing an order.

Jakkin walked, then almost ran to the small barn where the red dragon waited. He slipped through the dark passageway and into the birth room. Nothing was there but empty, broken shells. She had already been moved by one of the bonders into the larger room next door.

A chuckle of wavery lines came into his head as he entered the bigger room. So Heart's Blood had realized that he'd gone into the wrong room first.

"Ah, but I have much to tell thee," he said aloud.

In answer, the red dragon moved her head, forcing him to look beyond her. There were the hatchlings, almost doubled in size, one almost as high as his chest. They romped around him, and the tall one, its eggskin nearly all gone, gnawed at the straps of Jakkin's right sandal. The five hatchlings shared an evenness in color, uniform all over their bodies instead of sprinkled with freckles, but Jakkin knew better than to hope that any would be the same red as Heart's Blood. "Color fast does not last" was nursery wisdom. He patted the smallest on the head, and it shot a broken group of rainbow arches through his mind.

Jakkin turned from the hatchlings and asked Heart's Blood, "Thee will have many fights soon, beloved worm. Can'st leave thy hatchlings?"

In answer, she showed him the oasis with the blue ribbon of water and waving reeds, not as it had been a week ago, when they had splashed in the water, but an older picture. In that scent a young dragonling, the red just barely visible beneath the firstskin, leaped into the stream, its oversize wings pumping madly.

"Yes, a hatchling *can* make it on its own as long as it is fed. How could I forget thy own progress?"

The chuckling lines bounced through his mind once more, and he squatted by her side. She put her massive head in his lap, and he scratched behind her ears, starting a low thrumming sound deep behind her sternum. It grew in volume until the entire room seemed to vibrate.

The little dragons stopped playing at the sound and stared with round dark eyes at Jakkin, almost as if they were thrumming, too. The sound soothed him, and he sat down on the floor, putting his arm around the dragon's neck.

"Now I must tell thee of S'Blood."

As if she'd spoken, he knew that she already knew—and forgave him his inability to save the hamstrung brown. He put his head on hers and, for the first time, cried. The hatchlings crowded around him, so that their heads touched him, but they didn't intrude into his mind. They let him sob until he had no more tears, and when he was done, they sent a landscape of sun and rain and rainbows of six different patterns to comfort him.

~

ERRIKKIN FOUND THEM that way when he came to fetch Jakkin for dinner and again before lights out.

"I know I am only your bonder by sufferance, though I don't know why," he said rigidly, "and that it is not my place to say it—"

"About that . . ." Jakkin began, but Errikkin interrupted.

"But you spend too much time treating that worm like a person and treating people like worms. All we've had are rumors about the fight."

Jakkin laughed. "And you love rumors."

"The least you can do is tell me what happened, straight. And I'll still all the gossip." Errikkin smiled winningly.

Jakkin snorted. He should have guessed that all of Errikkin's concern came down to this, that he wanted to be the first to know the gossip. Well, he'd give it to Errikkin, tell him the whole thing, and let him make of it what he would.

"S'Blood put up a wonderful fight—and he won. But the big monster he fought, one of those gross lumberers, hamstrung him in the end. So Sarkkhan had him put down in the Stews. It was bloody and awful, and a man is supposed to accept it. A master takes it in stride. Well, I haven't and I won't. I'll never sell any of Heart's Blood's hatchlings to the Stews or send them off as culls to be turned into pastel-minded beauties. So you're mine, bonder, until I can figure out another way to get rid of you." Suddenly ashamed of his outburst, Jakkin stood and left the barn. A trail of scolding from Heart's Blood echoed in his head, though Errikkin was silent.

*Let him be silent,* Jakkin thought. *The rebels would make short work of him!* Cleansed of his anger and a good part of his sorrow, he went to the bondhouse to sleep.

~

CAUTIOUSLY AND WITH many apologies, Errikkin woke him in the morning. When Jakkin tried to apologize back, Errikkin smiled away his words, saying, "A master is always right." Because he had no answer for that, Jakkin became frustrated all over again, and his anger returned. It was a terrible start to a new day.

At Sarkkhan's order, Likkarn was waiting for Jakkin at the barn, his staring eyes clear for once of the telltale red of a weeder. Rumor had it that this time the old man had really cured himself of his dependency, having been off blisterweed for several weeks. But nursery rumors were as often wrong as right, and Jakkin reminded himself of the saying "Once the weed, always the need." Blisterweed addiction was an old man's vice, the young bonders having found that drinking gave them short-time highs and nothing worse than a hangover from the weed wine the next day.

Likkarn's mouth twisted when Jakkin entered the barn. They wasted little love on each other. Likkarn's jealousy of young masters and talented bonders was long-standing. And because of his weed addiction, no one trusted him in return.

Jakkin glanced at Likkarn's face, seamed with the red tear lines that were the ever-present scars of the addict. They were like the brands placed on the backs of the first convicts when they had been shipped out, speaking silently and permanently of the owner's crimes. Jakkin chuckled at his own flight of fancy, and Likkarn houghed at him like an angry dragon.

Seeking to make amends—he hadn't meant to laugh *at* Likkarn, for he needed Likkarn's advice and help—Jakkin tried a different approach.

"We have to get Heart's Blood in shape to take over S'Blood's schedule. There're two other fights in two days' time at The Rokk that were to have been his. And Sarkkhan and I . . ." He evoked the nursery owner's name, for Likkarn and Sarkkhan had a strong bond of friendship. He'd fix it up with Sarkkhan later.

"I like you no better than you like me, *Master* Jakkin," Likkarn replied. "But if Sarkkhan wants it, I'll do it. I like your dragon. She's smart, and she's got heart and fire. Maybe we can get her ready, and—with a lucky draw—she'll do. But the Majors are a lot different from the Minors. Even a dexad could lose there, lose badly."

"I know the Majors. I was just there. I ran S'Blood, and he won."

"He lost his life. Some win!" Likkarn spat on the ground.

It was no more than the plain truth, and Jakkin wondered again if he might have saved S'Blood. Not from the Stews . . . He knew that. Sarkkhan was right about the awful slow death by strangulation. But could he have saved S'Blood from being hamstrung in the first place? Had he been so concerned with finishing quickly so he could get out onto the streets and find Akki that he had overlooked the dragon's strengths and weaknesses? He didn't dare do that to Heart's Blood.

Likkarn noted his hesitation and rubbed his fingers together.

"Regrets fill no bag," he said. "But remember this: Never let a bigger dragon back you into a wall. Never. That should be rule number one.''

"It worked well until—"

"Bah! Every disaster starts, 'It worked well until . . .' '' Likkarn said, his voice a cruel parody of Jakkin's. "But if you listen to me, we'll get your red in shape. I've had a lifetime with the dragons, and that's more than three times what you've got, boy.''

Suddenly Jakkin heard again, "Ask questions, but keep your own counsel.'' Twice he had been so cautioned. He would try it. "What would *you* do?'' he asked, being careful to keep the bite from his voice.

The old trainer looked at him intently. "Watch and I'll show you,'' he said.

Jakkin forced his face into a smile and preceded Likkarn into the barn.

They worked for several hours with the wands and dummy until both men were sweating. Heart's Blood, though, was as cool at the end as she had been at the beginning. Jakkin, tuned to her internal rhythms, could hear no major changes in them.

Likkarn slumped for a moment against the wall. "She's fit, that worm,'' he said at last, speaking in short gasps. "Egg laying seems to agree with her. A fine fighter, fine brood hen. You chose well when you took her.''

"It was luck,'' said Jakkin, trying his best not to argue with the old trainer.

"It was *not* luck. Bonder's luck is all bad. That I know. It was talent. You have it. I have it. Luck is something else. Don't confuse them.''

Jakkin didn't answer. It was a stupid thing to be arguing about, whether he agreed or disagreed. It was dinner-table fighting, so Jakkin said nothing. The silence became a challenge between them that lasted through lunch and well into the afternoon.

Jakkin watched as Likkarn evaded the slash of the dragon's claws. In training sessions dragons always sheathed the lanceae, but the hard sheathing could still deal a sizable bruise. Only once did Heart's Blood catch Likkarn with her sheathed claw. The bruise appeared almost instantly on his upper arm—he disdained wearing the top of his trainer's whites as if to show off his stringy muscles and the medallions of a life with dragons. That bruise joined a series of other older, fading bruises that sat next to the blood scores on his back and chest and arm. Likkarn had nothing else than these blood scores and bruises to show for his lifetime with dragons. One way or another, Austarians bore the marks of their lives on their bodies.

Picking up Jakkin's musings, the dragon turned her head toward him, and Likkarn sprang forward with the wands, tapping her on the neck. She bit at the slender, flexible sticks, but he snapped them away too quickly.

"You were distracted," Likkarn called out to him, "and that distracted her. When she's fighting, you must concentrate, too."

He handed the wands to Jakkin.

Jakkin settled the wands into their holsters, spun around, and attacked Heart's Blood with renewed vigor, but the dragon, so tuned to his thoughts, had no trouble avoiding most of his thrusts. Three times the metal tips scraped across her hard chest links, and once he almost managed to touch her beneath the chin. All in all, his performance was embarrassing since Likkarn had managed at least three touches on her neck.

"You have talent as a trainer," Likkarn said as Jakkin flopped down beside him on the sandy floor. "That's no secret. But you don't use it yet. You have youth and speed—and so does your worm. But I've got the years. Touching dragons in practice takes timing—and some trickery. Mostly it takes shielding your thoughts. In the Pit it's the same. You must teach your worm what you yourself also must learn—not to broadcast to her opponent."

Jakkin, still catching his breath, nodded his answer.

"She's more than ready for her first Major. Will you be ready to return to The Rokk?"

Jakkin wondered for a minute if Likkarn could read *his* mind, for he had been wondering the same thing himself. He was both anticipating and dreading the trip. He wanted Heart's Blood to fight, but he was afraid of endangering her. He wanted to find Akki, but he didn't want to compromise her with the rebels. It was almost as if doing nothing would be best. Danger to himself he considered an acceptable risk, but putting either Heart's Blood or Akki in danger— those were things that worried him now. The problem with waiting games was that they left a person too much time for thinking, and he didn't need Henkky or Golden or Sarkkhan or Likkarn to advise him about that.

"I'll be ready," Jakkin said at last.

# *15*

DESPITE HIS MISGIVINGS, Jakkin was pleased that Likkarn worked hard and without complaint. Only once did their tempers fly, and it had been Jakkin's fault entirely. He'd let his attention wander once again, rehearsing what he'd say to Akki when he saw her, and the dragon had grown distracted as well. It was at a moment when Likkarn was charging her with the wands, and he drew blood from her nose.

Though mute, the dragon could scream mentally, and Jakkin's head rang with pain. He turned furiously on Likkarn.

"What are you doing?" he shouted.

Likkarn stood his ground. "Ask yourself that."

A touch from the dragon's mind recalled him, and Jakkin realized his mistake. He half bobbed his head, as if a bonder to a master, and Likkarn, mollified, turned back to the session.

After that, both Jakkin and Heart's Blood responded well. She moved with grace as he called out her gaits to her. Touch and feint, wing-back and hind-foot rise—it was a dance of controlled power that Likkarn could only applaud.

"She's a rare beauty," he said, leaning back against the fence, watching, his fingers unconsciously rolling an invisible weed, as if the fingers had a memory of their own.

"A rare beauty indeed," echoed Sarkkhan, coming through the gateway to watch.

Jakkin was relieved that Sarkkhan said nothing more. He didn't want Likkarn to know that he'd lied about Sarkkhan's orders. Lying—which was fast becoming a necessity in the game of rebellion—made him uneasy, fitting him as badly as did the waiting, as did the master's role.

But as though to confound his sense of right and wrong further, Sarkkhan simply assumed Heart's Blood was to take the dead brown's place at the Majors, making the lie true. Truth and untruth suddenly seemed as mirrored as the windows of The Rokk.

~

ALL THE WAY back to the capital city, Jakkin repeated Likkarn's rules of fighting in his head: "Never fight with your back to the wall" had been the first. Then there was "Never show all your tricks at once." And "The most useful trick of all is surprise."

Likkarn had offered these rules as if they were treasures uncovered after long digging, which, Jakkin mused, in a way they were. But the most important thing Likkarn had said had been as an afterthought the last morning, when the two of them had slumped together, resting from a two-hour session, while Heart's Blood groomed herself in the center of the ring.

"You have to be one move ahead of your own dragon and two ahead of your dragon's foe."

Jakkin wondered why that particular bit of wisdom should have hit him with such force. After all, Heart's Blood was already a dexad, and he had carried her through all those fights by himself and all through the first year of training without any help from Likkarn. In fact, for most of the training year Likkarn had been his enemy, spying on him, reporting his movements to Sarkkhan. But despite his distrust of the old trainer, Jakkin knew that Likkarn had a lot to teach him. "Watch your foe," Likkarn had said, meaning the opponent in the Pit, "and learn from him." It applied to Likkarn as well.

But it also applied to the rebels—and to Golden. That was why, Jakkin was sure, the warning had struck him so forcefully. In many ways he was Golden's dragon, being used against the rebels. Golden seemed to be at least one move ahead of him all the time. Golden alone knew what this was all about, which side was which. All Jakkin could see was a future of danger and blood.

The truck, under Sarkkhan's capable handling, made fast time, and they were in the city well before night. Jakkin refused to leave Heart's Blood alone, even for dinner, so the nursery owner went out alone. He promised to return with word of Akki, but he returned without any word at all. Golden's house had been dark, and no one had answered Sarkkhan's knock.

"We don't dare make trouble on our own," Jakkin cautioned him, masking his own bitter frustration. "We don't know where to start."

"I'm going to start at the Pit," Sarkkhan said. "I'm going to start by asking questions."

Remembering Golden's warning about Sarkkhan, Jakkin begged, "Please don't say anything. At least don't mention Akki by name. It could endanger her further."

"Fewmets, boy! We don't even know if she's alive. The last word we had of her was more than a week ago." Sarkkhan slammed his fist against the wall.

"He promised he'd let us know," Jakkin said. He'd been half expecting some word as he bedded Heart's Blood down; it had been one of the reasons he'd remained in the stall. Since he couldn't find his way back to Henkky's baggery and there was no contacting Golden, he tried to convince himself that the lack of news was a good sign. But as the night wore on, his thoughts grew wilder. The dragon felt them and slept poorly. They all had a bad night of it.

~

IN THE MORNING Heart's Blood was in the second fight, with a pit-wise female named Cat's Cradle. Her way of fighting was as complex as the string game after which she was named. She streaked back and forth across the Pit, trying to confuse her challenger with improbable moves. It was evidently a maneuver that had won her a number of fights before, since no dragon in a Major Pit was a regular loser. But Jakkin held Heart's Blood steady, and they let Cat's Cradle tire herself out early.

Then, on one of the Cat's streaking runs across the Pit, Heart's Blood suddenly snaked out a claw while simultaneously flying up a few feet over the Pit. It was a dangerous move because it put her off balance, but the surprise outweighed the danger. Cat's Cradle, already committed to the run, couldn't shift position fast enough. Heart's Blood snagged her tail and flipped the yellow dragon over on her back as easily as a marsh lizard turns a hundred-footer. The throat slashes came within five minutes of the fight's start, without a drop of blood more.

The crowd, cheated of a long, bloody fight, did little betting and actually grumbled as they left the Pit for the food stalls and the pay-offs. One man in a starship jacket shouted at Jakkin and waved his fist.

"Not a good fight, that," Sarkkhan said when he met Jakkin at Pitside.

"She won," Jakkin answered shortly.

"Winning isn't all," Sarkkhan said.

"Her back was never to the wall. She gave none of her tricks away. She surprised everyone. And most important, she wasn't hurt. Not a scratch."

Sarkkhan shook his head. "You should have prolonged it. Let the yellow get up again and let Heart's Blood knock her down a bit. Drawn some blood. That's what the crowd wants, even though it was obvious that Heart's Blood outclassed her. But the punters wanted to hear the Cat roar. Without a roar, they had no reason to put up more gold."

Jakkin's hands went up in frustration. "But Heart's Blood has no roar. She's a mute. And *you* bred her that way. Why complain that the other dragon was silent, too?"

Sarkkhan's meaty hands slapped Jakkin's away. "Think, boy, think! If neither dragon roars, then being a mute is no advantage. And that's what dragon fighting is all about—advantage and betting."

"I'm not a boy, and dragon fighting is about life and death."

Sarkkhan laughed. "Tell me about it, you who know so much. If it were about life and death, there'd be no more dragons left in the world. No, Jakkin, it's about money. And advantage. And blood lust. All ways of saying *power*. But what does a boy know about that?" He turned and walked away, saying over his shoulder, "I'll collect our gold and meet you below."

Jakkin's hands had made fists, but he willed them to uncurl. "He's wrong, you know. You are a man." The fluting voice came from behind.

"Golden!" Jakkin cried, and turned.

The senator stood with one arm around a starship trooper and one around a smudge-eyed girl. He spoke to his companions. "You can tell he's a man by his wide shoulders and his big mouth."

They laughed, the girl with a high giggle and the trooper with a kind of drunken bark, but Jakkin took the words "big mouth" as a warning.

"How's your head, Master Jakkin?" Golden asked.

"My head?"

"A doctor friend of mind told me she had to bandage you up last week." He smiled.

"Oh, that." Jakkin's hand went up to his forehead. "A dark alley . . ." he began. "Nothing serious."

Golden smiled. "Then you'll probably be celebrating your *win* tonight?"

Feeling his heart pound loudly, Jakkin spoke carefully. "I'll probably make the round of the stewbars. Do you know any good ones?"

The girl giggled again, and Golden ignored her. "The *good* ones are no fun. You want something down and dirty. A little dangerous even."

Jakkin nodded.

"What do you say, Lieutenant?" Golden addressed the trooper.

The trooper shrugged. "What about Blood Scores? Me and my mates broke that one up once."

"Excellent choice. And maybe after that, the Hideout."

"Oh, Golden, don't send him there," the girl said with a simper. "It's full of—you-knows."

"Rumor, my dear. You-knows are everywhere." Golden opened both arms wide, then closed them on his companions, turning them both. "The next fight is about to commence. Shall we?"

Jakkin raced down to the stall, where he found Sarkkhan stacking another bale of wort in front of Heart's Blood. Her afterfight hunger was already beginning.

"Where were you?" Sarkkhan asked.

"Let's celebrate," Jakkin said. "I'll prove to you I'm a man, not a boy. We'll go through the stewbars, and if we find some lizard lumps called rebels, we'll take them on."

Sarkkhan's eyes showed a spark of interest. "We'll shake Akki's name out of them. The two of us." He slammed one meaty fist into the other.

Then they bedded down the dragon and went out into the warm afternoon.

# 16

BLOOD SCORES WAS one long room with flickering lanterns that illuminated the ill-assorted tables and chairs. The bar itself was made of white dragon bone, fancifully shaped. It looked as if it had been in place the better part of a century. Carved into it were initials and dates. Jakkin saw that one was KK373/'23: some convict's number and year. He shook his head and thought that the room hadn't been cleaned since that time either, smelling worse than a dragon's stall, all sour sweat and old fermentations.

"Why did you want to come here?" Sarkkhan asked, looking around.

"I heard someone at the Pit say it was . . . down and dirty and full of rebels."

"Down and dirty all right," Sarkkhan said. "But these stewers are too far gone to be rebels. Their brains are all scrambled. Look."

There were only half a dozen old men in the stewbar, most sleeping noisily. Two who were still awake were arguing in hoarse whispers.

Sarkkhan chose a corner table and sat with his back against the wall, watching the scene. Jakkin sat next to him, imitating his caution. At last the steward came over and asked what they wanted, his tone implying that they were an intrusion on his valuable time.

"Earth shot," Sarkkhan said. "And give him a glass of chikkar." He dumped two gold pieces onto the tabletop, and the steward swept them with a practiced flourish into the pocket of his leather apron. He returned with a small glass of golden liquor for Sarkkhan and a large glass of sweet-smelling fruit wine, which he set in front of Jakkin.

Sarkkhan raised the tiny glass. "Here's fire in your veins," he

said. "This stuff is as hot as dragon's blood and twice as expensive."
He laughed. "It could almost keep you warm during Dark After—
but I wouldn't count on it." He drained his glass and set it down on
the table with a sharp rap.

Jakkin sipped the chikkar. He liked the soft furry taste. The drink
made his tongue feel strange, as if it had lost its ability to move
quickly, as if it had filled up the entire cavern of his mouth. He
laughed silently at his own fancies. After a moment the furry sensation
disappeared from his mouth and traveled like a flash of lightning up
to the base of his skull. It exploded there, tickling his brain, making
him laugh out loud. Suddenly he remembered what bonders called
chikkar—giggle juice. It never made you really drunk, just happy. A
good choice for his travels with Sarkkhan through the stewbars, he
thought. They had another round.

Sarkkhan got up abruptly just as Jakkin finished his drink. "This
place is too quiet. And it stinks. Let's go."

Jakkin rose and went after him, surprised to find that the light
outside was already beginning to fade. They had been in the bar far
longer than he realized. The chikkar had skewed his sense of time.

They turned left into the darker maze, glanced at the overhead
ramps, where a couple of girls ran, laughing. Jakkin had a sudden
attack of vertigo. He slumped against a wall.

"Not much of a drinker, is he?" a man asked.

Sarkkhan grunted and pulled Jakkin to his feet. "Where to now,
boy?"

"The Hideout," Jakkin mumbled. "There should be rebels
enough there."

Sarkkhan grabbed a passerby by the arm. "Do you know a place
called Hideout?"

The man was dark-skinned, an offworlder, with hands stained a
peculiar blue, marking him as a rocket jockey, a maintenance worker
on one of the starships.

"Just off ship, mate. Can't help you," he said pleasantly, slipping
the noose of Sarkkhan's grip.

Sarkkhan shrugged his thanks and grabbed another man. "The
Hideout. Do you know where it is?"

The man nodded. He pointed vaguely toward a square two blocks
away. "See that four corners? It's on one of the sides, I forget which.
But be careful. It's a rough go, the Hideout."

"Thanks, but we can take care of ourselves," said Sarkkhan.

Jakkin added, "We're a match for anyone." He smiled.

The man shrugged and left.

Sarkkhan walked on, and Jakkin shook his head, cleared it of the chikkar-induced fog, and caught up quickly. They matched stride for stride, silently, until they came to the square. On the west side was a dim storefront with a grimy sign above the door announcing the Hideout.

"There it is," Sarkkhan said.

They crossed the square and peered through the mirrored glass window. Jakkin could just make out a knot of men standing near the door and a darker clutch of bodies around what must have been the bar.

"Popular," he said to Sarkkhan.

Sarkkhan found a spot on the glass where the silvered surface was eroded and looked in. "Pickings here!" he said. "If we don't find one or two rebels in *that* crowd, you can slap me with a prod. Let's see what we can stir up."

He turned quickly into the doorway and shoved his way through to the bar. It was obvious he was looking for a fight. Afraid to lose him, Jakkin followed in his wake.

This bar was also of bone, deeply carved. The letters and numbers were grained with dirt. What caught Jakkin's eye, though, was the strange light-colored hide hung to one side of a mirror. It was as pale as a young dragon's skin, and pocked with colored circles—red, blue, green, and brown. At first Jakkin thought it was some kind of map or a counting device for unlettered Austarians. In the nursery they used knotted strings for totting up supplies.

Jakkin was still staring when a voice said, "What'll you have, son?"

Jakkin started. The steward was a tan-skinned man with greying hair and a mustache that trailed along the sides of his mouth like two parentheses.

"Have?"

"To drink. This is a bar, you know."

"Chikkar, I guess," Jakkin said, running his hand through his hair. Beside him Sarkkhan was talking to a rough-looking man.

Next to Jakkin a man not much older than he laughed. "Chikkar—that's a *boy's* drink."

"We don't make that distinction here," said the steward. "See that?" He pointed to the skinmap that Jakkin had puzzled about. "That's a man's hide, the back of one of the first KKers here. The blue dots, those meant he killed someone. The red, he was a thief as well. The green was for crimes against the state—politics or treason or maybe just writing down something the home world didn't like."

"And the brown?" Jakkin asked.

"No reprieve. Not that any was ever given. They say the branding was done under hospital conditions so it didn't hurt. Didn't hurt—what did *they* know? Once a man was branded, it was for life. The only way those brands came off was that way." He gestured over his shoulder at the hide. "Skinned. After death."

Jakkin found he couldn't keep his eyes off the skin.

"That one," the steward said, jerking his head toward the hide, "was a man. Not because he could meet a bond price but because of what he had to endure here."

Sarkkhan shifted in his seat and spoke loudly. "You sound like one of those beslimed rebels."

"No, sir. I'm an Austarian and proud of it. But a man is a man. I make no distinctions here." The steward looked at Jakkin. "I'll get you that chikkar now."

When it arrived, in a glass with a slight nick on the rim, Jakkin found he no longer wanted it. Sipping it as slowly as he dared, he stared up at the hide. He felt as if the brands had been burned into his retinas. His hand went first to the dimple in his cheek, then down to the bag lumping beneath his shirt. He took another sip of the chikkar and sighed. Looking around, he wondered: *How do you tell a rebel?* Was that man, the yellow-haired, sallow-skinned, pockmarked one downing glass after glass in frenzied animation, a rebel? Or the man sitting morosely in the corner, red tears leaking from his weed-coarsened eyes? Or the man, eyelids blackened with some sort of paint, talking to Sarkkhan? Was he? The man pulled at a ring in his ear and laughed, but did that make him a rebel? Or a Federationist? They were just men, after all, like the ones home at the nursery, arguing about dragons and starships and politics.

Jakkin got up. They wouldn't find Akki this way. He tapped Sarkkhan on the shoulder. "Can we go?"

"Go if you want, Jakkin," the nursery owner said, not even bothering to look around. "But this lizard brain needs straightening out." He gestured to the man next to him. "He seems to think that Bankkar's Mousekin could have beaten my Blood Bath in his heyday." He continued haranguing the man about the virtues of his first and mightiest fighting dragon while the man responded by laughing and pulling again on the ring in his earlobe. They argued, more or less good-naturedly, without really listening to each other.

Jakkin guessed it would be another hour at least before Sarkkhan would be done, all thoughts of the rebels gone. No rebel sent by Golden could possibly find him in this crowded place, Jakkin thought.

He'd have a better chance outside. Since Sarkkhan would not follow, it might be just the time to go.

Slipping through the tangle of men at the door, Jakkin went out into the gathering dark.

~

HE MEANT TO keep an eye on the turnings so that he could make his way back to the Hideout, but his attention was caught instead by the grimness of the streets. In the flickering half-light of the bars, the alleyways took on a grey and shadowed sameness that was broken only by an occasional man or woman staggering by.

Jakkin walked very slowly, hoping to be stopped by Golden's messenger, but no one seemed interested in him at all. Used to the open, clear desert air and the cleansing action of the wind-whipped sands, he was profoundly depressed by The Rokk. It was closed in, ugly, fetid, grey.

As he walked on, he saw men and women crouched in alleyways, sipping on bottles and passing them on to their companions. They didn't speak but rather signed to one another as if speech—the prerogative of higher animals—had been denied them.

To slow his progress, Jakkin straggled into a number of the bars along the street; Pit Stop, Thieves' Den, Kelley's were three he remembered. Each time he ordered a chikkar and drank a sip or two before the close, dark, dingy quarters made him nervous enough to leave. Then it was back to the streets, which were even worse.

He kept turning around, trying to catch someone following him. Once or twice he thought he saw the furtive movement of a man slipping quickly into an alleyway. And several times he recognized faces in the stewbars of men he had seen along the way. But whether it was coincidence or not, he couldn't say. And if he heard a rebel argument in any of the bars, after hours of listening to stories of Pit fights, a dozen new Ferkkin jokes, and the recommendations of a dozen different baggeries, he couldn't tell. All of a sudden it seemed a strange, solitary, useless odyssey, and at last he was determined to give it up and make his way to the Hideout and find Sarkkhan. They'd go to Golden's house together, break in if they had to, and find out what they needed to know. Jakkin had had enough games, enough waiting. It was time for him to act—act like a man.

He paid for the chikkar with his last coin and, without a backward glance at the stewbar, went out. Trying to remember the way back to the Hideout, he recalled Sarkkhan's instructions to orient himself by the light of the Pit dome. But he must have made a wrong turning, for he suddenly found himself on a black street that seemed narrower than the rest, an alley really, without doors. It was a dead end, and he realized his mistake at once. He was starting to turn back when he heard a noise behind him. Spinning around quickly and remembering too late Likkarn's warning about being backed into a wall, he saw a dark figure coming slowly toward him.

"What—what do you want?" he asked breathlessly, his hand going to his pocket for the baling knife he kept there. He had no more money, so he wasn't afraid of being robbed. And he certainly didn't intend to get beaten up. He'd try to give as good as he got. "What do you want?"

The alley was suddenly hot and close. Jakkin found he was having trouble breathing. He had to admit he was scared. Except for good-natured wrestling with his bondmates and an occasional slap from Likkarn, he'd never really been in a fight.

The figure hulked closer, a big man walking with a kind of shuffling gait. From his mouth came a single bubbling word. "Golden."

"Oh," Jakkin said, suddenly relaxing, "you're the one."

The man began speaking in that same hesitating gurgle. "Be careful. The bar, the rebel hideout." He moved forward, hand outstretched, and then, as gracelessly as a marionette whose strings are suddenly cut, he fell heavily to his knees and then onto his face.

Jakkin knelt and turned him over. The man had a strange, surprised expression on his face. His eyes were open and staring. The lids finally closed once, then opened again.

"Help . . . for . . ." he said suddenly quite clearly, and touched his bondbag with a trembling hand. Then, with a hissing sigh, he closed his eyes again, his face surprisingly peaceful.

Jakkin felt for a pulse, and there was none. He knew, all at once, that the man was dead, and he moved back, scrambling away crablike from the body. He felt hot and cold at once; sweat beaded his forehead and the back of his neck. Flexing his fingers, he felt an irresistible urge to wipe his hands on his pants, for his fingers felt stained with the unknown man's death. The only other time he'd touched a dead person had been when his father had been killed by the feral dragon and he'd helped his mother bury the body. For days after he'd wakened in the night, crying that his hands hurt. For months he'd washed his hands as often as he could. He had that same soiled, burning feeling in his hands now.

After jumping up, Jakkin edged around the body and out of the alley. Coming into the lighter street, he tried to catch his breath. All the giggle juice seemed to have evaporated, leaving him with an over-powering feeling of exhaustion. Rubbing his sweaty palms on his shirt, he began to walk, following the beacon light of the dome down the road.

He knew he had to find someone and report what had happened. And then he realized, with a sudden revelation, that he didn't really know what this was all about. Who was the man? Had he been sent by Golden? If so, then Golden should be informed. But Golden had indicated that the rebels weren't violent, at least not yet. Dr. Henkky said that Golden wasn't to be trusted, that he used people and then threw them away. The man back there had been used—and now was thrown away in a dark alley, his life ended with a cryptic message.

Jakkin felt himself reasoning everything out slowly, but nothing was clear. He stopped walking for a minute and thought about Golden and Henkky. They were the only two people he knew who lived in The Rokk, but he didn't know if he trusted either one of them. And he certainly didn't know how to find them. The only person to turn to was Sarkkhan, and that meant finding the Hideout again.

~

IT TOOK AN hour of careful doubling back. He asked three men, and only one had known the streets well enough to help him; but at last he found the square where the stewbar squatted on the west side. The window was still smeared with Sarkkhan's handprint. The crowds were gone. Jakkin pushed through the heavy door and stumbled in.

# 17

SARKKHAN WAS GONE as well.

After walking up to the bar, Jakkin set his hand on the top, feeling the group of letters under his hand. He traced them with weary, grimy fingers: "Fewmets Ferkkin, '47."

"My friend—the big red-bearded man. The dragon master. He was drinking here when I left. Do you know where he is?"

The steward smiled, and the mustache parentheses widened. "You mean Sarkkhan?"

Jakkin nodded.

"He's long gone, still arguing and boasting. Almost came to blows with his friend. Then he bought a round for the bar and made everyone toast his nursery, his dragons, and his daughter."

Jakkin suddenly felt his knees give. He sat down.

"You look as if you need a drink," the steward said.

Shaking his head, Jakkin tried to speak, found he couldn't, then tried again, and this time his voice worked. "Out there," he said. "A dead man."

The steward drew up close to him and looked at him intently. "Dead—or drunk?"

"Dead."

"It happens," the steward said, his voice curiously without inflection. "I'll get you that drink now. You'll need it. Then we'll think what to do about your dead man. It was chikkar, I believe."

"You remembered? But I had only one, and there were so many others here." Jakkin was amazed.

"Memory is my business," the steward said.

Jakkin touched his pockets. "I'm sorry. I can't have that drink. I'm flat."

The steward smiled suddenly. "Not even a grave coin."

Without thinking, Jakkin put his hand over his shirt where the bag lumped. "How did you know?"

Laughing, the steward said, "I'm an old hand at spotting bags."

"Another part of your business," Jakkin said.

"Not that it matters here."

"I'm not a bonder, though," Jakkin said quickly. "I'm a master. I own a dragon."

"So you do," the steward answered. He wiped a spot on the bar that was yellow with the stains of spilled drinks and age.

"I am. I do." Jakkin's voice grew unaccountably insistent.

"So your friend said. 'Tell Jakkin Stewart I've gone back to the stalls,' he said. 'A big, handsome boy with a slow smile and a shy manner.' That's what he said as a way of identification."

"The stalls!" Jakkin said. "I've got to go."

"He told me your dragon's name, too. Heart's Blood, isn't it?"

"You're *good* at your memory business," Jakkin said.

"That I am," the steward said softly, wiping the bar and setting the glass of chikkar in front of Jakkin.

"But I told you. I can't pay. And I've got to find Sarkkhan." Jakkin's hand left the bag.

"It's on me," said the steward, "because I want to know things. For example, I want to know about your dead man."

Jakkin suddenly felt cold again. "Not mine. Just a man who— who stumbled against me in an alley and fell down. Dead."

"Just like that?" asked the steward. "Without a word?"

"Just like that," Jakkin said, refusing to speak the dead man's words to the steward.

"What was he wearing?"

Jakkin closed his eyes and tried to remember. Only the feel of death returned. "I don't know."

The steward waited patiently. "What alley was it?"

Jakkin ran a finger along the bar top as if trying to pull out the memory. "I don't know. No, wait. The street was very narrow. And black. Blacker than the rest."

"Dead end then," said the steward.

"Yes, now I remember. It *was* a dead end. And it was near some other bars."

"Gold Dust? Bag's End? KKs? Blood Scores? Thieves' Den? Bailout?" the steward offered.

Jakkin put his hand to his forehead. "Yes. Thieves' Den, I think."

"Then I think I've got it," said the steward. "Don't worry. I'll tell the *proper* authorities. In fact, a few of them will be here soon. So wait. Drink your chikkar. There'll be time to find Sarkkhan." He smiled and wiped at the stain on the bar once again. "You know," he said slowly, "there are other things I want to know as well."

Jakkin looked up, the weight of the dead man off him now. "Like what?"

"Like you're a master, yet you wear a bag. You should be rich, but you're flat. You've never seen a skin before, yet you care about the scores. Son, I'm a very curious man, and I'll buy your answers with that drink."

Jakkin looked down into the glass. The scent of the chikkar was inviting, as ripe and as fresh as fruit. He knew it would warm him up. He'd been cold ever since touching the dead man. But he didn't drink it. Golden had mentioned this bar, the Hideout, for some reason. He was suddenly sure of it. And he sensed that his answers to this man were going to make a difference in the game. He wanted nothing to fuzz his tongue and make him giggle. The time for waiting was over.

"I wear a bag," he said, lying yet not lying, "because I don't feel like a man. In this time and in this place I don't feel like a man. When I can feel that I'm master of myself, then . . ." He hesitated, hoping that he'd made sense and wondering if he'd said what was expected.

The steward stared at him with eyes that were almost as dark and unfathomable as a dragon's. He ran his fingers along his mustache, the punctuation around his mouth. Then, as if he'd suddenly made up his mind about something, he leaned forward and whispered, "And then you'll take off the bag?"

Jakkin forced himself to nod.

The steward smiled. "Drink up, son."

*I've won*, Jakkin thought. *I've convinced this steward and won. Won . . . something.* He wasn't quite sure what, but in honor of his first small victory in the game, he sipped the chikkar, letting it explode softly at the base of his neck. He didn't think about the dead man or about Sarkkhan waiting for him at the Pit. He didn't try to guess who the *proper* authorities might be. He kept his eyes away from the skin hanging over the bar and concentrated instead on a quiet ebb and flow of the red ocean in his head. Although he was much too far from the Pit for a proper sending from Heart's Blood, he knew that red ocean was what she sounded like in sleep. And he felt—no, he *knew*—that he was finally close to finding Akki.

# *18*

JAKKIN HAD NO idea how much time had passed. The bar was empty except for the steward. While Jakkin sat, content to let the chikkar mildly tickle him, the steward had been busy sliding the woven reed shades down over the windows, blocking out the street. He locked the door. Jakkin took all this in but pretended not to. In his mind he heard Likkarn's voice, repeating once again, "Never show all your tricks in any one fight."

There was a sudden flurry of knocks on a back door that resolved themselves into a complicated pattern.

"Here they are now," the steward said. He left the bar and went into the back room, emerging with a blond man whose beard was carefully trimmed.

Immediately after the blond came a man about Jakkin's age whose bonder suit was belted with a lizard-skin lanyard. Both men wore bondbags ostentatiously outside their clothes. The bags were flat.

Before Jakkin could be introduced to them, there was another knock. The older man went back into the room and emerged leading a young woman who was scowling. Her white trainer's suit was stained at the knees. Long dark hair framed her face. Behind her came another tall young man who looked a lot like the first, except for the fact that he was beltless. He pushed the woman while the bearded man pulled.

"You needn't pull so hard. I'm not planning to run away," she said.

At her voice Jakkin felt his heart stutter. He bit his lip to keep from grinning foolishly and rose to greet her.

She saw him then and fear suddenly filled her eyes. She said quickly, "Another *new* one." There was a harshness in her voice that Jakkin had never heard before, and she had lost weight. Her hair was tangled and there was a smudge on one cheek, but she was still beautiful.

Smiling crookedly, she said, "Men don't believe in introductions. I'm Four." She held out her hand. Then she added, a note of sarcasm in her voice, "Currently not in very good standing, though no one has told me why."

Jakkin took her hand, remembering the softness of Bekka's. *React*, Dr. Henkky had warned him, so he squeezed her hand and, though he wanted to hold it longer, dropped it instead and smiled a stranger's smile at her. "I'm . . ."

"No names," she said quickly. "We're only numbers here."

"I have no number," Jakkin said, glancing over at the steward. "And *he* already knows my name."

The blond man moved forward with an angry gesture and pulled at the chain around Akki's neck. The bag, which had been tucked in her shirt, slipped out.

"Show your bag," he said, "or have you become too grand?"

She touched the bag briefly with her first two fingers, almost a prayer, then asked, "Where's Three?"

"I haven't seen him all day." The blond-bearded man's voice was rough, angry. "We were to meet earlier, then separate, then come here, and he never showed up. He knew what would happen if he was late again. Now I guess we'll have to take action. He wasn't too bright, Three, though he was loyal. But if we don't have discipline, we have nothing." He looked meaningfully at Akki, then spoke to the steward again. "Which is why I protest that you *dared* bring an unnumbered one to this meeting." His chin pointed at Jakkin, but his words flew directly into the steward's face.

The steward smiled, rubbing his right hand over his mustache. "He's here because he's someone you all should meet. He's the answer to a particular problem we've been having. And if Three doesn't show up, we can slot this one as Provisional Three."

"What makes you think that Three won't come?" Akki asked.

"Call it a hunch," said the steward slowly.

Jakkin suddenly felt cold and controlled a shiver.

Akki touched her bag again. "Well, we don't need a provo. I vote we get him out of here before he learns too much."

The beltless man laughed. "Your vote is pretty worthless these days, girl. And as for his learning too much . . . well, it's too late for that."

"Besides," the steward said, insinuating himself into the conversation, "he has information you might find interesting. An hour ago this young *master* stumbled onto a body near Thieves' Den, a special place of Three's."

"You know too much," said Beltless nervously.

The steward laughed. "Have you forgotten? The leader of a cell has to know everything about his people: their names, their backgrounds, their secret vices. But his people must know nothing about one another. It's the only system of checks and balances we have."

Beltless bit his lip and was silent.

"We have our cause and our loyalty to it," the blond reminded them.

"We may not all share the same loyalties," the steward answered blandly. "But we all do share the same risks. And when anyone's loyalty has been called into question, more risk is asked." He leaned his arms on the bar and smiled. "You, Two, and you, Five, go out the back way and find the dead-end street near Thieves' Den. Be careful. If you find the body, you'll know what to do."

"Cell," Jakkin whispered to himself as the two younger men got up. His voice was louder than he had intended.

"Tell him nothing," Yellow Beard cautioned.

The steward smiled again, and for the first time Jakkin noticed that he smiled only with his mouth. "I'll tell him what I think he should know. That's my privilege as cell leader. Afterward we'll *all* decide whether to keep him with us or not, though I think he can be turned. In fact, I think he's turned already. What do you notice about him?"

Akki answered quickly, "His bag."

Yellow Beard added reluctantly, "And it's empty."

"Yet he's a master," the steward pointed out. "Strange, isn't it? A master who wears a bondbag."

"He could be a plant," Yellow Beard said. "A spy."

The steward said, slyly, "He's still a boy really. Too young for a spy, his head stuffed with dragons and with dreams. And he's full of a boy's passions. Did you see how his eyes lit up when Four walked in? He probably holds pretty girls in high regard and thinks bravery and honor, might and right, automatically go hand in hand. Am I correct, son?"

Jakkin hung his head, saying nothing. He'd give them a *surprise*, a Likkarn surprise. He would act the boy, the farm clod, even in front of Akki. Then, when the right moment came, he would grab her and they'd escape back to the safety of the nursery.

"There," said the steward. "What spy could have resisted that moment to tell us all about himself, to give us a rehearsed speech about his awkward, angry, subsistence childhood? The beastliness of the masters and a life of unending drudgery? But this one blushes. Quite a spy, eh? Here, son, have another chikkar, and I'll tell you all about rebel cells." He poured a glass.

Jakkin wrapped his hand around the glass and looked up at the steward, willing innocence into his face.

Sitting, the steward began to speak with a quiet authority that reminded Jakkin of Golden. "Son, once the scum of the earth—the thieves, the murderers, the rapists, the muggers—were stuck away in small, overcrowded rooms called cells. And perhaps they deserved to be there. I'll not argue that. But when other planets were discovered, these same scum were given a choice—a cell or the stars. Most chose the stars. Instead of a small cell, they were given a cell the size of a world. Many died early deaths on those worlds because these were not the lush, soil-rich, metal-rich colony worlds. No, they were the marginal worlds that no proper star colonist would want. The KK worlds. The criminal lands.

"But not all the forced starfarers died at once. Some few managed to live. And to have children and grandchildren. And we who are the great-great-plus-grandchildren of those KKers, who bear no scores on our bodies but bear the scars on our souls, are still being punished for their sins. Even those we call masters can't leave the planet permanently. We have no starships, so we don't have the stars. We are, in effect, chained here. Paying a tithing to our captors. That is why we rebels choose to stand and fight our Galaxian overlords. The dungeon masters. The universal wardens. Fight them any way we can. Bring down this sick society and build our own world on the ashes of the old."

Jakkin saw Yellow Beard's head nodding, but Akki's mouth was drawn up in a crooked smile that gave no clue to her thoughts.

The steward went on. "To start, we form small cells, units of five with a sixth as leader. We call them cells because we know we're still prisoners. The leader, the trustee, knows the real names of his cellmates, and they know him. But within the cell, the others know one another only by number. We don't allow friendship or fraternization beyond cell business. That way, if anyone is caught by the wardens, he or she knows only numbers, not names. The trustee is known by other trustees as well and will be killed instantly if his cell is uncovered."

"You tell him too much," growled Yellow Beard.

"You worry too much, One." The steward smiled his cold smile again. "I know what I'm doing. Trust me."

One stood and was about to make another complaint when the steward cut him off with a chopping gesture of his hand. "Ask him why he wears his bag. Ask him as I did."

One turned away. "He could have been taught what to say."

Standing, Jakkin thought: *React.* "I wasn't taught to say anything. I fill my bag myself." He looked at the steward, but his words were directed to Akki. "A dragon I was running was put down in the Stews. And I saw men there laugh while it screamed itself to death in my head. I saw girls in the baggeries spending their early beauty for coins. A dying bonder stumbled against me in the street. I have been in bars tonight where men drink away what little freedom they have. And tonight, for the first time, I really heard about my great-great-plus-grandparents, not just bonder jokes and bonder stories. You're right, Steward, though I never saw it before. This world *is* a cell, but none of us need act like prisoners. Not anymore." His voice cracked at the end in a way it hadn't for almost a year. He was surprised at the conviction in his voice and wished he could have said all that to Errikkin. It might have persuaded him.

"All right," One said.

The steward nodded and smiled.

"But what of Three?" Akki asked.

Just then a noise at the back door startled them. The steward motioned for them to sit down and in a fluid movement put two bottles on the table. "If it's wardens, we're just friends in for an after-hours drink. One, put your arm around her."

The yellow-bearded man moved over to Akki and dropped his arm heavily onto her shoulder, effectively pinning her. Jakkin felt his hands make fists but stopped himself from saying anything. The steward brought a vicious-looking knife up from under the bar, concealing it in his sleeve. Then he moved silently to the back, and then his voice rang out. "Fewmets! Signal when you come in. I might have slit you without another thought."

Two and Five entered and sat down while the sound of the steward's locking the door followed them. They each grabbed a bottle and drank silently, quickly.

Then Five, the one without the belt, spoke. "It was Three all right. He was already stiffening. Dead some time. It must have been the wardens. His bag was cut at the bottom, and he had brands on his forehead."

Two added angrily, "They looked like two extra eyes, they did.

All the way to the bone. Worm slime, but it was awful. Five found him right away, though. We didn't have to look too hard.'' He drank another long draft.

"We left him there,'' Five said. "Nothing else we could do for him, and we know the rules.''

"Papers?'' asked the steward.

Five reached into his bag and drew out a card. "Here. It was in his boot heel. That was all.''

The steward put the card into an ashtray and struck a match. The card curled slowly in on itself as it burned. In a minute it was nothing but ash, and the steward poked it with his finger.

"He's nothing. He didn't exist.'' The steward looked around as, one by one, the others nodded. Even Jakkin, though his hands could still feel the man dying beneath them.

Jakkin touched his bondbag and kneaded it slowly. "Which wardens? What do you mean?''

"Police. Constabulary. Whatever you want to call them,'' said the steward.

"Murdering bastards,'' said Five.

"But don't they keep the law? Why would they kill a man?'' Jakkin asked. "What had Three done? If I'm going to be your new Three, I'd better know.''

"Maybe we ought to ask what you've done,'' Five said. "Maybe it was you that killed him.''

Jakkin knew there was no answering that.

"Why would he kill Three?'' asked Akki.

"To take his place with us.''

"But . . . I couldn't kill anyone,'' stuttered Jakkin. When the men laughed, he flushed.

"He's much *too* innocent,'' said One, stroking his yellow beard. "What are you, boy, right off the farm?''

"I've lived in a nursery most of my life, yes,'' Jakkin said, thrusting his chin out. "And what's wrong with that?''

Five spit to one side. "I thought I smelled worm on you.''

Jakkin started to stand, but the steward came over and put his hand on Jakkin's shoulder. Smiling, he said, "He didn't kill Three. That's obvious. His thoughts are printed on his face.'' He touched Jakkin's face, and Jakkin flushed again.

*It must be the chikkar*, he thought.

"He *is* innocent, and that's why he's perfect to replace Three. And he can get into places we can't go.''

"You guessed it was Three who was dead. You'd already planned this out," said Akki.

"That's why I'm the cell leader and you aren't."

Jakkin wanted to ask the steward what places he could get into, but he was afraid he knew. The nursery, the underpit stalls. Dragon places. He remembered that Henkky said the rebels would kill dragons. He kept silent.

"The wardens, son," the steward said, returning to his earlier mode, "they say we are nothing. We are ciphers. KK seven-eight-four-nine—that was my many-times grandfather. A number with a brand on his skin and a bag around his neck that held all he was allowed to carry away from Earth—one ID card and two gold coins. Gold. As if that could have bought him anything on this barren rock. They were like the coins the ancients put on the eyes of dead travelers, and about as useful.

"So we wear our bags and our numbers on our arms now, to show the wardens what we think of them." He rolled up his sleeve and showed Jakkin the number tattooed on the soft skin in the crook of his elbow. "And when they kill us, they slit our bags and burn a hole in our skins to show their contempt in return. And that's how I know you didn't kill Three, because it's clear that the wardens did it."

"But if they're the police . . ." Jakkin said.

"Not just the regular police," Akki put in quickly. "A special police, secret and deadly. Some people say they're really from the Federation."

"I say it," Yellow Beard added. "And I'm not afraid to say it out loud."

"Whatever we call them, *they* are the enemy, son," said the steward. He took the knife from his sleeve and put it back under the bar. "Now, let's make the cell."

The others drew their chairs into a circle, and Jakkin followed their lead. The steward pulled up another chair and sat with them. They sat in order of their numbers; that put Akki—who was number Four—next to Jakkin.

The steward slipped his chair between Jakkin and Two. He took up one of Jakkin's hands. Akki took the other and bowed her head. Jakkin did the same.

The steward began speaking. "I am a man. No one chains me. I am a man. No one brands me. I am a man. I am a man. I fill my bag myself."

They repeated his words three times, with Akki substituting the word "woman." Jakkin found himself chanting along with them. By the third time he could feel the phrases imprinting themselves on his heart. They were good words, strong words, words he already believed in. But the words were not enough to erase the other things in his mind: the violence, the intrigue, the bruises on Akki's arm. The man who had died had been unmarked. When had the wardens marked him? And hadn't Dr. Henkky said that the rebels would destroy the masters if they could? Was that what the steward had meant when he spoke about bringing down Austarian society and rebuilding on its ashes?

Jakkin set his jaw and lifted his face to look over at the steward's bowed head. To his surprise, the steward was watching him through slotted eyes that were cold and without pity.

"Business," the steward said. He stared right at Jakkin and pointedly let go of his hand.

# 19

THEY SPOKE QUICKLY of business matters that Jakkin didn't understand, something about the Galaxian command and the next starship
landings, about trustee meetings and senators leaning. After a while
Jakkin stopped listening and stared at Akki.

He had forgotten the exact shape of her chin that turned her face
into a heart and her funny off-center smile. He was desperate to speak
to her. Smiling, he shaped her name silently. She shook her head
almost imperceptibly and looked down. It didn't matter. He could
wait. He had waited this long already.

"... to Rokk Major," the steward was saying.

Startled, Jakkin turned toward the steward and began to listen
intently.

"And all they have to do," the steward continued, "is carry the
case into the stall area and leave it there for the pickup. She'll watch
him, and we'll watch them both." He smiled his cold smile at Jakkin.

Jakkin shivered involuntarily.

"No one will question a dragon master or the bag-girl he's decided to bring with him for the night."

"I'm not a bag-girl," Akki said.

The steward looked at her as if staring right through her. "No?"

Yellow Beard laughed. "Dressed like one, you might pass, though
you're too skinny for my taste."

The other men laughed with him.

Akki started to speak, but Jakkin interrupted, hoping he sounded
sincere. "I'll do what you want, but I'll do it alone. Leave her out of
this. No one would believe it if I showed up with a girl. And it's too
dangerous for her."

The steward nodded. "A boy's passion," he said. "You'll get over it. And you'll do as I say."

Jakkin looked down. "She's too pretty. I couldn't keep my mind on things."

They all roared, and when he looked up, Akki was glaring at him. He knew he'd have to explain it to her later.

"You'll take her."

Jakkin shrugged. "What's so important about this case anyway?"

"Papers," the steward said quickly. "Secret papers. So secret that if anyone but the right person tries to open the case, it will explode."

"Then why not hand the papers to this right person directly? Save yourself all this . . ." Jakkin gestured.

"No one must know that this right person has any connection with us, any connection with the *lower* levels of Austar society."

Akki gasped. "A Galaxian!"

"I didn't say that," the steward replied. "And you didn't guess it."

Around the circle the men nodded, suddenly privy to a secret. They seemed pleased. The steward ignored them.

"Just give me the case, and tell me where to put it," Jakkin said, hand outstretched.

"You'll leave it in the stall after the fights tomorrow. It will be found by our right person." Suddenly the steward's mouth got hard. "And don't think to turn us in because we *will* be watching you at all times."

"If you can watch him, why not use the watchers to place the case?" asked Akki.

"Because I want him to do it. To prove himself worthy of being a member. And to re-prove your loyalty," said the steward. He stood up, went into the back room, and returned with a small case that looked like a trainer's equipment bag. He set it on the bar and, after taking a key from his pocket, set it in the brass lock and turned it twice around. "Now the explosives are set, and only the person with the other key can open it." He pushed the key into his bondbag and very slowly tucked the bag under his shirt.

Jakkin let out a breath. He hadn't realized he had been holding it.

"Don't let the case out of your sight until the end of the fight." The steward folded his arms across his chest.

"But I can't take it up into the stands while I'm running a dragon or watching the fights," protested Jakkin. "It would look strange.

And security is tight about those things. Ever since the Brokka disaster—"

"I know all about the Brokka disaster. That's why you'll take the girl with you. She'll watch the bag while you watch the fight."

"But . . ." Jakkin began, hoping his protest sounded sincere. If he read the steward correctly, all these protests would solidify the man's resolve to send Akki along. The steward would insist now—and Akki would be free.

"Do as you're told, Provo Three. The girl goes, and that's final."

"I'm not going as a bag-girl," Akki put in.

*Oh Akki*, Jakkin thought, *don't make a mess of things now.*

"I'll go as myself," Akki said.

The steward's head nodded almost imperceptibly.

"Too bad," Five whispered as they left the bar. "I would have liked to see her in a bag-girl dress. Those trainer whites do nothing for her." He said something else in an undertone that the men all found funny, and Jakkin felt himself flushing.

"All right, you two," said the steward. "Take the case and go. But remember, we *will* be watching."

~

THE BACK ALLEY was dark.

"Hold my hand," Jakkin said.

Akki answered, in a peculiar, overloud voice, "Perhaps you'd better call me Akkhina. If we're going to be in public, numbers won't do." She moved her head slightly, and Jakkin heard the door snick shut behind them.

Just in case, he answered, "Then call me Jakkin. If you're coming to the Pit, you'll find that out soon enough."

"*Jakkin,*" she said in a kind of whispery voice he had never heard her use before. She slid her hand in his.

He wondered suddenly at the wisdom of naming themselves aloud. If the others knew their names, they would be . . . "expendable" was the only word that came to mind. Then he realized that the steward already knew them both but that once they left The Rokk, they would be going straight back to the nursery. He'd tell Sarkkhan, and Sarkkhan could tell Golden, and Golden could tell the authorities all about the dead man and the steward and the cell. Everything would be taken care of, and his part, and Akki's, would be over. They could go back to their dragons and forget about politics once again. He squeezed Akki's hand.

In the street Akki took the lead, showing Jakkin a way along the overhead ramps that brought them quickly to the Pit. The guard passed them through, calling after them, "I've got a coin on your red tomorrow."

"It's a safe bet," Jakkin said. "She hardly tired herself today."

"That she didn't," agreed the guard.

"Then put another on her. She's definitely going to win," Jakkin said, adding, "Meet Akki, she's a bag-girl."

The guard raised his eyebrows. "Really!" he said, his tone indicating disbelief.

Akki's elbow slammed into his waist. After they were inside, Akki whispered furiously, "You *don't* introduce bag-girls that way. Besides, in these clothes, I look anything but."

Jakkin smiled. "I think the whites look great on you."

Akki elbowed him again.

Once they had got down into the understall area, Akki held back. "What if my father is here already?" she began. "We have to warn him, and we don't know who the watchers are." She looked around quickly.

"Do you really believe we'll be watched?" Jakkin asked. "I didn't see anyone follow us."

"They didn't *have* to follow," Akki said sensibly. "They knew where we'd be going."

Jakkin turned around. Then he whispered to Akki, "I don't see anyone here except for the trainers and bonders who belong. They couldn't possibly be the ones."

"No?"

Jakkin bit his lip. "I'll go ahead and see if Sarkkhan is here. He told the steward this was where he'd be."

He found no one but Heart's Blood, who greeted him with a full sunburst, rising out of sleep and shaking her massive head. The sending paled into a soft yellow afterglow, then burst again in a portrait of Akki, haloed in gold.

"Yes," Jakkin whispered joyfully, "she's here."

~

THEY SETTLED IN for the night, sharing the heavy downer and clasping hands until they fell asleep. The dragon's contented thrumming helped lull them, and if they were watched while they slept, they didn't know it.

In the middle of the night Jakkin was suddenly awakened roughly. Akki, sitting up next to him, pushed at his shoulder. He sat up sleepily. "What is it?"

She put a finger to his mouth and shook her head. "I don't like it," she whispered.

"Hmmmmm," he murmured against her finger.

"It was too easy, too much of a coincidence that you became part of the very cell I was in without the help of Three. They all were furious with me, suspicious because I wouldn't go on any raids for stingers and other weapons. And I wouldn't have a number tattooed on my arm. I tried to explain that as a doctor I couldn't condone weapons and violence, that as someone who lived in a baggery I didn't dare put a number on my arm. But they didn't believe my excuses. They kept me locked up in a safehouse for a couple of weeks, and I couldn't contact Ardru or anyone. Then suddenly, tonight, on the steward's orders, they brought me to the cell meeting. And you were there. I don't like it. I don't like it at all."

Jakkin whispered back reluctantly, "The steward knew who I was. He knew Sarkkhan, too. By name. He said he had a good memory."

"Not *that* good," she said quietly. Her hands made the same wrangling motion that Sarkkhan's did when he was nervous. "But I don't think he knows that I came from the nursery or that I'm Sarkkhan's daughter. Only you and Golden know that."

"And Sarkkhan," Jakkin said, suddenly remembering the steward's saying Sarkkhan had toasted his daughter. Had he, Jakkin wondered, named her in that toast?

Heart's Blood woke and entered the conversation with a soft murmuration of color, like the ripples in an oasis pool.

"It's all right then," Jakkin whispered. "Let's go back to sleep." There was no point in worrying Akki further. There was nothing they could do now.

Akki shook her head, and her dark hair made a curtain around her face. "I don't know that it's all right, Jakkin."

She reached out and clung to him for a moment, and he wondered what had happened to the strong, willful Akki. What had the rebels done to her to make her so fragile? He could feel the bones in her shoulders. He traced the line from her cheek to her chin with a gentle finger.

"There's something else, too," she said.

"What is it?"

"Three—the dead man—was the one supposed to be guarding me; but he'd always half liked me, and while they kept me a prisoner, I made him fall in love with me. He wasn't very bright, but he did what I asked. The others were right—he *was* loyal, but loyal to one thing at a time. This time it was me. I asked him to take a note to Ardru—to Golden. And he told me Golden wanted him to follow you after a fight and bring you to the Hideout as a prospective member of the cell. Poor Three.'' She gave a little hiccuping sigh. ''He couldn't even say 'prospective.' Called you a prospector. I don't think the wardens killed him at all. I think the steward did. Which means *I* did.'' Her fingers began wrangling again. ''Poor Three. I didn't even know his name, just his number, and I killed him.'' She began to cry silently.

Jakkin reached out and untangled her fingers and brought them to his lips. ''It doesn't matter. None of that matters now. You are here, and after tomorrow we can go back to the nursery.''

''Of course it matters. I killed a man.'' She drew her fingers away from him angrily.

''His death matters. Maybe the wardens killed him or maybe not. But he was a rebel. You didn't ask him to be one.''

She turned her back on him. ''I asked him to help me.''

Jakkin touched her shoulder and pulled her back against him. ''You asked me to help, too. You said you needed me. Well, I'm here. Let *me* worry about things now.''

She turned to face him. ''Jakkin, *think!* These are not men playing at the dragon game but men who have probably killed other men, who'd think nothing of killing again. It's in their blood.''

''Our blood,'' he reminded her.

''I think these rebels are more dangerous than even Ardru realizes. They have great caches of stingers, and I know where they are. Three told me.''

Jakkin was silent, thinking. At last he ventured, ''Perhaps the stingers are just for a *show* of force. Men boast about such things, you know. I boasted about my first drakk kill when all I had really done was dip my knife in an already dead drakk.''

''I know that,'' Akki said. ''But it was a very small boast, and you were only a boy. But Three is dead—and that's no one's boast. I believe the steward when he says he's going to build a society on the ashes of this one.''

''A boast,'' Jakkin whispered without conviction.

''And I believe they're using us now, though I can't figure out how. Or why.''

Jakkin was fully awake, and so was the dragon. He could feel her inquiring mind send out tendrils of color into his; but he couldn't possibly explain politics to her. ''It is not for thee,'' he whispered to

Heart's Blood. Then he added to Akki, "Something the dead man said: 'Be careful.' "

"He was right."

"Dead right," Jakkin said, fighting a sudden awful urge to laugh at the unfunny joke.

"And more people, innocent people, might die the same way if we don't do something," Akki said. "The answer has to be in that case, in the papers."

"Should we look inside?"

"It's set to explode."

"Do you believe that?" Jakkin asked.

"Yes. Don't you?"

He hesitated, and Heart's Blood sent a barrage of dark, explosive bullet shapes through his head. "Yes," he admitted at last.

Akki put her hand on his. "Then what should we do? Should we find Golden now?"

"I don't know." He drew in a deep breath. "Dr. Henkky said we shouldn't trust him."

"What?" It was Akki's turn to breathe deeply. "But she was the one who introduced him to me. She loved him. They were pair-bonding."

"She doesn't sound very much in love anymore," Jakkin said. "She said he uses people and then throws them away."

"Not Ardru. He rescued me."

"I rescued you," Jakkin reminded her. "So now I don't know who to trust except you."

"And you," Akki whispered. She moved her shoulders restlessly. "We'll have to watch the case, see who takes it, and follow him. And once the case is properly opened, we can rush in and get the papers— and . . ."

Jakkin leaned over and put his arms around her. "No, Akki, you asked for a man, and now you have him. I'll watch. You'll take Heart's Blood to the nursery with Sarkkhan. You've already done much more than your share. I want to know you're safe at home where Kkarina can put some weight back on you."

To his surprise, she didn't argue, only gave a small noise, part yawn and part sigh, and lay back quietly. He lay down beside her and fell fast asleep.

# 20

THE DRAGON WOKE them both with a warning hough. Jakkin was stiff, and his throat hurt slightly from the chikkar. Stretching, Akki ran her fingers through her tangled hair. The leather case lay between them, and they looked at it guiltily.

Jakkin picked up the case and stuffed it deep into the downer, then turned to Akki.

"I've got to get Heart's Blood fed and ready. The fights start midmorning, and we can't call attention to ourselves by doing anything different. Besides, I have to concentrate on the fight. Anything else will send her reeling in the Pit."

Akki nodded.

Heart's Blood stomped her feet when her name was mentioned and sent tentative rainbows into Jakkin's head. She had been slow to greet him that morning as if shy to intrude.

"I'll work on her scales," Akki said. "You get the burnwort."

"Hey, *I'm* the trainer," said Jakkin. "*I* make the decisions. You do the scales, and I'll get the wort. The cloth is over there." He pointed.

Akki grinned at him, one side of her mouth lifting crookedly. "I've worked dragons before—remember? And Heart's Blood and I are old friends, aren't we, my beauty?"

"Shhh!" hissed Jakkin.

Akki put her hand up over her mouth, but her eyes smiled as the dragon bombarded them with firebursts. Jakkin could tell, by the glittering look in Akki's eyes, that she was feeling some of the dragon's reply, too.

As Akki began working on the dragon's scales with that circular motion that always brought out the shine, Jakkin left for the food mow. Akki's voice drifted back to him.

"So many scars, beauty. We both have so many scars."

"Medallions!" Jakkin whispered halfheartedly to himself, no longer proud of his own.

He was partway back with the wort bale when he remembered that Sarkkhan was due. What if he came on Akki alone and shouted out her name in his great, booming voice? He could ruin all their plans. Jakkin shouldered the heavy bale and tried to run the rest of the way.

As he came around the last curve of the hallway, he realized he was too late. The big man was already bending over the dragon, shaking his finger and giving Akki instructions.

"Sarkkhan," Jakkin shouted.

The nursery owner looked up, smiling. He called back to Jakkin, "Nice young lady you have here. Didn't think you had it in you."

Jakkin felt his jaw drop open as he closed the last few steps between them. Akki stood up and grinned.

"I've just met your friend, Master Jakkin," she said. "And told him at once who I was, before he could even ask, so he wouldn't think badly of you." She put her finger to her lips to keep Jakkin from saying anything. "And he's even invited me back to the nursery with the two of you. If after last night you'll have me, that is?" She batted her eyelashes in an outrageous imitation of a baggery girl.

"Have you?" Jakkin could say no more.

"Of course he'll have you, girl," Sarkkhan said. "There, and that's settled, I knew he was a man." He clapped Jakkin on the back. "Now let's get ready for this fight. We can talk later in the truck going home."

~

IT WAS NEARER lunch than breakfast when Heart's Blood's name was called. Her fight this time was with an old veteran of the Majors, a nearly black dragon named Murderer's Row. He was big, quick, and savage.

"But stupid," added Sarkkhan. "He doesn't listen to his trainer, and the few times he got into real trouble were when he tried something fancy—or something incredibly mean. So be ready. And . . ." He paused.

Jakkin waited.

"And this time I wouldn't mind a quick fight, blood or no blood, if you know what I mean," Sarkkhan said.

Jakkin passed the information on to the dragon, thinking at her, "So be thou ready. He will savage thee for the pleasure of it if he has the chance. Do not play into his claws. Be quick. Guard thyself here." He touched her throat. "And here." He drew his fingers across her eyes. "And here." He pointed to her silky, tough wings.

The dragon let the membrane down over her black eyes, shutting out the flickering dragon's fire for a moment. Then she flicked them open again, and Jakkin could see the red glow there. Around her neck the hardened collar of flesh began to rise.

"She's hackled and ready," he said to Sarkkhan.

"She's always ready, that one," Sarkkhan said, patting her flank. He slipped the rope off her head and helped Jakkin back her out of the stall.

The dragon went without urging to the dragonlock and flowed up into the Pit.

Jakkin took the stairs two at a time, making his way to the arena edge. He knew from her sending that she was still alone in the Pit. Leaning over the railing, he waved to be sure she sighted him. Then he thought at her, *Be thou a mighty fighter.* In answer, she roared with flashes of red, the only sound a mute dragon could make.

But another roar overbore the one in his head. With a terrible scream of defiance, Murderer's Row came through the second lock. Jakkin was startled. Though some dragons warmed to a fight with whining screams in their stalls, Jakkin had never heard of a dragon that roared as it entered the Pit.

His surprise communicated itself at once to Heart's Blood, and she backed up three small steps, putting herself slightly off balance. The great black dragon charged straight at her, and Heart's Blood raised her right claw in defense, the lanceae fully extended, the golden nails gleaming.

Row struck at the claw with his head and teeth, roaring as he came, heedless of any damage he might inflict on himself. Heart's Blood's nails raked his nose; yet still he pushed forward, and one of his front primary teeth ripped away a scale above her right claw. Heart's Blood backed away another step, and still Row kept coming.

"Up, up!" Jakkin cried out, seeing that the black dragon's rush would inevitably lead to her being pushed against the wall.

She heard him and leaped up, her wings pumping madly, her tail a blood-red rudder. She swept up and over the black dragon before he realized what was happening, and his forward movement carried him into a sprawl.

Heart's Blood dropped onto his back and ripped a strip of scales away. Then she winged back up again, the air under her pumping wings causing the sand in the Pit to eddy and swirl.

The black turned, going into a hind-foot rise, clawing angrily at the air. He was bleeding slightly from the nose, and several scales on his back were partially ripped away, hanging askew like a row of dangling medals. He roared that terrible roar again and was answered by the crowd in the stands, many of whom immediately doubled and tripled their bets.

Heart's Blood began to descend to meet Row's challenge.

"Don't be as stupid as he," cautioned Jakkin. "Let him go up to thee. Let him do the moving. It will cost him more. Let him tire himself out with his bluster and blowing; it costs thee nothing. Nothing."

Heart's Blood heard, and she waited, hovering above the Pit, a tempting red target. The black took several heavy hops forward, his front legs still raking the air. Stretching his great neck to its fullest, he blew out flames toward her and roared again.

The crowd went wild then, calling out to both dragons.

"Go to her, go," shouted someone in the upper tiers.

"Get him. Now!" came a loud voice from the masters' boxes.

Jakkin could hear the undercurrent of new betting that the double blooding and the roaring and the flames called forth. At his right he could see Sarkkhan conferring quickly with a tall man whose back was to the ring. Their voices came to him, Sarkkhan setting odds and the other man offering even greater ones against Heart's Blood. It was a familiar voice. He wondered why. He wanted to look full face but didn't dare. Heart's Blood needed his attention.

The black Row was incapable of waiting for Heart's Blood to descend. Urged on by the crowd, he began to pump his wings. The ribs strained; the fleshy feathers fanned out. Then he rose, banking slightly, to carry the fight into the air. In the opposite stands his trainer screamed at him to go back down, but the giant black didn't listen.

Jakkin smiled for the first time. It was, he thought, the wrong move for the heavier dragon to make. In the open his weight might be more of an advantage, but in the enclosed arena, under the dome, Heart's Blood's maneuverability gave her a greater edge. In the Pit the air game was hers.

She waited until the black was almost even with her, his wings slowly pumping. Then she cleaved her wings together, dropped under him, flipped onto her back—not an easy trick—and, as she fell, struck out with her left claw. It wasn't the lanceae that caught under his tail but the smaller, sharper razored back claw, the tricept, which opened a thin line on his vulnerable underside. The black screamed—a high, uneven keening. Heart's Blood righted herself, scraping the ground with her tail as she shot away again.

In that moment Jakkin knew whose voice it was that had bet with Sarkkhan. "Five!" he said, and turned to Sarkkhan. But the nursery owner was alone.

The roar of the crowd recalled him to the fight. He watched as the black, dripping tail blood that hissed onto the sand floor, sank slowly to the ground. The red dragon crowded him down, batting at his drooping head with sheathed claws, but the black was no longer in a fighting mood. He lifted his head as if he were sleepwalking, and she gave him the ritual slashes as gently as if she were admonishing a naughty child. Then she turned and stood in a hind-foot rise and waggled her great wings in a comic semaphore.

"Heart's Blood! Heart's Blood! Heart's Blood!" the crowd chanted in rhythm, on their feet.

She opened her mouth to roar and sent a series of skyrockets through Jakkin's head, then turning, found the dragonlock and flowed below.

Jakkin looked around the Pit once more, hoping to find Five. He saw no one he recognized except Sarkkhan. Half the crowd had left already to cash in its bets; the others jockeyed for better seats for the next fight.

"I'll get you your gold," said Sarkkhan. "You see to your worm's wound. It bled little, but a tooth slash over the claw can be nasty. It can get infected, or worse, it can permanently loosen the nail."

Jakkin nodded and went downstairs. As he walked, he kept looking around, straining to see if Five or any other watchers were nearby. He recognized no one.

# 21

AKKI WAS WAITING, case in hand. Jakkin gave her a quick hug.

"No one came for it," she said.

"They said they would collect it *after* we left," Jakkin pointed out.

"Remember, we don't trust them."

"They said they would be watching—and they were," Jakkin told her. "Five was there."

"You saw him?"

"How could I miss him? He was talking to Sarkkhan. He made sure I saw him."

Akki thought for a minute. Then she nodded. "They wanted us to know we were being watched."

"We have no time to fool with the case now. Just put it in Heart's Blood's stall and help. She's hurt her claw. If anyone comes for the case, he'll have to wait."

Akki went with him into the stall and put the case under the bale of wort. "I didn't even check her over," she said regretfully. "I was too worried about the case—and you." She bent down and looked at the wound. "That could get bad. There's little protection above the claw. We have to be careful of infection."

"Or a loosened claw," Jakkin said, echoing Sarkkhan. "Do you think that might happen?"

Akki did not answer but sat down on the ground and lifted the massive foot onto her lap. Then she bent over and put her tongue on the wound.

Jakkin knew what she was doing. There was something in human saliva that started the healing process in dragons. He had learned that a year ago from Likkarn, at Heart's Blood's first fight.

"There," Akki said, rubbing the back of her hand across her mouth. Her eyes were slotted. Jakkin knew that the dragon's blood had burned her tongue. She looked up at him. "Do you have a kit?"

No trainer ever traveled without a medkit. He took it from the stall shelf and gave it to her. She rummaged through it quickly, coming up with a surgical needle and the heavy thread used with dragons. After putting the kit on the ground beside her, she turned her attention to threading the large-eye needle.

All the while Heart's Blood munched loudly and contentedly on the bale, paying little attention to either of them, spurred on by the incredible hunger of dragons after a fight.

Akki began closing the edges of the wound on Heart's Blood's foot with sure, tiny stitches. Above the claws, around the eyes, along the vulnerable neck, and a patch on the belly were the only places that a needle could penetrate. Even a filed knife had trouble anywhere else, and a dragon wounded in unsewable spots healed raggedly. Infections were common.

As Akki sewed, she murmured to the great worm, "Hush, my lady. Sweet red, do not tremble so." For though the dragon did not stop eating, small earthquakes ran up and down her body as the nerve ends and muscles quivered.

Soon Akki was done. She pushed the red foot off her lap and stood, handing the needle and thread back to Jakkin. He stowed them in the alcohol bottle in the kit.

They both heard Sarkkhan's steps at the same moment. He came around the corner and was holding up a large leather bag in the air.

"Look at this, Jakkin. Look at this. Largest purse I've seen since I ran Blood Bath through his ten straight Major victories. And that's without some piece of worm slime who tripled his bet and then ran out on me. Tall, bearded man. If I ever find him, I'll . . . oh, the punters liked that fight, I tell you. Up in the air. Red against black. Male against female. Brains against . . ." His face was open, laughing.

Then he saw their faces: frightened, secretive. "What is it?"

"It's nothing," Akki said. "Heart's Blood will be fine."

"Then why look like that?"

"Like what?" Akki's eyes went down as if suddenly searching for something on the floor.

But Jakkin realized that Sarkkhan would have to be told something more, here at the Pit, not just fobbed off with a small lie until they were safely home. And he realized, too, that they were both too young and too inexperienced to deal with this alone. Someone else, some adult *had* to be trusted, and right now that someone was Sarkkhan.

"It's not Heart's Blood that worries us," Jakkin said. He pushed the bale back with his foot. "It's this."

The leather case lay exposed.

"Jakkin!" Akki whispered fiercely.

But his mind was already made up. Before she could stop him, he sketched the whole thing out in a quiet voice that did not carry beyond the stall.

Listening carefully, Sarkkhan interrupted him only once. "About the other rebels?" he whispered, turning to his daughter.

"I won't tell you that," she said, her face shuttering down as effectively as if she had drawn a membrane over it. "Some of the others are honest. They believe in what they do. And you hate the mere mention of the word 'rebel.' "

Sarkkhan grunted, but he didn't argue the point. Instead, he asked, "Then how does Golden fit in?"

Akki answered. "He asked me if I was afraid of joining, of being his eyes and ears in a cell. And I wasn't afraid—then. I was to tell him if there was any talk of violence. I reported as often as I dared, mostly through Dr. Henkky. Only the last time she was mad at him, and I couldn't get her to help, and before I knew what had happened, they took me from a cell meeting and kept me in housewatch. They asked me questions I couldn't answer. And some I wouldn't answer. They asked about Ardru."

"Who is Ardru?" Sarkkhan looked puzzled.

"Did they know he was Golden?" asked Jakkin.

"They guessed. Or maybe in the end Three told them. Maybe they killed Three because of that."

Jakkin nodded. "Three must have followed me from the Hideout when he heard my name mentioned. And he had a message for me from Golden. Only I guess he didn't really deliver it. All he said was 'Be careful. The bar, the rebel hideout. Help for . . . ' " He stopped. " 'Help *Four*' is what he meant. You, Akki."

"Not much of a message really," Akki said.

"Not enough to be killed for," Jakkin agreed.

Sarkkhan cleared his throat, and they both looked at him. "There's only one thing to do," he said. "*Both* of you will leave with the dragon and the truck. That's what they are expecting, after all. I doubt they will make a move until that happens. Obviously anyone who comes down here will have to be someone with a badge, someone allowed here. Security is too tight for anything else.''

"Akki got in," Jakkin pointed out. "And she didn't have a badge.''

"Bag-girls don't count," Akki muttered.

"If it's a trainer or one of the pitboys—or a Galaxian—chances are I will know him. And he won't be expecting me to have the case. That will be an advantage.''

Jakkin suddenly remembered Golden's warning about the nursery owner, that he was so hot-blooded he would want to be the center of any plan. He tried to argue.

"No," Sarkkhan said. "My way is the only way. It's not unheard of for me to stay and bet on other fights. Only I'll stay and watch the case instead. And when it comes to contacting the warden—well, they'll believe me a sight faster than they'll believe you two.''

"I don't like it," said Akki. "Something's not right. What if they suspect you and carry you off?''

Sarkkhan held up his meaty fists. "I've been a man for a long time, Akki. I trust these two friends. And my brain. And you two will be my backup. If I'm not home by tomorrow, you contact Golden. With what Akki knows, we can blast the bloody rebels offplanet. What we have going for us is surprise.''

"*Surprise!*" Jakkin remembered Likkarn's advice. Reluctantly he said, "I think Sarkkhan's right, Akki.''

At last she agreed.

~

THEIR PARTING WAS prompted by the arrival of several new dragons and their masters. After packing up the downers, the medkit, the extra bale of burnwort for the trip home, they both hugged Sarkkhan. Then they hid the case solemnly behind the remnants of an old bale.

"Remember," Akki whispered, giving Sarkkhan one last fierce hug, "don't try to open the case yourself. They've rigged a bomb to go off if you don't have the proper key.''

"I'll take care," he said. "We want the messenger as much as the message.''

They backed Heart's Blood out of the stall, each with a hand on her ears, and guided her quickly to the truck. She went into the trailer without complaint and knelt to groom herself.

"I'm going back to check on Sarkkhan," said Jakkin.

"No. Don't. It might look strange. He's ready and keeping an eye on things. He'll let us know as soon as he finds out anything.''

Jakkin nodded. "You'll have to drive," he said sheepishly. "I never learned." He climbed into the passenger's side of the truck.

"Then it's lucky Ardru taught me or we'd be stuck!" she said, laughing at his embarrassment. She got in the driver's side, started the truck up, and eased it out through the streets of the city. She needed no map but navigated with a casual familiarity Jakkin envied.

They passed only one truck on the way out and turned onto the long main road going east.

Jakkin glanced back at The Rokk skyline. He remembered that, when he had first seen it, it had looked like a great greedy dragon, the towers on each side stone wings. But it was not a dragon; it was just a city. The walls and towers and buildings and streets themselves were not what was dangerous. The danger came from what dwelt inside.

As the truck pulled farther away, Jakkin could see the yellow-green sun sitting on the nedge of the world. The buildings of The Rokk seemed to shimmer. And near the center the great dome of the Pit was just visible, looking like a dragon's egg just before the moment of hatching.

The late-afternoon light was a kind of creamy white, ringed with a rosy glow. In the back of the truck Heart's Blood stirred uneasily and sent a bizarre pattern of broken rainbows into Jakkin's mind. The ribs of the arches, like fractured bones, dripped flesh and blood.

"Stop!" Jakkin called out. "Something's wrong with Heart's Blood."

Akki guided the truck to the side of the road. "I hear her, too," she said.

They jumped out of the cab. As they ran toward the back of the truck, there was a strange color in the sky over the Pit dome.

"Look!" Jakkin cried.

As he spoke, the dome of Rokk Major began to split open with a jagged, running crack along one side, just as if a young dragon were about to emerge. Flames shot up as red as dragon fire, as dark as blood. Only afterward did they hear the roar of the explosion washing over them in wave after wave after wave.

# 22

FOR A LONG time neither of them spoke. A few trucks rode past, sending dust to bedevil them. The dragon, alerted by their thoughts, nosed the ziplock down and stuck her head out. She blanketed them with a mauve landscape.

Akki began to shake violently. Jakkin put his arms around her to try to stop the trembling.

"No," she cried. "No, no, no."

He held her, powerless to do more.

"It was us they wanted to hurt, not him. No. No. No." She babbled on and on, making little sense, in a high, stuttering voice about her life in the baggery as a child and about the time Sarkkhan had found her and claimed her and taken her away to the nursery. About the first time he had shown her a dragon and let her hold a hatchling in her hand. "I thought he was a giant for so long and was ashamed when I found out he was only a man," she said. "I wanted him to be perfect and hated him when he wasn't. I wanted him to love me for *me,* not for what he wanted me to be. And now he's gone, and I was so awful to him for so long."

"We don't know for sure he's gone," Jakkin said, meaning to soothe her. "We don't know what really happened. Maybe he'd already left the Pit. Maybe someone else opened the case. After all, we warned him not to try."

Akki shook her head, looking all the while at the ground. "You know him better than that. If he'd thought the case should be opened, and if he'd had the slightest doubt a bomb, he'd have opened it. He's so bullheaded—" She stopped herself. "He *was* so bullheaded."

"But maybe," Jakkin said.

As if suddenly clutching at possibilities, Akki looked up at him. "Maybe?" she whispered.

He nodded and forced a smile at her.

But the dragon denied them that comfort. She turned her head toward the scene of faraway devastation. And they heard through her, as though through a badly strained radio, in streaks of color instead of words, the final moments of the two with whom she had been most closely linked at The Rokk: the pain-ridden roar of the dragon Murderer's Row exploding with fear and the blustering red-gold light of Sarkkhan sputtering with surprise, then anger, then pain, and finally a strange kind of soft forgiveness that faded and went out.

Jakkin was surprised at how cold he felt. Even the waves of strength that Heart's Blood sent him couldn't warm him up. He hadn't felt this cold at Three's death or in any Dark After that he could recall. He clung to Akki and gave himself up to the cold.

How long they stood there, arms around each other, Jakkin didn't know, but at last he was able to speak again, his voice straining to be heard. He had to clear his throat twice to get the words out. "We— we—we have to get back to the nursery. We have to tell them."

"Tell them what?" Akki's voice seemed to come from far away.

"Tell them about the bomb. About us. About—I don't know. But the nursery is home, Akki. Heart's Blood's home. Your home. My home. Sar—" He stopped himself from saying the name. "It just seems right that we go there and then decide what to do next. I can go only one step at a time, Akki. I can't go any faster than that." He wondered if it meant he was just running away again.

"You're right. We must go home."

Jakkin watched her as she spoke and realized all at once that he was not running *away* from something but rather going *toward* it. That made all the difference.

Heart's Blood pulled her head into the truck, and Jakkin ziplocked it closed. Then he joined Akki in the cab. It was unfair to her, with her father just dead, with all the pain and anger she must be feeling, but she would have to do the driving. He felt like such an idiot, but there was no help for that now. He rubbed the back of her neck as they drove, and for a long while she said nothing.

Suddenly, her voice tight, she said, "I hate them. I hate *all* of them." Then she was silent again.

~

DARK CAME SOONER than they thought. Both moons rose.

"We're going to have to shelter. We'll never make it back before Dark After," Jakkin said.

They found one of the small roadside houses built for bonders caught out late at night. There was plenty of wood for the fireplace, and while Akki made a fire, Jakkin went out to let Heart's Blood fly free.

The dragon stood before him and nudged his shoulder with her nose. She sent him a picture of five separate rainbows, and he knew she would fly back to the farm.

"There will be wort and weed there for thee. And thy hatchlings wait. We cannot live in the cold as thee can. So wing away, beauty. We will see thee in the morning."

She stretched her wings to their fullest and then shook them. The fleshy feathers fluttered, and she preened the right one with her rough tongue. Then she turned and looked at Jakkin, but her thoughts were pale as if tuned to some faraway call. Leaping into the air, she pumped her wings, swooped once close to where Jakkin was standing. The wind from her passage blew his hair into his eyes. When he pushed his hair away, Heart's Blood was already a black smudge on the horizon.

He went into the house. Akki was already asleep in front of the fire. He was glad. That way she wouldn't hear him cry.

~

THEY WOKE BEFORE dawn with the sun still behind the eastern mountains but Dark After's hold broken for the day. Ignoring the residue of cold, they got into the truck. They cruised past Krakkow later in the morning without giving the small city even a glance.

By the time they reached the farm the spikka-lined drives were awash with red and the jagged crowns of the trees on fire with the sunlight.

They pulled up in front of the bondhouse and were surprised when most of the bonders ran out to greet them. L'Erikk was in the lead. Slakk, coming from the barn, still carried a pitchfork. Even Balakk, who never smiled, looked pleased. Only Errikkin lagged behind.

"You're alive. You're alive," L'Erikk shouted, pulling Jakkin from the truck and patting his shoulders. "When Heart's Blood came flying in last night and nearly knocked down the bondhouse door and Kkarina had to beat her off with a kitchen towel and Errikkin had hysterics, we didn't know *what* to think. Likkarn put her in the barn with her hatchlings."

"With no help from any of you," grumbled the old trainer.

"You wouldn't let us near her," Slakk pointed out. "Not that I would have tried. She was *wild,* Jakkin. What happened?"

"And where's Sarkkhan?" asked Likkarn. "Where's the master?"

Before Jakkin could answer, Kkarina had enfolded Akki in her expansive embrace. "Hatchling, my little Akkhina, you're home."

The circle tightened around them, and Jakkin turned slowly, unaccountably reciting their names out loud as if the litany could return what was lost to them: "Errikkin, Slakk, Jo-Janekk, Likkarn, Kkarina, L'Erikk." The familiar faces, their life histories crowding into his head, moved him deeply. He reached out a hand as if by touching each of them in turn he could touch a part of Sarkkhan. He said the name aloud. "Sarkkhan."

"Where is he?" Likkarn asked again.

Jakkin shook his head, the spell broken, and looked down at the ground.

"Jakkin!" Akki's voice cut through. "Look!"

He found her in the crowd and followed her pointing finger. Someone was coming down the path from Sarkkhan's house: a slim, elegant figure.

"Golden!" Jakkin suddenly shouted. He pushed through the bonders and ran up the path.

～

GOLDEN PRECEDED THE two of them back to Sarkkhan's house. Peremptorily ordering the bonders to remain behind, Golden had used the authority of his rank and presence to its fullest. They all obeyed, though Likkarn grumbled at it. Errikkin, bowing and smiling, had spread his arms and herded the bonders back toward the barn and bondhouse, eager to obey.

Akki stalked up the slight incline angrily. Jakkin was more wary. They walked apart, behind Golden, each a silent point in a triangle, bound yet separated by that silence.

Golden pushed the door open and entered first. As soon as they were inside, he turned and said sharply, "I didn't expect to see you both alive again."

"I bet you didn't," Jakkin growled. "You set it up that way."

But Akki read something different in Golden's face. "Did you betray us?" she asked, her voice an agony. "Ardru, I can't believe it of you. Did you have my father killed while you played at being a rebel?"

Golden sat down abruptly. "It is true then. He's dead?"

"You didn't know?" asked Akki.

"I didn't know what had happened except that Rokk Major is a disaster area. They'll be pulling bodies out of there for days."

"So you didn't plan it?" Akki asked again.

"No, little one. All along I've wanted only to stop the violence. That was my first goal. A peaceful revolution. No more masters, no more slaves. And my second was a free and open election to see if Austarians—all Austarians—wanted to be members of the Federation."

Jakkin snorted and turned his back on Golden. "Well, your peace has been bloodily bought," he said. "Sarkkhan dead. The dragons dead. And how many others?"

"Three," Akki added suddenly. "Don't forget poor Three."

Jakkin saw the staring face of the man again, felt death rising up under his fingers. In some ways, the death of Three was more real to him than Sarkkhan's. He was glad he had not seen Sarkkhan dead. This way he'd always remember Sarkkhan alive.

"Who is Three?" asked Golden.

"The man I sent to you with the note about where I was," Akki said, taking a seat herself. "For a nonviolent man, your toll is very high indeed." Her voice was bitter for the first time.

Golden put his hands in front of his face as if to ward off a blow, and his pose of studied elegance dropped away. Then he shook himself, straightened his shoulders, and stood up. The perfect control had returned. "I must explain."

"No need," whispered Akki.

But Jakkin disagreed. "I want to know what this is all about," he said. "I want to make sense of it."

"As Ardru I was on the rebels' Central Committee," Golden said. "Ironically, they called me the Golden Pirate because I always managed to find some gold for them. They never asked how. It was important that the Federation know what was happening with the rebels. And important for the Senate, too. I was able to satisfy them both. But the cells, which had once been under the Central Committee's control, were becoming more and more unpredictable. The cell leaders were often crazies, power-hungry anarchists like your steward. We tried to weed the crazies out, discredit them whenever possible. Originally I put Akki in that cell because the steward was a man gathering a lot of power to himself, and I could trust Akki to keep her head around him. *And* I could trust her judgments. She found out a number of important things for us. But when I learned that the steward had once been a dragon slayer in the Brokka Stews, I began to get worried. He liked blood a bit too much. That's when I knew I had to get Akki out of there and deal with the steward myself. But he'd already made his move, and before I could contact her again, she'd disappeared.''

Jakkin nodded. "Go on."

"So I came looking for you because I knew you were a friend of Akki's.''

"But it was Akki who sent the note,'' said Jakkin.

"What note?'' Akki looked puzzled. "The only note I sent was to Golden through Three. It was all I dared.''

"The note about *needing* me. About my being a man.''

"I sent nothing of the kind.''

They both turned to Golden, who shrugged and looked slightly embarrassed.

"Yes, I made that up,'' he said. "I knew that only a call from Akki would bring you into the game.''

Jakkin's hands balled into fists. "How did you know about Akki and me?''

Akki put her hand lightly on his arm. "Don't be angry. I told him, a long time ago, when I ran away and was lonely and hurt and he and Henkky were my only friends.''

Jakkin covered her hand with his and said nothing, but he suddenly remembered the doctor's phrase: "He uses people.''

As if reading his mind, Golden spoke urgently. "Yes, I used both of you—but for a cause.''

"Some cause,'' Jakkin said, "that lets us walk into danger with our eyes shut, that lets us bring a bomb into a building to kill innocent people and dragons.''

Golden shook his head. "Don't play the martyr, Jakkin; don't take the responsibility for that destruction on yourself. The explosive power of any bomb you could carry is not enough to bring a building the size of Rokk Major down. There must have been several bombs planted around the Pit, all timed to go off. You two were merely the scapegoats. Already a guard remembered you coming in with the case, a guard who conveniently escaped the blast. Everyone is happy enough to let the two of you take the blame, though I expect that once they realize you weren't caught in the explosion, both wardens and rebels will come looking for you.''

Jakkin broke in, "But if you thought we were dead, how come you're here? And how did you get here so fast?''

"I hoped that one of you *might* have escaped and would head here first. And being an offworlder, even such a one as I, occasionally has advantages," he said, his smile twisting bitterly. "There's a copter stationed at The Rokk, and since I know how to fly it, I borrowed it from the Federation."

"*Borrowed?*" Akki asked.

"Well, took!"

"Henkky was right," Jakkin said. "You belong to the Federation. You use people—and then throw them away."

"Of course I used you. I've already admitted that. Because the Federation can't officially mix into a planet's internal politics. If I hadn't used you, this entire world would already be bathed in blood," Golden said.

Jakkin turned away angrily and stared into the hearth.

"Like the blood of my father and the blood of the punters at the Pit and the dragons and Three. Doesn't their blood count?" shouted Akki.

Jakkin scarcely heard her. All he could think of was how easily he had been manipulated—by Golden, the steward, Sarkkhan, Henkky. If things were really fair, he, not Sarkkhan, would be lying buried in the ruins of the Pit. He turned back and asked quietly, "And was the rebellion the Federation's idea from the start?"

"Don't be a child," said Golden. "This rebellion arose because most of the men—and women—on this world are no better than slaves. The Federation didn't start it."

Akki, still furious, broke in. "The Federation started it two hundred years ago when it sent prisoners here."

Suddenly Jakkin felt a roar in his head. It translated into a bleak, jagged dunescape of blacks and browns. He stood up and touched his head, frowning a bit. "Akki," he said.

"I hear it, too," she answered.

"Hear what?" asked Golden.

"It's all dark and muddy. So angry. So afraid." Akki went to the window and looked out. "There are trucks out there I don't recognize. And men who aren't nursery bonders." She touched the bag at her neck. "Not rebels either, I wager."

Golden walked to her side and looked out. His voice was steady. "Well, they're here a full day sooner than I had expected. We have no more time. As your bonders like to say, dragon time is now! I recognize those men. They're wardens, the special anti-rebel squad. The leader, the one gesturing with his hand, that's Captain Kkalkkav. He's an old *friend* of mine. A senator as well. He's often hinted that he suspected my sympathies lay . . . elsewhere. But before today he had no proof. Just finding me here with you will be proof enough. He's already found the copter. Look—there are guards around it."

Jakkin joined them at the window.

"Who's the bonder, the one pointing up here?" asked Golden.

"Errikkin," said Jakkin, without surprise. "*My* bonder." He laughed without humor. "He respects authority."

"Kkalkkav has plenty of that," Golden said. "And it looks as if he has convinced your bonder that you're a rebel and therefore against authority."

"I'm not a rebel, but I don't think I'm particularly for authority."

Golden laughed humorlessly. "This is a fine time to try to make *that* distinction, because it looks as if *your* friend is betraying us to *my* friend. Is there a back door out of here?"

"Do we need to run?" asked Jakkin. "Can't we just explain?"

"Don't be thick, Jakkin," Akki said. "Explain what? That we didn't really know about the bombs—except for the one in the case, which wasn't really ours anyway? That we were forced to bring it in? I expect Kkalkkav doesn't care."

"I expect you're right," said Golden. "He has to bring in a bomber. And any bomber will do for now, just so the public is satisfied that something's being done. Now about that back door."

"This way," said Akki, starting toward a short hall.

"I'm not running anymore," said Jakkin. "I finally figured it out—*this* is where I've been running to."

"What do places matter?" asked Golden, grabbing his hand and jerking him along.

Jakkin yanked back, and the two scuffled briefly. Akki put her hand on the door handle and was about to open it when it was flung outward. Standing there, red tears following familiar tracks down his cheeks, was Likkarn. Akki gasped and cried out a warning.

Jakkin ran over and pushed her aside. He stared at Likkarn. "I thought you'd given up weed, old man."

"Oh, I had—I had—boy—," Likkarn said. "But you see, I'm going to need my blister fury in a moment."

Jakkin tensed then and, seeing the old man was not yet sunk into the comatose stage that preceded the angry rush of blister fury, put his hand out and pushed. "Let us by."

Surprisingly Likkarn smiled, a thin, wry smile, and stepped aside. "I got your dragon out of the barn. She's off to the mountains north of Sukker's Marsh. If you follow her there, you'll be safe from the wardens for a while if you can manage to live through Dark After. There are folk out there—and dragons, too. I know. I lived in the mountains nearly five years myself. There are caves. And berries. And mushrooms." He waved his hand vaguely toward the northwest.

Golden was out the door in a moment. Akki went after him. Jakkin stared at Likkarn but couldn't move. The old man's face was furrowed with tear lines, pocked with scores. It was an ugly, familiar face; once Jakkin had thought it the face of his enemy.

"Remember," Likkarn said suddenly, "the best trick of all is surprise."

"Why?"

"Because I don't believe a worm waster like that Kkalkkav. You might be a miserable piece of lizard slime, but you'd never knowingly endanger a dragon. And because Sarkkhan"—the red tears started up again—"because he filled my bag. And he loved you both. You and Akki. Remember that, boy, when you're out in the cold and the dark is pressing in. Now go. Go. I'll hold them off as long as I can. Go. Down the fields and through the marsh and over to the mountains. Go."

Jakkin nodded. "I'm sorry I ever called you boy," he said quietly. "You are a man!" But Likkarn's head was already beginning to sink to his chest. Jakkin pulled him inside, then went out the door and shut it behind him. It closed with a sharp, final snap.

# *The Fighters*

# 23

JAKKIN CAUGHT UP with the others at the bottom of the hill where the jigsaw-puzzle fields began. The red haze over the closest field was undisturbed, which was how he knew that they had waited for him, crouched in the shadows of the shoulder-high burnwort plants. Jakkin assumed the lead, showing them how to remain below the haze, guiding them along the rows of wort. He was careful to skirt the smoking plants, warning Golden away from the red stalks that could burn at a touch. Despite the warning, Golden's hands and shirt soon bore the marks of his passing.

Even Akki, though she managed better, had one long burn along her palm where she had held her hand up to shield her face against some of the tall jagged-leaf plants that were bending in the wind.

Past the first fields they had to wade across the stone weir channeling water from the Narrakka River into the dragonry. The water was thigh-high on the men, almost waist-high on Akki, but once they had emerged from the dike, the hot desert air dried their pants. Another group of fields, another weir, and they were out at the main road.

Jakkin signaled a stop, and they squatted in the dunes near the road. Screened by a sand mound, they could see without being seen. Heat streamed off the road, and mirage pools dotted the landscape; but they were not fooled.

"I hear nothing," Jakkin said at last. "Likkarn must have put up an incredible fight." Quickly he explained about the blister fury.

Akki nodded, holding her burned left hand with her right, and Golden scanned the area in a distracted manner.

Cocking his head to one side, Jakkin listened again. Still nothing.

Carefully he rose and checked the horizon. He could see no trucks along the road, although a long curve tended to obscure the northern passage. However, Jakkin knew that if the wardens were coming for them by the road, the fastest way would be from the south, for the nursery lay in a small pocket off the main road with exits both north and south.

He looked behind them and smiled wryly. Though they had no whiskers with them to broom away their footprints, a persistent wind was doing the job for them. The drifting sands would soon obscure any marks they had left. He hoped that Likkarn's blister fury had stalled their pursuers or that the comalike sleep that followed would keep him from telling the wardens about their final destination in the mountains. If no one noticed the few small eddies in the haze over the fields, they just might make it. And perhaps the other bonders, out of loyalty to Jakkin and Akki or awe of Golden's position, might spin the wardens a tale of Jakkin's oasis, which was entirely in the wrong direction. There was even the possibility that someone might send the wardens into the dragon barns. Jakkin chuckled at the thought of the wardens, their minds filled with disturbing thoughts, rousing the great worms. Kkalkkav and his crew would be in for a rough, uncomfortable, possibly even dangerous time if that happened.

But as swiftly, Jakkin reconsidered. Sarkkhan had been popular with his bonders. Most of the men had been together for years. If the wardens convinced them that he and Akki had been responsible for Sarkkhan's death, they might not hesitate to lead the pursuit. Errikkin was already helping, having transferred his bonder loyalty to the strong-minded Kkalkkav.

"Curse him," Jakkin muttered. "Curse them all." No doubt Errikkin had seen Heart's Blood winging off toward the mountain. He *could* have made a shrewd guess. Jakkin decided to keep those thoughts to himself for a while.

"Let's go," he said, gesturing with his head. "We'll head toward the spikka copse and then the marsh; otherwise the midmorning sun will be too much for us. But keep low."

Looking both ways, he raced bent over across the road and rolled down the sand dunes on the other side.

Akki and Golden followed.

There was still no sound of pursuit, and Jakkin prayed that their luck would hold, although it was hard to fight the conviction that bonders' luck was all bad. Well, he was no longer a bonder, nor were any of them. Neither bonders nor masters, neither rebels nor wardens.

Some new, unnamed breed perhaps. He stood again, looked, then ran toward the west and the copse, pulling the others along with him.

Out of breath, they came to the spikka trees where Jakkin had once helped kill a nest of drakk.

"In there," he gasped. "It will hide us and shelter us while we rest."

The high-crowned spikka forest was thick enough. There were perhaps forty trees in all, a large wood by Austarian standards. The nearby marsh fed an underground stream that kept the copse alive. Beneath the trees the ground was spongy, wet, and sandy. Unfortunately it would hold their footprints, but they had time on their side now. They sat down by an old spikka, its trunk crisscrossed with knife cuts.

Golden spoke first. "Turn out your pockets and your bags. What do we have with us?"

The results were disappointing. Jakkin's bag carried nothing; his pockets, the small sharp-bladed baling knife. He hadn't taken his Pit winnings out of the truck. Akki had a comb and a woven ribbon for her hair and a miniature medkit in her bag. Golden at least had an offworld knife that unfolded into several different blades. Jakkin had never seen anything like it. He also carried a notebook, pencil, a small flexible book without a title, the little makeup box, and some coins.

"No food," said Golden. "And no map."

"I have a map in my head," Jakkin answered. "What worries me is that we have no covering for Dark After."

"What worries *me* is that we have no real weapons," said Akki. "Those knife blades can help us gather food. I know enough of herbalry to keep us from starving. But we can't fight wardens with those little things."

"Or dragons," said Golden.

"Dragons?" For a moment Jakkin didn't understand. He ran his fingers through his hair; then he thought of their eventual destination: the rugged, wind-scoured mountains where the wild dragons and the feral escapees lived. He shook his head. "They shouldn't bother us if we don't bother them."

"I expect they are territorial," Golden said. "And how will we know what territory they are willing to defend?"

"*I* expect," Akki answered grimly, "that we will find that out soon enough."

"I'll think of something," Jakkin said. "Leave the dragons to me." He spoke with much more confidence than he felt.

"While you're thinking," Golden cautioned, "we'd better keep moving. The farther we get from the nursery, the better I'll feel."

Jakkin stood. "On the other side of the marsh and across the road are a series of Dark After houses about every fifteen kilometers. We'll need to stay in one tonight."

"That's the first place they'll look," Akki said.

"We've got enough time," Golden said. "Why not head right for the mountains and find those mountain folk Likkarn spoke of? We could send one of them to my people."

Jakkin looked annoyed. "First things first. It's going to take us awhile to get to the houses anyway. Then we'll hide until just at the snap of cold, when the wardens will have stopped looking for us, and go in."

Akki stood, too. "Then I'd better find us some food. Jakkin and I haven't eaten since yesterday. If we're going to hole up through Dark After, we have a little time now to look for something to eat. Too bad it's too early for scrolltops. This ground is perfect for them, and they make a lovely salad."

"Look for food later," said Jakkin. "Right now we'd better get moving." He started threading a path through the spikka trees. At the edge of the copse Jakkin stopped and checked the landscape for disturbing signs. He felt something as light and gentle and as quick as a marsh lizard touch his thoughts. It was a faint band of color, more like an aura, over a blank scape.

"Heart's Blood," he said aloud. The ribbon of color pulsed darker for an instant, then blanked out. She was simply too far away for understanding. But just knowing she was alive and searching for him was comfort enough.

～

THEY MADE A quick crossing of the muddy hundred meters between the edge of the wood and the beginning of Sukker's Marsh. Their sandals crushed hundreds of delicate golden jingle shells as they went; had they been barefoot, the slivers would have cut their feet cruelly.

Akki was startled suddenly by a tiny grass-colored lizard that flashed across the top of her foot. She jumped back.

"Just a streaker," Jakkin answered.

"I know that," Akki answered back. "I'm not afraid of them. It just surprised me."

A minute later she laughed as Jakkin leaped up. A larger streaker, this one sand-colored, had run up the inside of his pants leg. He shook it out with a loud expletive.

"Fewmets!" he shouted. "They come out of nowhere."

"But you're not afraid," Akki said.

"He's just startled," Golden added.

They all laughed, and it felt good.

They mucked their way through the early stages of the marsh, trying not to jump with the appearance of each new streaker. And Akki even tried to catch an orange by the tail, a difficult feat since the tails usually broke off, leaving the would-be captor with a quickly stinking piece of flesh that stained the hand.

"Everything in this world *smells*," complained Golden mildly. "Dragons, streakers . . ."

"You should smell a dead drakk," said Jakkin. "That's *really* bad."

Akki made a face. She let the tail fall into the mud, and only a streak of orange reminded them of the place it landed. Akki looked at the orange mark on her hand and made another face. "I don't know why I did that," she said. "They're inedible."

A sudden loud sound ahead of them caused them to drop to the ground. The sound was like a giant sucking noise, ending with a sharp bang. The echo of that shot ricocheted off the trees behind them.

"Wardens!" Golden whispered.

They forced their bodies into the mud.

Then Jakkin rolled over and began to laugh. "Call us lizard waste," he said. "That's not wardens. It's only marsh bubbles. They sound like gunshots when they burst."

Akki laughed nervously with him, but Golden's mouth was set in a sharp, tight line.

"We've been too lax," he said. "We have to hurry to get across the river and the main highway. If I read the sun right, it's afternoon, and once we get into night, Dark After comes too soon."

Jakkin and Akki did not argue with him. There was nothing really to say. They pulled themselves out of the mud knowing that it would dry quickly and could be brushed off later. They turned north again, and sighting the mountains, a good day's steady march away, they set their sights on the western rim of the cliffs as sharp as dragon's teeth and walked on.

# 24

THE SUN WAS starting down behind the first ragged peak when they reached a cliff that dropped off abruptly. The Narrakka ran sluggishly but noisily below them, giving back little reflection of the cloudless sky or the kkhan reeds that lined the riverbank. Jakkin marveled at how such a muddy, slow river could issue the clear, quick-moving waters in the weirs. But the stone dikes were veined at intervals with water sieves keeping out impurities. "Four screens pure," they said at the farm.

The waters of the Narrakka below looked anything but pure, and the climb down to its rock-and-reed shore was precipitous.

"Too steep for climbing here," was Golden's quick assessment.

"But the only easy crossing is back at the road," Akki protested.

"We *have* to cross here." Jakkin pointed. "It's nearly eight kilometers back by the road to the bridge, all open ground, and dangerously close to the farm."

They fanned out and tried to find an easier incline, but it was all the same steep, sandy soil cliff that crumbled and showered rocks down to the river whenever they came close to the edge.

"We'll have to ride it down then," said Golden. "Like a slide."

"A slide?" Akki and Jakkin asked together.

Golden explained, using his hands to demonstrate. "Go down feet first, hands at your side for steering, in a sitting position." Pausing for a moment, he looked cautiously over the edge. "Try to avoid the rocks."

"It's much too dangerous," protested Akki.

"What other choice do we have?" Golden said.

Before they could argue further, Golden sat down and slid over the edge. His body scooped out a long waterfall of sand, and it seemed to take him forever to reach bottom. But at last he made it safely, and without stopping to wipe off his clothes, he stood up and raised his hands. "Easier than I thought." His voice strained to reach them over the noise of the river. He looked extremely small and vulnerable below them.

Jakkin put his hands on Akki's shoulders. "I'll keep a watch out for the wardens. You go next."

When she hesitated, he put his hands on her shoulders and, when she sat down, gave her a little push. She uttered a sharp gasp as the bank crumbled around her. Sand sprayed away from her body, and she was followed by an avalanche of small stones. Near the bottom she began to slip sideways, but Golden caught her.

Jakkin suddenly realized that he had been holding his breath from the moment Akki had slid over the side. Only when he saw her standing and waving did he start to evaluate his own slide. The more he thought about it, the less sure he felt, so he decided to stop thinking. He sat down in the depression that Akki's and Golden's bodies had left, and before he could start to think again, the bank had collapsed around him, sending him down the sand in a spray of dirt and dust. Except for a stone that hit his cheek and stung and the dust that made him cough, it was amazingly easy. He was at the bottom and wiping himself off when an awful thought hit him.

"How will we get up the other side?" he said. "It's even steeper than this one." He realized that the same thought had just occurred to the others.

"Why don't we get across the river first?" Golden said.

Holding hands, they crossed the sluggish chest-high Narrakka, but it was clear, by the way they eyed the far cliff, that all they could think of as they pushed through the water was the wall of sand on the other side.

The northern bank was not only higher but straight up and down, as if a knife had sheared it off. It was of the same soft, sandy soil. Each attempt they made at climbing ended the same way. The cliff collapsed around them. After several tries each, they stopped.

Jakkin found a rock and sat down. He closed his eyes and caged his face with his right hand, trying to figure out what to do. In his mind's eye he saw the cliff side, and he tried to envision a way of climbing the unstable sand. Yet even in his imagination the cliff kept tumbling down. As he walked about the landscape in his mind, he kept seeing things as if in a hazy dream. And then, far away, a great grey blot seemed to form, almost a cloud on the dream horizon.

Slowly the blot grew, took on substance, developed great wings and a rudderlike tail. At last he recognized it as a shadow figure of a dragon. As it came closer and closer still, its color began to change, first a grey-pink, then a soft maroon, then a deep red, the color of blood spilled on the sands. In the dreamscape the dragon's beating wings stirred the sand cliff and brought it crashing down into a smooth road in an instant of transformation. Jakkin felt his fists clench and unclench. If only real life could be transfigured as easily as a dream.

"Heart's Blood!"

Akki's shout cut into the dream, and Jakkin opened his eyes. Akki was standing and pointing. Golden was up as well.

It had been no dream, but a sending, for there, winging toward them, her scales reflecting the rays of the retreating sun, came the red dragon, a giant fireball, haloed in gold.

Jakkin's head filled with rainbows, and he shouted up at her, heedless of the noise, "Thou great worm, thou beauty. Come to me. Come to me."

Heart's Blood circled lower and lower, her wings beating more slowly. At last, hovering, the sun riding on her right shoulder, she stretched her hind legs down for a landing, and settled gingerly beside Jakkin's rock, folding her wings against her sides. The sand spiraled around her like dust clouds.

For a minute none of them spoke; then Golden said, "We can ride up the cliff side one at a time."

Akki's mouth made its crooked smile. "Senator, you know nothing about dragons."

Jakkin added, "They can't be ridden. With a weight on Heart's Blood's back she couldn't even raise her wings. And if you sat there without a saddle of some sort, your legs and groin would be slashed terribly by her scales. The scales move when she moves, and they slice at a touch."

"Thanks for the anatomy lesson," Golden said, "but we have to risk it. What else can we do?"

"Ardru, you aren't listening." Akki put her hands on her hips. "It is *physically* impossible for her to fly with anyone on her back. As for sitting on top of those scales, I wouldn't try it. I've seen men who have tried to sit on a *walking* dragon, and they were all but crippled for life."

"She *can* carry us," Jakkin interrupted. "At least a little way, which is all we need. Look." He shrugged out of his trainer's tunic, twisting it quickly and knotting it in four sturdy knots. "If I can show her how to carry this in her claws, we could hold on to it, and she could lift us one at a time, at least as high as the cliff top.''

Akki looked thoughtful. "It might overbalance her. Dragons aren't predators used to carrying off large hunks of meat. And don't forget, she damaged one of her right lanceae in the Pit.''

With a start Jakkin realized he *had* forgotten. Guilt washed over him, soothed immediately by the dragon's wash of color. "We have to try,'' he whispered softly.

Golden agreed. "It's all we've got.''

"Can you make her understand?'' Akki asked.

"I think so,'' Jakkin replied. "I hope so.'' He closed his eyes and concentrated. "Take the shirt, thou great ship of the air,'' he mouthed, carefully visualizing what he wanted her to do.

To her surprise she stood at once and snatched up the shirt in her claws, stretching it between them. Then she unfurled her wings, pumped them twice, pushed off with her hind legs, and hovered several meters in the air.

"She understands,'' Akki shouted, clapping her hands.

"I'll try it first,'' said Jakkin, having to shout over the combined noise of the river and the wind from the hovering dragon's wings. "If she'll take anyone, she'll take me.''

He reached up and held on to the knotted shirt, his muscles straining as the dragon pulled him up. "Take me up the cliff, thou beauty.''

He felt the wind from the wings around him, battering him. The material under his hands suddenly seemed too flimsy to bear his weight. In his imagination he could already hear it rip. As the ground slipped away, his arms felt as if they were being pulled out of their sockets. He refused to look down but stared up and at the sky.

Suddenly his feet were again on solid ground. He glanced around. The dragon had carried him to the cliff and deposited him on the top. Realizing he might be seen from the road, he lay down at once. Then he thought at the hovering dragon, "Get Akki. Quickly. Down to the river again for Akki.'' He had to persuade the dragon to get out of sight. He might possibly be missed by any passing trucks if he hid in the dunes, but the red dragon was unmistakable. Ferals never came close to the road, and a dragon her size and color would be recognized as a nursery dragon at once.

The dragon banked quickly, pumped her wings once, and glided over the cliff edge.

Jakkin checked the road again, rising just enough so that he could see for several kilometers in either direction. The road was still clear.

"Now," he shouted, knowing that his voice would not reach the dragon but that his thoughts would. "Now!"

The red of the dragon's back rose slowly out of the river-cut canyon, and then her wings beat up and down once more. When she cleared the top and winged slowly toward Jakkin, he saw Akki hanging, one-armed, from the tattered shirt.

She flopped down next to him and said breathlessly, "I'm afraid your shirt is shorter now by a knot. I almost lost it. Her claws are shredding the material, but there should be enough left for Golden. I don't think you'll be wearing that shirt again, though."

He reached over and touched her arm, then shouted to Heart's Blood, "Get Golden. Down to the river. Get the man."

It was then, as the dragon disappeared from sight into the canyon, that Jakkin saw the dust from a truck barreling toward them from the east, the direction of the farm. He didn't know if it was a truck filled with wardens or if it was from one of the smaller farms that lay past the nursery. Jakkin pushed Akki farther down into the sand, and they lay there, trembling. All the while Jakkin thought desperately at the red dragon, "Stay. Do not rise. Wait. Stay."

The truck seemed to take forever to pass, but the dust it raised was sufficient to hide them. When at last it was out of sight, Jakkin and Akki crawled over to the cliff's edge.

"Now come up," Jakkin urged the red.

The red rose and hovered above the river with Golden dangling from the shredded shirt. But as the dragon moved toward the cliff top, the shirt ripped one more time. And as Jakkin and Akki watched, Golden's body tumbled through the air. He had no time for a scream.

The dragon back-winged, hovered once again, and wept great bloody tears in Jakkin's mind. He was too shocked to answer. He edged closer to the cliff's rim with Akki a few hand's breadths beside him. They lay down flat to distribute their weight, then peered cautiously over the side.

On the riverbank, next to a rock, lying face-down, was Golden. His arms and legs were spread-eagled. He didn't move.

# 25

AKKI TURNED TO him. "Is Ardru hurt? Is he dead?"

"Get back. If this rim crumbles, we'll all be down there."

They inched away from the edge and sat staring at each other.

"I'll have to go down," said Jakkin at last.

"No, I should go," Akki answered. "After all, I'm the one who knows about injuries. I'm the doctor. Almost."

Jakkin stood up. "He's too heavy for you. I'll deal with this."

Akki scrambled up and pulled angrily at his arm. "One of the first things a doctor learns is how—and when—to move a patient. You wouldn't even know if he could be moved or not. I'm the logical one to go."

Jakkin looked at her seriously. "Whether or not he *should* be moved, he *has* to be moved. That's why—"

Before he could finish his thought, the dragon's mind had intruded, a landscape similar to the one on which they were standing. In Jakkin's mind Heart's Blood played out a different scene.

Jakkin understood at once. "Go," he said. He held on to Akki's hand as the dragon back-winged carefully, descending once again into the river-cut crevasse.

A moment later she rose with her wings pumping furiously, claws firmly fixed in Golden's belt. His body hung limply. Heart's Blood barely skimmed the top of the cliff, and Golden's feet dragged along the ground. Jakkin and Akki ran over and took Golden from her. One of the lanceae on the dragon's right claw was torn, hanging by a thread of flesh.

Jakkin managed to carry Golden a few feet before depositing him gently in the sand. There was a nasty gash on his back.

Akki took off Golden's shirt. Sprinkling some yellow powder from her medkit onto the wound, she examined the outer edges of the tear.

"Not too bad," she said, ripping the shirt into lengths of bandage. She settled it over the wound, then around his waist and up over his shoulder. "There's a nasty bump on his head as well. Concussion probably. But since he's breathing, that's a help. We have to wake him, though."

She worked furiously for a minute at rousing him, and at last his eyes fluttered open. His hand went to his head.

"I feel awful," Golden said. "What happened?"

"You fell, and then the dragon carried you up here by your belt. You're bruised a bit, possibly concussed." Akki's manner was decidedly professional.

"You sound like a miniature Henkky," said Golden, trying to smile at his own feeble joke.

"Let's hope I'm near as good as she is," said Akki. "Can you see how many fingers I'm holding up?" She wiggled two in front of his face.

"Three," he said. Then, seeing her stricken look, quickly amended, "Two, I see two. I was just kidding." He put his hands to his head. "Still there, not in pieces. No time for sickness. We'd better be going." He added with another attempt at humor, "With or without me."

"*With!*" Akki and Jakkin said together, easing him to his feet.

Golden leaned on their shoulders for support.

An explosion of dark colors burst in Jakkin's head. He jerked around and saw the dust of a truck approaching.

"Jakkin," warned Akki.

"Down!" Jakkin shouted, pulling the others with him.

The small dunes hid them, but Heart's Blood was a mammoth red sign to any watcher.

"Away, away," Jakkin called to her.

At his desperate cry the dragon wheeled to her right and, wings beating rapidly, sped off toward the mountains. Her dark sending slowly faded.

The three waited breathlessly as the truck passed them. Either the driver had not seen the dragon or he was unaware of the significance of the great red worm hovering over the road. When the noise of the truck was more whine than roar, they stood up.

Golden seemed alert. In his old, high, fluting senator's voice, he said, "My dears, I can move by myself now. Except for my head and my back and my stomach and my heart (which is beating so fast because of the presence of that great beast of yours, Jakkin), I feel marvelous.''

They laughed, though Jakkin wondered how, in the midst of running for their lives, they could.

Making a dash across the road, they supported Golden between them. Soon they found a rough path leading into the foothills. But with the first moon just edging the horizon, the rocks of the countryside were part shadow, part real, and they stumbled frequently. Akki complained and Golden groaned at each misstep. Jakkin took on the role of cheerleader, encouraging them on.

"The second moonrise will give us light as bright as day, and then we won't fall over our feet," he said.

"The second moonrise will give the wardens enough light to shoot us by," snapped Akki. "And Golden should be lying down. Where *are* those Dark After houses? With the two of you shirtless, we'd better find one soon."

That started the old argument again. Jakkin, afraid the wardens would search all the houses, resisted. Akki countered that if they wanted to keep Golden alive, they needed to stop. Only Golden was silent, his face a mask of pain.

A vague memory began to tease Jakkin, part visual, part sound, as if he were receiving something from Heart's Blood. Yet it was not at all like the vivid landscapes she usually sent him; it was more a memory compounded of a dark, smoky interior and a woman's voice.

"Shut it, Jakky," said the voice.

The smoke made him cough, but his face was warm.

"Wait!" Jakkin said suddenly. "There *may* be another way. When my father was trying to train a feral, we lived in the foothills for a while, and after the first few nights I don't think we stayed in houses. We were in a cave. If we could find a cave and shelter in it, close up the cave mouth—"

"If—if—if," said Akki. "*If* we find a cave and *if* we can close up the cave mouth. We don't have the luxury of time, and the only *if* I see as possible is that *if* we don't find a place for Golden soon, he won't have a chance."

"Need a proper door," said Golden, parceling out the words.

Suddenly Heart's Blood's familiar signals announced she was near. Jakkin started to laugh. "How stupid we've all been. *She* will be our door." He pointed up to the dark shape winging toward them. "That's what dragons do in the wild to keep their eggs warm when they're hatching. They block up the mouth of a cave with their own bodies, a built-in furnace.''

The sound of the dragon's wings cleaving the air came to them. They started up the path toward her, heedless now of the shadow rocks.

~

THE CAVE THEY found was far bigger than they needed. The floor was damp and cold because of a spring that ran alongside one wall, but Akki swore the spring would be useful, so they stayed.

Akki tore a strip from one of the bandages, soaked it in the water, and cleaned the wound on Golden's back. Then they drank their fill of the clear springwater, using their cupped hands.

"I don't think I've ever tasted anything sweeter," commented Jakkin.

Once the moon had risen, Akki was able to find some edible fungi growing right outside the cave. It broke off like soft bread and was bread-colored as well, though it had no particular taste. Still it was filling, and Akki and Jakkin, so long without anything to eat, gorged themselves on it.

"Eat as much as you want, but eat it now," Akki said. "We can't save this stuff. Once it's broken off, it starts to go bad. After a few hours it's slightly poisonous. It wouldn't kill us—only make us slightly sick.''

Golden laughed. "I'm sick enough, thank you," he said, but he ate, too.

The first signs of the Dark After cold began, the slight crackling in the air when the twin moons squatted on the far horizon.

Jakkin and Akki went into the cave and moved Golden away from the stream onto the driest portion of the floor. Then the three of them curled together like spoons, Akki around Jakkin and Golden around them both so that nothing touched his injured back.

Heart's Blood circled in front of the cave entrance three times. When she finally settled, head on tail, her back mounded up into an arch that almost sealed off the mouth of the cave. She began to thrum contentedly, a sound that obscured any sendings. The heat from her body and the steam and smoke issuing from her nose slits raised the cave's temperature quickly.

Akki and Golden fell into exhausted sleeps, but Jakkin stayed awake a much longer time. He could hear, beyond the dragon's deep thrumming, the scrabblings of little claws on the cave walls as finger-size flikka darted about, wakened by the warmth. Twice Heart's Blood snapped up a mouthful of the tiny creatures and munched noisily.

Jakkin tried to count individual flikka by the sound and was up to thirty-seven when he, too, finally nodded off.

# *26*

WHEN JAKKIN AWOKE, the dragon had already gone to graze on the wild wort and weed in the valley. What had wakened him was not the dragon leaving, but Akki coming into the cave mouth, her hands full of berries.

"This was what I could find close to the cave," she said. "I was afraid to wander farther off while you were asleep. Do you know that you snore? I wish I'd thought to get us some cactus fruit when we were still on the desert floor."

Jakkin stretched and sat up. He looked over at Golden. The man was pale, and his body was covered with a shiny sweat. His eyes were open, and his breath was coming in short gasps.

"Golden!" Akki cried, and knelt, putting the berries by his side in a small pile. She looked at Jakkin. "He wasn't like this when I left. When did this start?" Then, without waiting for an answer, she put her arm under his neck and eased him up into a sitting position. His breathing became less torturous, but he started to shake. Akki held him, warming him with her own body.

"We have to get him outside, into the sun, out of this damp cave."

They made a chair of their arms and carried him outside, and when they put him down with his back to a flat rock, he smiled. "Guess I just couldn't stand the smell in there," he said.

"What smell?" asked Jakkin.

"Oh, Jakkin, the whole cave reeks of dragon," Akki said. "You and I are used to it. But other people find it—well—offensive." She stood up and went back into the cave. When she returned, she had washed the berries in the stream.

"I don't find dragon-smell offensive," Golden assured Jakkin. "Different. Alien even. And very, very obvious."

"Here," Akki interrupted, giving the largest share of the berries to Golden. "Breakfast."

They ate the sweet berries in companionable silence; then Golden said, "We can't stay here. We're still much too close to the road and to the farm. If there really is a community of outlanders somewhere in the mountains, we'd better head that way. There seem to be enough caves in these cliffs, and with your dragon's help we can shelter at night. Once we find those other people, we can have one take a message to the Federation representative and they can send a copter for us and fly us offplanet."

"Leave Austar? But why?" Jakkin felt himself go cold.

Golden answered slowly. "This society is in a very unstable condition right now, I'm afraid. I didn't see that soon enough. The rebels are much stronger and bloodier minded than any of us knew. And now the wardens will be out to crush anyone they even suspect of rebel sympathies. In their minds you two—and I—are rebels. Now is not the time to try to argue with them. We'll just lift you offplanet and then set you down again when things are resolved."

"No," Jakkin said.

"It won't be forever. Just a little while."

"No."

"Why?"

"Because you're only guessing that the Federation will help us. You don't know that for sure. You know, in a way, Golden, you are the Federation's dragon. They're running you in this fight just as you were running Akki and me. But we're refusing to play anymore. Not without knowing all the rules. I think you should find out all the rules, too, before you continue to play." Jakkin was adamant, and it showed in his voice.

"Is that all of it?"

Jakkin shook his head. "No. It's not. I've heard it said that anyone who goes offplanet can't talk to dragons any more."

"Rumors—that's all. You believe rumors?"

Jakkin smiled. "I'm a bonder, remember? Rumors play a big role in our lives. But think about this—offworlders can't hear the dragons. Even our great-great-grandparents, the first KKers, couldn't link with the dragons. Linkage was something that happened years later. So, rumor or not, I won't chance it."

"You don't really *talk* to those dragons," Golden said. "Not any more than a man on Old Earth could talk to his dog. Or his cat. Or his horse.''

''I don't know about horses or cats or dogs,'' Jakkin said. ''I've never seen one of those. But I know dragons.''

''They're animals, Jakkin,'' Golden said. ''You don't chance your life on them.''

Akki interrupted. ''But he *does* talk to dragons. A little. Even I can hear Heart's Blood.''

''And what does she say in these conversations?'' asked Golden.

''It's not words,'' Akki admitted. ''More like colored pictures in my head.''

''There, you see, Jakkin,'' Golden said. ''Your dragons probably have some slight esper sense. A level-two intelligence perhaps. Or three. But true language takes a level six, Jakkin. And in all the explored universe, only humans have that. Your dragon is an animal. Be sensible.''

''I am being sensible. I'm just not going to run away offplanet. But Akki is free to go.''

''Of course I'm *free* to go. But I'm not going anywhere without you, Jakkin,'' she said. She spoke with such intensity Jakkin looked at her in surprise. She stared back defiantly, chin raised.

Jakkin wanted to touch her cheek or hold her hand or hug her. But she looked so fierce he just nodded, his face a mask.

''We'll talk about this later,'' Golden said through a grimace. It was clear he was in pain. ''But we're going to have to go farther up the mountain. Farther and higher before we can head for The Rokk. And fast.'' He collapsed suddenly. It was clear he was in no condition to move quickly, even though he urged it, so they planned the day in easy stages because of him, leaving him to rest out in the sun for a while.

''I'll take the time to find us some food,'' Akki said. ''Give me your bag to carry berries in. And whatever else I find. With two bags, I should be able to get enough for today at least.''

Jakkin put his hand over the soft leather, kneading it with his fingers. His bondbag. He recalled his mother's placing the chain around his neck. ''Now you're a bonder,'' she said. ''But you're still a human being. Walk proudly. Let no man really own you. Fill your bag yourself.'' He pulled the chain over his head and held the bag in his hand. It was much lighter than he expected. He handed it to Akki, and she took it without a word. Then she was gone.

Jakkin rubbed his chest where the bag should have been. It felt strange not to have that lump of leather there. Turning to Golden, he said, "Funny how little things can be big burdens."

Golden was about to answer when they heard Akki scream.

"Akki, what is it?" Jakkin cried out. "Are you all right?"

The only answer was another scream.

"Here," Golden said, digging into his pants pocket and pulling out his knife. He snapped out the largest blade. It was serrated and very sharp.

Jakkin took the knife and fumbled in his pocket for his own. "You take mine."

"Keep it for Akki. Now go."

Jakkin needed no more urging. He ran down the hill sliding on the rough pebbles as he went. He shouted, "Akki, I'm coming." Then he heard a dragon's scream, feeling at the same time an alien flash of angry orange streaks in his mind. Heart's Blood was a mute, so he knew it was not she.

Akki's answer hastened him on.

"It's a feral, Jakkin. Hurry. *Please.*"

He made the final turning onto a flat ledge, and there was Akki, backed against the cliff face, a large white stick in her hand. Above her, lanceae fully extended and back-winging in order to hover, was an enormous brown male dragon with a spattering of blood-red spots along the underside of his wings. His hackle was a furious red, and smoke spouted through his nose slits.

As Jakkin ran toward him, he shouted furiously at the dragon, "Stop! Back! You!" He had thought to divert his attention from Akki; but the dragon had apparently decided Akki was the worst of the intruders, and he kept her pinned to the wall while covering Jakkin's mind with a pulsing, angry purple slime. Jakkin had to shake his head several times in order to turn away the attack.

It was the violent head-shaking synchronized with Jakkin's thoughts that at last caught the dragon's attention for a second, and Akki swung the stick hard, connecting with the brown's nose.

The dragon answered with a spout of flame that singed Akki's hand. She screamed, dropping the stick.

Jakkin charged in, the knife in front of him, slipped under the dragon, and came up with the blade at the dragon's throat. He made one slash and was starting the second when the dragon wheeled away. As he turned, he knocked Jakkin over with the hard secondary rib of his wing. Jakkin would have fallen off the cliff if Akki had not grabbed his arm and pulled him toward her. They fell back together against the rock.

"Why did he leave?" Jakkin asked.

"I don't know," Akki answered. She bent over to pick up the stick. For the first time Jakkin realized that it was a piece of dragon bone from the tail of a full-grown dragon.

"Where did you get that?" he asked.

"In a cave down there," she said, suddenly looking past his shoulder at the sky.

Jakkin felt Heart's Blood at the same moment, an overwhelming, angry, jagged attack of colors, bursting like great violet bombs in his head. He looked up, following Akki's pointing arm. In the sky two dragons spiraled up in a midair fight, first one, then the other on top. They tumbled so quickly they began to blur.

Suddenly one broke away and began a fast, downward plunge. The other followed.

From the mountainside Jakkin and Akki watched as if paralyzed. Finally Akki spoke. "It's Heart's Blood. She's falling."

Yet in his mind Jakkin did not hear the agonized death scream of a dying dragon. It was not a fading color, going out like a candle. Instead, he felt a deep, sly pulsing, a golden glow with a steady rainbow heartbeat beneath. Still, as he watched, she plummeted, and the brown male followed. Her wings were by her side, as if they had been clipped. The brown was having trouble keeping up in regular dive, so he slammed his own wings by his side, dropping after her. They fell without a sound.

At the last possible moment Heart's Blood unfurled her wings and back-flipped, landing jarringly. Too late the male tried to do the same. Heavier than she and already injured by Akki's blow to the nose and Jakkin's slash to the throat, he let his wings out a fraction of the second past the time he needed. He hit the ground on his back, slamming down with a terrible noise, as if the ground were breaking open. Three cracks appeared beneath his body, zigzagging like scars. Heart's Blood walked over slowly and gave the brown two more slashes on his throat, but he was already dead. She stared at him for a long time, scratched a little dirt over him, then turned her head up toward Jakkin.

From so far above her he could not see her eyes. But he knew from her sending that she was exhausted. Her rainbow signature was shaking, faded and ragged around the edges and shot through with a strange, ugly series of blood-red lines. Jakkin watched her limp slightly, favoring the right front paw with the torn lanceae.

*Go down, beauty. Eat thou, and rest,* he thought at her.

But as if denying her weariness, the red dragon pumped her wings twice, leaped into the air, and flew upward.

Jakkin put his arm around Akki's shoulder. Her arm went around his waist. Together they turned and went back up the path while overhead the dragon marked their place, a red banner against the bright morning sky.

# 27

GOLDEN WAS NO longer leaning against the rock. He had fallen over and lay on his side. Akki ran to him and felt his wrist, then listened to his chest.

"He's breathing, but his pulse is awfully weak."

"Can we get him to walk? Or carry him?" asked Jakkin.

Akki shook her head. "I don't think so."

Golden managed to whisper, "Leave me here."

They both stared at him, then ignored his command.

Golden tried again. "You *must* leave me. Whoever finds me will take me back. Then I can contact the Federation forces. They will rescue you. Take you offplanet."

"He doesn't give up," said Jakkin to Akki. He knelt. "Stop talking. Save your breath. We'll move back into this cave for one more night. The rest will do you good. No one seems to be following us, so obviously they have no idea where we are." He hoped he was right.

Standing, Akki spoke with a soothing voice. "I'll go on up the trail and gather what I can for food. Heart's Blood is overhead. She won't let any other dragons by. And Jakkin will watch the path below. We'll move you out of the direct sun, and you can rest."

It was obvious Golden had used up what strength he had. He just nodded his head and closed his eyes.

Akki pulled Jakkin by the arm, moving him down the trail a bit and whispered urgently, "He looks really bad, Jakkin. It's not just the head or the back. He must have injured something internally when he fell. And then when the dragon picked him up . . ."

"It wasn't her fault," Jakkin said.

"Of course it wasn't her fault," Akki answered quickly. "I'm just stating facts."

"What does he need?"

"Nothing we can give him here. Rest. A bed. Good food. An operation. I don't know." She touched his arm again, and he felt the warmth of it.

"Akki," he said.

She must have heard the longing in his voice. After hugging him briefly, she ran up the path, past Golden, around a turning, and out of sight.

Jakkin made Golden comfortable, laying him under an overhang to keep the sun from shining directly on him. Then he went back down the path to the turning where Akki had fought the feral. There was another cave, smaller than the one they had sheltered in, but half-hidden by a flowering berry bush. That must have been why they had missed it the night before. Jakkin pulled the bush aside and peered in.

There was the skeleton Akki had found, its bones scattered by the smaller creatures that had sheltered in the cave in the years following the dragon's death. The mound of yellow-white dragon bones was only a small reminder of what had once been a worm of great power. Its foreleg bone was almost as long as Jakkin was tall. He wondered if they could make some use of it. He carried it with him as he backed out of the cave and leaned against the rock face. Closing his eyes, he tried to remember for a moment what it felt like to be back at the nursery with nothing more to worry about than the next round of cleaning stalls. The sun felt warm against his upturned face. He dozed.

A hand on his arm woke him in an instant. He turned, ready to fight, and saw it was Akki.

"I've found lots more berries on a plateau about a kilometer up. There are enormous amounts of chikkberries and warden's heart." She held out her hand. The right one held the pink chikkberries; the left was already stained with the wine-colored juice of the black warden's heart. "Go on. Eat. I already gave some to Ardru."

He had eaten all the tart chikkberries and was halfway through the overly sweet warden's heart when he thought to ask, "Did you have any yourself?"

She laughed and pointed at her white suit. It was stained with several shades of red and black. Some of the stain was berry juice, and some was Golden's blood. "While I picked, I ate. I'm no martyr, Jakkin. I was hungry—and the berries were there."

Jakkin wolfed down the rest.

"I brought back enough in my shirt and my own bag to satisfy us for now. But I can't find your bag, Jakkin. I must have lost it fighting the dragon. I had just been holding it, not wearing it around my neck. I feel awful. I know how much it meant to you. But now it's gone."

Jakkin's hand went instinctively to his chest. He thought he should have felt a great loss, but somehow he only felt relieved. "I think I wanted it gone for good," he whispered. "Only I couldn't just *throw* it away."

"Well, it's gone for good now," she said. "You'll have to find something else to hold on to when you're worried."

"Did I do that?" he asked. "Did I really do that?"

She nodded. Then she stood on tiptoe and kissed him on the cheek. "Don't be embarrassed. It was . . . endearing." She laughed.

He felt his face burn, and he put his hand up to his cheek. Then he grinned. Feeling a tickle in his brain, like an echo of that grin, he looked up. Heart's Blood was still circling, a lazy scripting against the clean slate of sky. Jakkin called up to her, "Keep watch, my worm."

Her answer was a blood-red circle against a clear dream sky, a sentinel sign.

~

IT WAS MIDAFTERNOON, the kind of lazy, hazy, and hot afternoon that had always made Jakkin want to nap on the farm. Jakkin had scouted halfway back down the mountainside while Akki had gone up. Each time Jakkin checked on Golden, the man had been asleep, his forehead wet and feverish. Several times he had mumbled incomprehensibly about dragon's teeth and armed men and dragon's blood turning a man invisible. When he finally woke, Jakkin had asked him what the dreams had meant.

"Not dreams," Golden had said, sipping water Jakkin brought in his hands. "But Old Earth stories. Made up by men and women who had never seen real dragons, who could never have dreamed of Austar."

Jakkin tried to consider what a life without dragons would be like, but such a thing was incomprehensible to him. If he had to go offworld and so shut himself away from the big worms, he might as well die.

Akki returned with cave apples, the round reddish mushrooms that grew deep in certain caves. She had found more warden's hearts, too. Jakkin thought he would never get that sickly sweet taste out of his mouth. The leaves of chikkberries she claimed made good tea, but without a pot or fire, they could not even draw a stain from the leaves. They were forced to drink the water plain.

Akki used the soft tie of her suit dipped in the stream to sponge Golden off, and they tried everything they could to make him comfortable. He never complained but seemed to spend less and less time awake, more and more time in that half-conscious, mumbling state. His voice changed back and forth, too. Sometimes he raged in the high fluting, and other times it was pleasant and low. He spoke in tongues neither of them could decipher and once cried out Henkky's name and would be quieted only when Akki held him close.

The afternoon sun had started on its downward swing when the dragon sent an early signal of alarm: a march of red dots, bristling with fiery heads, across a sand-colored plain. At first Jakkin did not understand.

"What is it?" he asked aloud.

Akki looked at him, puzzled.

The signal came again, and this time it was unmistakable. Someone *was* on their track now. The easy trail they had left since Golden had been hurt had been discovered. They had lost too much time nursing him. And now a line of many men was marching toward them.

"Wing away," Jakkin commanded, hoping that Heart's Blood might lead the searchers off. She wheeled away east and south across the plain, across the river, far out of sight.

"She's heading back to the nursery," Jakkin exclaimed.

"To get her hatchlings?"

"It's probably too soon for them to fly this far," he said. "Maybe she's just going to feed them. Maybe she's just going to rest. But we can't. We have to go higher. We still have time to get away. She'll return at Dark After. She'll find us."

"We can't leave Golden." Akki was adamant.

Jakkin put his hand to his chest, fingers searching for the bag that was no longer there. "Of course not. We'll take him with us. Between us we can carry him."

Golden struggled to talk. "Can't move."

"He's right. He can't be moved. At least not up and away from civilization." Akki's face was dark.

Golden fumbled in the pocket of his pants and drew out a little book. "Take it. Keep it safe." He handed it to Akki.

"Is this about the rebellion?" she asked gently. "About the Federation?"

He laughed softly. "No, sweet child. I have been writing down

Old Earth stories. About dragons. For the children . . . of Austar. Take it. In case.''

"In case what?'' asked Jakkin.

"In case I don't see you again.'' He smiled, and in that high-pitched voice he added, "I can't wait to see my old friend Kkalkkav. I have some wild tales to spin him.''

Akki took the book and slipped it into the pocket of her stained shirt. She didn't bother to look in it. "I think we'd better move you back into the cave,'' she said. "Way back. There's a niche beyond the stream where you can be comfortable, and we'll lead them a merry chase, Jakkin and I. We'll come back as soon as we can.''

"We'll leave the rest of the berries, too.''

"And the cave apples,'' said Akki.

"All the comforts of home,'' Golden added, his eyes closing once again. "Don't worry, and don't explain. Years from now we all will make up a song about this. It will . . . it will be sung in the dragon nurseries.''

" 'Golden's Stand,' '' Jakkin said, smiling.

"As long as it's not 'Golden's *Last* Stand,' '' Akki said.

"It's more like 'Golden's Sit.' I don't think I'm up to standing. Don't lose that book.''

Akki shook her head. "I won't.''

They carried him into the cave, across the stream, and placed him in a half-sitting position with the berries and cave apples close at hand.

"Now go,'' he whispered to them.

They ran out of the cave and started up the cliff path without looking back. For the first time they could hear sounds of people on the pathways behind them.

"Did we do the right thing?'' Akki asked when they rounded a turn that put the cave completely out of sight.

"We did the only thing we could,'' Jakkin answered.

A sunburst exploded in his head as Heart's Blood appeared once more in the sky above them, bright against the fading blue of sky.

"Heart's Blood!'' they whispered to each other, waving at her as she dipped her right wing before diving straight down at something beneath her. As they watched, she suddenly threw her wings out and went into a stall. She raked the ground below her with flames.

There were answering flames from below as an extinguisher threw its punishing rays up at the dragon. But the range was much too great, and Heart's Blood banked to the right and flew away. A great deal of shouting and cursing followed her flight.

"She's keeping them busy. Maybe they'll think she's just a feral defending territory. She'll buy us time."

"The only way they'll believe *she's* a feral is if none of the bonders are with them. And if they find Golden . . ." Jakkin paused.

"What else? There's something else, Jakkin. You must tell me."

"I'm worried about Heart's Blood. She's worn out. She broke that claw carrying Golden. She had that Pit fight yesterday and the day before, and the fight with the feral today. She has been circling above us since then, not even taking time to eat."

Akki put her hands on his. "*She* knows what she's doing. We're the ones who do not. We have no weapons to fight stingers. At least she has flames. And claws."

"We have *this*," Jakkin said, holding up the knife.

"We have these," Akki said, pointing to her feet. "And *this*." She pointed to her head. "And that's what we are going to have to use now, or all of Heart's Blood's fighting will not help us."

She ran up the path, and Jakkin reluctantly followed.

~

THEY CAME TO the plateau where Akki had picked the berries. It was about three kilometers wide and covered with a grey-green furze broken by occasional berry bushes. Outcroppings of rock protruded like veins. A path seemed to wind around the edge of the field, a gnarled finger pointing upward. They stayed on that path, and it led them to a group of cliff faces, sitting like the crown of a hat on a brim of the plateau. The cliffs themselves were pathless, unclimbable, but honeycombed with caves. Some were shallow niches in the rock face, dents in the crown. Still others were deep, seemingly bottomless pits.

They had tried half a dozen, looking for a way through the cliff, and had just come out of a narrow, water-filled slot when they saw the red dragon appear over the plateau's rim. She was back-winging furiously, and her flames were sputtering. Without meaning to, she was leading the wardens right to them.

"Send her away, Jakkin," Akki cried out to him. "Her flames are almost out. She can't help anymore."

*Away! Away!* Jakkin thought at her, not daring to shout.

Her answer was to turn and fly toward them, a dark red angel with mountainous wings. She crouched on the path in front of them, and they shrugged back into the narrow wet cave.

*Against the wall,* Jakkin thought hopelessly. *We're trapped with our backs against the wall.*

Heart's Blood used her great body to seal them in and shut out the rest of the light.

Jakkin put his hand on the dragon's back and thought at her, *Thou beauty, thou great and loyal friend, remember the oasis. Remember the ribbon of water. Remember that thee has eaten from my hand.*

The dragon thrummed at him, and the sound of it made the tiny cave hum, sending little waves lapping against the cave wall. Jakkin could feel the vibrations in his bones as his head filled with the dragon's colored memories of their past together.

Akki slipped her hand in his. "I love you, Jakkin," she said.

After a moment he squeezed her hand. "I know," he said. "I know that. I guess I've known it for a long time, though I was always afraid to ask. In case you said no, knowing how much I love you." He turned to look at her, but it was too dark to see more than the outline of her head. He was glad, for that way he was forced to remember just her face, with its frame of dark hair and the crooked smile that had once been so happy and unafraid.

Dropping Akki's hand, he took the knife from his pocket and opened it by feel. Then he pushed the dragon aside and slipped out under her right leg. He looked at the plateau. The first moon was just rising, and he could see about two dozen shapes crossing in front of it, coming toward them through the furze. With the moon behind them they were faceless, dark, armed men moving through the low bushy brush. There was something electric in the air. Surprisingly he felt incredibly alive and unafraid.

"Are they wardens?" he whispered to Akki. She had pushed out of the cave to stand beside him. "Or rebels?"

"Does it matter?" she asked back.

He shook his head.

# 28

UNDER JAKKIN'S HAND Heart's Blood's thrumming slowly faded. She sent one rolling landscape of color—calm blues and greens with a swelling tide of red coming up from behind. Then waves of red—blood-red, wine-red, takk-red—rolled over and swamped the blue, roiling and boiling in a tidal wave. The dragon arched up and held her damaged claw in front of her. One lancea hung raggedly, but the other was fully extended. Behind them Jakkin could see that the unum, sedundum, and tricept were rigid. She opened her great maw as if to roar. Smoke streaked from her nose slits, followed by a furnace blast of fire. Jakkin felt the silent roar echo in his head; he was almost felled by it.

The line of marchers in the furze held back.

"Master Jakkin, give it up," came a shout.

"Errikkin!" Jakkin murmured. "I should have known."

A small knot of color, a tangle of many colored strings, crept into his head. Slowly one thread, a bland yellow, was unraveled from it.

Jakkin smiled quietly. "All right," he whispered to the dragon. Then he shouted out to Errikkin, "No man owns *me*, bonder. And I own no man. I manumit you. You're free now. Make your own decisions. Be your own master."

Tiny pops from the stingers were the marchers' answers. They came from three places, on both flanks and in the middle. *Pop-pop-pop* and then silence. *Pop-pop-pop* and then silence again.

"I think they have only three stingers," said Akki.

The dragon flamed one more time.

Only three match points answered her.

"I think you're right," said Jakkin. "For what good it does us. Even one is too many."

Jakkin concentrated on the dark line. It seemed to be moving only on the edges, and at last he could see that they were trying a pincers movement, circling around the edges of the field while leaving the center in a wide arc. They were hampered by the fact that the only path was guarded by the dragon.

"If we can hold them off until just before Dark After, they'll have to leave," he said urgently to Akki. "They'll have to get back down the mountain to a shelter."

"And then we can go get Golden," she said.

He did not want to tell her that he thought Golden was probably already dead—or as good as dead. Their only hope was to go higher, not lower, or find a way through the catacombed cliffs, but they could never go back down the way they had come.

"We *will* go back to get him, won't we?" Akki asked again.

Before he could answer, a voice called out, "We have your friend. We found him in a cave."

Jakkin's hand sought Akki's. "Don't answer. You know that even as an offworlder he'd have to answer to Austarian law. We're a Protectorate, not a state. But I bet that the Federation will do what it can for him. And if you give up now, the Federation will probably help you, too."

She held on to his hand. "Oh, Jakkin, you haven't been hearing me at all. Don't you understand? I'm staying with you. Nothing could make me leave."

Heart's Blood flamed again at the nearest marchers, but her flames lacked the deep blue heart. Still, some of the furze caught on fire and smoldered, sending up a smoke screen that popped with sparks each time a pocket of sap boiled. Straggles of grey haze came from the dragon's nose slits, adding to the smoke.

On their right flank one of the stingers blazed. Because of the distance as well as the smoke screen, it did not come close to them. Something hit the rock face high above the dragon's head, and small boulders rained down on her back, bouncing harmlessly off her scales. Slivers of granite sliced into Jakkin's upraised arm as he sheltered beneath it. Stone dust made his eyes tear for a moment. Akki began to cough.

Another burst from the stinger was even farther off. But the marchers moved closer.

"Hold thy flame, my beauty," Jakkin cautioned. "Let them come into thy range."

But the dragon could not be held. The anger in the marchers' minds reached out and goaded her. She leaped into the air, pumping her wings madly, fanning the blaze in the bushes. The smoke and the fire forced the marchers to retreat to the plateau's edge. Heart's Blood chased after them, slashing wildly at their backs, then returning when she had pushed them to the path down the mountain. She circled slowly and landed on the spot she had just left, her back to the cliff and to Jakkin and Akki.

It took a long time for the small fires to burn themselves out and the smoke to lift.

"Dark After is almost here," Akki said breathlessly. "Look!" She pointed to the western rim to their right, where the second moon was just now settling close to its brother on the horizon. Soon they would leak color along the edge of the sky.

"The wardens will *have* to leave now." Jakkin said the words, hoping they were true.

Just then the dragon hauled herself up in a hind-foot rise, her front legs raking the air, sensing something that they had not yet seen or heard. A thin scream ripped through the air, a harsh yellow bolt of lightning shot into Jakkin's head, and he saw what the dragon saw. Under the cover of the smoke, the three wardens with stingers had crept back and were within firing range. The scream had been Golden's warning to them, but it was too late.

There was a burst from the three stingers at once, as bright and near as the eyes of a scavenger, and as merciless. One shot struck the rocks right above the dragon's uplifted head. One hit beside Akki, showering her with stone. The third hit Heart's Blood in the throat, the unblemished, unscarred throat with its tender neck links of dark red scale. A bright flower seemed to bud and bloom there. Then, slowly falling, falling as though the world were ending, the dragon collapsed on top of Jakkin, on top of Akki, pushing them into the rock-littered ground. The rainbow of her mind went out color by color: red, orange, yellow, green, blue, indigo jewels fading one after another until all that was left was a faint violet glow.

"Leave them for Dark After," came a shout. "We don't have much time ourselves. Let's get back down the hill."

There was the sound of a general scramble down the mountainside. Then all was silent. The plateau lay charred and ruined under the darkening sky.

# 29

"Jakkin. Jakkin." The voice calling him came from far away, and Jakkin had to swim up through muddy waters into consciousness and the cold. He was lying under a heavy weight. Someone was slapping his face.

"Jakkin, please. Oh, please. You have to get up."

He opened his eyes and saw Akki bending over him, her body outlined by the wash of white-gold that signified the false dawn and the start of the bone-chilling, killing cold of Dark After.

He wondered where the rest of the night had gone and what it was that was weighing him down. He murmured, "Dark After, nothing after," a saying drilled into Austarians, from birth. He reached for his bondbag by habit and found nothing but his bare chest. Only then did he remember.

"Heart's Blood!" he screamed out, his throat raw with the sound of her name. He knew now what the weight holding him down was. He pushed out from under her leg. "Heart's Blood," he whispered passionately, but the great dragon did not move.

Jakkin stood and put his hand on her massive scaled body. He traced the zigzag scar that ran down the length of her leg. Then he closed his eyes and tried desperately to reach her with his mind.

"She's dead, Jakkin," Akki said as gently as she could, though nothing could soften the brutality of the words. "She shielded us with her body even as she died. But she's dead."

"No," said Jakkin, his voice sounding reasonable. "No, she's not dead." He searched in his mind for some lingering sending. "She wouldn't have died without my knowing."

Akki put her arms around his waist, trying to lend him some

comfort. She spoke softly. ''We'll be dead, too, if we don't find some shelter. Please, Jakkin.''

He turned in her arms and held her.

''No,'' he said.

She looked up at him. Her face was streaked with tears, and there was a blood score at the corner of her left eyebrow that had not been there before.

Jakkin looked away. ''What does it matter now if we die?''

''Matter? Matter? Your life matters. And mine. That's what Heart's Blood died for, defending us with flame and claw. That's what she took a shot in the neck for. In a hind-foot rise, defiant to the end. *I* heard her, Jakkin. And she didn't give up because she wanted you to live.'' She shouted at him, and he was forced to look at her again. Her face was blazing with anger. Her hair was in tangles. The blood score on her face was bright red, and she had burns on both forearms. She looked both terrible and beautiful, helpless and fierce, and he could feel that fierceness inside, filling him with new strength.

He held out his hand. ''All right. We'll go down to the cave.''

''No. Without Heart's Blood to stopper it, we'd be dead before morning. Any of these caves are useless as well.'' She pushed her tangled hair behind her ears.

''Then what could we possibly use for shelter? We can't make it all the way down the mountains in time.''

''We'll shelter in *her*.''

Jakkin looked at Heart's Blood's body, the scales too dusty now to catch the matte rays of the false dawn. He felt terribly cold. ''What do you mean?'' he asked slowly, afraid he knew.

''We can shelter *inside her*. Her body will hold its warmth for at least the four hours we need until Dark After breaks.'' Her voice was flat and matter-of-fact.

''*Inside* her.'' There were no words for his disgust, his terror.

''Like a hatchling, Jakkin. We'll be her hatchlings. She protected us with her body during the fight. She would want to do it now as well. She would. I promise you.'' Akki held his wrists with her hand and spoke urgently.

''Inside her.''

''I've thought it all out,'' Akki said. ''And it's the only way. But we have to hurry.'' She was already shivering with the cold.

Jakkin was shivering, too. He wasn't sure it was only from the cold. ''And how do you propose to do it?'' he asked, dragging the words out. ''This . . . this surgery?''

Akki held up the baling knife. She looked at him quizzically. He held up Golden's knife in return.

"With these? Dragon's scales are like stone. Only another dragon's claw or the special diamond-tipped knives of the Stews . . ."

"That's it! Her claw." Akki ran to the front of Heart's Blood's corpse and round the right paw. The torn lancea was almost severed from the rest of the claw. Using her knife, she sawed through the last bit of dangling skin and picked up the nail. It was larger than her two hands.

Jakkin turned his face to the rock and was quietly but efficiently sick. When he looked back, Akki was carving through the mound of belly, slicing carefully under the scales. Her face was awful to see, and her arms were covered with the dragon's blood. It no longer had the power to burn.

Jakkin wiped his hand across his mouth, willing the terrible taste of sickness to leave him. Then he walked over to her. "Here," he said, "let me do that." He finished the carving and lifted up the door of flesh, all the while fighting down another round of sickness.

Holding up the flap, he could see into the dark, steaming cavern of muscle and beyond it the great arches of bone. There was another wall before him, white and veined with red.

"The birth-chamber," Akki whispered into his ear. "Where the eggs are formed." Then putting her hand on his, she guided him into making a new incision along the largest vein.

The chamber wall irised open and a fresh burst of warmth greeted them. Without willing it, Jakkin felt himself pulled in.

Her teeth chattering, Akki slipped in after him, thinking of nothing more but the inviting heat, the red body heat.

Jakkin felt drunk with the warmth. He tripped over a polyp of flesh and fell to his hands and knees onto the spongy floor. He curled up where he fell. Akki curled around him, and they slept.

*His dream was all color and no sound. He opened his eyes and saw a translucent cream-colored casing around him. It was hard to the touch, yet by tapping on it, he could start tiny cracks running through it, a map of an unexplored alien land. Then one of the cracks opened, and he was bathed in blood, red and hot, that stripped off his skin, leaving his body a landscape of veins and sinew. He flexed his arm and watched the play of muscle and bone. The rivulets of his blood ran through the hard, skinless flesh, carving valleys.*

*He turned over and found another body next to his, but who it was or who it had been he did not know, for all the skin had been flensed as well. He saw only the armature of bones upon which all the rest was hung like an old coat. He wondered for the first time about the identity of skin.*

*Then the body turned and smiled, and he wondered only that he had not been able to identify her before. It was Akki. She took his hand, and at her touch skin leaped into place, a complete transformation.*

*Together they crawled through the house of flesh, through a long, curving tunnel, and into the bright white of the first day.*

They emerged out of the dragon's body well after light. Akki's hair was matted with blood; her suit, permanently stained. Jakkin tried to push the hair out of his eyes, and he could feel how stiff and coarse the strands were. But they were alive; they had got through the cold of Dark After.

He smiled at Akki. Even his smile seemed stiff. He had to touch his face with his stained hands to make the smile crack through the patina of blood.

Akki smiled back and pointed up.

Jakkin looked at the sky. It was no longer the familiar blue of Austar but a myriad of colors, a rainbow of violets and greens, browns and reds and golds. Colors that he could not put a name to, that he could scarcely have imagined, moved and flowed across the pathways of air, pulsing with life. He heard voices in the air as well, some angry, some challenging, others full of a coasting joy. He knew that they were dragons.

"Look," Akki was calling to him. "Look how much is out there. I must have been blind before. I must have been deaf. I never suspected. I never knew."

He wondered if they were drunk on dragon's blood, if they were crazed by it. He wondered if they had died.

Then five separate voices came to him, sharp, clear, distinctive. They called his name in a language he should not have known yet understood totally. The voices were young, almost baby voices, and they came to him over the miles; but he could tell they were moving closer and closer. Far out over the desert, he saw them, outlined by auras as full as rainbows: five baby hatchlings, still awkward in the air, winging toward him, joy-filled and free.

"Dragon's eyes. We have dragon's eyes," Jakkin said.

"We were born as they were," Akki said. "Out of Heart's Blood." She turned toward him.

Jakkin realized that he could read Akki's mind. It spoke in bright, clean colors to him.

She smiled and held out her stained hands.

Jakkin took her hands in his. Raising them to his lips, he spoke to her. "Thou beauty," he said, though he used no spoken words.

She blushed and threw a rainbow into his mind.

# 30

THE SECOND MOON lipped the horizon as Jakkin turned back into the mountains. Below him the desert of Austar and the farms were shadings and shadows of color. He had watched the changes for two days and each time was amazed anew. He glanced down at his feet. The ground was a dark purple glow.

Then he heard Akki running toward him and looked up. Light rainbowed under her skin. In her hands she carried cave apples and berries, and she called as she ran with her mouth and mind. Above her two of the hatchlings circled.

Jakkin smiled. No one would ever find them here in the mountains. Neither wardens nor rebels. He and Akki could hear intruders long before they were seen. Like the dragons of Austar, they could speak to each other over long distances with their minds. The very landscape of Austar talked to them now, now that they had been born again in dragon's blood. Yet still they reasoned and ran like humans.

Jakkin no longer worried if he was, at last, a man. He guessed he was part man—and part dragon. And though he did not fully understand the changes that had taken place, he knew that he was something new, the first true human Austarian.

Akki ran into his arms, and they turned to watch the moons start their pavane across the color-filled sky. Some day soon he and Akki would bring this gift of dragon's sight out to the others, for surely it would change Austar. But for now they had a world to explore.

# A Sending
# of
# Dragons

*For Jonathan Grenzke,*
*dragon master,*
*shatterer of a thousand shields,*
*who lives right down the road*

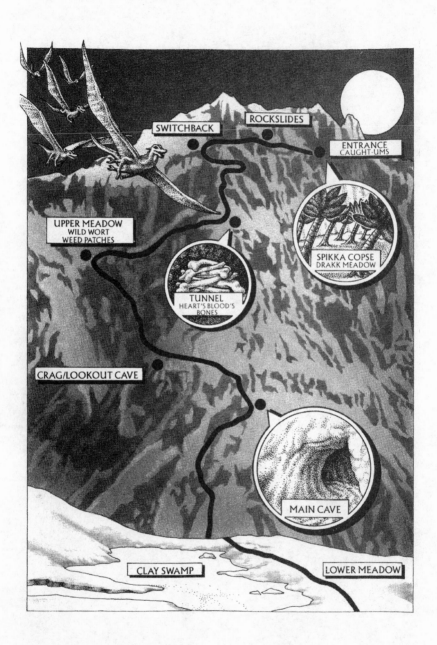

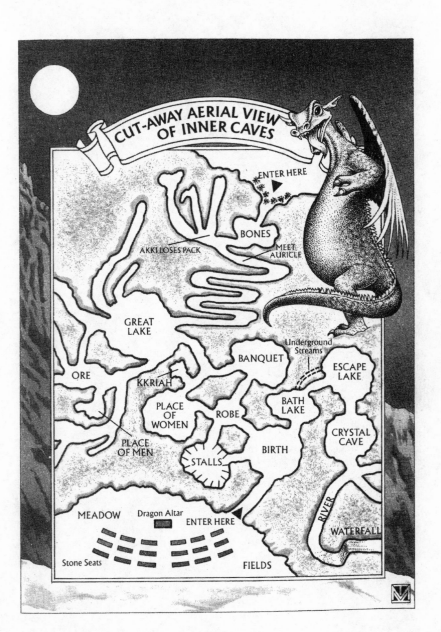

# *The Hatchlings*

# 1

NIGHT WAS APPROACHING. The umber moon led its pale, shadowy brother across the multicolored sky. In front of the moons flew five dragons.

The first was the largest, its great wings dipping and rising in an alien semaphore. Directly behind it were three smaller fliers, wheeling and circling, tagging one another's tails. In the rear, along a lower trajectory, sailed a middle-sized and plumper version of the front dragon. More like a broom than a rudder, its tail seemed to sweep across the faces of the moons.

Jakkin watched them, his right hand shading his eyes. Squatting on his haunches in front of a mountain cave, he was nearly naked except for a pair of white pants cut off at mid-thigh, a concession to modesty rather than a help against the oncoming cold night. He was burned brown everywhere but for three small pits on his back, which remained white despite their long exposure to the sun. Slowly Jakkin stood, running grimy fingers through his shoulder-length hair, and shouted up at the hatchlings.

"Fine flying, my friends!" The sound of his voice caromed off the mountains, but the dragons gave no sign they heard him. So he sent the same message with his mind in the rainbow-colored patterns with which he and the dragons communicated. *Fine flying*. The picture he sent was of gray-green wings with air rushing through the leathery feathers, tickling each link. *Fine flying*. He was sure his sending could reach them, but none of the dragons responded.

Jakkin stood for a moment longer watching the flight. He took pleasure in the hatchlings' airborne majesty. Even though they were still awkward on the ground, a sure sign of their youth, against the sky they were already an awesome sight.

Jakkin took pleasure as well in the colors surrounding the dragons. Though he'd lived months now in the Austarian wilds, he hadn't tired of the evening's purples and reds, roses and blues, the ever changing display that signaled the approaching night. Before he'd been *changed*, as he called it, he'd hardly seen the colors. Evenings had been a time of darkening and the threat of Dark-After, the bone-chilling, killing cold. Every Austarian knew better than to be caught outside in it. But now both Dark-After and dawn were his, thanks to the *change*.

*"Ours!"* The message invaded his mind in a ribbon of laughter. *"Dark-After and dawn are* ours *now."* The sending came a minute before its sender appeared around a bend in the mountain path.

Jakkin waited patiently. He knew Akki would be close behind, for the sending had been strong and Akki couldn't broadcast over a long range.

She came around the bend with cheeks rosy from running. Her dark braid was tied back with a fresh-plaited vine. Jakkin preferred it when she let her hair loose, like a black curtain around her face, but he'd never been able to tell her so. She carried a reed basket full of food for their dinner. Speaking aloud in a tumble of words, she ran toward him. "Jakkin, I've found a whole new meadow and . . ."

He went up the path to meet her and dipped his hand into the basket. Before she could pull it away, he'd snagged a single pink chikkberry. Then she grabbed the basket, putting it safely behind her.

"All right, worm waste, what have you been doing while I found our dinner?" Her voice was stern, but she couldn't hide the undercurrent of thought, which was sunny, golden, laughing.

"I've been working, too," he said, careful to speak out loud. Akki still preferred speech to sendings when they were face-to-face. She said speech had a precision to it that the sendings lacked, that it was clearer for everything but emotions. She was quite fierce about it. It was an argument Jakkin didn't want to venture into again. "I've some interesting things—"

Before he could finish, five small streamlike sendings teased into his head, a confusion of colored images, half-visualized.

*"Jakkin . . . the sky . . . see the moons . . . wind and wings, ah . . . see, see . . ."*

Jakkin spun away from Akki and cried out to the dragons, a wild, high yodeling that bounced off the mountains. With it he sent another kind of call, a web of fine traceries with the names of the hatchlings woven within: Sssargon, Sssasha, and the triplets Tri-sss, Tri-sssskkette, and Tri-sssha.

"Fewmets!" Akki complained. "That's too loud. Here I am, standing right next to you, and you've fried me." She set the basket down on an outjut of rock and rubbed her temples vigorously.

Jakkin knew she meant the mind sending had been too loud and had left her with a head full of brilliant hot lights. He'd had weeks of similar headaches when Akki first began sending, until they'd both learned to adjust. "Sorry," he whispered, taking a turn at rubbing her head over the ears, where the hot ache lingered. "Sometimes I forget. It takes so much more to make a dragon complain and their brains never get fried."

"Brains? What brains? Everyone knows dragons haven't any brains. Just muscle and bone and . . ."

". . . and claws and teeth," Jakkin finished for her, then broke into the chorus of the pit song she'd referred to:

> *Muscle and bone*
> *And claws and teeth,*
> *Fire above and*
> *Fewmets beneath.*

Akki laughed, just as he'd hoped, for laughter usually bled away the pain of a close sending. She came over and hugged him, and just as her arms went around, the true Austarian darkness closed in.

"You've got some power," Jakkin said. "One hug—and the lights go out!"

"Wait until you see what I do at dawn," she replied, giving a mock shiver.

To other humans the Austarian night was black and pitiless and the false dawn, Dark-After, mortally cold. Even an hour outside during that time of bone chill meant certain death. But Jakkin and Akki were different now, different from all their friends at the dragon nursery, different from the trainers and bond boys at the pits, different from the men who slaughtered dragons in the stews or the girls who filled their bond bags with money made in the baggeries. They were different from anyone in the history of Austar IV because they had been *changed*. Jakkin's thoughts turned as dark as the oncoming night, remembering just how they'd been *changed*. Chased into the mountains by wardens for the bombing of Rokk Major, which they had not really committed, they'd watched helplessly as Jakkin's great red dragon, Heart's Blood, had taken shots meant for them, dying as she tried to protect them. And then, left by the wardens to the oncoming cold, they had sheltered in Heart's Blood's body, in the very chamber where she'd recently carried eggs, and had emerged, somehow able to stand the cold and share their thoughts. He shut the memory down. Even months later it was too painful. Pulling himself away from the past, he realized he was still in the circle of Akki's arms. Her face showed deep concern, and he realized she'd been listening in on his thoughts. But when she spoke it was on a different subject altogether, and for that he was profoundly grateful.

"Come see what I found today," she said quietly, pulling him over to the basket. "Not just berries, but a new kind of mushroom. They were near a tiny cave on the south face of the Crag." Akki insisted on naming things because—she said—that made them more real. Mountains, meadows, vegetations, caves—they all bore her imprint. "We can test them out, first uncooked and later in with some boil soup. I nibbled a bit about an hour ago and haven't had any bad effects, so they're safe. You'll like these, Jakkin. They may look like cave apples, but I found them under a small tree. I call them meadow apples."

Jakkin made a face. He wasn't fond of mushrooms, and cave apples were the worst.

"They're sweeter than you think."

Anything, Jakkin thought, would be sweeter than the round, reddish cave apples with their musty, dusty taste, but he worried about Akki nibbling on unknown mushrooms. What if they were poisonous and she was all alone on the mountainside?

Both thoughts communicated immediately to Akki and she swatted him playfully on the chest. "Cave apples are good for you, Jakkin. High in protein. I learned that from Dr. Henkky when I studied with her in the Rokk. Besides, if I didn't test these out, we might miss something good. Don't be such a worrier. I checked with Sssasha first and she said dragons love them."

"Dragons love burnwort, too," muttered Jakkin. "But I'd sure hate to try and eat it, even if it *could* help me breathe fire."

"Listen, Jakkin Stewart, it's either mushrooms—or back to eating dragon stew. We have to have protein to live." Her eyes narrowed.

Jakkin shrugged as if to say he didn't care, but his thoughts broadcast his true feelings to her. They both knew they'd never eat meat again. Now that they could talk mind-to-mind with Heart's Blood's hatchlings and even pass shadowy thoughts with some of the lesser creatures like lizards and rock-runners, eating meat was unthinkable.

"If meadow apples are better than cave apples," Jakkin said aloud, "I'm sure I'll love them. Besides, I'm starving!"

"You and the dragons," Akki said. "That's all they ever think about, too. Food, food, food. But the question is—do you deserve my hard-found food?"

"I've been working, too," Jakkin said. "I'm trying to make some better bowls to put your hard-found food in. I discovered a new clay bank down the cliff and across Lower Meadows. You know..."

Akki did know, because he never went near Upper Meadows, where Heart's Blood's bones still lay, picked clean by the mountain scavengers. He went down toward the Lower Meadows and she scouted farther up. He could read her thoughts as clearly as she could read his.

He continued out loud, "... there's a kind of swamp there, the start of a small river, pooling down from the mountain streams. The mountain is covered with them. But I'd never seen this particular one before because it's hard to get to. This clay is the best I've found so far and I managed a whole sling of it. Maybe in a night or two we can build a fire and try to bake the pots I've made."

They both knew bake fires could be set only at night, later than any humans would be out. *Just in case.* Only at night did they feel totally safe from the people who had chased them into the mountains: the murderous wardens who had followed them from the bombed-out pit to the dragon nursery and from there up into the mountains," and the even more murderous rebels who, in the name of "freedom," had fooled them into destroying the great Rokk Major Dragon Pit. All those people thought them dead, from hunger or cold or from being crushed when Heart's Blood fell. It was best they continue to believe it. So the first rule of mountain life, Jakkin and Akki had agreed, was *Take no chances.*

"Never mind that, Jakkin," Akki said. "Don't think about it. The past is the past. Let it go. Let's enjoy what we have now. Show me your new pots, and then we can eat."

They walked into the cave, one of three they'd claimed as their own. Though Jakkin still thought of them as numbers—one, two, and three—Akki had named them. The cave in the Lower Meadows was Golden's Cave, named after their friend who had fled with them and had most certainly died at the wardens' hands. Golden's Cave had caches of berries for flavoring and for drinks. Akki had strung dried flowers on vines that made a rustly curtain between the main cave and the smaller sleeping quarters, which they kept private from the dragons. Higher on the mountain, but not as high as the Upper Meadows, was Likkarn's Lookout. It was as rough and uncompromising a place as the man it was named after, Jakkin's old trainer and enemy Likkarn. But Likkarn had proved a surprising ally in the end, and so had the lookout cave, serving them several times in the early days of their exile when they'd spotted bands of searchers down in the valley. But the middle cave, which Akki called the New Nursery, was the one they really considered their home.

What had first drawn them to it had been its size. It had a great hollow vaulted room with a succession of smaller caves behind. There were wonderful ledges at different levels along the walls on which Jakkin's unfired clay bowls and canisters sat. Ungainly and thick the clay pots certainly were, but Jakkin's skills were improving with each try, and the bowls, if not pretty, were functional, holding stashes of chikkberries, dried mushrooms like the cave apples Jakkin so disliked, and edible grasses. So far his own favorite bit of work was a large-bellied jar containing boil. It was the one piece he had successfully fired and it was hard and did not leak.

The floor of the cave was covered with dried grasses that lent a sharp sweet odor to the air. There was a mattress of the same grass, which they changed every few days. The bed lay in one of the small inner chambers where, beneath a natural chimney, they could look up at night and see the stars.

"There!" Jakkin said, pointing to the shelf that held his latest, still damp work. "This clay was a lot easier to work."

There were five new pots, one large bowl, and two slightly lop-sided drinking cups.

"What do you think?"

"Oh, Jakkin, they're the best yet. When they're dry we *must* try them in the fire. What do *you* think?"

"I think . . ." And then he laughed, shaping a picture of an enormous cave apple in his mind. The mushroom had an enormous bite-sized chunk out of it.

Akki laughed. "If you are hungry enough to think about eating *that*," she said, "we'd better start the dinner right away!"

*"We come. Have hunger, too."* The sendings from the three smallest dragons broke into Jakkin's head. Their signature colors were shades of pink and rose.

*"We wait. We ride your shoulder. Our eyes are yours."* That came from the largest two of Heart's Blood's hatchlings. They were already able to travel miles with neither hunger nor fatigue, and their sendings had matured to a deeper red. Sssargon and Sssasha, the names they had given themselves with the characteristic dragon hiss

at the beginning, spent most of the daylight hours catching currents of air that carried them over the jagged mountain peaks. They were, as they called themselves, Jakkin's and Akki's eyes, a mobile warning signal. But they were not needed for scouting at night because there was nothing Jakkin and Akki feared once the true dark set in.

*"Come home. Come home."* Jakkin's sending was a green vine of thought.

*"Yes, come home."* Akki's sending, much weaker than Jakkin's, was a twining of blue strands around his brighter green. Blue and green, the braiding of the cooler human colors.

*"Come home,"* called the blue once again. *"Come home. I have much food. And I have a new song for you."* The sending was soothing and inviting at the same time. The young dragons loved songs, loved the thrumming, humming sounds, especially if the songs concerned great flying worms. Baby dragons, Akki's thought passed along to Jakkin, thought mostly about two things—themselves and what they wanted to eat.

# 2

"THEY'LL BE HERE SOON," Akki said in the sensible tone she often used when talking about the hatchlings. "So we'd better eat. You know how much attention they demand once they're down—rubbing and coaxing and ear scratching."

"Nursery dragons are worse," reminded Jakkin. "They can't do anything for themselves. Except eat. At least these are finding grazing on their own. And they groom themselves. And . . ."

"They're still babies, though."

"Some babies!" Jakkin laughed and held his hand above Akki's head. Sssargon's broad back already came that high, and with his long ridged neck and enormous head, he was twice Jakkin's height and still growing.

"*Big* babies!" Akki amended.

They laughed aloud together and then walked to the pathway, where they sat down on the flat rocks that flanked the cave mouth. Akki shared out the bits of mushroom and then the berries. She had found three kinds: tart chikkberries, black and juicy warden's heart, and the dry, pebbly wormseye. They washed the meal down with a cup of boil, the thin soup made from cooking the greasy brown skkagg grass of the high meadow. Boil was only drinkable cold—and then just barely. Jakkin made a face.

"I still miss a cup of hot takk with my dinner," he said. He wiped away a purple smear from his mouth, a trace of warden's heart, and slowly looked up at the sky. A dark smudge in the west resolved itself into a dragon form. As it came closer, Jakkin stood.

"*Sssargon come.*" Sssargon always announced himself, keeping up a running commentary on his actions. "*Sssargon lands.*"

His wings stirred the dust at the cave mouth, and for a moment obscured his landing, but Jakkin knew it was a perfect touchdown. For such a large and clumsy-looking beast, Sssargon was often quite dainty.

*"Sssargon folds wings."* The great pinions swept back against his sides, the scaly feathers fluttering for just a moment before quieting. Sssargon squatted, then let his large ribbed tongue flick in and out between his jaws. *"Sssargon hungers."*

Jakkin went back into the cave and came out with a handful of wild burnwort, just enough to take the edge off Sssargon's hunger and to quiet his pronouncements. Though Heart's Blood's hatchlings had begun to graze on their own in the various high meadows full of wort and weed, they hated giving up their ritual of sharing. Jakkin had to admit that he also hated to think about giving it up. He smiled tenderly at the dragon.

"Big babies," Akki whispered.

Jakkin ignored her and focused on Sssargon. "Here, big fellow," he said aloud, adding a quick green-tinged visualization of the wort.

Sssargon's rough tongue snagged the plant from Jakkin's hand, and his answer was the crisp snip-snap of wort being crunched between his teeth.

Sssasha landed just as Sssargon began to eat, with neither fanfare nor commentary. She stepped over his outstretched tail but folded her wings a second too soon, which made her cant to one side. She had to flip her outside wing open again in order to right herself.

The red flicker of amusement that Sssargon sent through all their minds made Jakkin sputter. Akki broke into a cascade of giggles, but Sssasha was too even-tempered to mind. She was as sunny as the splash of gold across her nose, a slash of color that—along with her even disposition and placid ways—would have made her unfit either to fight in the pits as had her mother, Heart's Blood, or to be considered for spaying and dwarfing as a *beauty*, a house pet. Jakkin realized, with a kind of dawning horror, that Sssasha would have been one of the early culls in the nurseries, where hatchlings were bred for only one of three destinies. The bonders said, *pit, pet, or stew*. Jakkin swallowed hastily at the thought of Sssasha in one of the stews, a green-suited steward standing over her, placing a stinger to her ear, a knife at her throat. He bit his lip, all laughter gone.

*"What pain?"* Sssasha's question poked into his mind.

"No pain," Jakkin said aloud, but his mind transferred a different thought.

*"Yes, pain,"* insisted Sssasha.

*"Old pain. Gone."* Jakkin made his mind a careful blank. It was hard work, and he could feel himself starting to perspire.

*"Good,"* said Sssasha.

*"Yesssssss, good,"* Sssargon interrupted suddenly, exploding red bomb bursts in Jakkin's head. *"Sssargon have great hunger."*

Akki, who had been following this silent exchange thoughtfully, soothed them all with a picture of a cool blue rain, holding it in mind long enough for Jakkin to go back into the cave for two more large handfuls of wort.

Once in the cave, Jakkin was able to let his guard down for a minute, though he reminded himself that even in the cool darkness of the cave, behind walls of stone, he could not be private. His mind was an open invitation to Akki or any dragon who wanted to enter it. Only with the most careful and arduous concentration could he guard its entrance. He had to visualize a wall built up plank by plank or a heavy drapery drawn across it inch by inch. And usually by the time he had carefully constructed these images, the traitor thoughts had already slipped out. He wondered how dragons kept secrets or even if they had secrets to keep. Everything he thought or felt was now open and public.

"Open to me, anyway," Akki said as Jakkin emerged from the cave.

He realized with sudden chagrin that she had been listening to his self-pitying thoughts. The more powerful the emotion, the farther it seemed to broadcast. Akki, listening quietly, had sent nothing in return. Flushing with embarrassment, Jakkin looked down at the ground, trying to think of a way to phrase what he had to say out loud. He knew he could control words, because he didn't actually have to *say* anything until he was ready. At last he spoke. "Sometimes," he began reluctantly, "sometimes a man needs to be alone." He held out the wort to Sssargon and concentrated totally on that.

"Sometimes," Akki said to his back, "sometimes a *woman* needs to be alone, too."

He turned his head to apologize. Words, it seemed, could be slippery, too. But Akki wasn't looking at him. She had her hands up to her eyes, as if shading them from the too-colorful dark.

"Jakkin, this is a strange gift we've been given, being able to sneak into one another's minds. But . . ."

"But at least we're together," Jakkin said, suddenly afraid of what else Akki might say, suddenly afraid that the words, more than any thoughts, might hurt terribly.

"We may be together more than we ever meant to be," Akki said. But even as she said it she touched his hand.

He concentrated on that touch and let the rest of it go, making his mind a blank slate like the evening sky. At last little spear points of violet blue pushed across that blank and Jakkin realized Akki was worried.

"Where are the triplets?" she asked. "They should have been here by now. And that's a worry I don't mind sharing."

"*Sssargon not worry. You not worry.*" Munching contentedly on the last few straws of wort, the dragon gave off waves of mindless serenity. His mood changed only when he noticed that he had finished what was in his mouth, at which point he stretched his neck out to its greatest length and stole a few bites from his sister.

"*That's very reassuring, Sssargon,*" Akki sent.

Jakkin could only guess at the sarcasm behind her thought. There was no color translation for it.

Sssasha let Sssargon take the last of her wort and rose clumsily. She clambered toward Jakkin to see if she could nose out some more food. Bumping against his shoulder, she nearly knocked him to the ground.

"Fewmets!" he cried out. "I may be able to see and hear like a dragon now, but I still can't fly, Sssasha. If you knock me off the mountain, I'll land *splat!*" He tried to send the sound of it with his mind.

"*?????*"

"Splat!" Jakkin said, then shouted, "SPLAT!"

Akki cupped her hand and slapped it against the dragon's haunch. It made a strange sound.

Sssasha blinked, then sent a barrage of red bubbles into Jakkin's mind. Each one burst with a noise that sounded remarkably like *splat!*

"Exactly," Jakkin said aloud. "And if you think that sounds funny, you should see how funny I'd look *splattered* all over the landscape." His laugh was a short barking sound.

But the joke was untranslatable to the dragon and all she received was an unfocused color picture of Jakkin's mood: a net of wistfulness, a slash of anger, and a wisp of lingering self-pity. She turned her head away and gazed out across the mountains that edged into the valley below. If she was amused or worried or upset, no one could tell from her rosy sending and her casual stance.

"Dragons!" Jakkin muttered to himself. Even with his dragon sight he could not pierce the darkness to see what drew her gaze, so he settled down next to her on his haunches, ran his hands through his hair, and waited.

It was five minutes before the triplets began sounding in his mind.

# 3

THE HIGH-PITCHED twittering chatter of the three hatchlings began to reach them. The sounds the trio made were unlike any of the full-throated roars Jakkin had ever heard from dragons in the fighting pits. It was as if the three had invented a language all their own, which they occasionally slowed down so that listeners could make some sense of it. Their sendings, too, sputtered with color, which sometimes formed into readable pictures but as often remained unclear.

Moments later they sailed into view, wingtips apart. They flew in formation, their favorite trick. Inseparable, they might as well have emerged from the same egg, though in fact the eggs had been in totally different parts of the clutch. Still, they looked alike, a rough brown color undistinguished by any markings, and their sending signatures were remarkably alike, too. In honor of their being such close triplets, Akki had named them Tri-sss, Tri-sssha, and Tri-ssskkette. They had accepted those names without a murmur of dissent. But all together they were addressed as Tri, and all three answered to the one name. If they had any others they preferred, it was a secret they shared with no one.

Landing together on the upper edge of the ledge, they waddled in step single file down the trail.

*"Men coming, men coming, men coming,"* they sent, one right after another.

"It's dark and will soon be Dark-After," said Jakkin.

Rubbing Tri-sssha behind the ears, Akki added, "And you know men can't live in the cold."

*"You men. You men. You here."*

Tri-sssha, earflaps vibrating from the special attention, managed a different phrase.

"Yes, but we're different," Akki explained patiently.

*"Men coming. Men coming. Men coming,"* insisted the little dragons, ignoring both Akki's explanation and the food that Jakkin held out to them.

The minute they turned their heads aside to look up at the darkened sky, Sssargon stretched his long neck, moving his head within inches of Jakkin's. His tongue snaked out and deftly removed the wort from Jakkin's hand. Jakkin slapped at the dragon's nose an instant too late.

And then Jakkin heard a strange mechanical chuffing, the sound of a copter in the distance. It was a noise rarely heard outside the Rokk, the main city, where such devices belonged only to Federation officials or starship crews. No one on Austar was allowed them.

"Akki!" Jakkin cried out loud.

"I hear it," she said, fear touching her eyes before her mind sent its notice.

*"Men coming, men coming, men coming,"* the trio of hatchlings sent out again in arrow points, and the larger two dragons, from their perch on the mountain, picked up the chorus. They'd been linked to their dragon mother, Heart's Blood, when she had died under the guns of men, and they harbored a great distrust of humans, except for Jakkin and Akki.

Sssargon lifted his head and swiveled it about like a periscope. A bright light in his black eyes flickered for a moment. Then he addressed Jakkin formally, mind-to-mind. *"Sssargon flies."*

"No, Sssargon!" Akki cried, stretching her hand out to him.

"No!" commanded Jakkin, deliberately using the tone of voice he normally reserved for the training sessions in which he taught the dragons the fighting moves of the great pits.

But this time Sssargon, usually the most eager at training, ignored Jakkin's demand and stretched his wings. Pumping them twice, he leaped off the cliffside, immediately catching an updraft, and sailed away.

"He's only a baby," whispered Akki. "A baby."

Jakkin strained to watch the dragon as he disappeared in the night sky. "Are we so much older?"

"I feel about a hundred years older," said Akki in a quiet, tired voice. She herded the hatchlings into the cave before her and looked over her shoulder at Jakkin. "A hundred hundred years."

He followed them in.

The cave was large, but the four growing hatchlings crowded things considerably and Sssasha, as usual, managed to bump into a shelf, knocking off two of the new bowls.

*"Splat?"*

Even Jakkin had to laugh at that. He sat down with his back to the cave wall and hoped the cool rock would keep him from sweating too much. Four dragons, even small ones, were like furnaces in the closed-in cave. He could feel the temperature beginning to rise.

Akki sat across from him with Tri-sssha's head in her lap. Her fingers caressed the dragon's earflaps, scratching all around. Humming an old pit ballad about a hen fighter who was matched against one of her own hatchlings, Akki was totally caught up in the sad, haunting melody. So was Tri-sssha. Jakkin could feel the dragon begin to thrum, her initial fears of the men in copters subsumed by the deep sounding of her own body. Tri-sss and Tri-ssskkette joined her, and soon the cave vibrated with it. When Sssasha finally lent her own deeper thrums to the lot, it was overpowering. Jakkin's head buzzed with the hum and the heat, and he felt it as a great pressure on his temples and chest.

"Stop it!" he cried out angrily, standing up and bumping his forehead on a jutting rock. The pain communicated in a way his anger had not.

Akki lifted her hands as if warding off a blow. The thrumming stopped.

"We have to think," Jakkin warned. "We have to think and watch and listen. Pay attention."

As he spoke an image formed in his mind, a sending from Sssargon. The helicopter was making a series of quick spiraling passes over the mountains. Sssargon drifted along lazily, looking like any wild dragon out for a late evening fly. He buzzed the helicopter once, then banked away as if satisfied that the metal bird was not a threat. Jakkin saw the copter through Sssargon's eyes: a heavy, mindless object in the middle of wind eddies, communicating great heat and nothing else. It had no feathers and no smell and seemed, in Sssargon's view, pilotless.

*"The men inside,"* Jakkin sent to the dragon, trying to make his images clear. Landscape, emotion, things of the senses passed so easily through a sending, but other things . . . *"Look at the men inside, Sssargon. What do they wear? What do they look like?"* If Sssargon could send a description, they would know who the men were—Federation rocket pilots or wardens or rebels. *"Look at the men."*

But the questions didn't seem to interest the dragon and neither did the men in the copter. He sent only a vague impression of a human at the throttle, and then, having tired of this latest game, banked to the right and returned to the ledge. They caught his sending announcing a perfect back-winged landing. *"Sssargon lands."* A slight thumping outside the cave as his heavy hind legs touched down confirmed this.

*"Sssargon home, Sssargon home. Sssargon home."* The three jubilant sendings heralded him.

*"Sssargon home. Sssargon hungers. Scratch Sssargon."*

"Hush!" Akki's voice overrode the sending. "And stay put. We're already too crowded in here." The hushing was really for Jakkin's benefit, for Sssargon had made no outward sounds. Like his mother before him, and like Sssasha, Sssargon was mute. Only those who could tune in on a dragon's sending could hear him. But his sendings were always louder than necessary, like a young boy clamoring for attention. "Hush," Akki repeated, her tone still commanding. But her sending to the dragon was far gentler.

Sssargon swept his wings back and lay down at the cave entrance, looking for all the world like a dozing dragon guarding his cache.

The copter flew by once more and, apparently satisfied, the pilot found an updraft and the copter was quickly gone.

# 4

THE WHIR OF the copter had faded long minutes past but still they sat in the cave, waiting. Sssargon hulked in the entrance.

At last Akki sighed. "We can go out now," she said, but she said it in a whisper. Then she laughed. "What an idiot I am. What idiots *we* are. They couldn't possibly hear us with all that noise anyway."

Jakkin stood and started toward the cave entrance, wiping the sweat from his forehead as he went. The others followed after.

Sssargon refused to move.

*"Sssargon stays. Sssargon needs scratching. Sssargon hungers. Sssargon wants—"*

"Sssargon shuts up!" Jakkin hissed at him, and pushed at the dragon's nose while simultaneously sending large blue daggers into the worm's mind. The dragon rose reluctantly.

Akki caught up with Jakkin. "Who are they?" she asked. "Who was in the copter?"

"And why are they here? Were they looking for us or just flying by?" Jakkin countered.

Questions, like little scurrying animals, rushed back and forth across their bridged minds. The dragons broke through with their own questions about food. They cared little about the copter now that it was out of sight.

Jakkin shrugged and went back to the cave, emerging with a handful of wort. He shared it out, saving the largest portion for Sssargon.

*"Brave Sssargon. Sssargon eats."* After his announcements the hatchling finished his wort in a single bite, then rose onto his hind legs and gave a hop that sent him some three feet straight up into

the air. He pumped his wings at the same time and took off, rocketing up.

As if on cue, the triplets went after him, throwing themselves over the cliffside to catch different parts of the air current, tumbling and bumping in a kind of midair brawl.

Finally Sssasha stepped to the cliff edge. She moved her long neck up and down, head bobbing, as if she were trying to figure out the winds. Her sendings were rosy bubbles in a slow-moving stream, calm and indecipherable. Then, apparently satisfied, she stepped off the cliff and, after a long, slow fall, unfurled her wings to their fullest with a soft *shushing* and floated to the valley below as if she weighed no more than a feather.

After a quiet minute, Jakkin said softly, "They've landed."

"Yes," Akki replied. "And they're grazing. When they eat, their minds go blank and all I get from them is a kind of quiet chuckling." She laughed. "I wonder if we do that, too?"

Jakkin walked away from the cliff edge and sat back down on his haunches. "Maybe dragons can afford to be mindless, but *we* have to think, Akki."

"About what?" She flipped her braid to the front.

"About the copters and who may be searching for us and—"

"What makes you so sure they're looking for us? They could be looking for anyone. They might be looking for dragons. Or sightseeing." She shrugged. "It's been months since we 'died.' "

"Who else would they be looking for?"

"Rebels."

"The rebels are in the cities, blowing things up. Why would they come out here? There's nothing to destroy." His tone was bitter. "It has to be us the copter was searching for. The Fedders wouldn't waste a copter on anyone small. Sightseeing, ha! What can *they* see at night? As for dragons, if they want to see dragons, they go to the pits."

"Are you sure?"

"I'm sure!" Jakkin's mind added a solid exclamation point.

Leaning against the rock face, Akki mused, "If they're looking for us, it can't be the Fedders. What Federation rules did we break?"

"That bomb we were tricked into carrying must have killed a lot of Federation starship crewmen at the pit," Jakkin said.

"Jakkin, I know you dislike politics, but even you know that we are a Protectorate world, not a member of the Fed Congress. Not yet, anyway. That means the Fedders have no rights here. They're bound by *our* laws. It's the wardens who enforce those laws. If the

Federation doesn't like what's going on here, there's only one thing it can do.''

"Embargo!" Jakkin said.

"Exactly—embargo. No Fedder ships in and no Austarians out."

Jakkin added grimly, "And no outside bettors for the pits. No imported metals. No contact with the Federation worlds for fifty years. If that happens, we won't be popular."

Akki laughed, but there was nothing happy in the sound. It was brief and hawking, more like a cough than a laugh.

"Well, it can't be the rebels looking for us, can it?" Jakkin said, as much to order his own thoughts as to ask for an answer. "They don't have copters, unless they've stolen one."

"They'd like to do that, I'm sure," Akki put in.

"But stolen copter or not," Jakkin continued, "why would *they* be looking for us?"

"I could still identify them," Akki said. "At least some of them. At least Number One, the leader of my rebel cell."

A picture of the man who called himself Number One exploded with an orange-red ferocity that startled Jakkin because Akki rarely sent anything that strong. One minute the rebel leader was there in Jakkin's mind, his mustache a parenthesis around a slash of mouth, the next he was gone into a million blood red pieces all shaped like tears.

Jakkin stood and shook his head vigorously to clear it. "Akki, that doesn't make sense. We've been out here for months and too many things will have changed for the rebels. No one will remember you or care."

"It may seem long to us, but Number One is the sort of man who'd pick at his own scab to keep a wound fresh. And you and I are the only ones who could identify him as the real bomber."

Jakkin looked over at her, his eyes wide. "There were other members of Number One's cell besides you, Akki."

Her answering smile was grim. "Do you honestly think they're still alive? That wasn't his way. He thought we would die in the pit. If he found out we'd survived that, he'd check until he heard how we 'died' on the mountainside. He'd want to be sure."

Jakkin thought a minute. "Someone must have come back and found . . . they must have discovered Heart's Blood's . . . they must have seen her . . .''

Akki came over and put her hand on his shoulder. "Say it, Jakkin. Say it and be done with it. If you never say it, it's not real. Say *Heart's*

*Blood's bones.* Someone must have found her bones and not found ours. Say it.''

"I don't have to say it to know it.''

"Say it so you can be done with grieving. And done with the guilt.''

He moved away from her touch. "I'm not grieving. I'm not feeling guilty.'' But his mind betrayed him again, for the pictures were all of red dragons lying in horrible bloody parts and a boy with a bloody knife standing beside her. Knowing the sending had reached her, Jakkin turned away and spoke in a low voice. "I didn't cry when my father died under the claws of a feral dragon, though I was just a child when it happened. And I didn't cry a year later when my mother died of overwork and loneliness. I didn't cry when my friend, your father, Sarkkhan, was blown up in the Rokk Pit when it should have been me. And I won't cry now.'' But his sending turned gray and was shot through with blue tears, speaking a different truth.

Akki used the same quieting tone she used with the hatchlings. "It's all right. It's all right to cry, Jakkin.''

He shook his head. "We don't have time for tears. We have to think. Someone knows we're alive and is looking for us.''

"They may know we're alive, but they don't know everything,'' Akki said. "They don't know how we've changed. How we can see and hear with dragons' eyes and ears. How we can talk to dragons and each other with sendings. How we can survive the cold of Dark-After.''

Jakkin nodded slowly.

"And they don't know that we're living here!'' Akki said triumphantly.

"*Here* is where we shouldn't be. Fewmets, Akki, why didn't we see that before? It's been crazy to stay so close . . . so close . . .'' His voice stuttered off again, though his mind sent a picture of the mountain landscape broken into shards, the pieces looking remarkably like the bones of a dragon.

"You're right,'' Akki said. "If they look in Golden's Cave or the Lookout or here . . . why, there's no way anyone is going to believe dragons made those cups.'' She gestured toward the cave.

"Or the braided vines,'' Jakkin added. "Or the mattresses.'' He looked out over the mountain pass, now hidden by the darkness. Once he'd seen it as a jagged, threatening landscape. Over the last months he'd come to know its beauty. And how it reminded him of a dragon's necklinks, not only handsome but essential for defense. He and Akki knew these mountains as no one else did. They were part of the land-

scape now. But if the rebels found them, their lives would be forfeit.
If the trackers were wardens or Fedders, and they were caught—well,
there were worse things than death. Austar had no physical punishment excepting *transportation*. Break the laws a little, and you were
fined. Break the laws a lot, and you were sent offworld, transported
to another of the penal planets where life was even harsher than on
the tamed Austar. Ice planets like Sedna or water planets like Lir,
where the voices of dragons and the color patterns would be gone
forever.

"Jakkin, please don't do this." Akki's hands were pressed to her
head. "Please talk to me. All I'm getting from you are sendings of
windstorms and fire, snowstorms and storms at sea. That may be good
enough for the dragons, but I need words as well."

"Words? All right, then, how about these words—we're leaving.
Now. We'll take jars of berries and boil but leave everything else."

"Fine," Akki said, her voice hushed. "We can find other caves.
Better ones." Her tone was cheery, but the picture from her mind was
of empty, cheerless rooms.

Suddenly Jakkin wished she had disagreed and put up a fight. He
wished she'd come up with an argument to make them stay. Yet he
knew the decision to leave was the right one. Then why did he feel
so bad?

"It's all right, Jakkin," Akki said. She put her arms around him.

He broke away angrily. "Lizard waste, Akki. How can I be strong
when every little doubt or fear broadcasts itself to you. I hate it!"

Akki turned away, biting her lip and letting a stray apology wind
into his mind. He fought the sending for a long, bitter moment, but
at last accepted it, twined it with a blue braid, and let the two colors
slowly fade as he walked back into the cave.

~

USING CARRY-SLINGS fashioned from woven weeds, they packed the
jars, carefully separating them with mattress grass. They corked two
jars of boil with pieces of wood Jakkin shaved down to fit. Then he
helped Akki slip the smaller sling over her shoulders. She in turn
helped him take up the heavier load.

Besides the food, they packed Jakkin's knife, the old book of
dragon stories Golden had given them, and a spear Jakkin had made
by sharpening a dragon femur he'd found in one of the lower caves.
They knew they'd have to browse for other food, but they were both
expert scavengers by now. In the mountains berries, mushrooms, and
skkagg for boil were common all year around. If they were lucky, in

the higher meadows they might find lizard eggs and even kkrystals, the translucent six-legged insects that lived in lizard nests. A kkrystal dipped in beaten egg and crisped over a fire was delicious. Insects had no sendings, or at least none they could hear, and so Jakkin and Akki felt no remorse about eating them.

Akki walked around the cave one last time, as if memorizing it. There was so little there, yet it had taken them months to make it seem like home.

"We might never see it again," she whispered.

"If we don't leave soon, we might never see *anything* again," Jakkin answered. Quite deliberately he shaped a picture of a copter in his mind, a blood red copter winging toward them. There were three men in it, one wearing a Fedder flight cap, one a warden's hat, and the other had a mustache over a slash of mouth.

"If we don't leave soon, I might change my mind," Akki added.

Jakkin was glad she had said it, and he worked very hard to keep the same thought out of any of his own sendings.

Walking into the false dawn, they scarcely felt the bitter cold.

# 5

THEY WALKED UP the path for an hour in silence, both intent on masking their minds, the only sounds the occasional rattling of a loose pebble rolling down the mountainside or the *pick-buzz* of flikka wings. Then the path widened and made a great turn and they found themselves in the Upper Meadows, a plateau some three kilometers across.

Even in the dark Jakkin knew the place. He did not need to see the gray-green furze cover broken by the mounds of berry bushes to recognize it. He knew there was a cliff face on one side that sat like the crown of a hat on the plateau's brim. The place was engraved forever in his mind. It was here that Heart's Blood had died for them. He drew in a deep breath, and when he let it out again it sounded like a sigh.

Akki reached over and touched his hand.

"I finally found a path, you know," she said. "It's through one of the caves. Well, not exactly a cave, but more like a tunnel."

He didn't answer, but they both had the same awful thought leaping in lightning strokes from mind to mind: If they had found the tunnel those many months ago, Heart's Blood need not have died.

"Close your eyes, Jakkin, and I'll lead you past."

He knew she meant past the remains, the bones, all that was left of his beautiful red dragon. Obediently he closed his eyes and held out his hand. At her touch his mind replayed the final scene when Heart's Blood, smoke streaming from her nose slits, had risen in a hindfoot stand. Front legs raking the air, she had taken three shots fired at them from the near dark. One had struck the rocks right above her uplifted head. One had shattered the cliff beside Akki. And the third had raised a bloody flower on Heart's Blood's throat. He recalled how she fell, slowly, endlessly, forever.

Akki pulled him by the hand, whispering encouragements while he concentrated on not crying. When she stopped suddenly he almost fell over her.

"Bend your head," she said, "and walk forward."

Shuffling along, he felt the cool dampness of a tunnel surround him, like a dash at the end of a long sentence. He opened his eyes.

"The bones are outside," Akki said quietly. "But that's all they are—just bones. Not ghosts or demons or—"

"They're Heart's Blood's bones," Jakkin said. "And we both know it."

She nodded. There was nothing more she could say.

~

THE TUNNEL WAS short and opened onto a steep pathway where strange half-shadows played on the path under a sky lightening into gray dawn. For several more hours they climbed, winding upward without speaking.

Jakkin could feel Akki's longing for the caves they'd left, caves that were now only minor pocks in the landscape. That longing crossed his mind as an endless gray sending, but he didn't let her know how much she had let her feeling leak out, for it began to occur to him that one way to become private was to respect another's privacy. Instead he hummed monotonously to disguise his reaction.

When they reached a sharp switchback they both rested for a moment, drawing in deep breaths that slowly synchronized. Akki leaned against the rock wall and made no move to go on, but Jakkin stepped around the turn, doggedly determined to continue.

Around the bend he saw that the way flattened and then widened into an unexpected barren arena, as large as a minor dragon pit, the carved-out bowl of a mountaintop.

"Akki, come see this!" he called.

She rounded the bend and was as surprised as he.

"I've never made it this far before or seen anything like this," she said.

Jakkin scouted the base of the eastern slope and Akki the western. Since they'd come up over the southern rim, they had to find some alternate descent or else just go back the way they had come. But the best they found was a small handscrabble and rock-strewn trail running up the northwestern side.

"Maybe it widens later on," Jakkin said cautiously.

Akki shrugged, her mind a careful blank.

The path did widen after about a hundred steps up the slope but only slightly. What was worse was that at every turning there seemed to have been a rock slide. Great plugs of granite blocked the narrow, twisting trail and at each one they had to scramble hand over hand over the rocks. Jakkin went first, after giving his pack to Akki. Once on top, he leaned down and took both packs from her, hauling them to the top, then sliding them down the far side. Then he extended a hand down to Akki and helped her up. It was slow, exhausting, sweaty work, and they didn't make good time.

Sitting atop the third pile of rocks, Akki took a deep breath. "How many more of these do you think?"

Jakkin shook his head, too winded to talk.

A moment later Akki managed another sentence. "Couldn't we call the hatchlings in? After all, Sssargon says he's our eyes. Let *them* tell us what's ahead."

"Good idea," Jakkin said. "Why didn't we think of that earlier?" He shaped a careful sending of red and gold flags flapping in the wind, wound about with his signature color of green. He kept it quiet at first so as not to hurt Akki's head and after a while felt her blue braid winding around the green. They broadcast the sending as loudly as they dared until Akki's part of it began to waver and she put her hand to her head. Still there was no answer.

"They must be miles away," Akki whispered, rubbing her temples.

"Or just not answering," Jakkin added.

"Like babies."

He nodded. "Big babies."

They both laughed and the ache in their heads bled away.

"Wouldn't it make life simpler if we could ride a dragon?" Jakkin said at last.

"That's impossible."

"I knew you'd say that. But wouldn't it be nice if we *could*."

"You *know* that any extra weight on a dragon's back presses against the flight muscles and—"

"Anatomy lessons?" he asked innocently, referring to her medical studies in the Rokk.

"Oh, you worm pile, you're just egging me on." She tried to look grim but started to giggle and, as if to tease him back, formed very graphic sendings of the kinds of wounds dragon scales inflict on the inner thighs of any humans foolish enough to sit on them. When she saw Jakkin flinch Akki grinned broadly. "Now *there's* a real anatomy lesson," she said. "All the muscles laid bare. I had to stitch up a number of drunken bonders who tried to sit astride walking dragons."

Quite deliberately, Jakkin stuck his tongue out at her and was surprised—and embarrassed—at how much better it made him feel.

"So, we're even now," Akki said. "And I could use something to drink." She slid down the rocks to the sling packs below and took out a jar of boil. Taking a deep draft, she passed the jar up to Jakkin. He made a face, more for her amusement than for real, and drank his share. Even boil tasted good after hours of climbing.

"What would happen, do you suppose," Akki mused, "if we tried to clear a path instead of climbing over each and every rock?"

"It'd take forever," Jakkin said, wiping his hand across his mouth. "And time is important. It'll be day soon, and the copter will probably be back."

Akki nodded. "We'd probably start an avalanche anyway."

"And alert every wild dragon around," Jakkin added.

"Bury villages, too," Akki said, smiling, her ironic tone clear in the words. At the same time her sending was of an idyllic picture of a peaceful village.

Without meaning to, Jakkin sent back a scene of the same village with a series of small blue-gray people, shadows of shadows in an endless line, standing in front of the houses.

Akki touched his arm. "Are you lonely?" she asked.

Immediately a fall of rocks buried the shadow people and their village. "I have you, Akki," Jakkin said. "And the hatchlings when they bother to answer. How can I be lonely?"

Akki corked the jar and banged her fist on the cork. "That's what I asked," she said. "And you answered me with another question."

~

THEY WALKED ON until the path made a particularly bad turning, with only a foot's width between the cliffside and a steep drop. Their slings overbalanced them precariously.

Akki, who was in front, clung to the cliff and moved one foot at a time, then disappeared around the bend. Jakkin heard her cry out, "Look! Oh, Jakkin, look!"

He couldn't move quickly, and his heart was pounding madly by the time he'd come around the same precarious bend. Then he saw what had so astonished her. After the turn the path was nothing but jumbled rockfall for a few feet and then, below that, an unexpected meadow covered with deep purple gorse and dotted with bright green trees.

Akki slid down the rockfall, but Jakkin, conscious of the jars of boil in his pack, picked his way carefully.

"One, two . . . three. Look, Jakkin, there are seven spikkas."

The trees, with their crowns of spiked leaves, were unmistakable, though they were shorter and spindlier than valley spikkas. They all leaned toward the eastern slope at a comical angle.

Jakkin counted quickly. "You're right—seven—and over there a few smaller ones sprouting." He pointed to the far edge of the meadow where the gorse ended suddenly in a sharp, spectacular drop. "How could spikkas grow so high up? And look how they lean."

"They lean because of the prevailing winds," Akki said. "And they're up here because dragons fly."

Jakkin snorted. "Of course dragons fly."

"When they fly the seeds of the trees often stick to their under-bellies or go through them undigested and out in the fewmets, and if they land here and—"

"No lessons," Jakkin said. He smiled. "It wasn't that kind of question."

Smiling back, she nodded. "No lessons."

"It's morning and getting warm. We should rest here, under the trees. They may lean, but their crowns are full enough to hide us from copters overhead. We can look for food later on." He wasn't afraid to admit his exhaustion, and besides—he reminded himself—Akki had probably already read it in his thoughts.

Running over to the closest spikka, Akki dropped her sling pack and began to dance around the tree. Then she stopped, looked up at the leaves as if counting them, and shook her head. "Not this one. We, my friend, are going to sleep under the prettiest one in the copse."

"Some copse," Jakkin said. "Seven spindly trees widely spaced is not a copse."

"Who says?"

"I say."

"Where is it written?"

"Here!" He pointed to his head and sent her a very vivid picture of a book with words illuminated in fiery colors: *7 TREES NOT A COPSE.*

Laughing, Akki picked up her pack and walked over to what was, without a doubt, the tallest and handsomest tree of the seven. She dropped her pack and flopped down under it, signaling Jakkin with her hand.

He walked toward her humming an old nursery melody.

Akki took up the melody and added words.

> *Night is coming,*
> *See the moons;*
> *Softly thrumming*
> *Dragon tunes.*
>
> *Sky above is*
> *Filled with laughter,*
> *Dragons care not*
> *For Dark-After.*
>
> *Dawn . . .*

*"We come, we come, we come."* The sending was clear.

And then, from farther away, almost an echo, came the sendings of the two largest hatchlings.

*"Sssargon feeds now. Sssargon comes soon."*

And then Sssasha's languid message. *"I ride the winds. I come after."*

Turning on her side, Akki mumbled something.

"What?" His voice was a whisper.

Out loud, in imitation of Sssargon's sendings, Akki announced in a deep voice, "Akki sleeps."

Jakkin laughed and curled up by her side. "We'll both sleep now and eat at dusk. Then we'll find a way down from here when the moons begin to rise. It will be much safer that way."

Akki's only answer was a light, bubbly snore. Jakkin was still trying to figure out whether it was fake or real when he slipped into sleep himself.

# 6

IN THE MIDDLE of a dream in which he and a great red dragon were lazing by the side of a stream, Jakkin stirred uneasily. A dark cloud entered the dream, raining drops of fire onto the sand. He woke to an overpowering stench, a landscape in his head as barbed and as angry as any he had ever felt, and a steady babble of dragon voices churning across the picture.

*"Sssargon kill. Sssargon save."*

*"Help. Help. Help."*

*"Do not move. Do not thrash, Help comes."*

Jakkin leaped up and looked around, sleep still lapping at the edges of his sight. Akki, sitting on the ground, was as puzzled.

Then in front of the first of the rising moons they saw their hatchlings flying, four of them, in a tight circle. They were backwinging, tails linked, holding up the fifth, whose wing drooped strangely. Around that circle was another circle of fliers, an attack force of silent winged shadows with long snaky necks and blunted heads.

"Drakk," breathed Jakkin.

"Up this high?" Akki's voice was strained. "I thought they ranged the lowlands."

"They roost in trees. In spikkas . . ." He looked up the trunk of the tree warily but could see only the jagged teeth of the leaves. His hand went quickly to the knife on the braided belt. Then he shook his head. "Useless," he muttered. "Useless against one drakk, and look—there's a whole pod of them."

"Hush. Listen."

Jakkin tuned in on the ring of dragons. Beyond their babbling he could feel the heavy dark thoughts of the drakk. Unlike smaller lizards, whose minds were uniformly pale pink or gray, the drakk's sendings were sharp: blue-black, barbed, eternally hungry. They fed on the fear of a wounded dragon long before they stripped the meat from its flesh. The pipings of a dragon hatchling roused them to a frenzy. And one of the triplets was piping its fear.

Akki whispered, "I thought drakk hunted alone."

"So did I," Jakkin said. "But these are mountain drakk."

"That awful drakk smell," Akki added.

The smell. Jakkin turned. That smell meant that somewhere nearby was a wounded or dead drakk. He looked below the ring of dragons and, by the edge of the meadow, saw a dark shape he had not noticed before, broken upon the stones.

"There," he said, pointing. "The dragons have already gotten one."

Akki nodded. "How can we help them? As long as they're up in the air, what can we do?"

"Lend me your mind. Think as I think. They have a bit of training. Maybe enough. Fewmets, I wish I'd taken more time with them. But Sssasha is pretty big and listens well. And Sssargon is nearly full grown." He reached out and Akki put her hand in his, for touching seemed to strengthen a sending.

Concentrating, Jakkin sent a message to the dragons. *"At my signal, breathe out fire."* He knew that, large as they were, they were still young, and he'd had no supply of burnwort to help stoke the flames. Of the five only Sssasha and Sssargon could even trickle smoke yet. But he also knew that fear and anger sometimes triggered a fiery display. Perhaps a flame or two would be enough of a surprise to move the ring of drakk back.

"Wishes fill no bags," Akki reminded him. Then she squeezed his hand as if in apology.

The bit of nursery wisdom focused him. He nodded. *"At my signal,"* he reminded the dragons. *"Breathe fire and then at the next, drop down to me. All at once."*

He repeated the instructions twice. He felt sure that the drakk, with their wordless, dark minds, couldn't understand the plan.

Above them, dipping and rising against the first pale moon, the two circles continued their deadly dance. Thrust, retreat, thrust, retreat. Below them, at the ridge, the second moon's aura was just beginning to show. The drakk ring tightened like a noose. Guided by the dragon smell and the constant piping of the wounded Tri, the nearsighted monsters closed in.

"When I count to three," Jakkin said to Akki, "think about the hottest flames you can. It will help them concentrate, and flame is something they know instinctively. The moment the drakk move back, think—*drop!*'' He handed Akki his knife and picked up the femur spear, which he'd left lying against the spikka.

Akki held the knife before her and bit her lip.

"One . . ." Jakkin whispered aloud.

Akki nodded.

"Two . . ." He could feel her tension.

"Three. Fire!" Jakkin roared aloud and Akki screamed with him. They sent picture after picture of blazing firebombs and roaring flames, shouting and waving their arms about as an added distraction.

In response, Sssargon trickled some smoke from his nose, enough to make the sky around them hazy. But it was Sssasha, placid Sssasha, who suddenly flared out with a tongue of flame as long as a mature fighter's. It licked at the face of the nearest drakk, which banked out of the circle, hissing wildly, and crashed onto the rocks below.

Sssargon tried again. His smoke forced the nearest drakk to blink its near-dead white eyes and back away. Sssasha managed another fire flash. It raked the side of a drakk that had not been pushed back by the smoke. The drakk turned and the circle was broken.

*"Now drop!"* Akki and Jakkin screamed, their minds linking as one.

The ring of dragons plummeted to the ground, frantically back-winging at the last moment so as not to crash and further injure the wounded Tri.

No sooner had they dropped than Jakkin instructed them, *"Form a ring on the ground. Now—hindfoot rise."* He sent the kind of controlled messages he'd used when guiding a fighting dragon in the pit. Only this was not for gold, but for life, so there was an added edge of fright in his sending.

Sssargon understood at once and Sssasha was not far behind. Even little Tri-ssskkette, the wounded one, tried to stand, front claws raised and waiting.

For a moment Jakkin closed his eyes, remembering Heart's Blood. He felt tears beginning in the corners of his eyes. Blinking them back, he forced himself to look, but his grip on the spear tightened.

The lead drakk and the flame-racked second dived.

Jakkin flashed out with the sharpened spear, catching the front drakk in the head above the eye. He did not pierce its hide, but he jarred it enough to disrupt its perfect dive and Sssasha ripped its neck open with her claws. Then she grabbed the drakk in her mouth and flung it with such force, it tumbled to the edge of the cliff.

The second drakk banked sharply and winged away.

The fallen drakk lay on its side, still except for the pulsing sensor organs on the underside of its wings. Its malevolent, blind snake eyes shuttered and unshuttered rapidly. Viscous blood oozed from its neck.

Akki ran over to the cliff's edge and picked up an enormous rock. Holding it over her head, she walked purposefully to the drakk, ready to drop the stone on the dying beast. She bent over it and Jakkin ran up behind her and yanked her back.

At that moment the drakk's hind claws razored through the air just where Akki's legs had been seconds before.

"It's not dead!" she cried out in horror.

"It's dead," Jakkin said. "Or near enough. But even dead it'll make a final fatal pass, a kind of reflex, because of those sensors." He pointed to the fleshy sensors. They were still pulsing. "Didn't you study *that* in your anatomy lessons?" he asked.

"I never studied drakk," she said softly.

"Someone at the nursery told me he knew a man whose leg was nearly severed in two by a very dead drakk."

Akki shivered and let the rock fall.

Hot, foul-smelling drakk blood oozed onto the gorse.

"Last time," mused Jakkin, "the smell of that blood made me sick."

"Last time you weren't part dragon," Akki said, but her voice was strange, and Jakkin suddenly realized it was because she was holding her nose.

Sssargon walked stiff-legged over to the dead drakk and, using only the tip of his tail, poked and prodded it gingerly, waiting for a response. When there was none he pushed the drakk slowly—from the backside only—through the ground cover and over the edge of the cliff. When it landed, after a long fall, Sssasha sent a chuckling thought into Jakkin's head.

"*Splat!!!*" Then she turned her attention to helping Tri-ssskkette, slowly licking the torn wing. When the wound was clean she swiveled her great head toward Akki. *"Fix?"*

Akki smiled weakly and went back to the spikka. Her sling pack lay under the tree. In one of the jars were the remains of her medkit. She whispered to Jakkin, "I hope the needles I have are strong enough for dragon skin." Threading the needle, she went to work. Her small, careful stitches patchworked the flesh and scale feathers that had been torn. "See," she said to Jakkin, "luckily the *bande dominus*, the big wing bone here, is untouched. Otherwise she would have been in real trouble."

Jakkin nodded, muttering under his breath, *"Bande dominus."*

After a few minutes, except for the strange nobbiness of the thread, the wing looked as good as new.

"No more sleeping under trees," said Jakkin. "There are still a number of drakk there. And since they usually fly in a straight trajectory"—he hesitated—"they probably nest right here in the meadow. In the top of one of these spikkas."

Sssargon's anger suddenly forced its way through to them in red hot splashes. *"Sssargon fight. Sssargon flames."* And to everyone's amazement he shot a spearhead of flame out half a meter.

"Sssargon has lousy timing," said Akki, but she reached out and scratched him under the chin.

"Thou brave worm," Jakkin said, unconsciously falling into the elevated formal language that pit trainers used with their dragons.

Sssargon preened under their attention, oblivious of the ironic undertones. He even sent a wilder thought to them: *"Sssargon kill. Kill all. Sssargon flames once more."*

"Worm," warned Jakkin, "we can't be running off to fight now."

"Yes, brave Sssargon," said Akki, holding up the medkit. "We have little thread left for sewing up thy mighty wings."

"And only one small knife and one small spear and . . ."

Sssargon's fiery reply shot through them. He did not understand, nor did he *want* to understand, human reasoning. He wanted blood and earth and air and fire. When Akki tried to send a soothing gray cloud to cover his burning landscape, he shook it off, pumped his wings, and leaped into the air. They could feel the backwind as he flipped to the left and flew out over the valley, his defiance screaming into their minds.

"Lizard waste," shouted Jakkin after him. Turning to Akki, he said, "I've never had a dragon act like this."

"You're used to nursery dragons, trained and pampered. These hatchlings are wild."

"Well, they weren't born wild," Jakkin said.

"His temper will burn off up there in the sky. He's a bit put out, I think, that Sssasha was the great hero of the fight when he thought he should be," she said, putting the medkit back in her pack. "Reminds me of a boy I once knew." She smiled.

"Not funny," said Jakkin, but he couldn't keep from smiling back at her. "However, *that's* a dragon long overdue for some hard training."

"You're not exactly the picture of a trainer now."

He looked down at his shorts, the dirty remnants of his white trainer's suit. They were patched and repatched, the earlier, crisper darns done by Akki, the later ones, his own coarse handiwork. "Well," he admitted, "I guess I don't *look* like one. But I still know training. And a certain amount of discipline is necessary, as today proves. If we're all to survive, we have to find ways of working together."

Akki was silent and her thoughts blank.

"Fewmets, Akki, wasn't that the first lesson we learned in the nursery? Isn't that what our grandfathers learned when they were dumped on Austar?"

Akki's voice was very quiet. "I thought you said the first and best lesson was *I fill my bag myself.*" She touched his chest where the leather bag used to hang, the bag that signaled to all the world that he was a bonder, the bag he'd filled with gold enough to buy his freedom.

"We aren't wearing bond bags anymore."

"No, and we haven't for some time, Jakkin."

"Then why are we arguing?" Jakkin asked. "We don't have time for arguments. We've got to get away from this meadow. Now."

"Now, now, now. All of a sudden everything is *now* with you. And besides, we aren't arguing, Jakkin. We're discussing things, like sophisticated folk do."

"Like city folk?" asked Jakkin. "Is that what you learned the year you lived in the Rokk with the rebels?"

"I learned to talk about things that matter with Golden and with Dr. Henkky," Akki said. "I learned to talk out my feelings before they got so big . . . oh, never mind, Jakkin. How can you understand? You'd rather send to dragons."

"Akki, that's not true." But she had turned away. He picked up his sling and stood there, his mouth empty of words but his mind swirling and confused, and Akki, he was sure, heard it all.

# 7

WITHOUT SPEAKING TO each other, they walked the rim of the gorse meadow looking for a new path down the mountain. Their feet kicked up insects that chittered and flew away. Keeping pace with them were the four hatchlings, who trampled the purple ground cover with their massive feet.

Sssasha kept checking the skies, though it wasn't clear whether she was looking for more drakk or trying to find the sulking Sssargon. Unlike humans, dragons sent only what they wanted to send unless they were in the middle of a fight.

Tri-ssskkette's sendings kept breaking into jagged little markers of pain and, with the other two echoing her every mental whimper, it made concentration difficult for them all. Jakkin tried sending calming thoughts to the triplet, but nothing seemed to work until Akki began a light show of raucous, bumpy colors that finally took the hatchling's mind off her wounds.

Jakkin turned to Akki and drew in a deep breath. "Thanks," he whispered at last.

Akki shrugged. "Some patients need a lot of sympathy and some need a lot of distracting." She stopped for a moment, seemed to calculate, then added, "Dr. Henkky taught me that."

"She's a smart lady," Jakkin said. It seemed to make peace between them and Jakkin smiled with relief.

They continued to walk the meadow edge, but it was like looking over the rim of a bowl.

"I don't see any paths but the one we came up," Akki said as they circled a second time. She rubbed the side of her head. The light show was beginning to wear her down.

"Well, we can't go back that way," Jakkin said. "Not after all this."

"Without a path, we can't go anywhere else."

"What do you want us to do?" Jakkin asked. "Sit here and wait for the drakk to return? Or the copter?" His voice was over-loud.

"Jakkin, *I'm* not the enemy," Akki said. "Don't yell at me."

He was about to apologize, feeling stupid about losing his temper, when Sssasha sent a picture of a cave into his head. The cave had a long, winding thread of light running end to end.

Jakkin shook his head to clear it, but Sssasha's calling came again, steady, insistent. "In?" Jakkin asked. "You want us to find a cave and go in? That's no real solution. Fine for a night, maybe. Drakk don't go in caves. And copters won't find us there. But it won't last forever. We need a way down this mountain."

"Maybe she means a cave like the tunnel," Akki broke in.

"Maybe," Jakkin said. "But I haven't seen any caves, have you?"

Akki shook her head. The rock face had been solid.

Turning in a deliberate, lumbering manner, Sssasha headed toward the rock face beyond them. On a hunch, Jakkin ran after her, and then, with a burst of speed, reached the wall of rock first. The cliff was veined with a dark material and rose straight up, without handholds. At the bottom, where it met the meadow, instead of the ever-present gorse there was a thicket of prickly caught-ums. With his spear Jakkin gingerly parted strand after strand of the tangle. It seemed a hopeless task.

Sssasha moved slightly to the right and stared at the rock.

"Here," said Akki, catching up to them. "Try here, where she's looking."

Jakkin picked at the caught-ums with the spear and on the fifth try he spotted a low, dark hole. Akki carefully held apart the nearer vines, holding her fingers above and below the caught-um thorns while Jakkin used the spear to pull apart the rest of the thicket.

"How could she know it was there?" Akki asked.

"Maybe she saw it when she was flying? From above?" His answers seemed more like questions. "Or maybe dragons can, you know, sense caves?"

"Do you mean this one?" asked Akki, sending the thought simultaneously to Sssasha.

Sssasha's answer was another picture, this time of a close, pulsing darkness that reminded both Jakkin and Akki of the egg chamber where they had been sheltered and changed.

Jakkin looked again at the wall and the low opening, then turned to the dragon. But Sssasha, sensing some kind of signal that the humans could not read, was already pumping her wings in preparation for flight. The three smaller hatchlings fanned the air in imitation. Even Tri-ssskkette, her wounded wing stuttering in the small eddies, managed to rise up and hover for a moment over the bushes. The wind from the four pair of wings caused the caught-ums to sway, as if great waves were passing through. Then the hatchlings rose higher, banked in formation, and, led by Sssasha, disappeared over the top of the cliff.

"Stop!" Akki shouted. "Come back."

But the dragons were too far off to hear, and they ignored her sendings, even when Jakkin joined her. Soon they were out of sight.

Dropping to a crouch before the thicket, Akki said, "That's the first time they've *all* disobeyed." Then she added softly, "I sure hope those stitches hold." Hand up over her eyes, she continued to stare at the spot in the sky where the dragons had disappeared.

Jakkin examined the cave entrance. "I guess that's our only choice," he said, pointing.

Akki turned back and nodded.

They rounded up their packs, making sure nothing but the trampled gorse gave evidence of their stay there. Then, carefully, so as not to scratch their hands, they pulled apart enough of the intertwining branches of the caught-ums, hooking them on to peripheral strands until they had a clear if narrow path leading into the cave.

When they reached the rock Jakkin turned and, using his spear, unlocked the knot behind them. The brambles sprang back, once again obscuring the cave.

"No one could possibly know we're in here," Jakkin said, his mind sending its own version of a gate slammed shut.

~

THEY WERE COLD the moment they entered the cave. It was as if the cave were fed by some great belly of wind from below. And there was a strange hollow echo in it that gave them back breath for breath. Jakkin pulled his gray-white shirt out of the sling and put it on.

"I don't like it," Akki said, shivering. Parts of her voice, terribly distorted, came back to them from the black walls: *I . . . ikeit . . . ikeit . . . ikeit.* "It's not—not welcoming, like our other caves. There's something *ugly* here. I don't know what it is, but I feel it."

Although Jakkin didn't answer, his own mistrust linked with hers. They reached out and grabbed hands, as if touch alone could warm them, and together began to inch forward into the cave. It was dark inside, and though their gift of dragon sight usually meant they could see colors in the dark, the cave was void of any light. It was a darkness that matched the cold.

Rounding a bend, they found themselves in a secondary cave with a ceiling high enough so they could stand upright. Ahead was a faint gleaming that cast a grayish light on the shadowy walls. Instinctively they went toward the light, their fingers twined together.

The glow seemed to come from a pile of sticks stacked up so high, the top reached the cave ceiling.

Akki reached out with her free hand and touched one of the protruding sticks cautiously. "It's cold," she said. "And porous."

Jakkin put his hand on another stick. "That's bone," he said.

Akki looked more closely, horrified. "You're right," she said. She touched a different bone. "Oh, my God," she said. "Jakkin, look! Femur, fibula, humerus, another femur, tibia, and these little ones. They're caudal vertebrae." She went up and down the stack, touching the bones and naming them, until she added unnecessarily, "Dragon bones." The echo in the cave mocked her horror, whispering in return: *ones . . . ones . . . ones.*

Despite the cold, Jakkin felt a fine film of sweat on his palms as Akki counted out the bones. It took a moment more for him to get out the question that seemed to be echoing inside him. "What . . ." he began, his voice cracking, "what can be big enough to eat this many dragons?" He hesitated, then mused aloud, "Not drakk."

"What would be big enough to strip the bones—and then neat enough to stack them?" Akki added. "Stack them in an intricate, interlocking pattern?"

"We're leaving," Jakkin said. "Now."

The echo added its own mocking note.

They backed out of the dark, high chamber and reentered the lower room. The cave mouth, even shuttered with the caught-ums, suddenly seemed to blaze with light, and they started toward the opening.

A strange chuffing sound leaked through the thorny thicket and into the cave. Jakkin crouched by the cave mouth and listened. Something whirred around the clearing and settled in.

*"Copter!"* he sent to Akki, not daring to speak aloud or stir up the cave's echoes again, even though with the noise the copter was making, he knew he'd never be heard. Carefully he checked that the caught-ums were securely laced over the opening. As far as he could tell, they showed no evidence of entry.

"*We have disappeared,*" Akki sent back, forming a picture of a barred door. Jakkin recognized it as the sending he had envisioned earlier when they had first come into the cave. But there was a strange darker color in Akki's sending that might have been either grim satisfaction—or fear.

They edged backward till they came again to the bend. Fearfully they rounded it and huddled together against the wall in the chamber of bones. Akki's hand found Jakkin's and he was relieved that her hand was as moist as his own.

Two or three shouting voices reached them, any meaning lost through the filter of brush and stone. The cave echoed their own heavy breathing until it seemed as if the dark itself was filled with fearful respirations.

"Did we leave anything out there, anything they might recognize as ours?" Jakkin whispered into Akki's ear.

She was a long time answering. At last a quiet sending reached into his mind. It was of a landscape that, except for a few sketchy trees, was barren.

Jakkin wondered suddenly if the dead drakk puzzled the searchers. They could hardly miss it. The smell alone would warn them. He was glad he'd stopped Akki from beating in the drakk's head with a rock. Surely the searchers—whether they were rebels, wardens, or Fedders—would realize that the drakk had been killed by dragons. And Sssasha's heavy tread on the gorse should have wiped out any sign of their smaller feet.

One last shout came to them, then the whir of the copter.

A weak sending suddenly came through, a picture of a copter with the copse and mountain foreshortened. The copter in the sending rose up from the gorse and headed in a southerly direction.

"*Gone,*" came Sssasha's sending, ending with a quiet, bubbling "*Good!*"

"Yes, good," Jakkin said aloud, and sighed deeply. The sudden echo startled him: *ood . . . ood . . . ood.* It seemed to go on and on, finally dying off with a hissing, echoed sigh. He crept forward to the cave mouth and turned his head to see Akki in the darkness. "Come on," he said. "We can get out of here now."

"Wait," Akki said. "I hear something else. Not the copter. Not our own echoes. Something else."

When the tickling echo of her words had died away, Jakkin listened, too, straining into the colorless cold. He didn't know what to expect, perhaps the sound of lizards scrabbling on overhead ledges, perhaps the breath of dragons, perhaps whatever large predator had eaten the dragons and stacked their bones on the floor. What he heard instead was a sending, teasing and gray, as insistent as a trainer's command.

*"Come. Come. COME. COME."*

There was something else beneath the sending and around it, a wilder note, like singing.

Without willing it, he crawled back into the cave of bones, then stood and reached for Akki's hand once more. They walked around the pile of bones. Behind it was a tunnel.

*"COME. COME. COME. COME."*

The singing was higher now, like the piping of a flute.

Will-less, as if in a spell out of Golden's book of dragon lore, they plunged hand in hand into the tunnel, which closed around them, a narrow, stifling, winding tube.

# 8

AFTER THE FIRST few turns they had to drop hands, needing both to feel along the sides of the tunnel. Though the sides were cold, damp, even slippery to the touch, it was the grayness that amazed Jakkin the most. Outside, when the moons set and Dark-After was complete, there was always enough light to make colors. In the bone room the bones had lent a strange glow to the cave, and then the phosphorescent fungi on the walls of the tunnel had allowed them some further shades. But this part of the cave seemed just an endless gray shadow land that was more depressing and frightening than black night before the *change* had ever been.

Jakkin could not help himself, and his feelings broadcast to Akki. But when her own fear pulsed back at him, he felt only relief, as if her fear excused his. He relaxed into a yawn.

"I'm sleepy," Akki said just as he yawned. Her mind babbled at him, suddenly childlike, sending quiet little pictures of gray water and gray waves. "I think I'm going to sit down." It reminded Jakkin of one of Sssargon's pronouncements.

That seemed right—sitting down. They'd been walking hours, with little sleep. Jakkin struggled against another yawn, and when Akki sagged against him, he put his arms around her and let his own knees bend slowly.

Just then the strange faraway sending began again, steady and insistent, like an alien heartbeat.

*"COME. COME."* Then a pause and a repeat. *"COME. COME."* Entwining it, like a dark vine around a bright pillar of light, was another voice that sang to them a wordless, soothing song.

"Forward," Jakkin mumbled. "We've got to go forward." He

yanked Akki up with him, wondering only slightly why his voice sounded a register higher, childlike.

They plodded ahead, and when the tunnel's air got close Akki dropped her pack. Jakkin bent to retrieve it, dragged it after him for a few steps, and then let it fall.

*"COME. COME."*

The tunnel flared open again and little flecks of light, like the wild fire of a fighting dragon's eye, seemed to wink at them from the walls.

*"COME. COME."*

Akki shivered and Jakkin put his arm around her. He could feel the sweat through her shirt. She stumbled, went down on one knee, out of the protection of his arm, and gave a sharp cry. When she stood up she held something white in her hand.

"Our neat bone stacker is getting sloppy," Jakkin said, running a finger over the top of the bone. It was a *bande dominus*, the large knobby bone from a dragon's wing.

It provoked no laugh from Akki, who began to shiver again.

Jakkin's foot kicked something that clattered away in the darkness. He got to his knees to try to find it by its gleam, but there were no telltale white patches anywhere on the tunnel floor and he guessed it had fallen into a ditch or ricocheted around a bend. He lifted his head suddenly and realized that the singing and the command had stopped. It felt as if a headache that had long and mysteriously plagued him had disappeared. He shook his head.

"This is crazy," he said aloud, his voice back to its normal pitch. "What are we doing here? We have to find our way back and mark our passage or we'll be lost in here forever."

Akki grunted her agreement.

They turned, heading back the way they had come. With his head clear of the mental message, Jakkin found he could see a bit more. The gray was *not* complete, lit as it was by flickering jewels in the wall. He reached out to touch one, and when his hand came close to it, it winked out as if it were an eye, but where the eye had been was only a pinpoint of icy air.

He caught his breath and stumbled on, not mentioning this discovery to Akki, since he wasn't sure what it meant. Perhaps the mountain was only a shell and these tunnels were close to the outside. Perhaps there was some more sinister meaning. But she was already frightened enough, so he calmed his traitor thoughts and instead sent her a strengthening picture.

They walked along silently for some time, following the twistings of the tunnel. At last Akki spoke, though Jakkin had already guessed what she wanted to say, her absolute fear having snaked into his mind moments before.

"We're lost, Jakkin. I know it."

"How can you be sure?"

"We haven't stumbled over my pack, have we? We should have come on it long ago. And the path seems to be going down instead of up. If we were in the right tunnel, we would have found the cave opening by now."

He made more soothing sounds, but he knew she was right. He'd figured it out himself scant moments before, and his mind sent out a confirmation before he could stop it.

Akki sat down on the cold stone and, after a moment of hesitation, Jakkin did the same. For a long time they were silent, their bridged minds sending landscapes of gray despair back and forth, pictures compounded of nervousness and the steady drip-dripping of eroding confidence.

Jakkin forced himself to reach over and pat Akki's shoulder. That touch comforted them both. She moved over and snuggled against him.

And then they heard a sound, a quick scuttering, as if hundreds of tiny feet were coming toward them.

"The bones," Akki whispered. "The monsters of the bone pile."

Into Jakkin's head exploded the picture of that pile magnified by Akki's fear into a mountain of dripping blood, red blood, the first color he had been able to conjure in a long while.

The sound got closer.

They scrambled up, determined to face whatever it was on their feet, and they pressed their backs against the wall as if they could disappear into the resisting stone. Akki was holding her breath on and off. Each time she had to let it out to take another breath there was a tiny explosion of sound that echoed mockingly from the walls. Jakkin tried to slow his own breathing but it seemed to roar out instead, bouncing off the stone. He could feel his heart pounding, too, and that noise was so loud he wondered that there was no answering echo.

And still the slithering, skuttering sound came closer, as if the monster bone-stackers had rounded yet another bend in the tunnel.

Jakkin grabbed Akki's shoulder and she let out a high yip.

"I *know* that sound," he said. "The echoes confused me at first, but I recognize it now."

"What . . . is . . . it?" Akki asked.

"In the nursery," Jakkin said breathlessly. "When we unstalled the dragons and led them through the halls, the hens in heat dragged their tails behind them on the ground and made that shushing sound. That was when we first knew they were ready to mate.''

"Of course," Akki said, "the scent glands dragged along the ground and the *males* would smell it and track a female down." She stopped. "But all those bones . . . dragons don't eat dragons. They're vegetarians. Only people eat dragons. And drakk.''

"No one's been in these caves before. No one that I know of," Jakkin said. "Though old Likkarn said—"

And that was when the sending burst upon them full force.

It was a strange, wild, frenzied picture, a riot of grays shot through with angry, jagged blacks and icy silvers, reeking with fear. No common landscape, this one was tunnel-shaped and tunnel-twisted, but over and under and burrowing through was an unmistakable rainbow pattern, except that the only gradations of color were grays.

"That's Heart's Blood's pattern!" Jakkin screamed. "The rainbow. It's her. She's here!''

"Jakkin, no!" Akki cried, clawing at his arm. "She's dead. Heart's Blood is dead. No!" The walls returned her cry over and over.

But Jakkin was already running down the dark tunnel toward the sending.

Akki left the small safety of the wall and followed the sound of his pounding feet. Around a final bend she caught up to him and wrenched at the pack on his back, slowing him for a moment and slamming him against the wall. Just then something large and smelling of the familiar musk of dragon heaved past them, its dragging tail frantically whipping against the walls. The tail caught them both around the ankles and they fell heavily, Akki atop Jakkin's pack. She felt the jar of boil break and the wetness spread beneath her. She whispered frantically, "That's not Heart's Blood, Jakkin. She's dead. We carved her open. Remember? We sheltered in her. Remember? I saw her bones.''

His sobs began then, the racking sobs of someone unused to tears. At last he got hold of himself and sat up. "Sorry," he said, snuffling. "I know it's not her. But who—or what—is it?''

"I don't know," Akki said, putting her arms around him with a fierceness that astonished them both. "But I've got a feeling we're going to find out soon.''

Akki took a deep breath, then urged Jakkin to do the same. In and out, in and out, they timed their respirations until they were both calm. And then they felt it, a great trembling presence nearby: breathy, hulking, and frightened.

*"Man?"* The dark sending was knife sharp, though still within

the basic tunnel shape, still gray. Then, tremulously, the sharper image melted away into a river of softer grays. *"Not-man?"*

Jakkin stood and shed the soaking pack, then he walked slowly toward the creature with the sure step of a dragon trainer. All the while he thought cool and careful landscapes full of meadows and mountains, rivers and trees, gray-green, blue-gray. He put his hand out and rubbed down the dragon's enormous leg until the creature put its head to his hand and sniffed it carefully. It nudged his hand and he felt along the nose and over the bony ridge of the forehead till he came to its ears. He began to scratch around its earflaps.

Akki edged forward and tickled under the dragon's chin. She began to sing in a clear sweet voice:

> *Little flame mouths*
> *Cool your tongues,*
> *Dreaming starts soon*
> *Furnace lungs . . .*

And soon the tunnel was filled with a gentle thrumming and the dove gray sendings of the cave dragon.

# *The Snatchlings*

# 9

THE DRAGON'S THOUGHTS were confusing. They seemed to hop from one splash of gray to the next. Its mouthings were unformed as well, most of the time nothing more than the pipings of a new hatchling, as though it was almost mute.

"Can you get any sense of her?" Akki asked.

"If you've found out *it* is a *her*, then you're doing better than I am," Jakkin said.

"I can *feel* the difference, idiot!"

"By her head?"

Akki sighed. "All this time with dragons and you don't know a worm-eaten thing. Female dragons have a special ridge under the tongue. You can just barely feel it when they're not gravid, but it's there. It grows bigger to help with the egg breaking if a hatchling's birth bump can't do the job. Then it gets smaller again, after the hatching."

"I got all of that but *gravid.*"

"It means pregnant, Jakkin. Full of eggs. *Honestly!* I sometimes wonder about you."

Jakkin grunted. "You have a lot of head knowledge, Akki. But most of what I know comes from here." He tapped himself on the chest and his sending was a diagram of a human with the pulsing red point in the center of the body.

"That's the stomach, worm waste. Your heart is higher and on the left side." She laughed.

"I know that," Jakkin said quickly. But a moment later he joined in her laughter.

Sensing the lightened mood, the dragon gave a remarkable imitation of a chuckle, deep-throated and near a thrum. For an instant her mind seemed to clear and Jakkin caught a glimpse in her sending of a landscape so alien to him, he wondered if it was real. It was a dark hole in which hot fiery liquids bubbled, and nearly naked creatures, in stooped parody of human beings, bent over the boiling pit. Then the scene was gone, replaced by the same jumble of grays.

"Man? Not-man?" the dragon asked again.

"Of course man," Akki said.

The dragon leaped up, knocking Jakkin over with its tail as it stood and began to tremble.

"Oh, fewmets," Akki cried. "Jakkin, do something."

Jakkin scrambled to his feet and put both hands on the dragon's back. The only other time he had seen a dragon tremble that much had been in the pit when a defeated dragon had screamed until Heart's Blood began to shake in the tremors known as Fool's Pride. Such trembling usually led a dragon to forget all training and fight to the death. But a death wish was not what Jakkin sensed from the cave dragon. He could read only total and overwhelming fear, so he willed himself to send calmly, though he could feel sweat running down his back with the effort. Forcing the image that had always worked for him before, he sent a faded, grayed-out picture of the oasis where he and Heart's Blood had trained, with its ribbon of blue river threading through the sandy landscape.

But the dragon seemed unable to listen. Her own hot, bubbling fear images kept breaking into Jakkin's sending, boiling the gray-blue stream and turning the sand dunes into vast gray storms. Her trembling continued unabated.

"Man. Man. Man. Man." It was a kind of wail that ran through, around, under, and over the sending.

"I can't reach her," Jakkin shouted to Akki, his voice bouncing off the walls. "Either that or she can't hear."

"Maybe . . ." Akki's voice was thinned out, "maybe the pictures you're sending make no sense to her. Try something else." She'd begun trembling herself with the effort of soothing the dragon.

Jakkin moved toward the dragon's neck and put his arms around her shaking head. He blew into her ears, trying to get her attention.

"Listen, little flamemouth," he crooned, "I am not-man. I am part dragon. I had two mothers. Trust me. Trust me. Think of the dark. Think of the quiet. Think of the not-men." He forced cool, careful thoughts to her, stopping once to blow in her ears again, first the left, then the right. Then he started crooning again.

"I think . . ." Akki began, "I think she's trembling a little less."

He nodded, keeping up his croon. He babbled about caves and night and the moons and anything else that he could think of, but all the while he kept the sending as controlled as possible.

"She's *definitely* trembling less," Akki said.

Even Jakkin could feel it now, running his hand down the long neck where the scales, though shifting with small tremors, were moving more slowly. He doubled his effort then, sure of success. "I will tell you a story now," he said, his voice even, "about Fewmets Ferkkin, a fantastic fellow." He proceeded to tell the dragon seven jokes in a row without ever changing the tone of his voice. The important thing was to keep the words flowing.

Next to the dragon's leg, Akki relaxed into a giggle. "Jakkin— you're terrible," she said. But her mood, communicating directly with the dragon, helped even more.

As Jakkin began the eighth joke he realized he couldn't think of any more and finished lamely, "And that's all we know about Fewmets Ferkkin . . ." but it was all right, for the dragon had stopped shaking.

Jakkin sighed. "Now what is all this," he said softly, "about not-man?"

But the dragon, too, gave a tremendous sigh, lay down, and put her great head on her front legs and fell asleep.

"When you deal with hysterical babies," Akki said, "you'll find a surprising phenomenon—they fall asleep the minute the crisis is over."

"Some baby," Jakkin said.

"*Big* baby," Akki added.

They laughed, remembering their conversation only a day before.

"So now we have an enormous sleeping dragon on our hands," Jakkin began.

"And several enormous questions unanswered," Akki finished for him.

Jakkin was silent.

"One," Akki said, "is what is the difference between man and not-man and why did it scare her so much?"

"Two is—who is she and where did she come from?" Then, as if in afterthought, he added, "She's certainly too big to have come in through our entrance. And . . ."

"And if she came in elsewhere, where *is* elsewhere?" asked Akki.

"Three," Jakkin said, "who is she running from?"

"That's easy. The thing, whatever it is, that eats dragons and stacks their bones in neat piles.'' Akki gave an exaggerated shiver. It translated into wavy lines that streaked through Jakkin's head.

"Maybe. Maybe not," Jakkin said. "But that leads us right to question four, which is . . ."

"If man frightens her and not-man doesn't, then is it man who's doing all the eating?"

"*We* ate dragon meat before," Jakkin said.

They were both quiet for a moment, remembering.

"Maybe question five is—*what's down there?*" Akki said.

"Down where?" asked Jakkin.

"Question six," Akki said. "Which direction is *down there?*"

Jakkin squatted next to the sleeping dragon and put his back against the cave wall. "Question seven is—do we go forward or do we go back?"

Akki knelt next to him. "If we go back, we have to deal with the copter and whoever is in it."

Jakkin interrupted. "And the fact that there is no other way down the mountain."

She nodded. "But if we go forward, we have to deal with the dragon's fear and the man/not-man thing that eats dragons and licks the bones clean and whatever else in her sending we didn't understand."

"Hot bubbly somethings. And slope-shouldered creatures. And . . ."

"But that's all unknown," Akki said. "And maybe just in her imagination."

"Dragons don't have any imagination," Jakkin said. "They say only what is."

"But we *know* what's back there . . ."

"So the real question is?"

"Numbers eight, nine, and ten," said Akki. "Which is more frightening—what we know or what we don't know? The light world filled with copters and possible death or transportation, or this gray world filled with . . ." She stopped.

There was a long moment of silence. Jakkin tried to keep his mind blank, but it boiled with images. Finally he whispered to her, though his mind sent ahead what his mouth had formed reluctantly, "Both. They're both frightening. You choose. I'll do whatever you want."

"Hey," Akki whispered back, "that's *my* line!"

"Then we'll choose together."

"All right," Akki said. "We'll go . . ." Her mouth shut but her mind spiraled down and down and down into the unknown dark.

# 10

WITH THEIR MINDS made up, Akki and Jakkin began to plan, and their voices criss-crossed the echoing cave.

"We need to wake up baby here," said Akki.

"I don't like calling her *baby here*," Jakkin said. "She should have a name."

"I thought I was the one who named things," Akki said, smiling. "You're always teasing me about it."

"Maybe I'm changing," Jakkin said.

"Maybe you're growing up," Akki retorted.

"Maybe you're not."

"Maybe the dragon already has a name," Akki said.

"Maybe you've changed the subject."

"Maybe she has."

"Akki, think. If a dragon has a name, it announces it in the first sending."

"How can she be this old and not have a name?" Akki asked.

"Question number eleven," Jakkin said.

"Well, she had a gray rainbow in her first sending. How about Rainbow Gray?"

"I hate it."

"Ssstep-sister."

"Don't be stupid."

"Then *you* name her," Akki said. "It was your idea, after all."

"All right, I will. What's the big vein that carries blood to the heart called again?"

"Anatomy lessons, Jakkin?"

"Yes. Sure. What's it called?"

"You mean the aorta?"

"*Aorta?* No, that's awful. You can't name a dragon Aorta."

"That's what it's called," Akki said.

"You told me something else."

"You mean . . ." Akki paused and added, "during one of my anatomy lessons?"

"Enough," Jakkin said. "I give up. So they weren't lessons, exactly. Only I did listen. You know a lot and I learned a lot."

Akki sighed. "You couldn't have learned much if you can't remember."

"Wait, I *do* remember. It's not the big vein, it's part of the heart. It's called . . ." He stopped, shrugging. "I can't remember."

"Right and left auricles?" asked Akki.

"That's it. Auricle. That's what I mean." There was excitement in his voice. "We'll call her Auricle, which sounds like *oracle*, which is a kind of omen."

"A good one, I hope," Akki said. "We could use some good luck."

"Auricle. I like that. Because she reminds me of Heart's Blood," Jakkin said. "Get it? Part of a heart is an auricle."

Akki put her hand out and touched Jakkin's arm. "She is no relation to Heart's Blood, Jakkin. Don't keep hurting yourself that way."

"How do you know? Remember Blood's A Rover, one of the nursery dragons who went feral? He could have flown to these mountains. They're not far from the nursery. And if he did, and bred with other mountain dragons—well, Auricle and Heart's Blood *could* be related. Distant cousins. All of Sarkkhan's nursery dragons went back to a single breeding pair. So it's possible. No, even more than possible. It's probable. They're cousins."

Akki didn't answer, but her sending was dim and crackled around the edges.

"Anyway, we need to wake Auricle," Jakkin said.

As if on cue, the dragon began to grunt and snort, the usual sounds of a dragon rousing.

"Hello, Auricle," Jakkin said, stretching out the name itself and sending her a rainbow of grayish hearts.

The dragon ignored him and began grooming herself.

"Hey, worm waste, that's you!" Jakkin said. Then, switching to the more formal language of the dragon master, he added, "Auricle is thy name, little one." He punctuated it with a stronger sending.

The dragon looked up, its sending puzzled, fragmented. *"Name? No-name? Name? No-name?"*

"This one is either stupid, brain-damaged, or things are weirder down here than we imagined," Jakkin said.

Akki agreed, but put her hand on the dragon's neck and whispered into its ear, "Thy name is Auricle, little one. Auricle. For thou art part of Heart's Blood in that thou art part of something that belongs to the two of us, Jakkin and me."

At that the dragon's head snapped up, and in the not quite complete dark they could see the dark shrouds of her eyes.

*"No-name,"* came the sending. *"Dragons no-name."* It bent its neck almost in two and waited, a gesture of such submission that Jakkin was shocked.

"Well, No-name," he said at last in exasperation, *"get yourself up. We are going to search for your bubbles and your man/no-man. Now. Up."* He said the last angrily and the sending was laced with a different kind of fire.

Akki added, "Go!"

The dragon leaped to its feet, its sending a mumble of grays and blacks. *"Up. Go. Man says. Man says. Man says. Up. Go."* It turned carefully around in the cave and with a slow, lumbering, shambling walk began to go back the way it had come.

Jakkin grabbed Akki's hand and squeezed it once. "Up and go, us, too," he whispered directly into her ear, so there was no echo.

~

AS THEY WALKED down the spiraling tunnel, following the dragon, they expected things to become even darker, but instead the way seemed lighter. A fuzzy phosphorescence spattered the cave walls, spotty at first, and then in larger and larger patches. By the time they had gone around four or five deep bends, the tunnel was bathed in a gray-white glow that made the shadows they cast only darker.

Akki pulled on Jakkin's shirt and he turned, then gasped, for her face was gray and her mouth and eyes dark holes.

"You look strange," Akki said.

"You look like . . . a skull," Jakkin answered.

They didn't speak after that or look at each other, preferring to send little bits of comforting color back and forth between their bridged minds, reminders of the world outside, where gray was only a minor tint. But color was difficult to remember underground, and soon their sendings shaded off into the gray of the stone and shadow around them.

The walls grew damper to the touch, then progressively slimier. They could hear things dripping just out of sight. Twice Akki bumped into long fanglike pieces of rock that hung down from the ceiling, and once Jakkin tripped over a tooth of rock that protruded up from the floor. And still the tunnel spiraled down and down as they followed the large moving shadow that was the dragon's back and tail.

They heard a sudden loud splash and, turning a final bend, found themselves at the edge of a body of water.

Squinting his eyes, Jakkin realized that a small lake lay before them. He could just make out the dragon's head and neck protruding and throwing off ripples as it moved.

"Now what?" Jakkin asked.

Akki bent down and felt the water. "It's cold," she said.

"Well, we're part dragon," Jakkin said. "We should be able to stand the cold."

"The cold's not the problem," Akki said. "I . . . I can't swim."

Jakkin was silent for a moment, watching the dragon's head disappearing into the dark beyond.

"Maybe there's some other way around, some sort of ledge or path," Akki said.

"We don't have time," Jakkin said. "Auricle . . . she's getting away."

"Then you swim after her, Jakkin, and I'll keep looking for another way and follow along after." Her voice was thin.

"I don't want to leave you," Jakkin said.

"Go!" Akki gave him a push.

He stumbled backward into the water, which was colder than he'd expected, then he turned and splashed noisily after the dragon, his clothing slowing him down but not so much as to take him below. The sound of his swimming drowned out everything else. Once or twice he went under, but kept up his stroke. The water had a flat, metallic taste. When he opened his eyes under the water it was too dark to see anything. Blindly, he swam on.

The lake was not very large and he was on the other side quickly. But when he turned around the cave behind him was black. He couldn't see Akki at all.

"Akkkkkkkkkkki," he called out.

The sounds bounced crazily off the cave walls and it was some time before it was quiet again.

At last there came a tinny cry, neither plea nor call.

"Go on," said the voice. Or at least Jakkin thought that's what it sounded like. He mouthed the words back: "Go on."

He tried to send to her, but there was no response. All he received was a fuzzy static, a crackling that sputtered across his mind as if the water had somehow damaged his ability to receive. He shivered, more from fear than cold, then looked back over his shoulder to the passage where the dragon had disappeared.

"She said to go on," he urged himself. Then he hesitated for another long moment before he plunged into the passage after the worm.

# 11

STATIC STILL CRACKLED through Jakkin's mind, blanking out even the lightest of sendings, but he could track the dragon by the trail of large puddles in the middle of three tunnels leading away from the lake. Jakkin searched his pockets frantically for a marker to leave for Akki. Finding none, he tore off a pocket instead and dropped it on the floor of the cave. It was the best he could do.

The middle tunnel curved downward at a steep slope, but it, too, was lit with patches of phosphorescence. They were at such regular intervals, Jakkin wondered if they had been placed there.

"Question number twelve," he thought grimly.

The tunnel took one last abrupt turning, and then, suddenly, he could see light ahead. It wasn't the bright white light of outdoors, but rather a flickering reddish glow. For a moment he wondered if he should wait for Akki to catch up to him. He turned and looked over his shoulder, straining into the darkness behind, but he couldn't see her. In fact, he couldn't see anything. For a moment he listened, but his crackle-filled mind reached nothing. The only way to go was forward, so he edged slowly toward the red light.

As he got closer he heard a kind of steady growl above the mind-crackling. It came from the same direction as the light. He moved forward again and began to distinguish two separate noises, one a low clanging and the other an echo. The closer he got, the more he became mesmerized by the light and sound. After so many hours in the cave, the color and noise both assaulted and drew him. Finally, overwhelmed by it all, he stopped, crouched down, and put his hands up over his ears. He squeezed his eyes tight until white sparks seemed to jump around in front of them.

For a long time he squatted, unmoving. Then slowly his mind cleared, as if he were waking up and knew he was waking, but wasn't yet shed of a dream. He opened his eyes, took his hands away from his ears, and stood. His knees gave a protesting creak.

The scene before him was as odd as anything he'd gotten from the dragon. It looked as if it were a sending he couldn't read properly. He was on the far end of a large cavern lit by flames from a central pit that was as wide across as the Narakka River. Sitting on a grillwork over the flames were large pots filled with something that glowed now red and now shadow. Above the pots, on an overhang of rock, were half a dozen leaning figures stirring the pots with long sticks.

Were they men or not-men? Auricle's puzzlement became his own. *Men and not-men.* These creatures had a man's form, muscular and stockier than anyone Jakkin had ever known. But there was something really wrong with the shape. They were much too broad in the shoulder, much too short in the leg. Men and not-men.

One of the strange, stocky creatures saw Jakkin and pointed at him. Without a sound the rest of them all looked up at once.

Jakkin felt his head suddenly filled with strings of picture-questions. Like the sending of dragons, the questions were wordless and yet completely understandable.

*"Who you?"* The thoughts came in sharp stabs of light. *"You? You? Who you?"* It was not one mind but a number of them asking· the question. He could feel the differences as clearly as if they'd been individual voices.

Jakkin shouted at them across the pit, not yet trusting his mind, needing to feel the precision of words in his mouth. Akki was right about that. "I am Jakkin. Jakkin Stewart. From Sarkkhan's Nursery. Bondsman and trainer. Master now." He felt no need to disguise who he was. Surely these creatures knew nothing about the Rokk Pit. Unaccountably, his hand went to his chest, his fingers fumbling for the bond bag that had hung there for so many years. Then he gave a short, staccato laugh. None of that seemed to mean *anything* to them. He'd try another tack. "I am Jakkin Stewart of the mountains. Out of Heart's Blood. Who are you?"

That seemed to reach them. They put down their sticks and looked at one another, gesturing wildly but still not speaking aloud. Then, as if on a signal, they all turned and faced him, staring. Their eyes, even from so far away, seemed to glow like an animal's in the dark.

Jakkin felt his mind fill up again until he felt it would overflow, for the sending was so loud and overpowering, he couldn't move. It was like Akki's first sendings multiplied a hundredfold. Hot points of sizzling lights danced in his brain.

How long he stood there, stupefied, he couldn't have said, but suddenly he felt a painful slap on his cheek and he could see and move again, his mind cleared. In front of him stood the man who had delivered the blow, arm still upraised. A man. Definitely. Stocky, broad-shouldered, hulking, but unquestionably a man. He was stripped down to a skin loincloth, his feet in leather sandals, his chest hairy, his head smooth. But a man.

Despite the stinging cheek, Jakkin smiled at him. The man was a full head shorter than he was.

"I told you who I was," Jakkin said. "Who are you?"

The man raised his hand again. This time Jakkin saw the blow as well as felt it, yet he couldn't move from it or respond in kind, for at the same time a ringing admonition leaped into his mind.

*"Do not krriah, youngling. You not child. Still you give child's krriah. Be man."*

Bewildered, Jakkin felt himself cast loose of this second mind-spell. He put his hand to his cheek. He could still feel the heat of the blow beneath his fingers.

*"I Makk."* The sending was short, brutal, final. But whether that was his name, his title, or some other designation was not clear.

Before Jakkin could respond, Makk grabbed his arm and jerked him forward until his feet were curled over the lip of the rock. For a moment Jakkin was afraid Makk meant to push him over into the flames. For a short man, he was very powerful. As another protest started to form on his lips, Jakkin felt instructions insinuate themselves in his head. He glanced down at his feet. Below, where his toes curled over the rim, was a rough-carved set of steps.

*"Down!"*

He had no choice. With Makk at his back, Jakkin carefully made his way down the stone steps, hugging the rock as he went. He could hear the whisper of the man's feet behind him as he descended, and his head seemed filled with an alien presence he couldn't quite shake loose. The only thing he could do—and he did it with deliberate care—was to keep Akki's face out of his thoughts. She must not be caught, as he was, by the not-man men.

# *12*

THE STEPS FOLLOWED the curve of the cave wall and came out on the far side of the pit. Jakkin could feel the heat on his right side, and he longed to turn and say something to the man behind him, but the slap and the strange word *kkriah* were burned into his memory. Until he knew more he would not chance speaking aloud again.

Their steps echoed in the vast chamber, and Jakkin stopped for a moment, unsure which way he should proceed. He felt Makk's rough hand on his shoulder turning him toward the left, where there was another tunnel. Once they entered it he was cool again, and he welcomed the dark and the relative quiet.

Makk shoved him along the tunnel and Jakkin went slowly, trying to shutter his mind against the barrage of questions/instructions. The minute he closed the imagined door he felt a kind of release of pressure, as if the man had simultaneously stopped searching around in his thoughts. The oddness of it made him raise his eyebrows, but he kept moving.

The tunnel ended abruptly in another large cavern, but this one was not lit with fires. Instead there was a complete wall of phosphorescence that made the cave a place of deep shadows. Over thirty men were in the room, some sitting at long tables eating, some sleeping on rocky outcroppings, some apparently in deep conversations, for their hands moved as if shaping images, though their mouths were still. It reminded Jakkin of an evening in the nursery bondhouse, though it was certainly much quieter. And the memory ached like a rotten tooth when he probed it further.

"What is . . ." Jakkin began aloud, and was stunned into silence by the violence of a multiple sending. He began again, this time only with his mind. *"What is this place?"*

Makk put a hand on his shoulder again. *"This Place of Men."* The pictures he sent were straightforward and without any of the subtleties or undertones Jakkin associated with Akki's sendings.

*"What about . . . women?"*

*"Place of Women not here. There."* The image Makk sent was of a different cavern in which stocky, broad-shouldered women with long, straight dark hair ate, sat, slept in poses similar to those of the men. It was not a symbol of a place but the place itself, as sharply delineated as a picture.

Makk's sending continued. *"There, too, Place of Those Who Kkriah. There, too, Place of Great Mothers."* The last image he sent was that of dragons huddled together as if they were clutchmates, though they ranged in shape and age.

*"Dragons?"* Jakkin sent, and when there was no answer he added, *"Worms?"* Each image was slightly different.

Makk shook his head. He sent a gray picture of dragons hovering over a pile of eggs. The meaning was clear. *"Great Mothers."* It was reinforced by all the men.

Jakkin rubbed his head behind the right ear, where an ache was starting. A bad one, he guessed, and nothing to laugh at to help it bleed away. He drew a deep breath, ready to begin again. Sending this way was hard work, like speaking a strange language. Just then his stomach rumbled and all the men laughed. Their laughter was silent, a bubbly mind-sending that made him almost giddy.

*"You hunger,"* Makk sent. *"You eat."*

*"I'd love to eat,"* Jakkin sent back, his images laced with an ironic edge that spoke of other kinds of hunger: sleep, the need to understand, and a very dim image of Akki, which leaked out unbidden and which he quickly suppressed. But Makk seemed oblivious to anything but the central message.

*"You eat,"* he sent again, signaling one of the sitters with those curious finger waggles. The man stood and brought over a bowl for Jakkin.

Jakkin sniffed at the bowl. It smelled like dragon stew. Hungry as he was, Jakkin's stomach revolted. He could not eat such a meal. *"Dragon?"* he queried. Then, remembering, he added, *"Great Mother?"*

The sending that came back to him, so solid and unemotional, chilled him. *"What else?"*

He put the bowl on the nearest table and shook his head. *"No!"*

*"You insult Great Mother's gift?"* Even the sleepers stirred at that sending.

*"I'm not that hungry. I can't eat."* How could he explain to these crude cave dwellers that once he'd made full contact with dragons, eating their meat was impossible. His stomach chose that moment to growl again.

The bubbling response of the men was far out of proportion to the joke, and Jakkin suddenly wondered if any involuntary body noise was funny to these silent men. He tried to explain his refusal to eat meat as clearly and directly as he could. *"My . . . people . . . do not eat Great Mothers."* It was not exactly a lie. He and Akki were a separate people now.

*"Ancestors warn of such people."* Makk's sending seemed tinged with an emotion other than anger for the first time.

*"Your ancestors. Tell me."* Maybe, Jakkin hoped, careful to keep the thought hidden, maybe here was a real clue, a way out of this place.

Makk's face softened, as if the question somehow pleased him. His sending began and it had the rhythms of a story long rehearsed and often told. *"First were The Men. Strong Men. Men of Bonds."* He held up his wrists, and for the first time Jakkin noticed he wore metal bracelets.

Metal! Jakkin gasped aloud. There was so little metal on Austar that what there was had to be carefully husbanded for use in the cities. The cost of metal was far beyond the ordinary bonder. Even most masters could afford little. He remembered the grillwork under the great pots in the fire cavern. And the pots themselves. And the sticks! They were all metal. How could he have been so blind? These strange men had a secret the outside world would love to have—a secret metal cache. If he listened carefully, perhaps he could find out more.

Makk was continuing. *"One man, First Makker, knew to take Stone. Knew to turn Stone to Ore. From Ore comes The Fire That Is Water. From The Fire That Is Water come Bands. For we were of Bonds who now are of Bands."*

There was a poetry in Makk's sending that almost obscured the story he told. Drawing a curtain between Makk's mind and his own, Jakkin tried to find the real meaning. Could First Makker have been an escaped prisoner back in the days of all their grandfathers? Someone with a working knowledge of metal making who had somehow managed to live through the deadly cold. Jakkin knew that not all the early prisoners were murderers and thieves. A few had been political prisoners sent away from Earth or other planets to the metal-poor desert world of Austar. Some of those prisoners must have had skills beyond the ordinary. What if that First Makker was one? And what if other escapees had joined him and remained hidden within the bowels of the mountains, generation after generation? It made sense. Makk said they were Men of Bonds. And if the secret of the metal making had passed down from father to son over the years ... He suddenly realized Makk had stopped sending and was staring at him. Jakkin stared back, the wall around his thoughts carefully constructed again.

Makk nodded and the sendings came again. *"We Men of Great Mother, Flesh of her flesh. Blood of her blood. One day go to place of Bonds and throw them over."* The sending was dark red, the red of anger and fire and blood, but Makk's hands were raised as if in ecstasy.

Jakkin didn't understand what that meant at all. Some ritual of eating, perhaps? What if they insisted he eat with them? Could he do it? Did he dare refuse again? And if these strange men really did plan to go outside and fight, shouldn't he warn the outsiders? After all, the closest civilized place to these mountains was Sarkkhan's Nursery, where he had grown up. His friends were there. But if he managed to get out, the last place he should go would be the nursery. Surely any searchers would have spies there.

His mind in a turmoil, he drew in a breath and carefully drew aside the curtain over his thoughts to let a sending out. *"The Great Mothers, where are they? And where is the Place of Women?"*

Makk lowered his hands and came close to Jakkin, touching him on the shoulder. *"What place you? Too high for here. Too thin for here. No Bands. Yet speak without noise. Not like Others."*

*"Others? What others?"*

*"Long ago Others."* He did not elaborate.

A man who had been sitting at the far end of the table stood up and came over to Jakkin, placing his hand on top of Makk's. *"What place?"*

Jakkin thought a long time before answering, careful to cloak his mind till the last. Sweat beaded his forehead. *"I come from another Place, another mountain, another cave."* He knew suddenly that to admit being from the outside was inviting death. *"There we wear no Bands but we, too, know the Great Mothers. I am blood of the blood with a great red."* He wouldn't tell them how he'd shared the dragon's blood, though her rainbow sign broke across his sending, a memory of that generous spirit he couldn't keep out.

The colorful sending seemed to startle the men. Makk's hand dropped from his shoulder and everyone drew away mentally. Jakkin wondered if it was the color or the joy in the sending that had so provoked them. Then he shook his head, continuing:

*"I came to your place with my . . . woman."* He bet Akki would be furious if she knew he'd called her that.

Makk nodded, but still kept his distance. *"Yes. We know this. She in Place of Women."*

It was Jakkin's turn to be startled. He walked over to Makk and put his hand on the man's broad shoulder. At the touch he was able to see right into Makk's mind. So that was it! He made the sending as strong as he could: *"I want my woman. That is how it is done in my place."* When he took his hand away Makk's mind snapped shut like some kind of trap.

Makk's fingers moved swiftly, then his sharp sending pierced Jakkin's mind. *"Now you eat."*

*"Not that stuff."*

Turning, Makk signed toward one of the men at a table. He rose and brought over another bowl. This one was filled with a dark jellied substance. Jakkin took the bowl and tipped it eagerly into his mouth. He recognized congealed boil and chikkberries, but there was also a greenish, bittersweet taste that lingered after he had finished the food and made his mouth feel clean and good.

Only later did he realize what that meant: chikkberries and boil. The men of the cave didn't just stay inside. Somewhere there had to be an easy access to outside, to a meadow. He wondered when and how he might dare to ask.

# 13

MAKK MADE IT clear, though it took many sendings, that if Jakkin didn't work like the other men, he wouldn't be fed again. Nor would he be allowed to go to the Place of Women when it was time.

*"Time?"* Jakkin had sent, hoping for an explanation. He'd already given up on the food. Somehow, somewhere, there was a supply of fresh growing things, but certainly not in the bowels of the cave.

But Makk had only reiterated the same images, of sun and moons, clear notations of time. And since there was no way for Jakkin to find the Place of Women on his own, or to feed himself, for that matter, he worked. He wasn't happy about it, but he worked, reminding himself to stay alert and learn as much as he could.

Standing on the high shelf of rock and taking his turn at stirring pots of fire, Jakkin felt alternately hot and cold. The flames seared his front, but there was a cold breeze across his shoulders and along the backs of his knees. His arms ached from the unaccustomed labor and his mind was weary from the twin efforts of cloaking and listening. But the more he saw of the metal-making operation, the more he realized its importance. And the more he realized bitterly that he was powerless to let the rest of Austar know.

After hours with the great iron rod, Jakkin was relieved by a silent, hulking worker who signaled him with a hand on the back. When Jakkin turned away from the shelf there was Makk again, ready to lead him to another portion of the cave where men were grubbing around the walls, using metal picks the size of fewmet shovels, mining out the stuff Makk called ore. Following behind these men was a crew of workers with sling bags full of phosphorescent moss, which they placed wherever a vein of the ore had been picked out. Despite

Makk's attempts at an explanation, and the instruction of his own eyes and ears, Jakkin wasn't sure if the moss was used as tunnel markers for the pickers, for light, for decoration, or a combination of all three.

By the time it was his turn on the moss detail, Jakkin was openly yawning, but no one seemed to notice. The bag's straps were made for broader shoulders than his and kept slipping. The cool, flaky mosses were not as easy to set in place as he'd thought. They had to be bent and shaped and tucked into the ore holes, and most of the time they crumbled between his inept fingers.

He was just beginning to get the feel of it, under the gruff tutelage of a one-eyed man he called Brekk (his sign was simply a single staring eye), when there was a loud gonging that echoed and re-echoed off the cave walls. At the sound, so loud in the enforced silence of the tunnels, the men set down their tools and bags and shuffled to the main cavern. Jakkin followed them.

It was only when he was back in the main cave that he realized it was a shift change, much like Sarkkhan's Nursery, where a few of the bond boys had night-watch duty and others worked in the day. He almost laughed aloud remembering his friends Errikkin, who loved being in bond, and Slakk, who'd try anything to get out of work.

Brekk pushed him toward a small crevice where there was a grassy pallet set upon the stone. He gave Jakkin a brief smile that shut his one good eye and left the empty socket staring.

"*Sleep!*" he commanded, the picture being one of a face with both eyes closed. It was accompanied by a kind of mental hum-song.

Jakkin needed no further urging. He climbed into his sleep crevice and lay down on the grass. He was just wondering that the grass was so fresh and sweet-smelling when sleep overcame him, and with it strange dark dreams.

~

THAT SAME PATTERN of work and sleep, broken by silent meals, continued for a number of rotations. In the half-light of the caves, Jakkin had no idea whether he worked for hours or days at a time, but simply slogged along until the gong. After a while he almost forgot there *was* anything but the caves, holding only to Makk's promise that they would eventually go to the Place of Women, where Akki was being kept.

As he found himself slipping into the same kind of somnambulant shuffle as the others, he tried to rouse himself with spoken speech. He worked as far from the men as he could manage, whispering little ditties in a voice that carried no farther than his own shadow. He knew if he didn't talk to himself, he would eventually lose the use of ear and tongue. So he recited Fewmets Ferkkin stories, hummed old ballads, even found he'd a gift for verse. He made up seventeen different stanzas of a poem that began "There once was a bond boy named Jakkin . . ." using *lackin', snackin',* and *trackin'* among the rhymes. When he really became bored with his own company and felt himself slipping back into the half-sleep, he invented imaginary dialogues with Akki. She ended every one of these conversations with a hug. He got so he could feel her arms around him, the softness of her cheek on his.

One time he tried to slip away down an empty passage, but Makk caught him before he was around the first turn, and cuffed him soundly. Jakkin returned to the others, his ears ringing and his mind filled with the angry mutterings of the other men. But he noticed he wasn't the only one cuffed. Brekk had his head knocked a few times, and another man, Orkkon, was roughed up for dropping his iron stirring stick. But Orkkon was ill, not lazy, and after a second beating he lay on his pallet three rotations, tossing and sweating. He never moaned aloud, though his sendings were filled with formless dark clouds that Jakkin read as fever.

It was a wonder to Jakkin that the men bore the endless drudgery without complaining. What they did was not any more difficult or arduous than the tasks he'd done at Sarkkhan's Nursery, but there was no variety. And there were no voices. He decided that it was the human voice he missed the most—that and the brightly colored sendings of the dragons. Sound and light. Without those, how could a person survive?

And yet—his traitor mind continued—these men of the mountains survived, and thrived. Men—and not-men. Survived but at a price. Jakkin guarded his thoughts as he made a list of the things these cavemen lacked: warmth, emotion, laughter, love—all those things that made life worthwhile. The list comforted him.

"I *will* get out of here," he whispered to himself. "I'll find Akki and go. Anything on the outside will be bearable after this boredom. Anything." And then he remembered Heart's Blood dying, shook his head, and was silent.

~

IT WAS THE ninth or tenth rotation—he'd lost count somewhere along the way—when a runner came to the men as they ate. Jakkin knew him for a stranger even from far away because he was younger than the rest and dressed differently. He was wearing a kind of light-colored woven cloth instead of the loin-cloths of the ore workers or the darker coveralls of the miners, which were made of the eggskin that hatchlings shed.

The boy's sending was frantic, emotional, full of color, which further marked him.

*"Great Mother trembles,"* he sent, a maelstrom of dark tones. *"She pants. Her birth hole swells. It does not open. All our women fear."*

Makk and the other men made a tight circle around the boy. Putting his hand on the boy's shoulder, Makk sent, *"I come. Orkkon comes, whose father's father was First Healer."*

The circle broke apart and re-formed around Orkkon, who still lay sweating on his pallet. Jakkin, on the far edges of the circle, watched as Makk knelt by Orkkon and put a hand on his head.

*"You come,"* Makk sent.

Orkkon managed, with Makk's support, to sit up. Jakkin could see the sweat running down his chest and the flush on his cheeks. He seemed to be having trouble breathing.

*"You come with me,"* Makk sent again.

There was no answering pattern from Orkkon. His mind seemed as flushed and sweaty as his body.

"Wait!" Jakkin cried aloud, wincing as the men turned toward him with another brutal, dark sending. At least he had gotten their attention. *"Wait,"* he sent. *"I am a Dragon Healer in my own place. Let Orkkon stay here. He is too sick anyway. Let me go instead."*

Makk pushed the sweating man back down on his bed and stood. As he walked toward Jakkin, Jakkin put out his hand. Puzzled, Makk stopped for a moment, then moved forward again. He took Jakkin's hand in his. The instant they touched Jakkin could feel his mind being invaded and he willed it to show pictures of himself and Heart's Blood in the cavernous incubarn. His memory flooded back and he took the memory, shaping it to his own use. There was the dark barn and the great hen towering over him, the fire in her eyes now warm and inviting. Then the great red circling the room in the peculiar halting rhythm of the pregnant female. Next he showed her squatting over the shallow hole dug into the sandy floor. All the while Jakkin soothed her. "Easy, easy, my beauty, easy, easy, my red." He moved the sending forward, concentrating on the nest itself as the eggs cascaded from the dragon's birth channel into the hole. *"This I have done many times,"* his sending promised. He masked his traitorous afterthought that *many* was a gross exaggeration.

For a moment Makk didn't respond, though there seemed to be a murmured sending from the other men, approval of some sort. At last Makk sent a black ropelike form shooting into Jakkin's sending, whipping around the arm of the boy pictured there and dragging the dream boy away. Like all of Makk's sendings, it was unambiguous in its meaning.

"*Come,*" said his sending. "*Great Mother needs. Come.*"

# 14

THE THREE OF THEM trotted down the tunnels, and though Jakkin tried to mark the way, they made too many turnings and switchbacks for him to remember. Yet, fast as they traveled, Makk and the boy never hesitated; the tunnels seemed to be as familiar to them as the hallways in a nursery bondhouse.

Jakkin wondered what he would find when they reached the Place of Great Mothers. Would the dragon giving birth be Auricle? He doubted that. She hadn't been obviously pregnant and, in fact, had dragged her tail like a dragon in heat. Besides, it took four months for eggs to develop, so there couldn't have been time. But a little fear nagged at him. What did he really know about time inside the caves? It felt like a week or two, but without access to the sun and moons, he couldn't tell day from night, much less the passage of a week.

Besides, these men were so different—thicker, heftier, duller, speechless—perhaps dragons in the mountains were different as well. Certainly Auricle had seemed odd, almost brain-damaged, or like an infant unused to either light or sound. Of course, now that he'd met and worked with the men of the cave, he understood the dragon better.

Makk and the boy stopped suddenly and Jakkin caught up with them. They had paused just inside the entrance to another large cavern. It seemed lighter and airier than the tunnels, and Jakkin squinted, looking around. High above them was a small opening and, far above that, a wan light like a pale lantern. He stared at it for several moments before he realized it was one of the moons. So—they *could''* see outside; they *did''* have a way to measure time. He laughed out loud and was cuffed by Makk for the sound.

Clenching his fists, Jakkin turned on Makk, but the man was already walking away, through another arched doorway. That it was a doorway and not just the beginning of a tunnel became clearer to Jakkin the closer he came to it. The stone on both sides of the arch had been intricately carved with figures of dragons: dragons fighting, dragons flying, dragons mating, dragons giving birth. They were illuminated by torches set on either side of the doorway.

Jakkin raced through the doorway after Makk and the boy and gasped in surprise. Unlike the rough, unadorned caves where the men lived, in this well-lit cavern was a series of stalls chiseled into the stone. In places the stone itself was fluted like curtains, in others there were detailed carvings of men, women, and dragons all entwined.

In the stalls to the left close to twenty dragons were roped, their shadows moving sluggishly against the walls. Silent gray-brown presences, they sent only beige images into Jakkin's mind, so different from the usual raucous colors that challenged him whenever he'd entered the nursery barns. The beige sendings were pale questions that floated slowly across his mind before drifting away, like clouds across a sky.

Jakkin looked carefully at the dragons in their stalls and sent back his own questions, trying to locate Auricle. But if she was there, he wasn't able to identify her.

*"This is the Place of the Great Mothers?"* Jakkin queried, puzzled because none of the stalled dragons looked old enough to be mated.

*"Place of Little Mothers,"* Makk sent back. *"We go farther."* He motioned with his head and walked on.

They went through another arched door, this one decorated with a pattern of egg-shaped bulges.

*"Who did all this?"* Jakkin's mind buzzed with the question. He hadn't meant to send it, but his curiosity couldn't be contained.

*"The Makker made this."* Makk stepped through the archway. The boy remained behind, but Jakkin went after Makk.

If the outer cavern had been a surprise, this room was an astonishment. It held only three stalls, but each was as spacious as a room in the nursery incubarn. The first stall was occupied by a greenish gray dragon a little smaller than Sssasha, placidly munching on something Jakkin didn't immediately recognize. The second stall contained a pale red dragon who seemed to be sleeping. Both dragons were pregnant, their stomachs bulging, their tails flattened and drooping on the floor.

He heard a panting noise in the third and largest stall. Jakkin peered in. Two broad-shouldered women were kneeling over a large brown dragon. The dragon was lying on her side and breathing noisily, tongue lapping the side of her mouth and her earflaps trembling.

*"The Great Mother fails."* Makk looked over Jakkin's shoulder; his brief judgment brutally apt.

The women looked up simultaneously. Although as thickly built as Makk, their faces as blunt and unattractive, they had more emotion in their expressions. The older one pushed her lank dark hair away from her eyes; the younger one sighed. One of them sent a tired gray thought: *"Yes. She fails."*

Jakkin went into the stall and moved around the women. He knelt by the dragon's head and touched one earflap. The skin vibrated against his hand in a fast, erratic manner. Not a good sign. He pried open one of the dragon's eyes with his fingers, being extremely careful not to tear the inner membrane. A dulled eye stared back at him but did not respond to the torchlight. Another bad sign. He noticed the tongue. A healthy dragon's tongue was rough and ridged. This one was smooth and velvety, and that meant fever for sure. A very high fever.

He stood, stepped over the dragon's neck, and walked beside the spine toward the tail.

Gesturing downward, he sent an order to the women: *"Hold the tail away from the Great Mother's body."*

The younger woman stood and came over to the tail. She picked it up, exposing the birth canal.

Jakkin ducked under and examined the channel. It was clogged with pulpy masses, angry swellings the color of a bruise. When he touched one with a tentative finger, the dragon moaned out loud, a sound so foreign in the cave, it echoed eerily. The woman dropped the tail.

Jakkin stood and turned to Makk. He knew he might not get another opportunity and so he formed his sending with great care. *"My woman. The one you found. She is a healer. She makes sick ones well. If we are together, she and I, we can save this Great Mother."* He made the sending as positive as he could, though under his breath he murmured, "I hope."

Makk was concentrating too hard on his sending to notice.

When Makk gave no answer Jakkin sent again; this time his image was unambiguous and linear. He pictured Akki as tall and clean, bright-eyed, narrow-shouldered, and beautiful. Very beautiful.

*"No!"* Makk sent suddenly, his sending knifing across Jakkin's. *"This one"*—and his picture was of a girl thin, malformed, ugly— *"this one can bear. Only women past bearing serve Great Mothers."*

Jakkin thought a minute. He would have to lie. He wondered whether these people understood lying. It must be very hard to lie if all you had were the thoughts in your head. Lying was much easier with words. He drew in a deep breath and began, *"My woman is a healer and in my Place healers do not bear children."*

Makk's eyes grew wider and he gave what might be mistaken for a smile. *"Good!"*

*"When?"* Jakkin's sending was as clipped as Makk's, a single sharp stab of light.

*"Soon."*

*"If it is not soon,"* Jakkin sent, kneeling again by the dragon and slipping his hand under her tail, *"this Great Mother will die and her eggs will crack open inside her."* He touched one of the pulpy masses again, put his hand around it, and quite deliberately squeezed.

The dragon screamed.

Makk and the two women placed their hands over their ears and the younger woman fell to her knees. But Jakkin, even though he hated bringing pain to the beast, nonetheless reveled in the sound.

# 15

BY THE TIME the echo of the scream had faded, Jakkin was once again at the dragon's head, checking her eyes and tongue. There was no change. He put his head down by the dragon's mouth and breathed deeply. The smell was slightly sour, not unusual for a dragon, but also strangely bland. In the nursery such a smell usually meant a worm needed extra rations of burnwort, but he'd no idea what they fed dragons here.

At the head of the stall was an iron hook on which several handfuls of dry grasses hung. Jakkin walked over and tore out some. Crumbling it between his fingers, he spread it along his palm. He could identify sedgeseeds and skkagg grass, but there were other things new to him, including a fleshy wine-colored fungus. In the nursery they'd never feed a dragon that. What was it Likkarn used to say? *Mushrooms red, dragon dead.* He held out his hand and pointed to it. *"This?"* he sent bluntly.

The older woman came over to him and stared at his hand. She didn't meet his eyes, and her sending was so tentative, he couldn't make out any name for the fungus. But it was obviously no surprise to her.

Still, he asked again because of Likkarn's warning and because food was always the first thing examined when a dragon fell sick. It was just too easy to poison one of them, large as they were, especially a fighting dragon at one of the major pits. He held out his hand and this time sent directly to the woman before him, *"This?"*

The woman's answer was clearer this time, though she still wouldn't look up at him. *"That makes bearing easy. Women eat too."*

Jakkin nodded and let the stuff drift to the floor. Both women were quick to broom it away, which made Jakkin smile. No wonder these stalls were so clean. No fewmets, no extra straw, no pieces of half-chewed meals. The women were quicker at their tasks than any stallboy he'd ever known, including himself. He turned back to the dragon. Her tail was twitching ever so slightly.

*"Lift that tail again!"*

This time both women hauled the tail up and to the side.

Jakkin knelt down. A grayish fluid was leaking from the birth channel. He put his hand in and discovered that the swelling he'd squeezed had burst. The smell of it was over-powering.

Hearing a noise behind him, he turned around. Akki was standing at the entrance to the stall.

"Akk—" he started to say aloud, and her hand went immediately up as if to cover his mouth.

*"Shhh,"* came her sending, a bright green cloud covering the mouth of a golden sun. It was the loveliest color he'd seen in ages. *"Later."* She smiled.

~

IT WAS ONLY after Akki knelt to examine the dragon that Jakkin realized she'd lost weight and her hair was dirty and tangled. There was a bruise under her right eye and a scratch along her right arm. He wanted both to hold her and to shout at her and shake her. But when she turned around at his bubbling sending, he suddenly remembered he'd told Makk she was a healer and not to be thought of as a woman-who-bears. He had to treat her with the cold deference due such a one as long as Makk's people could overhear their sendings.

*"I'm glad you have come, My Healer. I have told Makk and his men of your many skills."*

Akki understood at once and nodded at him, gesturing that he kneel by her side.

He kept a careful distance between them, sketching in what he knew of the dragon's condition. It was hard to do in a sending. Akki was right about words. But as he formed the pictures Akki followed along, performing the same tests he'd just done. The dragons ear-flaps still vibrated erratically, and the eyes remained fixed. But the tail had a tiny touch of resilience now.

When she finished her palpation of the birth channel, Akki turned and looked directly at him. *"You're right. The channel is clogged and we'll have to lance those boils."* She wrinkled her nose. *"But without the proper tools . . . I can't guarantee a worse infection won't set in."*

The women didn't stir as her complex sending filled their minds.

If they understood it, they gave no sign. Makk shuffled self-consciously. But Jakkin just grinned. Her sending had been filled with wonderful asides, bright-colored pictures that told him more in a single sending then all the dull patterns the mountain clan had offered the whole time he'd been there. But her sending had hidden messages as well: oblique warnings of other dangers, plus a joyous rainbow under which a green tree was twined with a bright blue vine. He knew Makk would never guess what those private images meant. Akki was saying she loved him.

Akki stood, brushed her hair back over her ears, and looked straight at Makk. He seemed uneasy with her direct gaze, shifting his eyes right and left.

*"Bring me water,"* Akki said. *"Boil it. Bring me knives but first put them in the fire. Bring me cloth. It must be clean."* Then, as an afterthought, really more a mental sigh, she added, *"What I'd give for my pack. It had my medkit in it."* The picture of the kit lying on the cave floor was skillfully rendered.

Makk's eyes seemed to shutter for a moment, and then, as if making up his mind, nodded to a man standing in the doorway and broke into rapid hand signs. The man nodded back and took off down a tunnel to the right of the stalls.

Jakkin watched him go, his curiosity uncurtained. He was still staring after the man when he felt a hand on his arm. Turning, he saw it was Akki. She pulled him close, whispering so quietly he had to strain to hear it, "I think they know where the pack is, Jakkin. It's got your knife in it, the one Golden gave to you."

He didn't dare answer her, not even with a sending.

~

THE MAN RETURNED in minutes with the unopened pack. He handed it carefully to Akki, as if he were afraid of her, making sure their hands did not touch. She took it coldly, then knelt again by the dragon's tail.

At the same time the two women came back with an iron pot filled with steaming water, the younger woman also carrying two fairly crude knives and strips of yellow weaving.

Rooting around in her pack, Akki found the silver knife. She plunged it into the pot of water and held it there, as if ticking off seconds. Jakkin could feel her visualization of a clock and wondered if the others knew what it was. At the count of sixty she withdrew the knife and held it up to the torchlight, examining it.

*"If you know any prayers . . ."*

To Jakkin's surprise, the women immediately began a sending that was a repetition of patterns, like a chant. It had an intensity beyond anything they'd sent before.

Akki gestured for him to kneel beside her and he scrambled to do her bidding.

*"Now!"* she sent.

He held the dragon's tail away while she slid the knife into the birth channel and punctured the first of the bruise-colored boils.

Jakkin had never participated in an operation before, though he'd had some experience with minor doctoring in the nursery. One of the nursery stud dragons, Blood Sucker, had frequent mouth infections that always needed attention. And he'd watched countless wing-tips sewn up after fights. But this was different and he marveled at how calm Akki remained.

He knew enough to soak the woven strips in the hot water. Then, holding the tail away with his left hand, he wrung out the strips with his right, using the cloth to soak up any infection. When he withdrew the rag and dropped it onto the floor, the waiting women whisked it away. Over and over they repeated their tasks until the work assumed its own rhythms, which coincided with the dragon's labored breathing.

All of a sudden Akki withdrew her arm from the channel, sat back on her heels, and sighed out loud. She was soaked with sweat. The bruise under her eye seemed to reflect the yellow of the light and the infection. Jakkin guessed he looked as bad, but he smiled at her.

Wiping a filthy hand across her forehead, Akki stood and looked at Makk, focusing a sending on him. *"The Great Mother will live. The women must keep cleaning her. In a day or two she should be healed. Then the eggs will drop."*

Makk nodded. *"Good."*

"Damned right!" Akki said aloud.

Automatically Makk raised his hand, but Akki stared him down and slowly his hand lowered. It happened so fast, Jakkin hadn't had time to stand, but as Makk's hand went down Jakkin got to his feet. He touched Akki's shoulder.

Akki sent, *"We need to wash. We are covered with sickness. Take us to a place of water."*

Jakkin added, *"Place of much water. Like a lake."*

Makk made a face and looked uneasy. Then he nodded curtly and signed to the two men in the doorway. Squaring his shoulders, he turned and left.

~

THE MEN LED them through a wide, unadorned tunnel whose turnings were sparingly lighted by widely spaced phosphorescent mosses. After only half a dozen bends they found themselves at the edge of a small lake.

For a long moment Akki hesitated, and Jakkin remembered that she couldn't swim. He reached out for her hand and led her, fully clothed, into the cold dark water. When they were waist deep he let go and let himself sink down to the lake bottom, thankful for the touch of the clean water on his face and through his hair. When he surfaced Akki was standing where he'd left her, staring out into the darkness. He tried to reach her mind to assure her and was rewarded instead with a crackling sound. He realized that once again his mind had been closed by the water to any sendings.

Motioning with his hand, he tried to call her toward him but she didn't move, only stared at him strangely. So he went over and led her into even deeper water, away from the two men who glowered at them from the rock ledge.

"I can't hear any sendings now," he whispered. "The water blocks it. You go under, too, Akki."

She turned her back on the men and whispered back, "I wondered why you didn't answer me."

"Put your head under and you'll see."

Dipping her hands in the water, as if she were still washing, Akki hesitated. "I can't," she whispered.

"Can't what?"

"Can't put my head under."

"Why not?"

"I'm too scared and . . . owwww!" Her hand went to her forehead.

"What is it?"

"The men!" She gasped. "They've just sent a double command to return. And, Jakkin, it hurts. I have to . . ." She stopped talking and a blank look crept into her eyes. She began to turn around.

Jakkin grabbed her by the waist and pulled her underwater. She struggled violently against him and her right hand smacked his chin. He let her go and she burst up into the air, spluttering and gasping.

"Jakkin, that wasn't funny!" She stopped, put her hand over his mouth, and stared at him. "My head," she whispered, "it's crackling. And . . . and I can't hear them anymore. I'm all alone in here!"

"It'll last for only a little while," he said, glancing quickly over his shoulder at the men and waving at them. They looked puzzled. He turned back, whispering frantically. "Listen, Akki, I don't think they'll come into the water unless they have to. Remember, they've got only the sendings, no words. They wouldn't want to lose it. So tell me quickly what you know. I didn't see anything but the Place of Men. It's nothing but a dreary cave where they pick out ore and turn it into molten metal. But *metal*, Akki. Do you realize what that means?''

She nodded, lacing her fingers together.

"I didn't even know much about the dragons or these caves until today. Or tonight. Or whatever worm-eaten time it is."

Akki took a deep breath and her words came to him in a rush. "I don't know much more. The Place of Women is filled with women and children, though there are only a few babies and a good number of them are sickly. They seem to spend a lot of time preparing food. And weaving. And making clothing.''

Jakkin thought a minute. "What about the food? Where does it come from?''

"Come from? I don't . . . oh, I see what you mean, Jakkin. If they're growing food—or gathering it—they have to have access to the outside.''

Jakkin nodded.

"But where?''

"And," he added, "how do *we* get there, wherever *there* is?''

Puddling her hand in the water, Akki sighed. "Jakkin . . .'' she said.

He waited.

"Something else. It's been puzzling me a lot. Those babies. They cry like ordinary babies, you know—sounds. But the older ones, the toddlers, they don't make any noise at all, even when they fall down taking their first steps. They just sprawl on the cave floor and send unhappy-feeling patterns. Somehow something—or someone— teaches them to forget language and use only their minds. *And I don't know what it is!*'' Her hands ran through the tangles of her hair.

Jakkin reached over and took her hands in his. Just as they touched, the crackle in his mind stopped and he could feel her puzzlement and fear.

"Quick!'' he said. "Duck down into the water again.'' But it was too late. The men on the ledge had been joined by Makk. Their sending, strengthened by linking hands, was too strong to be disobeyed.

*"COME. COME. COME.''*

Jakkin's last coherent thought was that he'd heard that command before. Then he took Akki's hand, and they walked out of the lake to stand before the waiting men.

# 16

FOR TWO SLEEP periods—Jakkin couldn't be sure they were actual nights—they'd been forced to remain by the dragon's side. They slept on the stone floor by her stall without even the comfort of grass pallets. Hulking, expressionless guards watched over them, ready to slap them if they tried to speak out loud. Anytime Jakkin tried a sending he was painfully aware that the guards were listening in, painfully because they often doubled their sendings, leaving him with an aching head. He and Akki were reduced to passing looks to remind themselves that they were not stooping, silent cave dwellers.

In her frustration Akki began a frantic round of nursing that was at first welcomed by the dragon, then tolerated, and at last shaken away with tail thumpings and fierce houghing. Jakkin, in his turn, groomed the dragon until her scales were polished to a shine that even old Likkarn, Old Likk-and-Spittle, would have admired. But finally the dragon shook him off, too.

When the dragon started stretching her neck out to the fullest, Jakkin knew she was well again and ready to lay her eggs. Neck stretching was an unconscious gesture left over from the days when dragons had scouted for danger in the mountain caves where they gave birth. Sarkkhan had told him that.

Always before when Jakkin had been near a layer, he'd been caught up in her sendings, violent maelstroms of color. But this dragon's sendings were in black, white, and gray, and while they were no less violent, Jakkin found himself outside the waves of her emotions rather than caught up in them. However, the cave people, whose own sendings were as colorless, seemed to be buffeted by the dragon's wild sendings, and they fled the cavern as soon as she began, leaving Jakkin and Akki alone.

They stayed, partly because they were delighted to be shed of the guards, but primarily because Akki feared there might still be problems with the newly healed canal.

"It's too soon," she whispered, even though there was no one else in the room. "The eggs might tear open the scabs."

"That'll be a mess," Jakkin said.

"And painful," Akki added.

As they watched, the pressure in the dragon's birth canal began to send waves rolling up under the sternum and along the heavy stomach muscles. She reared up, her head scraping the rounded ceiling. Fluttering her wings, she pressed them to her sides, the edges touching her belly. Jakkin could see her earflaps vibrating steadily as she slowly settled back down.

"Easy, easy, my beauty," he murmured, remembering with a sudden shudder the last time he'd spoken these same words to a laying hen. It had been to Heart's Blood, and the eggs she'd dropped contained Sssargon, Sssasha, and the triplets.

Akki's head snapped up and she grinned. "The triplets," she whispered. "Lizard lumps, how I miss them."

Jakkin didn't even mind that she'd read his thoughts, but he pointed to his mouth. "Use words," he said.

"Where do you think they are now?"

"Who?"

"The triplets."

"Outside." He sighed.

"I wish we were outside," Akki said.

He touched her hand, stroking it with his fingers. "We *will* be soon. I promise."

And then the dragon's panting began, in and out, in and out; the ragged breathing filled the cavern and settled over them like a heavy mist. They stopped talking as the rhythm enveloped them.

The dragon heaved herself to her feet and backed out of the stall, pushing Akki to the floor and squashing Jakkin against the wall. Mindlessly the worm stomped around the room three times, as if searching for something. Her frantic pacing disturbed the two dragons in the outer stalls, and they houghed at her. She responded by whipping her tail back and forth.

At last she found a shallow depression filled with sand at the far end of the cavern. Eyeing it for a moment, she tested it with a claw. Evidently it satisfied her, for she squatted over it and began to push down. Eggs popped out between her back legs, cascading continuously into the sandy nest for the better part of several hours.

Higher and higher the pile of eggs grew until at last the pile was so high, she had to stand to finish the job. As she did a sticky yellow-white afterbirth tinged slightly with red trickled out of the canal, coating the eggs and binding them together.

"See the blood," Akki whispered to Jakkin. "Some of the scabs must have come off."

The dragon shook herself all over, stepped over the pyramid of eggs, and waddled slowly back to the stall, where she began cleaning herself.

Jakkin pulled Akki out of the stall just in time. They were as drained as if they'd done all the hard work of laying themselves. Akki slumped against the cave wall and fell asleep. Jakkin sat down next to her and was soon snoring gently. Their dreams were full of color and light and the smell of the open air.

~

THEY WOKE WELL before the dragon, who was in the comalike sleep that followed egg laying. Jakkin knew that was how the first dragons had been captured, during the vulnerable aftermath of birth.

As they woke they were buffeted by new storms, not from the dragon but from many individual human sendings. Surprised, they looked around the cavern. It was filled with silent men, women, and children jostling one another for a look at the eggs. The most surprising thing of all was that they were all dressed in white robes, a costume oddly unsuited to their heavy bodies.

Makk left the crowd and came over to them, holding out his hands in a gesture of greeting. *"Good. Much good."* Then he waved his hands at the white-robed people behind him.

What followed his wave was such a clamor in the mind that Jakkin could think of it only as a cheer. It made him shiver with its intensity, and ended by giving him the worst headache he'd ever had.

As quickly as it had arisen, the silent cheer stopped, but the ache above his eyes continued. Jakkin rubbed at his forehead but it didn't help.

*"Come!"* Makk's sending was both an invitation and a command.

Jakkin stood and pulled Akki up after him, and they joined the crowd surging out of the cavern down a long, straight tunnel and into a small, niched cave, where they were helped into white robes of their own.

Jakkin turned to Akki, mouthing, "What's going on?"

She shrugged, pointed to her head, and rubbed her left temple with a finger.

Before he could answer, they were rushed away again, moving like part of an underground river racing through the tunnels into yet another cave.

This cave was enormous and vaulted, its ceiling strung with lanterns. Tapestries hung along the walls, the pictures on them, while primitive, clearly showed dragons and children superimposed upon one another. Long unadorned wooden tables sided by benches covered most of the cave's floor space.

Jakkin was pushed toward a bench and made to sit, strangers on either side of him, Akki across the way. The table was piled high with dishes of steaming stews and salads, boiled mushrooms both gray and white, and cups of a liquid the color of fresh blood.

There was no ceremony. Just as in the bondhouse, everyone reached out for whatever he or she wanted. The clattering of dishes and the banging of hands on the table contrasted strangely with the wordlessness of the people in the room.

After so many days of limited fare, the sight of so much food was overwhelming. Jakkin could feel saliva pooling in his mouth. A strange smell pervaded the room, and it took him a moment to realize it came from the tallow candles set at the table ends. Hungry as he was, Jakkin suddenly felt sick to his stomach. The only thing that could make that much tallow would be dragon fat. Even though his plate was piled high with a variety of inviting foods, he no longer felt like eating. His head ached still, his stomach revolted at the smells. He shook his head.

The man on the right clapped Jakkin on the shoulder before turning back eagerly to his food.

Jakkin sat back and made his mind a blank. Slowly he built up a wall, concentrating on each block until it was as high as his head. He felt rather than heard someone standing in the front of the room and he looked up.

Makk had his hands raised above his head in a kind of benediction, fingers semaphoring to all who watched him. Jakkin raised himself carefully over his mental wall to listen, and Makk's sending came to him full force:

*"Eggs are high. Now we eat. Now we sleep. Not-now we watch hatching. Not-now we count eggs. Time we celebrate. Time we praise. Time we birth again. Blood to blood."*

All around the room people were leaping to their feet, raising their hands overhead.

*"Blood to blood,"* their sendings repeated. For the first time a river of color, bright red, washed through their black-and-white minds. *"Blood to blood."*

In the end only Jakkin and Akki, across the table from him, remained seated. Akki was weeping silently, tears channeling down her cheeks. Jakkin hissed at her and she opened her eyes and stared at him. He sent one word across their bridged minds:

*"Why?"*

She bit her lip, then whispered, "Oh, Jakkin, I'm afraid. I don't know why, but I'm so horribly afraid."

Suddenly Jakkin caught her feelings and they rushed through him, pushing out the bloody sendings, his headache, and everything else except that fear. And he knew he was afraid, too. That he didn't know why only made it worse.

# 17

As MAKK SAID, they ate and slept and then ate again, an enormous display of gluttony that made Jakkin so sick he refused to go back in the dining room.

The watch was set: three men and three women at a time, with a child between them, waited by the nest. Jakkin supposed they were there to guard the eggs from any flikka, though the caverns had seemed curiously without life. *And* to report when the eggs started hatching.

Jakkin and Akki were dragged along to make up one of the watch teams. They kept their vigil for less than an hour, or so it seemed, squatting on their heels and staring silently at the now-hardened pyramid of eggs. Jakkin's stomach was still queasy and he wondered if he were *clutched*, which is how trainers linked to a dragon often felt when the hen was laying. But this wasn't his dragon and he was hardly linked with her, at least any more than the rest were. He suspected it was just plain fear. And what was that fear? It had something to do with the bloody sendings, that much he knew. And something about the way the cave people greedily devoured their dragon stew. But he'd had friends like that at the nursery and they'd never frightened him. It was just a feeling he had. And Akki, he knew, felt the same.

When his watch was over Jakkin stood with the rest of the white-robed guardians, but instead of filing down the tunnel with them he moved over to the dragon's stall. She was getting restless in her sleep and he knew she'd be waking before long.

Akki came over to the stall and touched his shoulder. They stood that way as the new watchers entered the cavern to take their turns.

The silence in the cave was unbearable. Jakkin was ready to say something aloud, whatever the consequences, when the dragons in the far stalls began to rock back and forth in place. Jakkin welcomed the creak of bone, the muffled thud of the dragon feet. The rhythm was compelling and he began to sway with them.

And then the dragon sleeping by his feet awoke. Shaking her head from side to side, she stood and backed out of the stall. The watchers at the nest scattered as she moved purposefully toward the pyramid of eggs.

Stopping by the nest, she lowered her head slowly until her nose rested on the topmost egg. For a moment she didn't move, then houghed a mighty breath out through her nose. The wet, warm breath touched the eggs and a kind of vapor surrounded the top three or four. For a moment the hard shells seemed almost translucent. Jakkin imagined he could see into them and judge the contents. Then the moment passed. The dragon rolled the topmost egg off the pile and onto the floor. It seemed a miracle it did not break, but the hard elastic shell was almost impenetrable from the outside. Only the hatchling within, with the birth bump of horn on its nose, could easily crack open the shell.

Soon the floor by the nest was littered with the cream-colored eggs. There seemed to be nearly a hundred.

A babble of sendings filtered through Jakkin's concentration and he looked around. The cavern was fast filling with people jostling for position; the children pushed to the front. Unmoved, the dragon continued her work.

Touching each egg in turn, she shoved them around with her lanceae, the twin nails on the front of her foot, almost as if she were counting them, as if she knew already which eggs held live hatchlings and which were just slime-filled decoys for the flikka and drakk.

She tapped an egg that lay close to her right foot. *Tap. Tap-tap.* She paused. *Tap-tap.*

There was a tiny echo from inside the egg. *Tap-tap.*

She touched the egg again with a more vigorous stroke.

*TAP!*

A thin dark line formed on the shell, the barest whisper of a crack. Jakkin let out a breath.

Suddenly the line became a wider crack, zigzagging like a river around the smaller end of the egg.

The dragon gave the egg a final tap and it split apart. In the larger half lay a crumpled form, curled tightly around itself. It was the color of scum and was covered with a yellow-green fluid.

The hen dragon overturned the shell and the wrinkled hatchling stumbled blindly onto the cave floor, its eyes still sealed shut with the egg fluids. She gave it a perfunctory lick, then turned her attention to the inside of the shell, which she cleaned with her rough ridged tongue. When all the fluids were gone she went back to the hatchling, licking it clean. Once free of the fluids that had coated its overlarge wings and head, the hatchling flopped down to sleep. The hen ignored it and once again picked through the eggs.

Seven times she tapped an egg, once biting an egg open with her under-tongue growth. In four of the shells were live hatchlings. Two of the eggs contained deformed dragons, one that trembled for a minute in the air before it died, the other long dead and stinking. The third shell held nothing but a bright yellow yolk with a coin-sized spot of blood in its center. She gobbled the yolk down eagerly.

When it was clear the Great Mother was through picking over the eggs and had fallen back into sleep, the crowd surged forward to clean up the nest and its scattered contents. Each person took an egg or a handful of sand as a souvenir. The dragon was shooed back to her stall with her hatchlings. Then the floor was swept up by the same two women who had been with the dragon from the first. It all happened so quickly, it was as if the hatchling had never occurred.

Jakkin was shocked that the cave people had not let the mother dragon crack open and eat the rest of the eggs. There might even be a singleton, an egg that opens late with a slowly forming baby dragon in it. Every nursery bonder knew how important it was for the mother dragon to get those extra rations to replace the fluids and protein she had lost in the hatching. How else could she recover?

Yet even as he worried about the dragon's condition, Jakkin had to smile. The five new hatchlings, wrinkled, ugly, and ungainly, were already nestled by their sleeping mother's side, their butter-soft baby claws pushing against one another in their sleep.

# 18

HOW LONG THEY sat by the dragon's stall, half dozing in the dim light, Jakkin didn't know. What wakened him was a rumbling noise that began as a low growl and rose steadily into an angry roar. He looked around and couldn't see anything, but an uneasiness invaded his mind, a misty sending that suddenly resolved itself into a tunnel-shaped blackness shot through with familiar gray rainbows.

Jakkin's head jerked up and Akki whispered, "That's Auricle. She's here. Why didn't we notice before?"

Jakkin shook his head. "She never sent anything before."

"And we were too worried about the egg laying," Akki added.

They stood and followed the sending to the side stalls, where two dragons were rocking nervously from foot to foot.

"Which one is Auricle?" Akki asked.

Jakkin sent a pattern of blues like lazy rivers meandering across the dark sendings from both dragons. "I'm not sure," he said to Akki. "We never actually *saw* her. It was too dark in the tunnels."

"And I was too scared."

"Me, too." He laughed aloud. "Me, too."

"So, which one?"

Jakkin sent Auricle's name, bound about with colorful rainbows, and the larger of the two dragons, the pale red, raised her head to stare back at him.

*"Not-man?"* Her large dark eyes grew larger still.

"Akki, it's the red. She's *got* to be Heart's Blood's cousin."

"Don't start that again, Jakkin. There's no way to know. Not for sure. And she's not your dragon anyway. She belongs here, in the cave."

*"Not-man?"* the red dragon sent again.

"What is it?" Jakkin whispered, molding the question into a sending as well. But no sooner had he sent it than a different sending filled his mind, so loud his head hurt with it.

*"COME. COME. COME."*

The rumbling noise and the sending seemed to blend together until the command was irresistible, and Akki and Jakkin stumbled toward the tunnel entrance. But the dragons, cuffed as they were by iron bonds at neck and foot, didn't leave their stalls, only started rocking again. The sleeping mother dragon stirred uneasily, lifting her head for a moment in a dazed fashion before sinking back into her stupor.

At the entrance Jakkin could see movement down the tunnel and soon he could make out the figures of Makk and six of his men hauling an enormous wheeled cart. Jakkin put his hand out and dragged Akki back inside the cavern as the men pulled the cart through the arch.

Stripped of their ceremonial robes and wearing only leather shorts, the men's arm muscles bulged and flattened, then bulged again as they tugged the cart over the uneven cavern floor. Behind the cart, pushing, were another half dozen men similarly stripped down. Beyond them Jakkin could make out the entire company of cave people still dressed in their white robes. The women were now garlanded with strings of dried chikkberries and warden's hearts and some kind of yellow-centered flowers. Five in the front carried naked infants in their arms, babies whose heads were crowned with circlets of leaves.

As the cart rumbled into the cavern Makk directed the men toward the stall where the sleeping dragon once again tried to shake herself out of her stupor, but the lack of extra birth fluids had already taken its toll and she could scarcely move.

The five women came forward, walked in front of the cart, and into the sleeping dragon's stall. The first touched the dragon on the flank. Her sending was restrained but perfectly clear.

*"Great Mother, my child, your child, be one."*

She bent down and picked up one of the hatchlings with her free hand. It was the same size as her infant, small enough to fit comfortably into the crook of her right arm.

The second woman entered the dragon's stall and touched the hen on the shoulder.

*"Great Mother, my child, your child, be one."*

"Jakkin, I don't like this." Akki's mouth was right against his ear. He put his hand up as if to silence her but never took his eyes off the unfolding drama.

The third woman touched the dragon on the head, the fourth over the heart, and the fifth placed her hand on the dragon's belly. Each woman's sending was the same and each, in turn, picked up a hatchling and cradled it against her breasts.

Akki whispered frantically in his ear, "They're going to kill the hatchlings, Jakkin, I know it." Her breath was hot. "What kind of people are they?"

Jakkin shook his head. What kind of people? He remembered his own nursery's culling day, when unsuitable hatchlings had been taken from the screaming hens and sent off to the stews. What kind of people were these men and women of the cave? What kind of people were *all* the people of Austar?

The women holding the hatchlings turned, walked out of the stall in a line, and with slow, measured steps walked across the cavern to a small holding pen of wood and stone. They placed the baby dragons in it and closed the gate.

Akki let out a relieved sigh that almost deafened Jakkin, then slipped her hand into his, masking her feelings behind a carefully constructed wall he couldn't penetrate. Silently they continued to watch.

The robeless men crowded into the stall, six on either side of the sleeping dragon and Makk by her tail, holding a plaited net. The men at the dragon's front rolled her onto her back and Makk slung the net down at their feet, then spread the net where she'd been. When they let her go she rocked back on top of the net.

Then the men in the back did the same and Makk pulled the net through so that it spread across the entire stall floor. When the dragon was settled again each man grabbed a handful of net and, on a mental signal, heaved her toward the cart. It took a lot of grunting and straining, and more than once a man let out a mental curse that struck Jakkin's mind with the force of a hammer blow. Though he'd heard many curses in the nursery, they'd never made him physically ill before. Jakkin rubbed his temples, trying to ease away the pain.

At last the dragon was positioned on the cart, her tail dragging off the end. Makk and his twelve helpers took up the rope at the front. Six robed men came around the back to push. The five women carrying infants each helped pick up the dragon's tail so that it wouldn't scrape along the floor. Then they began to haul the cart and dragon out of the cavern.

Jakkin had no idea of their destination, though he feared it was the pile of white bones at the tunnel's end. He sent a picture of that pile to Akki, and she squeezed his hand. Puzzled, he looked at her. She was smiling. Turning her head toward him, she whispered, "The bone pile is near the entrance, Jakkin. We could escape."

He knew she was right, yet something about the ceremony they'd just witnessed kept him from celebrating. The chanting women, the white-robed men all seemed destined for some dark purpose, and he followed them hand in hand with Akki because they knew no other way.

~

IT WAS HARD, sweaty, backbreaking work, but Makk and his men never faltered. Surprisingly, none of the other men offered a hand. It was as if towing the dragon were a singular honor that only certain men were given, though Jakkin couldn't figure out why. The rest of the people, who trailed behind the cart, seemed enveloped in a carnival atmosphere, smiling and waving their arms, their sendings shot through with unexpected colors, though their silence lent a bizarre note to the whole proceedings. The only noise was the constant rumble of the cartwheels broken by an occasional high, piping cry of one of the infants in its mother's arms.

Just when Jakkin was beginning to believe there was no end to the journey, only the parade through a maze of tunnels, he saw a pinpoint of bright light ahead, beyond the surging crowd and beyond the cart with its comatose burden. Then the pinpoint became larger, irised open until it filled him completely. Only then did he realize he was not just seeing the spot of light but receiving it as a sending as well.

It took him another moment to understand that the light wasn't torchlight or lanterns or the light from phosphorescent mosses. He threw his hands up over his eyes to help filter out the intense brightness as he continued forward with the crowd. When he finally pulled his hands away he saw they were in a large meadow dotted with copses of trees. The meadow was entirely surrounded by the steep, sloping sides of the mountain, as if they were at the bottom of an enormous bowl.

It was night. What Jakkin had thought was a single bright light was really the pale glow of the sand-colored moons, Akka and Akkhan. He'd been so used to the dim caves that the twin moons seemed uncomfortably bright. Squinting, he stared up at them. A dark figure swept across Akkhan's face. *A wild dragon*, he thought.

And then, as if in a dream, came the familiar rainbow pattern, filling him with hope.

*"Sssargon waits. Sssargon watches. Sssargon hunts. Sssargon . . ."*

Then the sending was gone, blotted out by the closer patterns of the people around him and the dark rumblings of the cart.

The cart moved more easily now, along well-worn ruts, toward a great stone enclosure in the center of the meadow. The ring reminded Jakkin vaguely of some of the country pits, with their stone seats around a center maw.

The men drew the cart through a stone archway and into the center of the ring, where, with a ceremonial heave, they hauled the dragon off the cart. She lay where they dropped her, panting and blinking sleepily up at the light.

Herded into their seats by the crowd, Akki and Jakkin sat next to one another but didn't touch, afraid that their thoughts would thereby be doubly broadcast to the cave folk. And soon Jakkin's attention left Akki and was focused on the ring.

He wondered if there was to be a fight. If so, there'd be nothing but a straightforward slaughter, for the hen could barely get her head up. In fact, if she weren't fed soon, she'd die. He didn't like the way she was breathing, and *everyone* knew that a hen right after egg laying and hatching needed extra rations. The irony of it wasn't lost on him—that he and Akki had worked so hard to save her and were now helplessly going to watch her die. He thought about that a moment. He *wouldn't* be helpless. Shaking himself loose of the crowd-induced torpor, he started to stand and protest. But as he stood everyone else stood, too, as if reacting to some signal he'd not even registered.

Once again in their white robes, Makk and his men entered the ring and formed a tight circle around the dragon, as if guarding her. The five garlanded women, infants in arms, stood by the dragon's tail.

The familiar chant began again. *"COME. COME. COME."*

For a long moment no one moved except the hen, whose tail beat a feeble tattoo on the ground.

Then, from the left side, through the stone arch, marched a figure in dark red. Her robe was stiff and fell in peculiar rigid folds from her shoulders. A cowl covered her head, a veil her face. Only her eyes showed, ringed with black paint. She carried a long white stick in her right hand.

Coming to the circle of men, the woman stopped until they moved apart, then walked to the dragon's head, where she raised her hands above her.

*"Great Mother,"* she sent, and the people echoed it, a dark black-and-white picture of a towering dragon form that seemed to shimmer in the mind from so many sendings. *"Where your children cradled, cradle mine."* She brought her hands slashing down toward the dragon's exposed neck.

In that instant Jakkin knew what it was she carried: a forefoot bone with the nails still intact. Only a dragon's nail could slice efficiently through dragon scale, though the underneck links were the tenderest part.

Blood gouted from the dragon's neck and covered the woman's robe and cowl, staining it a deeper red. The hot, acidic blood spattered on the rocks below and splattered on the woman's hands. It must have burned her, pocking her wrists and fingers, but she never dropped her weapon. At the very moment of the cut she broadcast a high, piercing sending of triumph and light. The answering image from both the dying dragon and the people around the ring was a tidal wave of red: bright red, blood red, an ocean of it that threatened to drown them all.

Jakkin closed his eyes, hoping to shut out the sight, but the sending went on and on, replaying the scene endlessly in his horrified mind.

~

MINUTES LATER THE woman in red cut open the dragon's belly and one by one the women laid their infants in the dragon's birth chamber, closing the flap of skin over them to ensure the babies' invulnerability to cold and to open their minds to the linkings of dragons and men.

Akki wept openly through it all, but Jakkin forced himself to remain dry-eyed. He felt hardly anything but guilt, for as soon as the bloody sendings from the crowd had ended, his own bloody memories had begun. He remembered, before the change, the three dragons in his life who had died because of him. The great stud Blood Brother, killed in the nursery, because Jakkin had been careless. He remembered Brother as he last saw him, in a hindfoot rise, pulling his leather halter out of the stall ring and screaming his defiance over Jakkin's prone body until Likkarn brought him down with a barn stinger. Then there was the pit fighter S'Blood, that Jakkin had allowed to get badly wounded in a fight. He remembered S'Blood's last moments, protesting groggily in the slaughterhouse stews as the steward, in one economical movement, shot him through the ear while Jakkin and Master Sarkkhan watched, helpless, from the walkway above. And then there was Heart's Blood. *Heart's Blood.* That memory was the worst of all. The great red towering majestically above Jakkin and Akki, taking the shots meant for them, death blossoming on her neck like a hideous bloody flower.

*No more*, he thought. *I will allow no more. Not Auricle. Not the new hatchlings. Not even if I have to die to prevent it.*

# *The Fighters*

# 19

JAKKIN DREAMED OF it all that night, the woman in the blood-stiffened cloak so triumphantly slashing the throat of the weakened dragon, then carving open the worm's belly, and the five infants being cradled in the birth chamber. His dreams were as red as the blood that had covered the babies when they were lifted out of their fleshy nest, changed forever by their contact with the dead dragon's body. In his dream the dragon was no longer the unnamed brown that he and Akki had saved for the knife but his much mourned Heart's Blood. And the infants all wore his own face. He dreamed he was drowning in the blood, and when he woke up he was covered with sweat.

He'd fallen asleep in the bowl of meadow along with Makk and the rest of the people, all of them exhausted by the awful ceremony and its equally bloody aftermath. But, unlike the others, he and Akki hadn't feasted on the raw dragon meat, hadn't helped carve away flesh from bone with nail and knife and teeth. Instead they'd watched in horror as the bones, still spotted with the bloody bits of meat, had been piled in a pyramid atop the cart, a pyramid that made mockery of the eggs the dragon had so recently laid. They didn't even need the wild sendings of the crowd to tell them that soon the cart would transport the bones to the great white pile far off in the caves where scavengers would do the rest.

Akki, eyes swollen from weeping, had turned to run and hide somewhere in the tunnels. Her sending was an agony that flashed through to him despite the blood red frenzies of the crowd.

"We can't go now," Jakkin had whispered to her. "Think, Akki, think. If we run now, we leave Auricle. She'll die the same way. We let Heart's Blood die. We let the brown. We can't let Auricle go like this.''

She'd turned toward him, nodding reluctantly.

He'd put his arms around her. ''We'll stay and watch and plan. We've got only one chance to get it right.''

Akki had kept her face hidden against his chest, but Jakkin had borne witness to the rest of the ceremony. Then they'd fallen asleep in one another's arms.

But because they had not taken part in the horrible feast, Jakkin and Akki woke early, Akki first, pulling at Jakkin's arm until he woke covered with sweat, the sun high overhead. The smell of the carnage was still heavy in the early morning air.

Akki, her eyes like dark bruises, turned toward him. Jakkin concentrated on those eyes, trying to forget his dreams.

''I feel so . . . so dirty,'' Akki whispered.

''I think I can get us back to the bath lake,'' he said with confidence, though his traitor mind sent uneasiness and confusion. ''At least I can try.''

They sneaked away from the sleeping people, careful not to step on outflung arms. It helped that they had fallen asleep on the edge of the crowd. Grabbing a torch that was still spluttering in its metal sconce, they plunged into the inviting darkness of the tunnel. Akki went on ahead, thankful to quit the meadow light, but Jakkin turned back for a moment. For the first time he looked beyond the crowd and the bloody altar and noticed carefully cultivated fields around the meadow's rim. His mind worked furiously. Could those fields have been worked by the same people who had torn apart a dragon in an hour of bloody worship? The acres of painstaking hoeings did not seem to belong to a folk who savaged a dragon hen just a day after she'd laid her eggs to their silent approval. He turned back onto the dark winding path into the mountain's heart, remembering his own home, a place where dragon breeders ate dragon steaks and men linked with dying beasts reveled in their cries in the stews. People—people were a puzzle. He guessed he preferred the dragons.

''Akki,'' he called, relieved to be able to use his full voice again. ''Akki, wait for me!''

~

THEY TOOK SEVERAL wrong turnings and had to back up three times, but it was Akki who noticed it first, at a juncture.

''Look, Jakkin, the phosphorescence isn't just haphazard. There's a pattern. Five lines here.'' She ran her hand over the nubbly moss and for a moment her finger glowed. A disembodied white finger pointed. "And three over there."

Jakkin looked. She was right. "That explains how they can run through the tunnels and never get lost." He laughed, holding an imaginary conversation with himself. "And where do you live, Master Makk? Why on number three, past five, second cave to your right!"

"So if we can remember the number patterns, we can find our way around," Akki said.

Just as she finished speaking they rounded a turning in the number five tunnel and stumbled into a small cavern with a lake at its center.

"I said I'd find it!"

Akki shook her head. "I don't think you found *it*—I think you found another one." She handed the torch to Jakkin, who set it carefully against the wall. "These caves must be riddled with lakes."

"You may be right," Jakkin agreed. "This one doesn't have the ledge where the guards stood."

"I'm always right." She laughed and stripped off her robe. She was wearing her own clothes underneath. Before he could react she'd waded in. When the water was as high as her shoulders, she stopped and turned around. "Come on, Jakkin. Why are you so . . . ?" She took one more step back and disappeared under the water, her mouth still open to speak.

Jakkin thought she was joking and waited for her to resurface, laughing. After a moment he began to get worried. He knew she couldn't swim. A moment more and he ripped off his own robe and dived in. The water was icy cold and he was afraid it was going to be pitch black underneath. To his surprise, when he opened his eyes the water was dark green and, the farther down he went, a piercing light green shot through with gold. Ahead he could see a dark, slim shadow. It had to be Akki. He swam as fast as he could toward that black spot and at last he could make her out, arms above her head, legs limp, her hair spun out around her head like a web.

He grabbed a handful of her hair and drew her toward him. Her eyes were open and staring, her mouth a black O. Putting his right arm around her waist, he started to kick upward when he realized he wasn't really sure, in this crystalline world, which way was up and which was down. But trusting to memory, he went away from the light, paddling desperately one-handed toward the black wall.

They shot up and out of the water. He gasped for air, but Akki did not. He dragged her toward the shore and, when he finally got his footing, hauled her up onto the rock. He knew little about healing, less about someone who had almost drowned. All he had was his body's desperate knowledge.

"Oh, Akki, please. *Please!*" he cried. "Not now. Not when we've escaped." The echo of his voice was dampened by his water-filled ears. He couldn't reach her by a sending for there was only that crackle in his mind, the water-induced static. He pulled her close to him in a last mindless embrace and the pressure of his body against hers caused water to spew from her mouth.

Frantically he turned her over onto her stomach and pushed against her back, reasoning that he might be able to pump more water from her that way. Water drained from her mouth and nose, but still she didn't take a breath. He pushed and pushed until he could coax no more out, until his arms ached, then turned her over and stared.

Her eyes were closed. Her mouth was slack. There was a reddening bruise on her cheek from the stone.

"Oh, Akki, *please,*" he cried again. "Take my breath. *Please!*" He put his mouth on hers, as if he could force air into her, and blew. Once. Twice. Three times.

And then, as if rejecting his breath, she coughed, a frothy rough hacking that sent both breath and water back into his mouth. He gagged. She opened her eyes and they were like water-filmed stones. Then life seemed to spark in them again slowly. She coughed once more and Jakkin hugged her, burying his face against her neck. He didn't want her to see him cry.

"Oh, Akki," he whispered hoarsely, his lips against her cold skin, "I thought you were dead."

"Not . . . not dead yet," she whispered back, her voice unnaturally low. "But awfully wet. And cold."

Tenderly he wrapped her robe about her shoulders. "Don't move," he said. "Just get warm. And get your breath back. There's something I have to check out. But I'll be back."

He turned and dived into the water, an inelegant splashing. Just before his head went under his mind cleared and he could feel her sending, still pale but clear:

"And where would I go without *you*, Jakkin?"

# 20

As HE WENT down, down, down toward the piercing green light, Jakkin concentrated only on his swimming. He was an instinctual but untrained swimmer and had never gone any long distances before. Most of his swimming had been of the splash-and-wade variety, done in the water that threaded through the oasis where he'd raised Heart's Blood. But he pulled strongly with his arms, kept his feet kicking steadily, and headed into the center of the green light. He *counted* on that light—it had to be a way out.

Just when he thought his lungs would burst the green turned a brilliant white and he followed it up and into the air. He grabbed great gulps of breath and his chest heaved up and down. When his eyes were no longer water-filmed he saw he was in a cavern of green-white crystals. Overhead and on the cave walls were strange, faceted rocks that pulsed with light. Above the water, rainbow shadows danced and shimmered. Then he realized that instead of being in a lake he was in an eddying river whose slow-moving current was carrying him along. He paddled in desultory fashion, letting the river do the work, and in this way rounded a great curve. Suddenly an enormous opening was before him. It was as high as the nursery studbarn and opened on to endless sky.

The water carried him through. He turned over and floated along on his back, looking up into the clear blue Austarian sky where a black dot was scripting an elliptic message. His mind still crackled with the water's static, so there was no way he could receive a sending that would tell him if that dot was a dragon—or a copter. He flipped back over onto his stomach, took three strong strokes, and clambered out onto a bank whose grass came right down into the water.

From where he stood, shaking himself like a dragon just emerged from a bath, he could see that the river wound on for another couple hundred meters, and then disappeared precipitously, as if the end were suddenly sheered off. There was a constant low deep sound, which seemed at once comforting and ominous. He wondered about it, but it wasn't like any sound he'd ever heard.

Behind him the mountain climbed straight up, as if a second mountain stood atop the first, its dark rocks broken and ugly. On the other side of the river was a grassy slope similar to the one he stood on, and beyond it a sheer drop. He could see a stretch of desert land below with scattered green-black clumps of trees. And even farther on there was a black snaky line he guessed was a river, perhaps even the Narakka.

He became aware of the untrammeled grass between his toes, cool and tickling. Smiling at last, he threw himself facedown and let the strong familiar earth smell surround him.

But all the while he was thinking furiously, questions boiling up inside. How was he to get Akki, who could not swim, through the water to this blue-and-green haven? How could he convince a dragon already beginning to swell with eggs to swim to an unknown and unknowable destination? How could he hold both girl and worm through the terrifying moments underwater when none of them would be able to link minds? And, above all, how could he do it so that the cave people didn't know their plans ahead of time or follow them into this light and open place?

Shaking his head, Jakkin let the sun warm and dry him. Slowly his mind cleared of the static, and as it did he felt it invaded by a faraway sending, faded but familiar:

*"Sssargon rides. Sssargon turns. Sssargon soars."*

Jakkin chuckled to himself, waiting for the dragon to become aware of his presence. Then as the dragon monologue continued unabated, realization dawned on Jakkin. Sssargon simply didn't hear him. He, Jakkin, was broadcasting none of his feelings. The habits he had learned in his long days deep in the cave held. Without even worrying about it, without working at visualizing a wall or a curtain or a fence, he could now cloak his feelings. Thankfully he opened his mind and let out a whoop of color. "Sssargon!" his sending shouted. "Sssargon, shut up! And Sssargon—come here!"

The dot did a complete loop-de-loop and started toward him, its sendings blasting out a parade of patterns—reds, golds, purples. In its wake there came four other sendings, related yet individual.

The hatchlings, Heart's Blood's five, had all heard him and were on their way.

~

THEY NEARLY BROKE two of his ribs and fairly suffocated him once they had landed, crowding around him in boisterous delight. Sssasha had to buffet the triplets away from him with a broad sweep of her tail. And Sssargon, undaunted by their teasing, continued his commentary throughout the reunion, a colorfilled drone that soon had them all chuckling.

*"Sssargon laughs. Sssargon feels joy."*

At last Jakkin caught his breath and cleared his mind. He looked carefully at the five, all of whom seemed overgrown after the stunted, dull dragons of the cave. He patted Sssasha's nose with its splotch of gold, then opened his mind to them slowly, like a storyteller beginning a tale. He made them feel the low, dark inside of the mountain caves and the low, dark minds of the cave's damaged inhabitants. He pictured the work details, the reunion with Akki, the healing of the dragon, and the silent, steady laying of the eggs. Then, with a kind of mental drumroll, he pounded out the rest of the story, ending with the great gout of blood red spewing over them all.

If dragons could weep, they wept. Crowding close to him, they rubbed against him in their need for comfort. Sssasha licked his ear carefully with her rough tongue.

Then Tri-ssskkette, with the mental equivalent of a sigh, sent a fluttering thought that flapped like the skin over her ears. *"Akki!"* She laced the picture of Akki in gold but the flutter lines kept breaking up the image. It was so plaintive, Jakkin reached over and hugged her around the neck.

"Akki," he said aloud, framing a simultaneous sending. Dragons recognized certain spoken words—names and specific objects—but the sendings were still necessary. *"Akki is under the mountain by the lake. I must go back. But thee will have a place in this ending, Tri—I promise thee that."*

The others pushed next to Tri-ssskkette, signaling their own willingness, and nearly knocked Jakkin over. He gave them each a pat on the nose.

*"This is my plan, and it will be better to say it to thee now, for once I am back in the water and under the mountain, I can send thee nothing."*

*"Nothing?"* Sssargon was startled out of his self-involvement for a moment.

"Nothing," Jakkin repeated, both out loud and in a sending. *"The water stops all sendings."*

*"Thee will be like other men then?"* It was Sssasha who understood first.

*"Almost."* Jakkin nodded. *"But the people of the cave can send to dragons, and their sendings are strong. If thee feels it, Sssasha, if they call thee in this way"*—and he looked at them fiercely— *"COME, COME, COME, then thee must all pump thy wings and leave at once. For these are worm killers, bone stackers, blood drinkers. Thee must all leave Akki and me. No more of Heart's Blood's line must die for me. Do you understand?"*

They nodded their great heads up and down, up and down, in slow agreement, Sssasha first and then the triplets and, at the very last and reluctantly, Sssargon.

*"Thee must wait here, ready to help. Thee must be my eyes and my ears."* Then he told them what he planned, so shapeless a thing that even as he spoke and sent it, he wondered if it could possibly work.

When Jakkin had finished Sssargon put his nose against Jakkin's ear and blew a warm breath into it. Then he twisted his neck so that he was eye to eye with Jakkin. *"Sssargon hears. Sssargon be eyes."*

*"We are thy ears, thy ears, thy ears."* The triplets emphasized this by fluttering their earflaps outrageously. Jakkin rewarded them each with a chuck underneath the chin.

Then he turned to Sssasha. *"And thee, my beauty?"* he asked, touching the gold slash on her nose.

*"I am thy heart, Jakkin,"* she sent. It was as clear and unambiguous as any sending the people of the cave could send, but it shimmered with light and with love, and he could read past, present, and future in it.

He turned, slid down the grassy slope back into the water. It seemed colder than before. As he started to stroke against the current, moving slowly upstream, he fought the impulse to turn and look back at the dragons. He needed every bit of strength for the difficult pull ahead. And he feared that if he saw them there he might not be able to go on. Water splashed up into his mouth and made him cough. His ears had begun to ring. The cold and the steady current sapped his fading strength even further. But he went on, one stroke after another, until he had battled his way back through the great opening in the mountainside and into the green crystal cave.

Treading water there, he looked about as if measuring something—the rocks, perhaps, or the walls, or his own fast-disappearing courage. Then through the static in his mind, as if it were a fresh sending, came the memory of Sssasha's words: *"I am thy heart, Jakkin."* Well, he would need the heart of a dragon to get through the rest of it. But for Sssasha, for all of them, for Akki and Auricle—and especially for Heart's Blood, who had sacrificed herself that they might live—he would be brave. Taking a deep breath, he dived down and swam swiftly and surely away from the light.

# 21

THIS TIME, TIRED as he was, Jakkin had been able to judge the amount of breath he needed, and he pulled himself through the ever-darkening water with growing confidence. Just as he began his ascent toward the green-black surface, something caught around his legs. Yanking and kicking, he brought the heavy object up to his eyes and saw, with horror, that it was one of the white robes.

His heart began to pound and his ears felt ready to burst. Fearing the worst—that the robe was Akki's and she'd *really* drowned this time—he pushed it away and watched it rise slowly. He swam desperately for the top, bursting up into the air, gulping mouthfuls into his exploding lungs, and then made for the shore. Rubbing the water from his eyes only seemed to make his vision worse, and he reminded himself to calm down. But when his eyes seemed clear at last he still had trouble seeing in the cave, and that was when he noticed the guttered torch lying in a puddle. The cavern was lit only by the water reflecting eerily on the walls. There was no sign of Akki. The robe in the water must be his own.

He cursed himself for leaving her there so long, alone and unprotected, and his curses rose in volume and originality until he found himself screaming her name. The walls echoed crazily, bouncing the two syllables back and forth, as if playing with them. But there was no answer, and his static-filled mind could find no trace of any sendings.

"Akki!" he screamed again, starting down a tunnel.

Hearing a sound behind him, he turned abruptly. Something on the far side of the lake was rising up from the shallows.

"Shut up, Jakkin," she said. "Maybe we can't send, with all the static, but no one could miss your shouting. The walls are ringing with it!''

''*Fewmets*, Akki, I thought you were gone. I thought ... I thought ...'' He found he could scarcely breathe.

She waded around the lake, careful to stay where the water was only knee-deep.

''What about what *I* thought, Jakkin?'' she said. ''You were gone so long, I thought you were drowned. And I can't swim, so how could I rescue you? And then I thought that if you really had died, your body would float up. So I had hope that you'd found another way out. But I didn't know if I could follow.'' She hesitated. ''But I always knew you'd come back for me if you could.'' She put her hand on his arm.

He shook it off angrily. ''What were you doing underwater?'' he asked. ''You nearly scared me to death.''

''Practicing!'' she said lightly.

''Practicing? Practicing what?''

''That's a joke, Jakkin.''

''I'm not in the mood for jokes.''

''Well, you sure could use something to sweeten you.''

He made a wry movement with his mouth.

''Actually it was the only way I could think to keep them from finding me. When they began that gathering call again, you know, '*COME, COME, COME,*' I was so scared I wouldn't be able to resist it, I ducked down into the water. Even held my nose. And the chant stopped, just like that! Or at least I couldn't hear it anymore because of the crackling. Then I remembered both our robes were by the lake, so I came up for air and dragged them in with me. If Makk saw those, he'd figure out where we were easily.'' She smiled. ''Smart, wasn't I?''

He was still not mollified. ''You left the torch.''

She looked over her shoulder at the guttered torch. ''Oh, dragon's droppings. They'd have known anyway.''

''Still,'' Jakkin said quietly, ''it was awfully brave.''

''It was awfully stupid,'' Akki insisted. ''Don't patronize me, Jakkin. I've done brave things in my life. Don't forget I joined a rebel cell to spy on them. I've lived in the wilderness with you. It just turns out that this wasn't exactly one of the bravest things I've done.''

''It was.''

''It wasn't!''

''It was, too.''

''It ... oh, listen to us, Jakkin. We sound like kids.''

"I still think it was brave."

"Never mind. It's a silly argument anyway. Tell me what you found down there." She pointed to the center of the lake.

Excitedly he sketched out the underwater passage, the crystal cave, the river, the grassy slopes, and the reunion with the hatchlings.

"Then they're all right?" Akki asked, relief in her voice. "What about Tri-ssskkette's wing? All healed?"

"I . . . I didn't look," Jakkin admitted.

"Well, you *were* a bit busy," Akki conceded. "Besides, if she could fly all that way up the mountain, she must be doing fine. Wish we could heal as fast!"

"You can check it out when we get there," Jakkin said.

"I'll do that," Akki said a bit too brightly. "And now that I've practiced my underwater swimming—or at least my underwater nose holding—I'm ready to go. As long as you take my hand, Jakkin, I'll make it." Her voice had gotten high and brittle sounding and she gave a little shiver, but she never stopped smiling.

Jakkin realized she wasn't feeling quite as brave as she was trying to appear, and he thought grimly that they'd both need Sssasha's heart for this.

"Why should I need Sssasha's heart?"

"Because . . . oh, never mind." Flustered, he could barely speak. She'd been able to pick up his thoughts, and he'd been so sure the automatic shielding worked. Perhaps it wasn't as complete as he hoped. Or maybe it worked just with dragons. Or self-involved dragons like Sssargon. Or perhaps it didn't work with someone who loved him, like Akki. Or . . . and then the further realization hit him. There was no more static in his mind.

"We've got to get out of here," he said.

"I'm ready." She started backing into the water.

"I mean back to the egg cave."

"The egg cave—don't be crazy. I can make it through the water, Jakkin. I *know* I can."

He put his hand out toward her. "I know you can, too, Akki. But we can't leave Auricle. They'll kill her. Just like the brown. Another bloody ceremony and more bones for the pile. We can't let them do it."

"Jakkin, we really don't have a choice. We have to save ourselves."

"No! We're not in danger. We can leave anytime. But we've got to save Auricle."

She turned away from him, shivering, and stared into the darkness. "We *are* in danger, Jakkin. In danger of becoming as brutish and dark-minded as these people. Can't you feel it? If we stay, sooner or later we'll be forced to join one of their bloody rituals, and then what will we be?"

"Akki, we're that already. Dragon breeders and stewards and trainers and all the rest of us on Austar, we've used and abused dragons for centuries. We've beaten them and eaten them, we've maimed and trained them as if they were simple animals. Even with all the evidence that they're more than that. And that's why we have to save the dragons, as many as we can—here and back at the nursery. At whatever the cost, Akki."

"Dragons? Plural? Do you have delusions of grandeur, Jakkin? Do you think you're a mighty hero? A moment ago you wanted to save only one dragon—Auricle."

"We have to save the hatchlings, too."

"You can't save them all, Jakkin. There must be twenty or thirty dragons in here. And saving even one of them won't bring Heart's Blood back. Let's just go ourselves, before it's too late."

He ran his fingers through his hair and sighed. "You're not listening, Akki. I realize there's no such thing as a trade-off in guilt—these dragons for Heart's Blood. It's much more. I feel as if I'm seeing clearly for the first time. Why can't I make you see it too? Humans and dragons *together* for Austar's greater good."

*"COME. COME. COME."*

She stared at him, though her face had a strange listening look, as if one part of her was already caught in the web of chanting. Then her thoughts came tumbling into his mind, obscuring the call for a moment. *"Together. Dragons and humans. Oh, yes, Jakkin, yes. I understand."* Aloud, she added, "You really don't need to save *all* the hatchlings here, only the females. They set the males free when they're old enough to fend for themselves. Didn't you know that? All the adult dragons in the cave are female. When one comes into heat they stake her outside in the meadow and the wild males battle for possession. That way the cave people don't have to worry about feeding and caring for males, who are so unpredictable and difficult. The males don't really matter to them anyway."

Jakkin snorted. "Don't matter?"

"No egg chamber," Akki said.

"Oh!"

"So you need me."

"Of course I need you," Jakkin said, pulling her into his arms. She looked up into his face, her eyes suddenly clear and laughing.

"Idiot—you need me because you still can't tell the difference between a male and a female hatchling—and I can. Some dragon master
you are."

He began to chuckle and she joined him, and their laughter rose
into a kind of hysteria until the chant began again, overwhelming them
both. Then, like the rest of the cave people, they marched unerringly
through the tunnels toward the source of the chant.

*"COME. COME. COME."*

# 22

THEY GATHERED ON the edge of the meadow and watched the sun go down, a crowd of silent, staring people bound together by their thoughts.

Then, as if the setting sun released them to their tasks, the crowd surged forward into the great open space. Some of the men moved away from the rest, going toward a section of meadowland that was fallow and fuzzed over with new grass. A few women with hand tools headed toward the planted fields. The rest paused around the altar, which was splotched with dark shadows.

One woman began gathering up discarded robes, passing through the crowd to collect any that were left. She made piles of them on the stones, though Jakkin couldn't tell whether the piles had to do with size or with the amount of dirt or rips or tears in the robes. When he and Akki handed their wet robes to her, she glanced at them oddly, then placed them in a separate pile.

Makk threaded his way through the crowd, placing his hand on an arm here, a shoulder there, choosing a cadre of workers, who in turn chose others. There were no arguments.

Coming toward him, Makk put his hand roughly on Jakkin's arm and his sending hurtled forward.

*"Stay with others now. Pull cart."*

Jakkin looked puzzled, and Makk pointed. When Jakkin made no immediate move Makk pushed him and hurled a sending after him.

*"Go Brekk. Brekk knows."*

Jakkin bowed his head at Makk, grateful the man hadn't noticed their absence. Searching out Akki, who'd been herded into a knot of women folding robes, he caught her eye and nodded. Then he concentrated on raising a heavy curtain over his thoughts with a tiny peephole showing through which he let out a carefully constructed sending. He was counting on the fact that these people, who shared every thought together, seemed to know nothing about acting or telling lies. His sending was a dark rendering of a dragon in pain. Not the pain of the slashed throat or the pain of a dragon in the pit, but the pain of a hen whose birth canal was blocked. He drew on his memory of the days just past and flung the sending directly at Makk.

Makk's head jerked up. Looking around, he found Akki in the crowd and walked over to her swiftly, placing his hand on the back of her neck.

Jakkin forced himself to relax and lower the curtain, letting Makk's sending flood through him. He knew he'd be able to eavesdrop on it because he didn't subscribe to the code of privacy these people had fashioned for themselves.

Makk's sending was direct and clear. *"Go dragons. Heal."*

When Makk took his hand away, severing the intensity of the connection, Jakkin insinuated a sending into Akki's still open mind.

*"Good. Go to the dragons. Pretend Auricle's sick. Check her bonds. I'll be back as soon as I can."* Then he closed his mind, turned, and sought out Brekk and the others, who had been detailed to the bone cart.

~

THE JOURNEY SEEMED endless, even with ten men pulling and pushing the cart, for it was a heavy, unwieldy vehicle that could navigate the twisting passageways only with a great deal of human help. Pulling was worse than pushing, for they had to be strapped into leather harnesses. They stopped often and traded back and front groups.

Jakkin tried to keep track of the turnings so that he could make his escape. But he lost count of the numbered patches when someone fell against him, shoving him into the wall. He bumped his head so painfully, he forgot his careful tally.

It surprised him that they never came to the original lake where he'd tracked Auricle until he remembered that Akki had been taken on the other side of the lake and brought to the Place of Women by an entirely different route. So, he reasoned, his head still throbbing from the fall, there were many roads in this intricate mountain maze. That thought didn't comfort him.

He recognized only three of the men from the ore shifts, one being one-eyed Brekk. If he'd had any hope that Brekk might treat him with an easy familiarity, he was wrong. As cart master, Brekk was a hard but fair leader and a tireless worker, taking many extra turns in the harness. In this he reminded Jakkin of Master Sarkkhan, who had outshoveled and outshouted every bonder at his nursery. Brekk's sendings were loud and snappish: *"Faster! Push! Here! Right turn! Stop!"*

In fact, they took only five rest stops altogether, and at each Brekk handed around several jugs filled with a cold, spicy red drink. Whether it was made of dragon's blood, like the hot protein drink takk, which was standard nursery fare, or of pressed berries, Jakkin couldn't tell. And he didn't ask. He drank it as eagerly as the rest of the men, for it was all they got on the long haul. When they'd each drunk their fill Brekk pushed them back to their feet with a powerful sending.

The cart and its bloody baggage rumbled on. Every once in a while one of the bones would tumble from the cart and someone would bend to retrieve it. Often the man picking up the bone would hold it up to his nose or lick it surreptitiously, snagging a piece of the stringy flesh. One time a *bande dominus* dropped down at Jakkin's feet, and when he stooped to pick it up he was aware that all the men were staring at him, waiting to see what he'd do. He stood up slowly and placed it reverently back on the cart, eyes smarting for while it was in his hands he could feel—as if in a sending—the mental screams of the dying dragon. He walked away from the back of the cart into a side tunnel and was quietly sick.

The men ignored him completely after that, as if he'd failed some important test. Jakkin remembered, almost as if in a dream, the easy camaraderie of the bondhouse: the silly jokes, the noisy songs, the raucous, teasing laughter. Suddenly he missed all the bond boys and girls he'd grown up with: the fat cook Kharina, the sluggard Slakk, the hard-handed trainer Likkarn, even Errikkin, whose ingratiating ways had often irritated him. He thought of them with an exaggerated fondness even as he wondered what they'd make of Akki and him should they ever return.

When he had to get into the pull harness, Jakkin placed himself in the worst position, closest to the cart, where the wheels threatened at every pull to bang against his heels. But at that position the growling and creaking of the cart overwhelmed everything else and he could lose himself in his own thoughts, forgetting the sweat around him and the stale air of the cave.

~

BY THE TIME they reached the bone pile Jakkin was walking in his sleep, every muscle aching. After all, he'd been up long before the others and the underwater swim had taken its toll on his strength. Though he hadn't shared the frenzy of the night before, he'd also not shared all of the sleep. So he pulled with his eyes closed, following the lead of the straps, oblivious of the time. That's why it came as a surprise to him when they rolled to a stop in front of the great pile of whitened bones.

The other men dropped down where they stood, but Jakkin couldn't even move that much.

*"Sleep,"* Brekk sent. *"Work not-now."*

Even before Jakkin could get his bearings, two of the men were snoring. When he finally got himself free of the harness, he found he couldn't just drop like the others into mindless sleep. He was too tired and too upset for that. So he stepped over the men in his way and walked up to the bone pile, craning his neck to look at the top. He remembered—how many days ago had it been?—when Akki and he had first seen the bones. They'd wondered what horrible beast could have done such a thing. And now they knew.

Walking slowly along the tunnel, he found his way back to the cave opening where he and Akki had first entered, pursued by the copter. He bent down and squinted at the bright light filtering through the interlacings of caught-ums. It was day again! They'd pulled the cart with its load of hollow bones the whole night long. It was clear that ordinary time had no meaning for these people. They went to hoe fields in the night. They slept when they dropped. All that mattered was metal—and blood. Dragon's blood. Because metal gave them their tools and blood gave them the ability to live in the cold, the ability to send, the ability to see the world through dragons' eyes.

And then a further thought hit him. *These* were the gifts—metal and the knowledge of the change through sheltering in the dragon's bloody birth chamber—that he and Akki had wanted to bring back to the daylit world.

He pushed aside the caught-ums, heedless of the briars that pierced his fingers. When he'd opened up a path he looked around. It would be so easy, he thought, to slip away down the hill, back to the three little caves where he and Akki had been so happy. But he couldn't slip away because there was Akki, left behind. And Auricle. And the hatchlings born of the slaughtered dragon. And because those three little caves were no longer an easy answer.

Finding a stick on the ground near the copse of spikka trees, he hefted it and went back through the thorny path, using the stick to unhook the caught-ums and close the way behind him. Then he found a place in the cave as far from the other sleepers as he dared, yet still within sight of them, curled his back against the wall, and slept.

# 23

THEY STACKED THE bones in an interlocking pattern and set them without ceremony next to the large pile. The unceremonious manner with which they treated the bones after the frenzied ritual of slaughter surprised Jakkin, and he was not asked to help. Because there were so many bones, it took a long time. When the men were done they began the long trip back without fussing. The cart was only marginally lighter on their return.

It occurred to Jakkin slowly, as they wound through the tunnels, that the pattern of bones was much too complex for these simple people to have invented. All their bowl ware was new and simple; the carved statues and the ironwork had been created generations before by the original Makker and his friends. Over the years of inbreeding and silence the cave people's minds had grown dull, lifeless. Jakkin knew enough about bloodlines to understand that. Dragon masters always said, *The wider the stock, the better the breed.*

The closer they got to the heart of the caves, Jakkin realized something else. He no longer feared the dark-minded Makk or the single-minded Brekk or any of the others. He pitied them. But—he was quick to remind himself—that didn't mean they were any the less dangerous for it. After all, they'd killed a full-grown dragon with the crudest of weapons and their combined sendings could stun a man into a stupor. What he and Akki had were quick wits and an ability to communicate through words as well as sendings. He felt equal to any battle. But he would not let his confidence get in the way of caution.

~

WHEN THE MEN returned they ate in the Place of Women, for it was the largest cavern available. The ceremony being over, however, they ate apart from the women, though Jakkin noticed several couples signaling one another with their hands and then slipping away down the tunnels after the meal. Briefly he looked for Akki, thinking they might do the same. Then he remembered that he'd told Makk she was a healer, not to be treated like an ordinary woman. For her own safety, he had to keep her apart.

As he thought about Makk the man seemed to materialize beside him, a blunt sending coming through without the help of a touch.

*"Go dragon. Help healer."* The sending seemed grayed over, as if Makk were tired.

Jakkin nodded and, with Makk's initial help, found the right tunnel, which was marked with three lines of phosphorescence placed vertically, one horizontally. He took careful note of it. Then, hearing a sound behind him, he turned to see Brekk, his single eye glaring. Jakkin stopped and Brekk stopped. When he started forward again Brekk followed. So, Jakkin thought, he had been assigned a guard. And there was nothing secret about it. Something he or Akki had done must have made Makk wary. If he could only find out what, he'd act differently. After all, he didn't want to alert them ahead of time.

The tunnel opened into the egg room, bright with the light of many torches, and Jakkin saw Akki standing by a large stall behind a pale red dragon. Auricle had been moved into a layer's spot, though it would be months before she was ready to birth her clutch.

Auricle greeted Jakkin with a gray rainbow and arched her neck, but Akki's greeting was all in her face. Then her eyes shifted to Brekk, who had paused at the tunnel entrance to lean against the wall. Akki's eyebrows went up, and Jakkin, with his back to Brekk, formed a single silent word.

"Guard."

She nodded, turning back to the stall, and Jakkin followed her in. There were two women on their knees fussing over the dragon's nails and a third woman picking up straw and fewmets by hand and dropping them over the stall wall into a pushcart. *By hand!* Jakkin smiled wryly, wondering what his bond friends, the lazy Slakk and the fastidious Errikkin, would say about that.

Sending carefully, he questioned Akki. *"How bad is this one?"* But he let the query broadcast to the women and Brekk.

*"This one seems well, but when I examined her I found many*

*potential problems. She needs exercise. And a bath.''* The picture she sent was of a greenish lake where a dragon frolicked and splashed.

"Careful," Jakkin whispered.

One of the women tending the nails looked up at the sound. Her mouth worked angrily, and her sending was sharp. *"Kkriah! Kkriah!''*

Brekk straightened up and started toward them, and Akki pushed out of the stall and met him halfway, putting her hand on his. *"The dragon must be moved. She must walk. Standing still so much makes the birth canal . . .''* Her sending faltered. She didn't find lying easy without words.

Jakkin broke in, finding the contact with Brekk made simpler by Akki's hand contact. *"Makes the birth canal close tight with sores. It is the way of this sickness.''*

Akki took a deep breath, adding, *"How do I set her free?''*

Brekk shrugged off her hand and turned away from her, going back to the wall. His contempt shaped his sending. *"Woman's work.''*

Wiping her filthy hands on her shirt, the woman who had been handling the fewmets signaled to Akki, *"Come. Come.''* Her sending had more tone and rhythm than most.

Akki went back into the stall, Jakkin behind her. The woman bent down and opened the metal cuff with a quick flick of her hands. She held the cuff up. It had a simple snap-on lock.

Akki nodded, then turned away as if she were no longer interested in the mechanics of the bonds, sending instead to the women still tending Auricle's nails, *"Get water. Boil it. Very hot.''*

They showed nothing in their faces but leaped up together and went out past Jakkin and Akki toward a far entryway.

*"And you,''* Akki sent to the other woman, *"I need knives for the lancing. Boil them. And wash that filth from your hands.''*

*"Filth?''* The sending was clearly puzzled.

*"Go!''* Akki let her exasperation show.

The woman left, wiping her hands down the front of her shirt.

Akki walked back to Brekk, who had been observing everything from his post, his single eye squinting. *"I need . . .''*

His sending cut across hers with the neat precision of a surgeon. *"I watch. I go no woman's way.''*

Akki controlled her mouth and eyes with an effort, turned her back to him, and opened her mouth in a silent shout at Jakkin. "Help!"

Jakkin gave her a lopsided grin, bent, and quickly flicked open the other three chains and removed one from its setting in the wall. Then he signaled to Brekk. *"A man is needed here. The dragon must be led to water. Do not help the woman. Help me."* He never thought it would work.

But Brekk seemed relieved, and he came over at once to take hold of the dragon's ear, pulling it so roughly that Auricle backed out of the stall with jerky steps. Jakkin waited until the dragon obscured him, then he pulled Akki close and whispered in her ear, "We can go *now*. Get the hatchlings. I'll take care of him."

She moved quickly to the stall where the five hatchlings were sleeping, climbed over the fence, and disappeared. Jakkin, holding the chain behind him, walked up to Brekk, who still had Auricle's ear in a twisting hold.

Brekk may have heard his step, or a bit of Jakkin's anxiety may have leaked out around the edges of his mind barrier. At the last moment, just as Jakkin was bringing the heavy chain down upon his head, Brekk turned and raised his arm, taking most of the blow there, but the shock of it nevertheless tumbled him in front of the dragon's forefeet. She fell on her knees on top of his leg, and Jakkin heard the crack of bone. At the same moment a sending rocketed through him, full of pain and anger and astonishment. Then Brekk must have passed out because only a lingering shard of the sending remained in his head.

Jakkin grabbed for Auricle's ear. "Up!" he commanded aloud. His sending was more emphatic. The dragon slowly rose from her knees and Brekk, groaning out loud from the pain, turned his head aside.

Out of the corner of his eye Jakkin saw Akki climbing out of the stall, a single hatchling in her arms.

"Only one?"

"All the rest are males," she said.

"Are you sure?"

"Trust me."

"Then let's go." He pulled at her arm.

"I'd better do something about his leg," Akki said. "I don't know if they can set it. And—"

"We don't have time, Akki. And when he comes to, he's not going to be happy with us."

"Jakkin . . ."

He bent and picked up the chain and dangled it in front of her. "Trust me."

"Yes, sir!" she said, giving him a mock salute.

"Sometimes I wish you'd obey as fast as those other women!"

She whispered a curse that startled him because he hadn't known she knew such language. Then he grinned and gave her a hug. "But I'm satisfied," he added. "Trust me!" Throwing the chain down, he grabbed a fresh torch lying against the wall and lit it. "Now let's go!"

~

THEY TROTTED DOWN the tunnel, careful to mask their thoughts, until Jakkin realized that the dragon's mind was wide open and broadcasting.

*"Shut up,"* he commanded in a frantic sending, but either she didn't understand him or she just couldn't stop. And then the hatchling began to send a piping that bounced from wall to wall.

"Well, so much for a sneaky exit," he said. Akki's laughter bubbled through his mind, a laugh on the edge of hysteria. He had to concentrate hard to keep from responding to that hysteria himself.

Whether it was luck or memory that brought them to the lake Jakkin couldn't say, but within minutes they had found the pool with its green-white center. Akki set the hatchling down and stretched her arms.

"All right, Master Jakkin, now what?"

"We dive in." He pointed.

"You're the only one who can swim."

"I can pull you through and you can hold the hatchling. And Auricle *can* swim. I've seen her. And . . ."

Akki shook her head. "Gravid dragons have extra buoyancy."

"What's that?"

"It means she's going to float to the top."

"Why are you telling me this now?" Jakkin asked.

"Because you never gave me time before," Akki said. Then she looked down. "Besides, I just thought of it."

"Are you sure about the buoyancy?" Jakkin asked.

"Pretty sure," Akki said.

He sighed. "Well, I could run back and get those chains."

"What for?"

"Added weight."

"Not enough."

"Well, we have to try something." He scuffed his foot on the stones.

The dragon suddenly sent a gray-and-tan rainbow and there was that same plaintive tone: *"Man? Not-man?"*

That determined Jakkin. He sent her a command to lower her head, put his hands on each side of her face, below the earflaps, and stared deeply into her eyes. Speaking and sending at the same time, he said, "Auricle, thee must dive in the water and go under, fighting the buoyancy to get down to the light. Else the *men* will take you. They will take you and . . ." He summoned all his strength and showered her with the bloodiest sending he could manage. As he did so he felt Akki's hand on his back, lending her strength to his.

Startled, the dragon pulled back, nearly squashing the hatchling, who piped her distress. The piping stopped the dragon in her tracks. She turned and nuzzled the little one.

Akki pushed past Jakkin and put her hand on Auricle's broad flank. "They will kill this hatchling and those females in thy eggs as well." Her sending was even redder than the one Jakkin had managed, and it was filled with images of mothering and babies' blood and bonds.

Auricle lifted her head and a strange red light flickered in the dark shrouds of her eyes. It was the first time they had seen such a reaction from any of the cave dragons.

*"Thou fighter,"* Jakkin sent strongly. *"Thou beauty."*

Akki picked up the hatchling and they walked to the edge of the lake.

# 24

As THEY SUMMONED the courage to dive, they heard the sound of footsteps in a nearby tunnel.

"Quick!" Jakkin's voice was suddenly hoarse. He plunged the torch into the water and, as it sizzled out, they were left in the half-shadows of the reflecting lake.

Akki waded in first, the hatchling clutched to her breast. Jakkin gave Auricle a shove with his shoulder against her flank, and she followed Akki into the shallows reluctantly. Jakkin entered the lake last, careful not to let his head get wet.

He whispered to Akki, "Comfort the little one but hold on tight. Once we go under she won't be getting any sendings from you and might panic. Take a deep breath when I tell you to and hold your nose."

Akki shifted the hatchling to her right arm and put her left hand up to her face in preparation.

"Good! Once we're under I'll grab the back of your shirt and tow you along. You won't have to do anything but hold on to the hatchling—and *don't breathe.*"

"I trust you," she whispered back.

He turned to the dragon. *"Open thine eyes underwater and swim toward the light. I cannot command thee under the water. Nor can any man."*

She answered him with a flash of color.

*"Freedom awaits thee outside, my beauty. There are no blood rites there. Thee shall birth thy hatchlings and live to see them fly."*

*"?????"*

"Jakkin," Akki hissed. "She doesn't know what you mean. Cave females never get to fly."

"Well, they've seen the wild males flying, haven't they?" He sent Auricle a picture of a male dragon in the sky circling a female below. *"That is flying, my beauty."*

*"!!!!!"*

The running footsteps got nearer, honing in on the sendings, and the first tentative feelers from the searchers drifted into their minds.

"Take a deep breath, Akki. Now!" Jakkin said. "Dive!"

The dragon went first, her tail whacking the water with a sound as loud as a thunderbolt, drenching them in the process. Akki was next, taking a noisy breath and ducking under. Jakkin followed immediately, grabbing a handful of her shirt back. With a powerful kick, he began to tow her down toward the inviting green-and-gold light.

As he swam Jakkin felt as if he were moving slowly through a nightmare. Each stroke seemed to take forever. Glancing back, all he could see of Akki was a dark, amorphous figure. He hoped she was still holding the hatchling because he couldn't tell. Her dead weight slowed his progress. By the time they'd come to the light-colored water, he was practically out of breath and he knew there was still a long passage under rock before he could start toward the surface again.

Ahead of him the green-gold light suddenly went dark and he felt the cold water chill his bones. For a second he considered surrendering himself to the cold. All he needed was one quick intake of breath and the aching in his chest and lungs would be gone forever. Then he thought about Sssasha and Sssargon and Heart's Blood. They flashed across his thoughts like pictures on a screen. At that very moment the light returned full force and he saw the outline of a tail moving ahead of him. Auricle's enormous body had been blocking the light. He'd known it subconsciously and that was why he'd thought about the other dragons. Relieved, he kicked his feet extra hard and surged forward, ignoring the fact that he'd no breath left, that he couldn't feel his towing arm, that his ears were popping. He kept swimming because it was the only thing he *could* do, for Akki and the hatchling and himself.

And then he was past the rocky overhang and into the pulsing light, bursting up into the air, sobbing and gasping at the same time. Already on the rock ledge, Auricle was shaking herself all over, spraying the cave with water and rainbows.

Jakkin swam toward the ledge, found a footing in the shallower water, and hauled Akki behind him. Her eyes were still squeezed shut, her left hand cupped over her nose. He grabbed the hand and pulled it away, and for a moment she fought him.

"It's all right, Akki," he cried, his voice ragged. "We've made it. We're here."

She opened her eyes slowly, all the while taking in great gulps of air. Her eyelids fluttered and her pupils seemed filmed over and unfocused. The hatchling began to squirm in her arm. They both moved with a slow deliberation, as if they were still underwater.

"Jakkin," she whispered. Then louder: "Jakkin?" Opening her right arm as if it hurt to do so, she dropped the hatchling into the water. It paddled in awkward circles until Auricle stuck her long neck out and nosed the dragonling to the ledge. It scrambled up, leaving patches of eggskin on the rocks.

Jakkin and Akki lay side by side in the shallows for a minute, neither one with enough energy to move or speak further. Their breathing was rapid and Jakkin could feel the pounding of his heart. After a while he tried flexing his hand, the one that had held on to Akki's shirt. His fingers were cramped and his thumb ached.

"You're no lightweight," he said at last. "Even in the water."

Stretching her right arm, Akki smiled but kept her eyes closed. "Neither was the hatchling. I don't think my arm will ever be the same."

Behind them, on the ledge, the hatchling piped for attention until Auricle stopped its noise with a lick of her tongue, simultaneously removing another small patch of eggskin.

"How do we get out of here?" Akki asked, sitting up at last. "There's only one tunnel and it's full of water."

"We float through," Jakkin said. Noticing Akki's dismayed face, he added, "We don't have to go under again. The river does all the work. Trust me. We just lie on our backs and it takes us through. I promise I'll hold on to you."

Akki nodded, but they had to wait a few minutes more, until their minds were free of the static and Jakkin could give Auricle her instructions. Then the dragon waddled into the water, where Jakkin placed the hatchling on her broad back, close up to the neck.

*"Stay there,"* he warned the hatchling with a stern sending, and touched it on the nose. *"There thee will be safe, little one."*

The hatchling piped an answer, but whether it understood, Jakkin wasn't sure. It looked as if it did, cocking its head to one side, a patch of eggskin peeling from its nose.

*"The river is slow,"* he sent to Auricle. *"There is nothing to fear."* He looked again at the hatchling and wondered if it was afraid.

Communication with it would be uncertain for days, even weeks. After all, it was only a baby.

"It's a she, remember?" Akki's voice had recovered much of its lighthearted quality.

"You stay out of my mind!" Jakkin said gruffly. "Unless I invite you in. That's one thing the cave people have right."

"The *only* thing," Akki added.

"Concentrate on floating," Jakkin said. "The rest is easy."

The current had already caught the dragon and was moving her along in a slow, majestic fashion. Jakkin was reminded of the way Sssasha had floated in the sky. He took Akki's hand and they pushed off into the middle of the lake. Soon they, too, were caught by the river's pull.

"The hard part is over," he called. "Relax and enjoy this."

Akki, her body stiff, shouted back, "Why do I wish you hadn't said that?"

"Everything's going to be just fine," Jakkin shouted. "Trust me!"

They floated through the round tunnel opening to the outside, where the sun was just rising on a new Austarian day.

# 25

As they floated they watched the sky, blue and unmarred by clouds. First one black dot, then a second, then three more suddenly peppered the horizon, rising and coming together in a triangular formation that moved closer and closer.

"Look!" Jakkin shouted, waving his free hand in the air. A wave swamped them, causing him to lose his grip on Akki's hand. They both went under, and Jakkin swam desperately after her, taking nearly a dozen strokes before he caught up with her again.

Grabbing a handful of her shirt, he headed them both toward the riverbank. Once his feet touched bottom he stood up, surrendering himself to a coughing fit. Akki found her footing at the same time and began pounding him on the back. Then they scrambled up the grassy slope and stared at the sky.

The five dots had become much larger, resolving themselves into dragon shapes. Jakkin knew they had to be Heart's Blood's hatchlings, but he couldn't reach their minds because his now crackled with static from his recent ducking in the water. He waved frantically instead.

But the dragons weren't watching him. They were hovering over a place farther downriver. It was Akki who understood first.

"Auricle!" she cried. "It's Auricle they're watching. She's still in the water."

Jakkin shaded his eyes, following the path of the twisting river until he could just make out Auricle's lumpish form. Knowing he couldn't reach her with a sending until the static cleared, he shouted, "Get out! Auricle—get out now!" But his voice couldn't compete with the sound of the water.

Akki grabbed his arm. "What's that sound, Jakkin?"

"You mean the crackle? The static? Or the river?"

"No, there's another sound. A kind of growling."

"I don't know. I heard it before. Why?"

They both strained to listen for a moment, and then Akki said softly, "Waterfall!"

Without another word they began to race along the grassy border, screaming as they went, even though they knew it was futile. Auricle couldn't hear them. At last they gave up screaming because the more they yelled, the less breath they had for running.

For a while they seemed to be gaining on the waterborne dragon, for her progress was slowed by the many broad river bends. Several times she was spun around completely, bouncing off dangerous-looking rocks. They could see the hatchling balanced on her back. And once she wallowed for a moment in a patch of reeds close to the far shore, giving them time to close the gap. But then the current caught her again and carried her farther downstream. As she approached the place where the river and land dropped away precipitously into the waterfall, things seemed to speed up and she was buffeted from side to side by the ever-increasing white waves, further endangering the hatchling clinging to her back.

Just then Jakkin's mind cleared and he stopped in order to read the frantic colors of Sssargon's sending. Akki began to slow down as well, and he waved her past.

"Sssargon worries. Sssargon calls. Sssargon hears nothing."

More sensibly, Sssasha broadcast advice to the drifting dragon: "Paddle thy wings. Use thy feet. Come to the shore."

But it was soon apparent to all of them that Auricle was too frightened to do anything but let the current carry her on. Her mind was filled with the same dull terror that Jakkin had first heard in the caves. He guessed the fighter's light in her eyes would be gone.

He sent instructions to the larger hatchlings. "Go in the water with her. Push her to the shore. Triplets—be my eyes and ears. Stay above. Let me see all."

Without waiting for an answer he began to run again, concentrating on the precarious footing, for the grass was slippery near the river.

Sssargon launched himself into the water, further drenching Auricle. One of his wings buffeted her and she spun around helplessly. Then Sssasha dropped into the river on Auricle's other side. Keeping her between them, they tried to ease her to the shore, but by now the water was churning angrily and a wild froth filled the air. All three were perilously close to the edge of the falls.

Standing on the bank, Akki urged them out with frantic shouts and sendings, but Sssargon's running commentaries had ceased and so had Sssasha's calm murmurings. Either they were all too intent on staying afloat or the water had once again performed its own strange silencing.

Jakkin caught up with Akki, shouting to her above the noise of the river, "It's no good trying to send, Akki. They must have each gone under at least once. The water's cut off any sendings. I don't understand it. The water in the oasis where I trained Heart's Blood never did this."

"Minerals, Jakkin. The same minerals that the cavefolk mined. That has to be it. It has to be. It has—"

He grabbed her arm, wanting to shake her into silence, and at the touch was drawn into the maelstrom of her mind. Taking a deep breath, he forced himself to blanket them both with a calming blue. Akki finally stopped mind-babbling.

In the water the three dragons were now fighting the tossing current individually, spinning away from one another, lost in separate whirlpools.

"Why don't Sssasha and Sssargon get out?" Jakkin cried.

"Because, you idiot, you told them to save her. And they'll do whatever you ask. You're both father and mother to them. They'll die rather than disappoint..." She closed her mouth but her mind finished off the thought and Jakkin felt both hot and cold at its touch.

And then the river took the three dragons and tipped them over the edge of the world.

Rushing to the cliff side, Jakkin cast a sending up. *"Tri-sss, be my eyes."*

Immediately a picture formed in his mind: three large figures tumbling down the falls. Sssargon, the heaviest, was first. For a moment he stopped, caught on a rocky outcropping. Then he pushed straight out from the water, plummeting through the air, his wet wings too heavy to carry him. As the wind dried his scaly feathers he unfurled his wings with a loud crack. Pumping them once, he flew straight back toward the falls.

"No!" Jakkin shouted.

Deaf to both sound and sending, Sssargon made one or two feints at the falls and then found Sssasha. He plucked her out of the vertical water and dropped her free.

Overweighed by the water she, too, fell straight down. Then suddenly she flipped, shot her wings out, and back-winged away from the plunging water.

"What about Auricle?" shouted Akki.

As if sensing the question, Sssargon and Sssasha both turned back to the falls. Jakkin could see through Tri-sss's eyes that Auricle was no longer falling but clinging to a rocky outjut, though water was steadily pounding around her. There was no sign of the hatchling.

As if on a signal, Sssargon and Sssasha dashed into the falls at the same moment, emerging again with the drenched Auricle in their claws. Once free of the water, they dropped her. She fell like a stone, tumbling end over end in the glistening air.

"She doesn't know how to fly," screamed Akki. "She's . . ."

Even though they couldn't hear her, Sssasha and Sssargon had come to the same conclusion. Sssargon swept his wings back hard against his sides and followed Auricle in a long, perilous stoop, diving headfirst toward the ground. Passing Auricle, he flipped over, snapped his wings open once he was below her, and readied himself to cushion her fall.

"If she hits him . . ." Akki began.

"She'll kill them both," Jakkin said, his voice flat. He closed his eyes, but Tri-sss's unrelenting sendings denied him any relief.

Just fifty feet from the ground, as if the air itself had ripped them open, Auricle's wings spread, fluttered, and caught an updraft that sent her into an off-balance soar.

Surprised, Sssargon almost fell to the ground anyway. At the last moment he turned and pumped his wings, scraping one on a large rock. Then he sailed up to Auricle's right. Sssasha banked and flew down to her left, sending a bemused thought into Jakkin's mind:

*"No splat!"*

"No splat indeed," Jakkin whispered. He threw his arms around Akki, unashamed of the tears running down his cheeks.

A horrible thought hit them both at the same time, though it was Akki who said it aloud.

"The hatchling!"

Already aware of the danger, the triplets were broadcasting simultaneous signals of distress: flashes of haunch and head as the little dragon tumbled head over heels through the water all the way down the treacherous falls.

~

IT TOOK JAKKIN and Akki nearly an hour to scramble down the cliff-side, but when they got to the bottom, where the falls puddled into several rocky pools before fanning out into five small fingerlike rivers, there were the triplets and Sssasha, Sssargon, and Auricle, all standing over the dragonling.

Akki screamed, "You didn't tell us! You let us think she was dead." She ran over and grabbed up the hatchling, who wriggled delightedly in her arms.

A splash of chuckles ran through Jakkin's head. *"No splat, no splat, no splat."*

Akki turned to him, her eyes full of laughter. "Jakkin, don't you see—proof positive that they're not just animals. Animals couldn't play a practical joke." She nuzzled the hatchling.

Jakkin nodded. "But what really happened?" he asked, letting his mind send the question to them.

It took many minutes of patchworked sendings before he and Akki really understood the whole thing. Each dragon added a part or contradicted another. But finally the story came clear. The hatchling, being so small, had tumbled easily and landed in the pooling water at the bottom of the falls without hitting any rocks along the way. She was hardly the worse for her hazardous trip and, in fact, had rather enjoyed it all.

If dragons could smile, they smiled.

Without her medkit Akki couldn't do much for the scratches and bruises. Sssasha had torn her secundum while carrying Auricle, and the endpiece of Sssargon's left wing was ripped. Auricle was missing some scales in both wings and there was blood on her nose. None of it was serious. Only the hatchling seemed unbruised, though its egg-skin was peeling off more quickly than was natural.

"We'll have to be careful with her," Akki cautioned, "or she'll get sunburned on her new scales."

The dragons licked their wounds and Akki reminded Jakkin that that was, after all, the best medicine for them, since there was something in the saliva that promoted healing.

"What really worries me, though," Akki said later, gesturing to Auricle, "are her eggs. She's taken quite a beating these last few hours. It may not show on the outside but . . ." She let the sentence dangle.

"Even if she loses this clutch," Jakkin said, "it won't be so bad. She'll be able to have another. And at least she's alive."

"Alive—and lost. Just like the rest of us," Akki said.

Sssasha, who'd been listening in on their thoughts, intruded a sending.

*"What pain?"*

*"No pain,"* Jakkin sent back.

*"Yes, pain,"* Sssasha said, coming over to stick her nose against Jakkin's chest.

*"We're lost, Sssasha,"* Akki sent.

*"Not lost. Trust me."*

Jakkin looked at Akki and they burst out laughing at the same time. Sssasha joined in with tiny, popping, rainbow-colored bubbles that seemed to march across a vast sandy plain.

# 26

EXHAUSTED, THEY SLEPT away the rest of the morning in a tight circle of dragons and humans. Akki woke before Jakkin, then shook him furiously.

"Sssasha and Sssargon are gone," she said.

Jakkin opened an eye, for a moment stunned by the sun's glare. He yawned and stretched, surprised at how stiff his body was, and remembered only slowly why his left hand was cramped and aching.

"Jakkin, wake up. Sssasha and Sssargon are gone."

"They're probably just off grazing, Akki." He rubbed his left hand slowly.

"There's enough grazing right here," Akki said, her sweeping hand taking in all the land around the fingerlike rivulets.

Jakkin nodded. The grass was rich and thick, and in the drier places burnwort and blisterweed were both growing in abundance, the red stalks a sign of healthy plants. Smoke ghosts swirled over the patches of wort and weed, signaling they were almost ready to leaf out.

"And I can't hear them," Akki said.

"You're worrying too much, Akki."

"I can't hear them, but I do hear something else," she said. "Listen!"

Shrugging, he listened. He could hear the *pop-pop* of the dragons' breath as Auricle and the triplets slept easily. He could hear the dull roar of the falls and beyond that a kind of echo that might have been the river. Nearer were the *swish-swash* sounds of the five streams lazing between banks. He could hear the *pee-up-up* of some river-edge creature protesting their presence, and the constant chittering of insects.

"I'm listening," he said as his mind filled with dragon dreams: soft, unfocused points of pulsing light, with darker undertones he suspected belonged to Auricle.

"Then you hear it?"

Shaking his head, Jakkin was puzzled. He tried to listen harder. And then he heard a strange faraway *chuffing*, deeper than the dragon snores but higher than the roar of the falls. He knew that sound.

"Copter!" he said, jumping up.

Akki grabbed his arm. "What will we do? Where can we hide?"

They'd been sleeping near the smallest of the five rivulets, for the grass was soft and sweet and relatively dry. But there were no rocks or trees to hide behind, and the falls were too far away.

"We could hide under the dragons," Akki said. "If they were on their feet, we could lie down under Auricle and the others could crowd around." She ran over to the dragons and started pulling on their earflaps to rouse them.

The copter sounds came closer even as the sleeping dragons began to wake. Auricle lumbered to her feet, sending a jumbled message, gray and questioning, but the triplets, still stretched out on the ground, sent a different thought:

*"Man coming. Man coming. Man coming."*

"Akki," Jakkin said sharply.

She turned at his tone and looked up at him.

"Akki—no." This time his voice was soft, almost pleading. "No more hiding. No more running. It's time to face this . . . this *man* coming. Face him and go home." He hadn't known what he was going to say until the words came tumbling out of his mouth, and then he realized he'd known it all along. The escape from the mountain hadn't been a running-away-*from*. It had been a running-away-*to*.

"Think, Jakkin, think." Her mind sent him arrow points of orange and red, charged with electricity. "We don't know who's in that copter, enemy or friend."

"It could be a stranger," Jakkin said. "Someone just out for a flight. One chance in three."

"Remember what you said when we first ran off from the copter, Jakkin. That whoever is in the copter *has* to be looking for us." She began to braid the ends of her hair nervously.

He walked over to her and put his arms around her, drinking in the clean grass and river smell in her hair. "Akki, listen to me. With your ears and heart and mind this time." He sent her a picture of a damned-up river, then slowly opened the floodgates. A wall of green water tumbled through, threatening to overwhelm her.

"It's time for us to open those gates, Akki."

"I don't know what you mean."

"Time to grow up and time to help Austar grow up, too."

She pulled away from him and stared at the ground. "Will you be telling them about the egg chamber and how it changes a person, how it lets us live in the cold and see the world through dragons' ears and eyes? If you do, you know, you'll be condemning every female dragon on Austar to an early death."

He shook his head.

"And will you tell them about the metal to be had inside these mountains? Because if they find that metal, they find the cave people. And then they'll find the secret of the change. Good-bye, dragons."

"*Them*, Akki? Who do you mean?"

"The rebels or the wardens—the bad guys. The ones who've been after us."

"Don't just worry about the rebels and the wardens, Akki," Jakkin said. "If it's a matter of metal and the change, *everyone* will be a bad guy. Even the good ones like Dr. Henkky and Golden and Likkarn. For all the *right* reasons, they'll slaughter the dragons."

"Then what will you tell them? All of them?"

Jakkin shook his head. "Very little at first."

She bit her lip. "Listen, Jakkin, I'm a doctor. Or at least I'm almost one. I bet I could help find some *other* way, other than killing dragons, to give everyone what they want—dragons' ears and eyes."

He nodded.

"But if we can't say anything, how are we going to help Austar grow up?"

He pulled her toward him again. "Slowly," he said. "From the nursery on. That's how babies grow."

"It won't be easy."

"Growing up never is," he said. "I guess I'm just understanding that."

She kissed him, her hands cool on either side of his face. And the flooding river of his sending turned a blue-green and then they needed no more words.

~

THEY WERE STILL in each other's arms when the copter came into view around the mountainside. Flanking it were Sssargon and Sssasha, though well out of range of the twirling blades.

Slowly the copter settled between two of the streams. The dragons hovered until the rotors stopped whirling, then they made perfect, graceful landings.

"Show-offs!" Akki whispered, but her arm tensed about Jakkin's waist.

The copter door opened and a man in a Federation uniform got out. He was a slim man who walked with a movement that was both calculating and loose. As he got closer Jakkin could see the blue of his eyes under beetling brows.

"Hello, Akki. Hello, Jakkin," he said, his voice full of warmth.

"Golden! It's Golden," Akki cried, letting go of Jakkin and running over to the man. "We thought you were dead."

Golden smiled and the scar on his cheek bunched. Jakkin was sure that this time it was a real scar, not the fake one he'd used so often in the past.

"The same was said about the two of you—in certain quarters. But the reports of our deaths, as an old Earth writer once said of himself, have obviously been grossly exaggerated." He disentangled himself from Akki's arms. "Be careful with me, Akki. These bones don't knit as swiftly as your young ones. Henkky hasn't been too pleased with my progress these last months. I seem to have several painful reminders of our last—outing—together."

They all laughed and Akki touched the scar on his cheek.

Jakkin shook his hand, surprised at the strength in the grip, and said, "You don't seem surprised to see us."

"I am—and I'm not," Golden said. "Can you say the same?"

"We're definitely surprised," admitted Jakkin.

"We thought you'd be wardens or rebels," Akki said.

Golden looked at them thoughtfully. "But still you didn't try to run off." He paused. "I'd say you've done a lot of thinking—"

"And growing up," Akki said.

"I always thought you two were remarkably grown-up for your age," Golden said. "Or I wouldn't have involved you in spying and—"

"Why are you here?" asked Jakkin. "Why now?"

"To find you, obviously. And bring you back."

Akki smiled but Jakkin's eyes narrowed. "Bring us back how? As friends? As prisoners? As criminals? As runaways?"

"Not exactly prisoners, otherwise I'd be home and the wardens would be here. But not exactly free either. Let's say you are wards of the state."

At their puzzled glances, he added, "An offworld term I learned

long ago. You see, I ran the investigation from my hospital bed—when Henkky allowed me!—and cleared you two of the charges of planting the bomb at Rokk Major.''

"How many people were hurt?" Akki asked.

"And how many dragons?" Jakkin added.

"Enough," Golden said.

*"How many?"* Jakkin insisted.

"Thirty-seven were killed outright," Golden said.

"And Sarkkhan?" Jakkin asked.

"And Sarkkhan," Golden said, nodding.

A small sigh escaped Akki's lips but nothing more. It was an old wound, and she'd never really believed her father had a chance of escaping. But Jakkin put his hand on her arm and her eyes widened.

"Hundreds of others were injured, some very seriously. At least twenty more died of their wounds over the next few months."

"And the dragons?" Jakkin asked again.

"Forty maimed."

"And sent to the stews," Akki whispered.

Golden nodded. "It was the worst disaster Austar has ever known. The Federation sent men and supplies, but the price was high. They wanted to run the search for you themselves and it took a lot of arguing in the Senate to rule that out. Meanwhile, Captain Khalkkav and his wardens declared you dead. He wasn't pleased when I proved your innocence from my hospital bed. It took away his hero status and made him little better than a murderer. He forgot how well connected I am. But he forgave me when I found him Akki's old cell of rebels and he and his men broke it—except for the leader."

"Number One!" Akki breathed.

"Your Number One got away. His name, by the way, is Swarts."

"There's no double *K* in that name," said Jakkin. "Is he a master?"

"Oh, yes," Golden said.

"Then why is he a rebel? I thought only KKs were involved in trying to bring down the system." Jakkin looked puzzled.

Golden smiled. "Still the innocent, Jakkin? There are as many masters who hate the bond system as bonders."

Akki whispered, "Golden is a master, Jakkin."

Golden ignored her and continued, "Wanting freedom to run a world is not a dream limited to the underclasses. Every master is not rich. Every bonder is not poor. And every rebel is not fighting to set his *brother* free, Jakkin. There are as many reasons as rebels."

Jakkin looked down at the ground, chafing under Golden's lecture.

"But freedom *is* a good and noble goal, Jakkin. I managed to get some of the best of the rebel ideas cleaned up and passed into law from my hospital bed. We set the bonders free. That brought a good many rebels into our camp, I'll tell you. Except for the ones like Swarts, whose interest is more domination than nation. You'd be surprised how effective and popular a man can become when he's lying near death and issuing pleas through an attractive lady doctor!"

"I don't understand," Akki said. "If you've cleared us of the pit bombing and all bonders are free, why aren't we—*exactly?*"

"Because, my dear Akki," said Golden, putting his hands on her shoulders, "I cleared the names of a romantic young *dead* couple. Once you return alive—well, there are bound to be some difficult questions, which, as my wards and prisoners, you won't be obliged to answer."

"What kind of questions?" asked Jakkin, sure he already knew.

"Questions such as why haven't you frozen to death many times over during Dark-After? How did you escape the night you were left? Where have you been living all this time? Which, by the way, no one will know because I destroyed the pots and garlands in your caves."

"You found the caves?" Akki asked, her voice rough. "You destroyed everything?"

"Everything," Golden said. "I hated to do it. It was clear you'd worked hard to make those caves your home."

"One of them was even named after you," said Akki in a small voice.

"How did you find them?" Jakkin asked.

Golden shrugged. "Bones," he said. "The tattletale of bones. We found Heart's Blood's bones—but we didn't find yours."

*"We?"* Jakkin and Akki asked together.

"Don't worry. *We* wasn't Kkalkkav or any of his minions. He really hasn't the brains to assume you were anything but dead. It was Likkarn."

"Likkarn!" Jakkin exclaimed.

"Funny old man. Years ago he'd managed to live for a while in the foothills, holed up with dragons in a cave. He knew it *could* be done, just didn't know if it had been done by the two of you. What he said was 'Jakkin and Akki have the luck and lust for it,' meaning if it could be done, you two could do it. He also said that if you hadn't made it, then we should bring back your bones and bury them at home. *'Among friends.'* That's what he said. He told me that in the hospital. We had a long time there together and I found him a fascinating, complicated man."

"He was in the hospital, too?"

"He'd had both arms and a leg broken when he fought off the wardens at the nursery to buy us running time, remember?" Golden said. "And he lost the use of one eye as well. Old bones heal slowly. But he says he's the better for it, for he'd been off the weed all that time. And I don't think he's going to backslide, either."

"So you went up to the caves together?" Akki said. "That must have been difficult for him."

"We took a copter and set it down in the meadow where your red was killed. I could hardly bring myself to look at the bones. Likkarn did that. He looked—and laughed out loud. Brought me right over. 'I told you they got luck and lust,' he said. There wasn't a human bone among them. Well, you'd know that, of course.

"We went along the pathway on three different days, checking the caves. Found three places with your stamp on them. We tore apart the mattresses and garlands, threw the pots over the cliffside."

"Oh," Akki said.

"But how'd you know to find us *here?*" asked Jakkin.

Golden gestured with his head toward the dragons. "They told us. The big ones."

Sssargon and Sssasha, squatting on their haunches on either side of the copter, managed to look bored.

"They'd been coming and going almost daily at the nursery these last two weeks, circling and then landing by the incubarn. Likkarn thought he recognized them as Heart's Blood's hatchlings. Said that golden slash on the nose of that one was a dead giveaway."

Jakkin sent a quick burst of color toward Sssasha, which she returned with a rainbow.

"Likkarn seemed to manage some kind of connection with them," Golden continued. "Even claimed he could understand them. I said he was a good guesser."

"Very good guesser," Akki said, laughing.

Golden rubbed his nose with his forefinger. "Of course, maybe there's more to it than I know." He said it carefully.

Akki looked at Jakkin, her eyes widening.

"Maybe," said Jakkin. "And maybe not. As your wards we won't be answering questions, or so you said."

"That's right," Golden answered. "That's what I said."

"Then what comes next?" Jakkin asked.

"I'll take you back to the nursery farm now," said Golden. "If you're ready to come."

"We're ready," Jakkin said.

Akki nodded her agreement and reached down to pick up the hatchling, who had been lying against her ankles. The hatchling snuggled into her arms, its tail looped around her wrist.

Jakkin watched Golden and Akki climb into the copter. He walked over to Auricle and placed his hands on either side of her broad head. *"Thou beauty,"* he sent. *"Try thy wings once more and, if thee will, follow the others to the place where we live, the nursery. It will be a safe place for thee and thy eggs."*

He didn't wait for an answer. Whether she came to the farm or stayed in the world, she was free of the tyranny of the caves. That was all that mattered now.

Climbing into the copter, Jakkin sat behind Akki in a seat that seemed much too soft for comfort. Golden turned and showed him how to buckle his seat belt across his lap. Then he turned back to the copter console. As the great machine engine started up the noise was deafening.

Golden shouted, his voice barely rising above the churring of the rotors, "We won't be able to talk much until we're down again. Too loud." He pointed to the ceiling, then bent to fiddle with the controls, a panel of winking, blinking lights that reminded Jakkin of fighting dragons' eyes.

Jakkin put his hand on Akki's shoulder and their minds touched, a clear, clean, silent meeting. Then he looked out the window as the copter rose into the air. Austar stretched out below him in great swatches of color. He could see the dark mountain with its sharp, jagged peaks and the massive gray cliff faces pocked with caves. He could see tan patches of desert where five ribbons of blue water fanned out from the darker blue of a pool, and the white froth of the waterfall. Running into the waterfall was a blue-black river that gushed from the mountainside like blood from a wound.

He sent a message to Akki full of wonder and light. *"This . . . this is true dragon sight, Akki. We're like dragons in flight above our world."*

Mind-to-mind they talked of it all the way back to the nursery and home.

7176222